Valerie

An Elusive Butterfly of Love

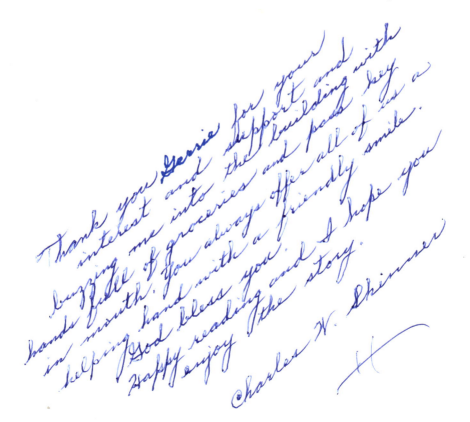

Thank you Gerrie for your interest and support and buzzing me into the building with hands fulle of groceries and pass'n bey in mouth. You always offer all of us a helping hand with a friendly smile. God bless you. I hope you Happy reading and I enjoy the story.

Charles W. Shimmel

Valerie

An Elusive Butterfly of Love

by

Charles W. Skinner

DORRANCE PUBLISHING CO., INC.
PITTSBURGH, PENNSYLVANIA 15222

ISBN # 0-8059-6222-0
Printed in the United States of America

First Printing

For information or to order additional books, please write:
Dorrance Publishing Co., Inc.
701 Smithfield Street
Third Floor
Pittsburgh, Pennsylvania 15222
U.S.A.
1-800-788-7654
Or visit our web site and on-line catalog at www.dorrancepublishing.com

Dedicated To

All of the women I have met and with whom I've kept
company through the years, for without their sensitivity,
compassion, affection, and love, this story could not
have been written.

I

At Newark's International Airport, Greg Ericsen moved hastily amid the scurrying crowds of Christmas travelers. It was evening on December 23, 1990, and the concourse was a maze of organized chaos. Anxious people flowed in all directions as they hurried toward their waiting gates.

The tall, handsomely built young traveler easily merged in and out of the swarms of nervous people as he worked his way toward the SAS departure gate. Greg was bound for Norway.

When he finally arrived at his gate, short-winded, he checked in with the attendant at the counter and noted the time on his watch. With fifteen minutes to spare, he'd arrived in time for his connecting flight to Oslo. After the attendant confirmed his boarding pass and window seat, Greg sauntered over to the waiting area and, with a sigh of relief, settled down onto a comfortable, soft-cushioned lounge chair.

Being an observer by nature and a people-watcher, Greg's dark blue eyes quickly scanned the faces of the people facing him in the waiting area. He enjoyed observing peoples' expressions. Then he briefly turned his attention to the intense faces of hastening travelers as they passed by the waiting area.

Finally he turned his attention and thoughts toward the huge terminal windows and gazed outside at the wintry evening sky. The overcast layer of thick gray clouds was tinged with a distinctive reddish-orange hue, while the roiling clouds appeared heavy and full as they hovered low over the terminal.

A thin blanket of snow covered the outlying area, but the huge mounds of snow piled high near the windows indicated to Greg the area had had a great deal of recent snowfall.

He contemplated a white Christmas in Oslo, but his thoughts were interrupted by the terminal's PA system.

A female voice from the SAS counter announced, "Passengers awaiting SAS Flight 909 will be boarding in a few minutes. This is just a reminder for those of you who have not checked in. Please do so at this time. You should have already received a boarding card. If you have not, please contact an agent at gate eighty for pre-boarding assistance for SAS Flight 909. Thank you."

While listening to the announcement, Greg continued to stare out the window at the grayish wintry scene and, momentarily, his thoughts shifted to his relationship with Valerie; to all the unanswered questions; and to all the unexplained circumstances that incessantly plagued his mind for the past fifteen months. The persistent questions were less frequent now and only in recent months did his thoughts of Valerie begin to diminish but, from time to time, they still returned to nag his brain.

Abruptly the PA system broke into his thoughts again.

"All passengers for SAS Flight 909 are requested to begin boarding at gate eighty," the female voice announced. "Those passengers with seating in rows twenty-five through forty are requested to board first. Thank you."

Greg got to his feet, picked up his carry-on bag, and made his way to the end of the line of people filing through the gate.

When he reached the gate, the agent tore the boarding pass from his ticket and handed back the ticket.

"Have a nice flight, sir." She smiled.

With a return smile, Greg thanked her politely and proceeded down the tunnel to the waiting aircraft.

As he entered the airplane, he ducked his head and lowered his broad Norwegian shoulders in order to pass through the plane's small doorway. Once inside, he straightened up, greeted the flight attendant with a smile and nod of his head, and proceeded down the aisle to find his seat.

At his seat, he stuffed his carry-on bag into an overhead compartment, slid into his seat by the window, and began to wait impatiently for the plane to take off.

After a thirty-minute delay, the aircraft finally backed away from the terminal and, within the next ten minutes, a tremendous thrust of power pushed Greg firmly against the back of his seat when the giant 767 sped down the runway and lifted off the ground.

As the huge aircraft slowly gained altitude, he peered out the window and looked down at the cars moving slowly along the streets and, within minutes, all the cars and houses appeared in miniature and were quickly reduced to mere specks. Eventually they were indiscernible from the panoramic and ever-expanding, picturesque scenery.

In a short time, at cruising speed altitude, refreshments were served to all the passengers and, an hour later, supper was served.

After supper, as Greg sipped his drink of cognac, he studied the giant television screen situated high in the middle of cabin. The screen simulation projected the course of the aircraft and presently displayed the plane being above Newfoundland. The simulated plane's image pointed toward Iceland and Greenland and showed the aircraft departing from the continental limits of North America. They were now flying over the Atlantic Ocean.

Soon the flight simulation disappeared and a movie flashed onto the television screen.

Since he was not interested in the movie, Greg turned his head toward his small window and looked below. The ocean could not be seen. The aircraft was flying high above the clouds, and when he leaned back in his seat to relax and observe the cloud layers, a flight attendant spoke over the plane's PA system.

"Would those passengers in window seats," she began, "please close their window shades to make better viewing conditions for those watching the cinema. Thank you."

Greg pulled the window shade down, pushed the button on his armrest, and dropped the back of his seat into a reclining position. Settling backwards, he rested his head comfortably on his pillow and turned his head sideways to face the window shade.

Then he closed his eyes and immediately focused his thoughts on the day he and his best friend, Tom Schaeffer, departed from their hometown of Rapid City, South Dakota, for their vacation to Oslo, the scenic Norwegian city where he first met Valerie.

CROCROCRO

Greg had met Valerie eighteen months previously, but to him it seemed as if their relationship began just a few short months ago.

It all began when he and Tom planned their Norwegian vacation three years ago, and when all travel arrangements and reservations had been taken care of months in advance and their time of departure arrived in June of 1989, needless to say, they bristled with excitement at leaving South Dakota for a European vacation. After all, they were small-town prairie folks and, never having traveled more than 50 to 100 miles away from town, they were leaving their hometown on a real vacation for the first time in their lives.

When they stepped off the Scandinavian airplane at 8 A.M. in Oslo, a rented car awaited them, and after they quickly stowed their baggage in the trunk, they climbed into the car and sped off onto the freeway in the direction of Oslo.

As they traveled into the city, they admired and gawked at all of the water inlets along with the passing tree-lined environment and rugged Norwegian countryside. In their excitement to satisfy their insatiable curiosities, they came within inches of sideswiping a few cars.

With no knowledge of the Norsk language and the inability to read road signs, their trip into the city was, to say the least, a harrowing ten-mile experience.

Once they reached the downtown city center, they began a fruitless search for their hotel which led them in circles. After a frustrating one-hour search, they gave up and finally asked a taxicab driver for directions to the Hotel Bonderheimen.

They all laughed when the cab driver informed them they were only two short blocks away from their hotel. After he instructed them to follow his taxi, he led them directly to their hotel within minutes. Whereupon they parked their car at the curb, thanked and tipped the cabby for his valued assistance, checked into the hotel, and went straight to their room to stow their gear.

Since they were only one block away from the downtown shopping district and with their excitement running high, they set out immediately to walk downtown and explore the city's shops.

At a corner newspaper stand, they stopped to buy a street guide and also obtained free brochures of all the city's guided tours and tourist attractions.

For the next half-hour they strolled down Karl Johans Gate, admiring the city's surroundings and observing the healthy-looking, ruddy faces of passing city shoppers, and soon they came to rest on a park bench to ponder their choices of guided tours. After agreeing on their first afternoon tour, they spent the rest of the morning casually window-shopping and wandering about the inner city.

For lunch, they chose the Egon Restaurant inside the small Paleet shopping mall, which provided an enjoyable, satisfying meal.

After lunch and after asking directions, they made their way to the bus stop for their first guided tour.

When the bus arrived, Tom stepped up quickly ahead of Greg, but when he lurched forward into the aisleway, his back foot caught on the top step. He took a header and fell flat on his face.

"Ooo! Are you all right, sir?" a soft female voice inquired.

Tom flipped over and stared up into two chocolate brown eyes that peered down at him with genuine concern.

Tom reacted to her pretty eyes with the thought, *Wow! How expressive!* Then he smiled broadly and quipped, "Ma'am, if I'm not all right, could YOU please nurse me back to health?"

Embarrassed by the unexpected flattery, the young woman's face flushed red, but she smiled in return and instantly turned her head to the side to face her female friend, who simply gazed out the window appearing to ignore the whole incident.

Tom jumped to his feet with Greg still following behind him and halfway down the aisleway, they settled into their seats on the opposite side of the bus from the two women.

"Hey, Greg, did you check out those two beauties?"

"How could I not check them out with all your dramatics?"

"Look at the sheen on her long hair," Tom observed while staring at the back of the woman he'd just embarrassed. "That brown-eyed beauty must brush her hair a hundred times a day, at least."

"I'd bet on it," Greg replied.

Tom continued to stare at her back and whispered, "C'mon, sweetheart, I know you're going to turn around. Anytime now."

Moments later, the brown-eyed woman turned around and caught Tom staring directly at her and two bright smiles abruptly lit up their faces.

Then she quickly turned back to face her friend and the two women began talking to one another.

"Ah-ha! I've got eye contact already, Greg. Did you see that smile? She's my pick."

"Yep, that was one great smile she gave you. So what else is new? You always take first pick." Greg laughed. He sat up straight and stretched his neck to try and get a good look at her friend but to no avail, so he slumped back in his seat. "Her friend won't even turn her pretty auburn head around for me to get a good look at her. All I saw was her profile when I passed by them," he replied.

"They're doing a lot of chattering," Tom remarked.

"Womens' favorite pastime wouldn't you say, Tom?"

Tom folded his arms and fixed his eyes on the back of the woman's head. He admired the beautiful sheen on her long dark brown hair and hoped for more eye contact and smiles, but none were forthcoming for the rest of the drive to the first museum.

When the bus stopped at the museum's entrance, the two women were on their feet and standing next to the driver. The brown-haired woman turned and gave Tom a big parting smile which he quickly returned in kind. Then the two women stepped down briskly into the stairwell and exited first from the bus.

The rest of the tour group followed behind the two women and strolled up the walkway in single file.

With Tom and Greg's eyes focused on the two women heading the group, Tom remarked, "Look at how straight her hair is cut across her back. It's an eye-catcher."

"Yes, it is. Very neat, too. I don't think her friend has a face, though. All I've seen is her back and wavy auburn hair."

"Yeah, me too, Greg."

Halfway to the museum's entrance, the brown-haired woman turned around, smiled again at Tom, and suddenly stumbled forward on the sidewalk.

Instantly her friend grabbed her arm to steady and prevent her from falling down. At first, the two women cupped their hands over their mouths and giggled with embarrassment. Then they straightened up and marched ahead with more rigid, deliberate steps.

"She has a pretty profile, anyway." Greg grinned while pondering his chances with the auburn-haired beauty, and she didn't seem too promising judging by her indifferent demeanor. She showed no interest in Greg.

Inside the building, the guide stopped the group at the bow of an old Viking sailing ship and talked about the ship's origin, but Greg and Tom were oblivious to her dissertation. Their eyes remained fixed directly on the backs of the two beauties standing several feet in front of them.

"It looks like you've got something going with the brown-haired one," Greg whispered while edging sideways, "but I can't even see the other one's profile now. I wish I could get a good look at her full-faced without starting a Norwegian war. Why, I can't even ignite a spark out of that Viking troll."

"Troll!" Tom blurted.

Instantly the tour guide stopped talking. A heavy silence fell as everyone in the group turned around to stare directly at Tom.

He glanced uneasily at all the pairs of eyes glaring at him. Embarrassed, he brought his fingers to his lips.

"Oops, excuse me. Sorry for the outburst, folks. It won't happen again."

"It's quite all right, sir," the guide replied cordially and continued with her lecture.

Tom quickly turned to Greg.

"Troll?" he whispered. "Don't you know, Greg, that trolls are ugly, fat, gruesome little fairy tale people who supposedly live under all the bridges in Norway? How can you call that beautiful woman a gruesome ol' troll just because she's ignoring you?"

"But INSIDE, maybe she IS an ugly ol' troll," Greg mused, "with a witch's power to appear elegant and beautiful on the OUTSIDE. Maybe her beauty is nothing more than a facáde–an illusion, perhaps. She's not nice to fool mother nature."

"You're spacing out on me, Greg."

"Well, what can I say? I know she can feel me staring holes through her and she hasn't given me the slightest glance. You talk about Norwegian icebergs–it's June already and she hasn't even begun to thaw out."

The two men inched closer to the two women until they stood directly behind them within earshot.

"Their perfume sure smells pretty," Tom remarked.

"Expensive, too," Greg added.

"Would you guess Joy or Chanel?" Tom grinned.

The brown-haired woman instantly nudged her friend with her elbow.

Then she turned, peered over her shoulder at Tom, and said, "Mine's Enjoli." Turning to her friend, she asked, "What's yours, Valerie?"

Valerie remained silent and distant, but the brown-haired woman continued, "So, you two fellows like our perfume, do you?"

"You betcha. Enjoli, eh? I'll try to remember the name. My name's Tom. What's yours?"

"Annika." She smiled demurely.

"This is my friend Greg."

"Glad to meet both of you, and this is my friend Valerie."

Valerie still remained silent, shrugged her shoulders, then turned and glared intently at Annika. Her ice-cold countenance expressed her obvious irritation. She showed no interest and ignored Greg and Tom completely. Then she returned her attention to the tour guide and preoccupied herself with the commentary.

Greg quickly gestured to Tom, saying, "Cool it!"

"Gotcha," Tom murmured. "We don't want any obnoxious behavior to spoil our chances, but she sure is one cold mackerel."

Valerie's iciness left much to be desired, but Greg felt her ice had cracked somewhat. He had her name and that's always a beginning.

The tour group continued on its way without any more trollish outbursts or close encounters of the female kind. However, Tom and Annika continued to exchange furtive glances, smiles, and occasional hand waves along with Tom's periodic winks.

At the end of the Viking ship tour, the bus arrived and returned everyone to their original stop on the boat piers. While most of the passengers exiting the bus dispersed in various directions, many of them hurried off for a shopping excursion at the marina mall with its inviting 100 shops to explore. Everyone except Annika, that is, because when she stepped off the stairwell, she stepped aside and waited outside next to the bus door.

When Tom exited the bus ahead of Greg, Annika quickly grabbed his arm and pressed a crumpled note into the palm of his hand.

"What's this—" he replied, looking down at his hand.

Annika smiled broadly but quickly turned away and ran off to catch up with Valerie, who was a block ahead of her.

Tom gazed at her running away as he unraveled the crumpled ball of paper.

"TOMORROW MORNING. 10 A.M. AT PIER 3. PLEASE COME." It was signed only with a friendly happy face.

When they looked up to observe the two women walking in the distance, Annika turned around and waved.

Greg and Tom waved in return and signaled mutual compliance to meet them by nodding their heads up and down.

"I can't believe I never got a good look at Valerie's face," Greg replied.

"Nope, nor did I, but even though you didn't get a peek at her today, you'll get your second chance come the 'morrow, pardner—thanks to Annika." Tom held up the small piece of paper with the fingertips of both his hands, pulled the paper to his mouth, and kissed it, saying, "You've got Annika the spy working for you."

Then he slid the note down into his jeans pocket; patted his pocket gently several times, as if to ensure its safe keeping; hitched up his pants, stuck out his chest, and sucked in a deep breath of fresh ocean breeze flowing in from the harbor. Afterwards, he slapped his stomach and rubbed it with both hands, saying, "I'm famished. C'mon, pardner, let's celebrate our beautiful female fortune with some delicious food and drink."

"After today's frosty experience, my only question is, 'How do I melt her kind of ice?'" Greg queried. "Brrrr!"

As they began their walk uptown, Tom patted his best friend's back and with reassuring words said, "Now, pardner, you can't quit on her just because we both know she was hatched from an iceberg. I've seen you take on tougher challenges in football and eventually win the game, so I know you'll also win this battle of the sexes game, too. I've got great confidence in you."

"Oh, I know I'll give her another try and I suppose the worst thing that can happen to my ego by the end of tomorrow is for it to be frozen and encased in a Norwegian block of ice. The one thing we DO know for sure, though. We know where we'll be at ten o'clock sharp in the morning, right, partner?"

Within a few short blocks, they found a fine restaurant and cocktail lounge where they could relax and plan a strategy for Greg's pursuit of Valerie.

Annika's flirtatious gestures with Tom were, indeed, positive and encouraging signs on which Greg could build his enthusiastic hopes and satisfy his curiosity in a meeting with Valerie.

II

Awakening early the next morning, Greg and Tom entered the hotel's coffee shop and huddled at a corner table to review their strategy for the day.

When ten o'clock drew near, the two men finished their coffee and left the café to walk the few blocks to the boat marina. Because they didn't want the women to leave on the cruise without them, the two men quickened their pace as they hastened toward Pier 3.

Approaching the pier, they saw Annika standing alone by the ticket booth. Valerie was nowhere to be seen.

"Uh-oh," Greg said, "Annika is by herself. Valerie didn't come with her. My ship is sunk."

"Now, don't give up the ship so soon, Greg. She may be waiting on board the tour boat or taking snapshots around the piers."

"I hope you're right, Tom."

A few seconds later, they walked up to Annika.

"Hi, Annika, how ya doin' this morning?" Tom smiled.

"I'm fine." She beamed. "And how are you, Greg?"

Already preoccupied scanning the piers for any sign of Valerie, Greg did a double-take and answered, "Aaaah at the moment, not too good, Annika." Continuing to gaze out over the piers, he asked, "How come your friend, Valerie, didn't join you today?"

"I wonder why I knew your first question would be about Valerie?" She laughed. "Valerie did come with me, but–reluctantly."

Still staring into the distance, he continued, "If she's on the docks somewhere, I certainly can't see her."

"That's because she's already on the boat waiting for us."

Instantly, Greg turned toward Annika and queried, "What kind of mood is she in?"

"I must say she's in a much better mood today, Greg. If you go slow, it's my guess you've got a chance with her. At dinner, last night, she did admit you were kind of cute."

"Kind of cute, huh? How 'bout that, Tom? A tidbit of hope. There's a crack in the iceberg, after all. Thanks for the tip, Annika."

"You're quite welcome, Greg, and thanks for coming today, fellas. It's always fun meeting new people on tours. Don't you think so, Tom?"

"I sure do. By the way, what's your last name, Annika?"

"Sissel, which makes me all Norwegian," she said proudly, "and what are your last names?"

"Mine's Schaeffer and Greg's is Ericsen with an e-n."

"I am of Norwegian descent," Greg interjected.

Looking at Tom, Annika added, "And you must be of German descent, I suspect."

Instantly, Tom stuck his thumbs down inside his belt, stooped low in a bowlegged cowboy stance and, with tongue in cheek, drawled, "You suspect right, ma'am, but also understand that we're from the good ole U.S. of A. Ya see, we were raised on the plains of the old Wild West where the reeeeal Americans once roamed. We come from Sioux Indian country. Dakota territory to you, ma'am."

While Annika cupped her hand to her mouth and giggled at Tom's cowboy antics, Greg grinned and stepped to the ticket window to purchase their tickets.

Afterwards, he joined Tom and Annika and asked, "What is Valerie's last name?"

Before she could answer, the ticket seller at the booth shouted out to them, "You folks better get to the boat. They're waiting for you and anxious to get underway."

The threesome looked toward the cruise boat at the end of the pier and saw the crew members waving for them to get aboard.

"We'd better hurry or they'll leave without us. Then it's a two-hour wait for the next departure. Thank you, sir," Annika called to the booth attendant as they began to run down the wharf.

At the mooring, they quickly jumped on board the glass-enclosed boat, scurried down the narrow stairway, and landed on the the lower deck.

On both sides of a middle pathway leading to the stern, ten or fifteen rows of benches awaited curious passengers.

Annika made her way toward the stern to join Valerie, who sat on the port side by a window.

However, Greg, not wanting to press his luck too soon, quickly slid into a second row bench closer to the bow. He motioned for Tom to follow him, so Tom slid onto the bench next to him.

"Hey, I finally got a good look at Valerie, full-faced. Did you see her, Tom? A real pretty fox, eh? A little intimidating, though."

"Now, now, pardner, don't get too excited. It seems to me—yesterday, as a matter of fact—I heard someone refer to her as an ugly ol' witchy troll, or was that just a figment of my imagination?"

"Okay, okay, so she's a beauty and now I'm chomping at the bit to crack her icy facade."

"This potential relationship could become a new version of 'Beauty and the Beast'," Tom chided, "and it's obvious who the beauty would be, huh, pardner."

After waiting a few more minutes for more last-minute passengers to board, the skipper finally started the engine, shifted into reverse, and backed away from the pier. When the boat safely cleared the dock, he shifted into forward gear, spun the wheel sharply to the right, and within seconds, the boat sped out into the spacious harbor.

"Check out the huge rocks on the shoreline," Greg observed. "Products of the ice age, I would think, and all of the beautiful homes—large and small—perched in the hills. According to our boat guide on the microphone, she just announced they're mostly summer homes and cottages. Their brilliant shades of reds, yellows, greens, and blues certainly paint a colorful landscape; so picturesque."

"Look up ahead, Greg. Far into the distance, you can barely see the blackish outline of the fjords standing in the misty horizon. They look like ghostly monsters spreading a large net of gray clouds over the entire land. Pretty spooky, eh?"

"Rapid City doesn't have anything like this, eh, Tom?"

"Certainly not, Greg, but we still have our good ol' Black Hills and forests, though."

As the boat cut through the choppy waves, the boat's female guide spoke into her hand-held microphone. In a calm and pleasant voice, she welcomed aboard the Norwegian passengers, first in Norsk and, afterwards, welcomed the English-speaking passengers. She was well-spoken in both languages.

When the boat reached a few tiny islands, the captain slowed the engine's speed, and while they cruised close to the rocky shorelines, the guide described the various points of interest on shore. Her informative commentaries always being spoken in both Norwegian and English.

At the halfway point of the tour, the skipper brought the boat to a standing idle with the guide announcing, "Refreshments will now be served to all passengers."

At that time, Tom turned around hoping for eye contact with Annika and saw her staring straight at him. Pointing to the bench in front of them, she gestured anxiously with her hand for him and Greg to join them.

Tom got to his feet and said, "Annika wants us to join them, Greg. We better go quick before they roll the refreshment cart into the aisle."

Greg stood up to follow Tom and snapped, "As Presley would say, 'It's Now or Never'."

Tom stopped short, turned round, pressed his palm against Greg's chest, and eyeball to eyeball, he winced, saying, "Just wait one minute here. We can do without Presley's innuendo's and song titles. If she doesn't like Elvis, your goose is cooked on the spot. Better to put Presley on the back burner, right?"

"Yes, you're right, as always. I'll just be 'Yo Teddy Bear'," Greg smirked. Tom stood fast with a disgusted look. "C'mon, c'mon," Greg urged, "let's go. This is my big chance to meet that beautiful troll."

"Then don't blow it with the Presley bit," Tom replied as they stepped into the aisleway.

Unrelenting, Greg whispered, "All women love Elvis."

They moved quickly down the aisle and when they stopped at the bench in front of the two women, Tom waited for Greg to scoot onto the bench ahead of him, thereby enabling Greg to slide all the way to the window and sit directly in front of Valerie.

Tom followed Greg onto the bench and sat in front of Annika.

Delighted with their company, Annika immediately said, "Greg, I'd like you to meet my friend, Valerie. Valerie, this is Greg."

Transfixed, Greg sat silent and simply stared into Valerie's incredible dahlia-blue eyes until Tom broke his fixation.

"Hey, Greg, you were just introduced."

Suddenly Greg shook his head, extended his hand for a handshake, and stuttered, "Er, ah, how ya doin', Valerie?"

While shaking his hand, Valerie replied, "I'm doing just fine, Greg, but do you always stare so intently at a woman when you're first introduced?"

"Yes—I mean, no, no I don't," he said, shaking his head. "It's just that your incredible blue eyes stunned me for the moment and I DO apologize for staring."

"Your apology is graciously accepted." She grinned with a nod of her head. "And your staring was actually quite flattering. I took it as a compliment, thank you. However, I do hope you don't always stare at women like that. Some women might be offended by it."

"You're the first woman whose eyes affected me that way, really." Greg smiled. "Of course you probably don't believe that, but it's true."

"In support of my best friend," Tom interjected, "Greg flatters very few women, Valerie. I must attest to that, scout's honor."

"Ohhh, and on whose scout's honor would that be?" Valerie questioned.

Tom drawled, "We're from Indian Dakota country, ma'am, so that would be on heap-big Injun scout's honor. Indians don't speak with forked tongues."

"True enough, but Indians also say, 'White man speak with forked tongue'." She laughed.

"Not us white men Indian scouts, ma'am. We no have forked tongues."

"Oh, you and that cowboy stuff," Annika said. "You were born a hundred years too late, Tom. Your mother should have delivered you on a horse."

"What's your last name, Valerie?" Greg asked.

"Nielsen. What's yours?"

"Ericsen. And can I safely assume you're of Norwegian descent?"

"I'm Norwegian-American; born in Tupelo, Mississippi; raised in Charleston, South Carolina; so I'm a Norwegian southern belle to you, suh."

"I thought I detected a southern accent." Greg smiled. "I like it. There doesn't seem to be too much about you I don't like today, but yesterday you weren't exactly the friendliest woman in Oslo."

Valerie winced, clenched her teeth, and said, "I must apologize for my prudish behavior yesterday. I was not at all sociable and in a very bad mood all day."

The guides arrived with the refreshment cart and the new foursome chose only four drinks, no food.

Since they were the last four passengers to be served, the guides back-peddled the refreshment cart to the bow of the boat.

Tom sipped on his Coke and surmised, "So, you women are from Stateside, eh."

"Oh, no," Annika snapped. "Valerie is from America. I was born and raised in Norway."

After another swig of his drink, Tom replied, "That's great. A real native Norwegian and a right pretty one, too, I must say," he added with a wink.

Flushed pink, Annika first drooped her head, then peered up at him impishly while she curled strands of hair around her index finger. Tilting her head to one side, she batted her eyes and flirted demurely.

"Do you always twist your hair around your finger?" he asked.

"Not always—only when I don't know what to say. It's a nervous habit."

Now the captain increased throttle so the boat would speed faster toward the north end of the harbor.

To the west, on the far distant horizon, were the ominous black militant fjords standing their protective guard and never-ending vigilant watch on the environment. The giant majestic mountains loomed formidable in the mysterious gray mist and stamped regal grandeur on the silent Norwegian landscape.

During the next hour, the boat cruised among the many tiny islands, then turned eastward to return to the piers.

It was high noon when the skipper docked the boat at the Pier 3 starting point.

When the new foursome disembarked, Greg snapped a photo of Monika, one of the tour guides, and turning to the captain, asked, "How about you, Skipper? May I take a picture of you, sir?"

"Yes—for ten dollars." The captain laughed.

Greg quickly snapped a shot of the skipper leaning against the boat's wheel and thanked him.

Then he rejoined Tom and the two women waiting for him on the wharf. When he noticed Valerie standing directly behind the other cruise guide, Kristina, he also asked the guide for a snapshot. She agreed and Greg grinned snidely at the opportunity to include Valerie in the picture.

When he brought the camera up to his eye, he called, "Hey Kristina and Valerie, say cheese."

Valerie turned toward him and when both women beamed spontaneous smiles, Greg snapped the shutter. Relishing his sneaky adeptness, Greg gloated over the capture of Valerie's beautiful face and radiant smile.

After thanking Kristina, he looked at Tom and Annika, saying, "You two make a cozy pair. How about a shot of you two together?"

"You betcha," Tom grinned.

Standing close together, with arms around each other's waists, they both smiled for the camera. After Greg snapped the picture, Tom squeezed Annika's waist tightly, bent down, and kissed her full on the lips. Greg quickly captured the embrace on film with a quick flick of the shutter.

"Excellent!" Greg laughed as Annika blushed in amazement, then continued, "Everyone must be hungry. Let's eat."

"Good idea," Valerie agreed.

"We could go to Saras Telt on Rosenkrantz Gate," Annika continued, "if everyone would like beer and pizza. It's an outdoor patio in the city center."

"They have very good pizza," Valerie confirmed.

"Sounds great to me," Tom consented.

"Me, too," Greg replied.

It took only a short time to reach the open sunlit patio and after the foursome took up chairs at a big round metal table with a short discussion about pizza size and ingredients, Greg and Tom went to place their order.

Within minutes, the two men returned to the table holding two glasses of red wine for the women and two large steins of beer for themselves.

"Pizza—Norwegian style," Tom exclaimed. "This is a real first for me."

Greg agreed, "For me, too; When in Rome, do as the Romans do, and when in Norway, do as the Norwegians do."

"And I'm sure the pizza will be delicious," Tom added.

As they began drinking their beer and wine, Greg pushed his stein into the center of the table. Holding it up with a propped elbow, he proposed a toast.

"Here's to the two most beautiful women in Oslo, Valerie and Annika, and to Norway with all its friendly people and magnificent scenery."

"I'll second that," Tom declared, clicking his stein to Greg's.

Annika lifted her glass and tapped it against their steins.

"Here's to lasting friendships." She smiled.

Valerie also joined in, touched her glass to the other three glasses, and stated, "May the future be full of happiness for all of us."

Then the foursome clicked their glasses together and in unison shouted, "Skol!"

Greg looked at Annika and asked, "Why are you Norwegians so healthy-looking, with your clean ruddy complexions?"

"I don't know." Annika beamed. "Maybe it's because we're an outdoor people. We love being outside in the fresh air and healthy climate."

"And it shows–terribly." Greg laughed. "Looking at you, Annika, I suddenly feel very sickly and unnecessary; as if I need to get to a hospital immediately, if not sooner, to find out how unhealthy I am."

"You don't look very sickly to me." Annika giggled. "In fact, I think both of you fellas look very strong and healthy. Don't you think so, Valerie?"

"Oh, yes, I certainly agree," Valerie said while sipping her wine.

The pizzas arrived in due time and as everyone bit into their tasty slices and enjoyed their drinks, the general conversation began to wane.

Eventually, Tom and Annika became preoccupied with themselves and whispered intimately to each other while Greg and Valerie also became engrossed in their own private conversation.

Soon Valerie, smiling and in a raised voice, stated, "You know, Greg, you really are a bit bourgeois."

"Bourgeois? What's bourgeois?"

"Since you don't know what it means, why don't you ask Tom?"

Greg decided to play her game and cried, "Hey, Tom, do you have a dictionary in your pocket?"

Tom stared intently into Annika's cat-like greenish-brown eyes and without breaking his gaze, answered, "Can't say as I do, pardner."

"Okay, since you can't define bourgeois." She grinned. "Let's try another word. How about *gauche*. Do you know what *gauche* means?"

"Ghost! I'm no ghost." He laughed.

"I didn't say ghost, I said *gauche*. It's slang for bourgeois. You still don't know the meaning?"

Greg continued to evade the question, saying, "Okay, so I'll be a ghost and you'll be a doll and this is the day when one beautiful doll met an ugly ol' ghost. I'd say that's great for starters."

Chagrined, Valerie smiled warmly and said, "You're impossible, Greg, not to mention weird and a bit strange."

Then Greg's expression became more somber and he mistakenly turned their light conversation into a more serious vein.

"Valerie, what I feel for you, right now, I've never felt for any woman in my life," he confided.

Valerie abruptly pushed her chair backwards away from the table, jumped up, and replied, "I'm not really ready for this, Greg. I don't think I want to hear what you're about to say, so I'm ready for some afternoon shopping." Turning, she added, "Are you coming, Annika? I'm ready to leave now."

"Yes, I'm coming, Valerie."

Valerie turned on heel and hastened from the patio to wait for Annika on the sidewalk.

At the same time, Annika got to her feet, whisked her purse from the back of her chair, and strapped it over her shoulder. Then she bent down, pecked Tom softly on the lips, and ran to join Valerie.

For the moment, Greg and Tom looked at one another in bewilderment. Greg hunched his shoulders and suddenly they both jumped to their feet and raced after them.

Valerie and Annika hurried on their way, but when Greg caught up to Valerie, he pleaded for her to stop and talk to him.

Finally, she stopped and with a roll of her head and eyes, asked, "Okay, what is it, Greg?"

"Valerie, I'm really sorry. I didn't mean to offend you. I simply wanted to express my feelings for you. That's all. I didn't mean anything by it—honest. Please don't be angry with me."

"Oh, I'm not angry, Greg. It's okay. I'm fine, now. I'm just not in the mood for any serious talk and I'm anxious to get on with my shopping before the stores close for the weekend."

"We need to get to the stores, too, Greg," Tom reminded. "Hey, maybe we can all meet somewhere later and have dinner and drinks together. It's been a terrific day, so far. Why not keep it going? What do you both say? Are you game?"

"That's free dinner and drinks for the two prettiest women in Oslo," Greg pressured. "C'mon, you two, you can't turn down a free offer from two honest guys from Dakota territory."

Tom stuck his thumbs down inside his belt, puffed out a cheek, closed one eye, and stooped like a bowlegged cowboy.

"C'mon ladies," he drawled, "we'd be much obliged ifn' you'd grace our dinner table with your presence this evening. We promise to be on our best behavior and we'd be much beholdin' to ya. Please say, yes."

While Valerie rolled her eyes, Annika laughed. "You guys are crazy. You know that."

"Crazy is right, Annika, with weird and strange thrown in."

Annika looked at Valerie and anxiously asked, "What do you say? Should we?"

Valerie shrugged. "I know you want to, so it's okay with me, too."

"Well, that settles it," Annika replied. "We'll meet you fellas at 5:30 P.M."

"Hey, that's great. Where shall we meet you?" Greg queried.

Annika pointed back down the street and said, "We'll meet you at that newsstand on the corner by the cafe where we just ate. It's across from the Bonanza restaurant. Do you see it?"

"Yep, I sure do," Tom confirmed. "We bought our street guide there yesterday."

Valerie smiled. "We'll see you guys later." Then she rushed across the busy boulevard with Annika. They quickly disappeared into the heavy flow of afternoon shoppers.

"I guess we'd better get on with our souvenir shopping, too, Tom."

Tom bowed slightly, extended his arm to point the way, and replied, "Be my guest, sire. The carriage is waiting. Our next stop is Oslo's Fifth Avenue shopping district."

Eventually, toward late afternoon, Greg and Tom found themselves back on the piers at the marina shopping mall where they mingled with the heavy crowd of people and browsed among the 100 gift shops and boutiques.

Soon, Greg spotted a stuffed, ugly, funny-looking troll and quickly picked it up to admire it.

"Now, don't be getting any ideas, Greg. I know who that might be for."

With sparkle in his eyes, his square jaw broke into a broad smirk as he scrutinized the doll.

"That's exactly who it's for, but study him, Tom. See the little grin on his face? I'll tell her he's a kind and happy troll who will bring her lots of good luck. He'll be a good luck offering. My good luck with her, of course, but I won't suggest that to her."

Tom folded his arms, leaned against a post, and said, "May his luck be with you, too, when you hand it to her or you and your little ugly friend could easily end up under a bridge together. At which point, I'd say your goose would be thoroughly cooked–cremated to be exact!"

"Being an observer of human nature, I'd say her display of standoffish indifference is her defense mechanism to move cautiously in a new relationship. Beneath her seemingly cold exterior, I detect a warm, sensitive, and affectionate woman."

"Well, well, listen to ol' Doc Ericsen giving his expert analysis of Valerie, the inner woman. When do you hang out your shingle, Doc?"

Greg nodded to the clerk and as he handed her the krona and troll, replied, "I'll offer Mr. Troll as a token of our fun weekend together. I'm confident she'll accept him graciously and hopefully our unique friendship will take root. I'll hang out my shingle back home if I have her figured right."

When the clerk handed the bag to him, she said, "I know she'll like it, sir. We love our trolls here in Norway."

Taking the bag from her hand, he thanked her with a wink of his eye, saying, "There, you see, Tom? I've already make points with one pretty young woman in Oslo and, if Valerie won't accept Mr. Troll, I'll come back and offer him to you. Ma'am? Would that be okay with your boyfriend?"

"Oh yes, I'd gladly accept him." She beamed. "I like ugly ol' trolls. I have a small collection of them."

"It's a deal." Greg smiled.

As he and Tom waved their goodbyes and sauntered off into the crowd, Greg pondered, "Now, I wonder where I can buy a nice friendship ring for her?"

Tom stopped in his tracks and stammered, "A friendship ring! Now I know you've spaced it. The Greg Ericsen I know NEVER, EVER has bought any woman a friendship ring. You've slipped a screw, man. This isn't a marriage safari, you know. We're only in Norway for a fun weekend, remember?"

"I know, Tom, but those beautiful blue eyes get to me. She's really got me bugged. Is there something wrong with that?"

Tom scratched his head, squinted his small brown eyes, and said, "Well, no, not really, I suppose, and I'm all for it, of course, but I've never seen any woman affect you like this. You're really stuck on her, aren't you? I guess it's all too new and scary for me. However, I must admit, I can't wait to see what happens next."

"Standby and tune in at the supper hour for the next episode." Greg laughed.

"Oh, my antennas will be out and I'll be all ears, for sure."

"You won't hear a thing—not for a second—because you can't keep your eyes and hands off Annika."

Tom lifted his index finger, saying, "Uh-uh, I can still hear."

"Not when she's whispering in your ear."

"Ah-ha! But she can only whisper in one ear at a time."

At that moment, Greg caught sight of a ring in a jewelry display case and stopped to bend low over the glass countertop to examine it.

"May I help you, sir?" asked the clerk.

"Yes," he replied, tapping the case, "I'd like to see that gold rose-colored friendship ring with the two fingers touching tips."

After the clerk reached inside the case and handed the ring to him, she stated, "It's 14-karat gold; an ideal friendship ring."

"It's perfect. I'll take it," Greg said, "and can my woman friend come here to have it sized?"

"She can come back at any time," the clerk replied, "and have it sized with no charge. We keep records of all sales, so she needn't worry if she loses the sales slip. Our gift box also serves as a receipt."

After Greg paid for the ring, the girl handed him the small bag, and having exchanged smiles and "thank yous," the two men walked off to continue their quest for souvenirs.

Later, with their shopping complete and before their scheduled rendezvous with the women, Greg and Tom stopped at a tavern to relax and wet their dry mouths with a couple of cold beers.

Soon thereafter they arrived at the corner newsstand, promptly at 5:30 P.M. sharp.

The busy newsstand was alive with people, so Greg and Tom stood back away from the steady flow of customers and waited for the two women to arrive.

Gazing up the boulevard, Greg commented, "I'll bet they don't show."

"How much says they DO show?" Tom quizzed.

"Would our evening's dinner and drinks suffice?" Greg queried.

"That's a bet," Tom snapped. "If they don't show, I'll buy your dinner and drinks and, if they do show, we'll split the tab, but you'll owe me for my food and drinks. Fair enough?"

"Fair enough, pardner," Greg agreed as they shook hands and slapped ten to seal the bet.

Suddenly a small car spun around the corner and stopped short at the curb.

Valerie rolled down her side window and called, "Hey, you two guys look lost. Need a lift somewhere?"

Tom gloated with a grin, "Looks like my free dinner and drinks just arrived, pardner."

"With pleasure," Greg chimed when they stepped to the car door.

As the two men scrambled onto the back seat of the car and before Greg could close the door, the car screeched from the curb, sped off down the street, and jerked to an abrupt halt at a red light only half a block away. Everyone shot forward in their seats amid the uproarious laughter of Valerie and Annika.

"Hey, where's the fire?" Tom shouted.

Valerie and Annika grinned impishly, then Annika laughed. "No fire, Tom. We're just hungry, aren't we, Valerie?"

"I'll say." Valerie laughed. "And since you fellas are buying, we're both salmon hungry."

As the two men straightened up in their seats, Greg declared, "Sounds great. Now where's a good restaurant that serves excellent salmon dinners?"

The light turned green and the car jumped forward to pass quickly through the intersection.

"There's a very good restaurant only a few blocks away," Valerie announced.

Annika spun a few right turns, merged in and out of heavy traffic, and after a harrowing ten-minute ride on the congested one-way streets, the car stopped short at the curb.

Everyone lurched forward again and as Annika straightened the car into a parking space, Tom remarked, "Whew! I guess we're all in one piece. I'll have to check all my moving parts, though."

The foursome were still laughing when they tossed their shopping bags into the trunk and walked across the street to enter the Theatercafeen restaurant.

Inside the restaurant, Greg asked the hostess for a window table, whereupon she smiled graciously and led them to a table by a window which overlooked the main downtown boulevard.

Outside the window, a steady flow of anxious passersby hastened to complete their Saturday evening shopping before the stores closed.

The waitress arrived shortly to take their orders and Greg ordered for everyone.

"We'll have four baked salmon dinners with four glasses of white wine, please," he said.

The waitress nodded politely, noted the order, smiled, and left their table.

Greg turned to Valerie. "Well, how did all your shopping go?" he asked.

"Mine went very well," she replied, "but Annika didn't do so well. She couldn't find everything she wanted. How about you, Greg? Did you get all of your souvenirs?"

"Yes, I was able to find something for everyone back home."

"And how about you, Tom?" she added. "Did you find everything you wanted?"

"Yes, I did, but I only had a few souvenirs to buy. It's too bad you couldn't find everything, Annika, but that gives you a good excuse to go shopping again next week, right?"

"Yep." She smiled broadly. "I love excuses to shop because I always have trouble finding exactly what I want, anyway."

Tom teased, "And I suppose, Miss Picky, you're very fussy and particular in what you do buy."

Annika squiggled her nose, curled her hair around her index finger, and stated curtly, "I've always been very particular about my clothes."

"So, I've noticed." Tom grinned. "Hey, do that again!"

"Do what again?"

"Squiggle your nose. That's sexy."

"You think this is sexy?" she replied as she squiggled her nose once more.

"Oh, yeah," he growled. "I'd like to reach across the table and kiss you right now."

"You ARE a strange one." She giggled while squiggling her nose again.

With a wink of his eye, he growled low.

Greg proposed a suggestion.

"While we're waiting for our dinners," he said, "why don't we tell each other about our deep dark secrets and reveal the skeletons in our closets. Is everyone game?"

"Great idea," Tom snapped as he reached across the table toward Annika's hair.

She jerked backwards, saying, "What are you doing?"

"C'mere, I only want to fix your hair."

Annika edged forward slightly and reluctantly permitted Tom to touch her hair.

He quickly slashed her soft, fine, brown hair neatly across her forehead. Then he leaned backwards to admire the look and sheen of her hair. "Now, it's perfect." He grinned.

"Ladies first," Greg announced. "So which one of you women would like to start with your secrets from the past?"

"Oh, I'll go first," Valerie smirked, "but I haven't any dark past. There really isn't much to tell about myself. I was born in Tupelo, Mississippi, and went to grammar school there. After eighth grade, we moved to Charleston, South Carolina, where I graduated from high school. From there, I attended the University of Virginia and received my teaching degree."

As he studied her milky-white clear complexion and almond-shaped eyes, Greg asked, "So what brought you to Norway?"

"My grandparents live in northern Norway," she went on, "and because my parents brought me here on their summer vacations, at a very young age I fell in love with the country and its people."

She glanced up momentarily to admire Greg's thick crop of unruly black hair and shook her head slightly. Then she moved on with her story.

"My father was a Norwegian merchant seaman and from time to time his ship docked in southern ports in the United States. Most of the time they docked in Charleston and that's where he eventually met my mother. She worked as a seamstress at the time in a downtown dress shop, and because she was a prim and proper southern lady from the town of Tupelo, she charmed Dad out of his shoes and right into marriage."

"You mean he married your mother in his bare feet?" Greg chided.

Valerie smirked, ignored his remark, and continued, "After they married, Dad gave up the sea and they moved back to Tupelo, where Dad farmed for about fourteen years. Eventually we moved to Charleston, where I finished high school. During college, I worked my summers as a waitress in Charleston to buy clothes and help with the tuition, and once I received my degree, I came to Norway to do postgraduate work and teach grammar school. I love children, and I always dreamed of coming here to teach the third grade, and I've been here ever since. So that's my life's story till now, everyone."

"How did you learn the language?" Tom inquired.

"From my father. He always spoke English and Norsk in our home. He wanted Norsk to be part of my education growing up. It was fun conversation for Dad and me." Then she looked at Annika and said, "Now it's your turn, Annika."

"Yes, I know," Annika answered, "but my story isn't as interesting as Valerie's. I simply grew up in Oslo and lived here all my life."

"Have you ever traveled to the United States?" Tom asked.

"No, I've never been to America, but I've vacationed in Finland and Sweden many times. My parents, like Valerie's grandparents, grew up on a farm in northern Norway—about one hundred miles south of Finland—and because many of my relatives live in Finland and Sweden, we visited them, or they visited us, mostly during the summer holidays. I've never been to Europe or the British Isles, either, but I intend to travel there some day. I graduated from high school in Oslo and after graduating from our city university I, like Valerie, also have a teacher's degree and teach grammar school. I love teaching the younger children, too, and I teach fourth graders. They are so full of curiosity and so eager to learn. I think of myself when I was their age."

Tom replied, "I assume you and Valerie have been friends for quite awhile and both of you teach at the same school."

"No, Tom, we don't teach at the same school and we only met for the first time yesterday on the Viking ship tour."

Tom reacted with amazement.

"You mean, you two women didn't even know each other before yesterday?"

"It's true," Annika confirmed.

"Yes, that's right," Valerie agreed. "I teach in Bergen."

Turning his head slowly from side to side, Tom continued, "Now that's a surprise. Greg and I thought you've been longtime friends for years, right, Greg?"

"Right, Tom, they sure had us both fooled."

Annika had finished her story, so Valerie looked at Greg, saying, "Now that you fellas have heard our dark secrets, let's hear all the lurid details of your backgrounds, including all love affairs. Who will be first with his closet skeleton?"

Tom stood up, leaned across the table eagerly to kiss Annika, and said, "If I have to play the game of 'kiss and tell', then I must have a kiss first."

Annika flushed, but met Tom's lips with an anxious, affectionate kiss.

Tom's dark brown eyes gleamed when he tasted her lipstick and exclaimed, "Now I'm ready to tell all. Like Greg, I was born in Rapid City, South Dakota. Because we both grew up there and attended the same grammar school together, we met and became best friends. Although we went to different high schools and played football and baseball against each other, we both did graduate together from South Dakota University. I majored in business administration and after college, I took a job with a company in Sturgis, about thirty miles west of Rapid City. I live in my own apartment there now, but Greg and I still see each other often. We play on the same softball team and neither of us has ever been married—scout's honor."

Tom held up three fingers to display the boy scout's salute and Annika quickly snared them with one hand and squeezed hard.

22

"Two of those fingers look crossed to me. Let me straighten them out." She smirked while twisting his fingers.

"Ow!" he squealed. "But it's true, Annika. Greg and I have never been married, honest."

"Then how about your love affairs? You haven't mentioned any steamy romances," she goaded with another strong twist of his fingers.

"Okay, okay, so I had one love affair," he admitted sheepishly. "One day, my girlfriend and I played 'doctor and nurse' together and I kissed her behind the barn. Now are you satisfied? You can let go of my fingers now."

Annika twisted them harder. "How old were you?"

"Oh, eight years old, I suppose." He grinned slyly while looking down. "We were in second grade."

Her eyes narrowed to slits and with pursed lips, she muttered, "Oooo, you're so evasive!" Then she twisted his fingers hard with a final hard twist, whisked her hand away, slumped back in her seat, and folded her arms. In feigned frustration, she pursued, "Okay, Mr. Slippery, keep going. Now I suppose, you're going to slither into your second grade high school and second grade college affairs, too. Where were those? Behind the haystack?"

"More precisely INSIDE the haystacks," Valerie murmured from the corner of her mouth.

"Thank you, Valerie, I believe it."

Instantly, Tom lifted his hands from the table, brought them to his eyes, and covered them with each hand. Then he brought them to his ears and covered each ear. Lastly he brought his hands to his mouth and covered it with both hands.

"See no evil; hear no evil; speak no evil. I plead the fifth to all female affairs and refuse to answer on the grounds that it might incriminate me." He grinned.

Because the waitress arrived to serve their dinner plates, Greg delayed his story until later. After the waitress left, everyone cut into their scrumptious-looking salmon first.

"This salmon is great," Greg commented. "It's as good as our steaks back home."

"Better than your steaks." Annika beamed. "It's Norwegian salmon, which makes it the best."

"Oops, that was a ridiculous thing to say in the land of Norway. I'll bite my tongue for that, Annika."

"See that it doesn't happen again," she scolded.

When Greg took a bite of his roll and munched on a piece of salmon, he began to relate his background.

"My degree is in physical education and presently I coach the track and football teams at Rushmore High School where I also teach American history. It is my hope to develop winning programs for both teams so that eventually I can step up to college coaching and perhaps someday reach the professional level. For young aspiring coaches, it's cheaper to live at home, so I live with my parents temporarily and, no, I've never been married. Tom doesn't speak with a forked tongue. I'm strictly a one-woman man who seeks the right woman for a permanent, lasting relationship."

"But we want to hear about your deep, dark, illicit affairs," Valerie teased. "Tell us about your closet skeletons."

"I'm not answering any questions until I see your badges." He laughed. "Now what about you two women? Have either of you been married?"

Valerie laid her fork on her plate, wiped her mouth with her napkin, and leaned back against the booth.

"Not me," she snapped.

"Me, neither," Annika replied, biting a piece of salmon. "I've never been asked."

"In that case," Tom interjected, "I'd say this dinner marks an auspicious occasion for us single people. It's an ideal happening to complete a perfect day with a perfect evening. I propose a nightclub with dancing and drinks. That is, if the ladies don't have strings attached to them; do you?"

Annika squiggled her nose. "Strings attached?" she queried.

"That means, 'Do we have boyfriends?'" Valerie said.

"Oh no, Tom, I don't have a boyfriend," Annika snapped quickly.

Then Valerie replied, "No, there aren't any strings attached to me, either."

"There's another stunner," Greg declared. "I would think all eligible bachelors in Oslo and Bergen would be huffing and puffing to blow your apartment doors down."

"As a matter of fact, Greg, I lead a very quiet life alone in my little apartment. During the school year, in addition to teaching the children, I take evening classes. I'm going for my master's degree, so I'm too busy and tired during the week to date. However, I'll date occasionally on weekends. Mr. Right hasn't entered my life yet, so I can take men or leave them right now."

"Would you take me, right now, for a dance partner?" he asked.

"Sure, it sounds like fun." She smiled while staring at the cleft in his chin.

"Then it's settled," Tom stated. "Let's go dancing. Where's a good dance club, Annika?"

"There's a nice club only a few minutes away. It's off the main boulevard on a side street. I think the band starts playing at eight o'clock."

After they finished dessert, Greg paid the tab, left a nice tip for the waitress, and the foursome left the table to walk to the front entrance.

When they stepped outside, it was raining, so Greg and Tom used their jackets to make a canopy from the downpour.

After spreading their jackets high over their heads, and Valerie and Annika ducked underneath, all four raced across the street and scrambled into the car.

"Whew! It does get wet in Norway, I see," Greg replied.

"It rains all summer long." Annika grinned.

Tom ordered haughtily. "Driver! Would you now take us to our evening of dance and spirits, please?"

"Yes, sir!" Annika reacted while starting the engine.

As the car pulled away from the curb, torrential rain pelted the car and pounded the pavement. Golf ball-size water pellets bounced up from the sidewalk and when Annika turned the car onto the main boulevard, she strained to see the street ahead of them.

The wipers slapped back and forth vigorously across the glass, but to no avail. A steady mass of water, which now streamed across the windshield, created only blurry images, so Annika swerved the car to the curb and stopped. It appeared all traffic on the boulevard was also stationary.

Within minutes the deluge subsided to a slow patter of raindrops striking the car's roof, and with Annika now able to see through the windshield, she drove off from the curb and continued down the boulevard.

In only a few minutes, the downpour flooded curbsides with shiny pools of water that glimmered from beams of light cast by the overhanging street lamps. The perpetual streams of water that glistened past the glowing street globes appeared to spread a sparkling carpet of water on the streets below.

In a short time, the foursome arrived at the nightclub, and Annika once again parked the car on the street curbside.

Greg and Tom jumped from the car and spread their jackets high to protect the two women from the pelting rain. Then the foursome scampered across the street for the nightclub entrance.

Safely inside the club, the men shook the rain from their jackets and after they handed them to the coat check girl, Valerie and Annika led Greg and Tom to an empty table from where the two women left to freshen up in the ladies room.

"It's good we got here early. There aren't many empty tables left," Greg observed. "It must be a popular club."

"Not many empty bar stools, either," Tom replied.

"You know I'm not much of a dancer, Tom. I hope the band doesn't play all fast stuff."

"C'mon, Greg, you've got rhythm. Get with it. Just jump around to the beat like everyone else. Nobody's even watching you. They're all too busy doing their own thing."

After Valerie and Annika returned to the table, the waitress came to take their order and returned shortly with their four drinks.

By then, each twosome had pulled their chairs close to one another and engaged in intimate conversation, but when the band started playing, Annika and Tom sprang to their feet. Joining hands, they rushed for the dancing area. They were the first couple on the floor and quickly boogied down to the rock music.

Within seconds, the dance floor was crowded with jumping, hopping, wiggling dancers.

"I thought you were my dance partner?" Valerie quizzed.

"So I am, but I'm not too cool with the fast stuff."

"Oh, I don't believe that. Move with the feeling and beat of the music. If you're out of step, who cares? Make up your own steps. Nobody notices you anyway."

Greg lifted his drink, swirled the ice cubes around the glass, winked at Valerie, and said, "After I drink up some more courage, I'll give it a try, but first let's start off with the slow stuff, okay?"

"Chicken!" she cried as she turned to focus on the dancers and clap her hands to the beat of the music.

After the first three fast numbers, the music slowed, and when the singer sang, "In the Misty Moonlight," Greg stood up, grasped Valerie's hand firmly, and whisked her off to the dance floor where they quickly danced into the crowd.

When Valerie's hair wisped across his cheek, Greg whispered in her ear, "Your hair is very soft and fine."

"Oh, is that good or bad?"

"More like sexy and titillating, which makes it good or bad depending on viewpoint. Your enticing perfume doesn't help, either. It arouses my animal desires."

"Dowwwwn, Tiiiger," she purred softly in his ear.

"Hey, I'm not a tiger. I'm a ghost, remember? I'm a ghostly apparition who just came into your life. I'm 'Ghosty', your dance partner for the evening."

Valerie pressed her soft breasts firmly against his hard, broad chest. Greg pulled her tight against himself and as they glided around the dance floor, his feelings for Valerie welled within him. He was smitten with her. He'd never felt so much emotion for any woman in his life.

When the slow music ended, the band broke into more fast rock and immediately, Valerie picked up the fast beat. Instinctively, she bounced to the tempo. Then as she wiggled and writhed to the sensuous rhythm, she danced seductively backwards away from Greg.

Entranced with her suggestive movements, Greg stopped abruptly to leer at her captivating body.

With a toss of her head, she flipped her long, silky, auburn hair over her shoulder and, with outstretched arms, gestured for him to come and dance.

"C'mon, chicken, get with it!" she teased.

Instantly, Greg reacted and jumped, hopped, and bounced frantically. His arms flailed and his legs gangled in wild frenzy.

"I really feel foolish doing this!" He laughed.

"That's the whole idea!" she cried. "Now keep it up."

Suddenly, Valerie stopped dead on the spot. Greg stopped, too, and stood fast, not knowing what to expect next from her.

Standing rigid, Valerie ran her right hand slowly up the side of her body to her face. Then sliding it slowly up the side of her face to her hair, she ran her hand through her hair, stroking long strands slowly through her fingers; and with a final flare, she threw her hair wildly forward to land sexily over her right eye.

Placing the palm of her hand on her thigh, she spread her fingers wide and with her other palm, she pressed her wide-open fingers firmly against her breasts.

Then she slowly unfastened two top buttons on her blouse and slid her blouse sideways off the end of her shoulder. With a pink bra strap and bare shoulder exposed, she struck a sultry pose momentarily before gyrating her bare shoulder seductively.

Finally she moved stealthily and sensuously toward Greg until she stood in front of him. She slid her long leg up and down the side of his leg, lifted one eyebrow, and with a menacing stare, purred, "I'm giving you an evil eye, Mr. Ericsen."

In a returned fixed gaze, he smirked. "You had better stop right now, sexy one, or you're in deep trouble."

"Oh, really?" she simpered lifting her eyebrow higher. "But you're just a ghost, remember? You couldn't cause trouble even if you wanted to, Mr. Ghost."

Suddenly she spun around, wiggled her buttocks at him, danced a few feet away from him, stopped, and wiggled her buttocks again. Afterwards, she turned her head around, peered at him over her bare shoulder, and rolled her shoulder teasingly. Then she batted her eyes, jerked her blouse back up over her bare shoulder, and re-buttoned it, then with a final provocative gesture, she swished her skirt sassily behind her, wiggled a few more feet away, and whirled around to face him.

Greg clapped, along with the circle of dancers around her, while he danced up to her. The number ended quickly with the band playing into a slower tune.

When the singer sang, "Love Is a Many Splendored Thing," Valerie leaned against his hard body and rested the side of her head on his broad shoulder. As they danced across the floor, Greg kissed her softly on her neck. He felt so relaxed and comfortable with her in his arms. He'd never wanted or desired a woman more than Valerie. At that moment he didn't want to let go of her.

When the song ended, the singer announced their first break, so the couples strolled off the floor and returned to their tables. Tom and Annika joined Greg and Valerie at their table and ordered a new round of drinks.

"Hey, pardner," Tom stated, "you did great on that dance floor." Then turning to Annika, he held up three fingers again and added, "That's the first time I ever saw Greg dance to rock. That's a fact–scout's honor."

Annika squiggled her nose, grabbed his fingers, and twisted them hard.

"Ouch!" he yelped, tugging his fingers back. "You do that once more and I'll turn you into an ugly old troll."

Annika squiggled her nose again, folded her arms in mock disdain, and smirked defiantly. "Oh, so now you think you're some kind of Norwegian wizard, I suppose." She squiggled her nose again, puffed out one cheek, and drawled, "I thought you was from Dakota territory. That's Injun country to you, ma'am?"

The other three laughed heartily at Annika's imitation of Tom until Greg said, "It looks like we've got a couple of sassy females on our hands, eh, Tom?"

Tom winked at Greg, puffed out a cheek, and drawled, "Looks that way, pardner. Should we turn them over our knees? Maybe a good spanking might do them some good."

Valerie sipped her drink, peered over her glass, and dared, "If you guys think you're big enough, come ahead and try."

As the humor and good-natured bantering continued, it was several hours later when a man in a wet trenchcoat entered the nightclub and hurried past the coat check stand without stopping to check his coat.

He walked directly to the end of the bar, slid onto an empty stool, and ordered a drink from the bartender. While waiting for his drink, his small eyes squinted and slowly panned around the room until they spotted and stopped instantly to focus squarely on the happy, slightly inebriated funsters.

Unaware to the oblivious foursome, an inconspicuous and unknown figure now sat at the bar observing them. The tall, heavyset, prematurely gray and balding man with tiny gray squinty eyes fixed a steely gaze at all of them.

When the hour grew late, the happy foursome left their table, proceeding toward the entrance door, and as they swaggered past the coat check stand, Greg and Tom stopped to retrieve their jackets.

While at the bar, the inescapable beady eyes of an unknown stranger scrutinized their every movement.

As the laughing funsters passed through the doorway into the nighttime misty rain, the lone figure slipped off his bar stool and followed them.

After the four hurried across the street to the car and after Annika fumbled through her keys to snatch the right one and open the car door, everyone finally stumbled gaily into their seats.

At the same time, back across the street, a lone silhouetted figure stood in the dingy yellow glow of the open doorway at the nightclub entrance, still eyeing their every move. Once they entered their car, he hastened to his own car parked on a nearby side street.

Inside their car, amid the giggling and laughter, Annika continued to fumble through her keys to find the ignition key and once found, she finally started the engine and drove off slowly down the street.

When they passed by the first side street, unbeknown to the happy four, lights flicked on instantly from a parked car. The black car pulled away from the curb, turned the corner behind them, and proceeded to follow their car at a distance.

Annika inquired, "At what hotel are you fellas staying?"

"The Bondeheimen," Greg spoke up, "but I sure couldn't tell you where it is from here. All I can tell you is that it's one block up from the main boulevard on a side street near the Grand Hotel and around a corner."

"I know exactly where it is," Annika slurred. "We'll be there in a few minutes."

As they continued on their way through the dimly lit, dark, and abandoned downtown streets, the undetected black car followed them at a distant, steady, and deliberate pace.

When Annika reached the hotel and parked across the street from the entrance, the black car also stopped two blocks behind them, doused its headlights, and sat unnoticed in the blackness.

As soon as Annika shut off the engine, Tom reached over and kissed her full on the lips while Greg and Valerie, sitting in the back seat, kissed passionately.

"You know, Valerie, no woman has ever affected me like this," he whispered.

Valerie pecked his lips and answered, "I'll bet you've said that to hundreds of girls."

"No, I mean it. I've never felt this way in my life. I've never even revealed my feelings to any woman."

"Do I turn you on, Greg?"

"In more ways than one, sexy lady."

The rain was heavier now and beat incessantly on the car's roof.

Greg pulled her toward him and embraced her tight against his chest. He kissed her long and hard. After a prolonged kiss, he rubbed the side of his face alongside hers. Then he kissed her neck softly and backed away.

"Can I see you tomorrow, Valerie?"

"Oh yes, I was hoping you'd ask."

"Hey, terrific! Would you fly with me to Bergen? We could fly early in the morning. All expenses paid, of course. Since you teach school there, you could show me the sights. We could spend the whole day and eat lunch and dinner there. I've heard it's a very picturesque fishing town with a cable car ride. At the end of the day I can drop you off at your apartment or we can catch a flight back to Oslo, whichever you prefer. How does that sound?"

"It's sounds like a wonderful day." She grinned, touching her finger to his lips. "You're on, pardner."

"Them's Tom's words. You're both stealing his act."

Greg reached over the front seat and shook Tom's arm, which was wrapped around Annika's neck.

"Wha . . . what do you want, Greg?" he moaned. "Can't you see we're doing business here?"

"Pardon the intrusion, Don Juan, but it's very late. If everyone wants to get an early start this morning, we'd better let the women get home to get their beauty sleep."

"Yes, I suppose so," Tom mumbled. "I will see you later this morning, won't I, Annika?"

Annika shoved her hands to her hips and cried, "Well, you better see me today. I'd feel very hurt if you didn't."

"Then it's all settled," Greg said, "so let these beautiful women be on their way. Let's get our bags, Tom."

When the two men slid out their side doors, Annika scooted out of her door, ran to the rear of the car, and popped open the trunk. Then she rushed back to her warm, dry seat inside the car.

After checking for their right bags and while Greg pulled the troll from his bag, Tom closed the trunk lid.

Even though the rain had slowed to a drizzle, the two men returned to the side windows and with dripping faces, motioned for the women to roll down their windows.

Valerie rolled down her window and as Greg handed her the wet doll, water dripped off the end of the troll's crooked nose.

"Oh, Greg, he's so ugly!" She smiled while studying his face. "And even though he's sinister-looking, he IS cute and he DOES have a friendly smile."

When she started to hand him back, Greg pushed her hand backwards.

"No, no, he's not mine. He's yours, Valerie."

"He's mine! That's sweet of you, Greg," she remarked, then frowned. "But he's quite ugly."

"Yes, he is, but he's also a very happy troll who will bring you good luck and good fortune."

"Thank you, Greg. I know he will," she replied, holding him up to admire. Then she brought the doll to her breasts, hugged it tightly, closed her eyes, and made a wish.

When she opened her eyes, he asked, "What did you wish?"

"Oh, I'll never tell." She grinned impishly while coddling the doll. "If I were to tell you my wish, the happy troll couldn't let it come true."

The two men reached inside the windows, gave each of the women a final kiss on the lips, and bade them good night.

"Is 7 A.M. okay?" Greg queried.

"Seven sharp." Annika nodded.

Then she started the car and as she pulled away from the curb, the two men waved and started across the street to the hotel entrance.

At the same time, the black car's headlights popped on, the back tires screeched from the curb and the car aimed straight at Greg and Tom, but within seconds, the two men entered the hotel and the black car passed slowly by the entrance without incident.

As the two men entered their room, they were still unaware of the black car following Annika on the streets directly below them.

Annika, at Valerie's direction, deliberately passed Valerie's hotel, which was only a half-block away from Greg and Tom's hotel, and now she was making continuous right turns in an effort to return to their hotel.

The trailing black car also circled the streets behind her.

After many turns, they finally reached the men's hotel again but drove on for another half-block and stopped at Valerie's hotel entrance.

As the two women got out of the car, the black car quickly turned into a side street next to the Bondeheimen hotel.

Annika helped Valerie gather up her bags from the trunk of her car. Then she assured Valerie she'd pick her up at her hotel entrance in a few short hours and after they bade each other good night, Annika got back in the car and sped off down the dark, abandoned streets.

Valerie walked toward the hotel's entrance, but stopped near the doorway. Silhouetted by the light streaming from the doorway, she stood momentarily and stared back at the hotel where Greg and Tom stayed, unaware that two beady eyes stared at her from inside a black car in pitch blackness. She entered the hotel and quickly disappeared into the elevator.

Once Valerie was inside the hotel, the black car's headlamps lit up and the car moved slowly around the corner and headed toward Valerie's hotel. At the hotel's entrance, the car stopped at the curb for the lone figure inside to lean across the front seat and peer out the window on the passenger's side. The mysterious stranger mentally noted the name of her hotel and its street number. Afterwards he leaned back behind the wheel and a flame flared instantly from a cigarette lighter. The flickering flame lit up the pock-marked craggy face of the ugly stranger, the same face that earlier observed the foursome in the nightclub.

The flame quickly snuffed out and the black car drove on down the darkened street into the blackness of the night.

So for what started out as a fun-filled weekend in mid-June for the happy foursome of Greg, Tom, Valerie, and Annika, none of them could possibly imagine the harrowing experience yet to befall Valerie and Greg.

III

Very early that same morning, around 6:15 A.M., the mysterious stranger entered the Bondeheimen hotel and walked into the small cafeteria adjacent to the hotel lobby.

He picked up a tray and sweet roll, along with pouring himself a cup of coffee, placed them on the tray, and slid it along the track toward the cashier who sat on a stool by the register. He was preoccupied reading the morning newspaper.

After paying the cashier, he carried his tray to the windows facing the main street. Choosing a corner table where he'd have an unobstructed view of Valerie's hotel, he sat down, but before he ate, he focused his steely gaze on the entrance of her hotel. Seeing no activity, he looked down at his sweet roll, took a bite, sipped his black coffee, and opened a paperback book.

Periodically he looked up from the book to take glimpses of Valerie's hotel entrance, which indicated the stranger was more interested in watching for Valerie than with reading the book.

His actions went unnoticed by the other four customers in the cafe, who were engrossed in newspapers and whispered conversations.

In a short time, Greg and Tom walked into the coffee shop preoccupied with their usual morning discussion.

Taking only one tray, they poured two cups of coffee, placed them on the tray, and slid it to the cashier for payment. Afterwards they walked to the windows and sat down at a table directly behind the stranger. Greg faced the stranger's back, but a potted plant blocked any vision of the man. It also obstructed any view of Valerie's hotel, which was only a short half-block up the street.

The stranger was well aware of Greg and Tom sitting behind him, since he had taken note of them at the cashier.

It was still raining outside as the two men continued their conversation and sipped their coffee. Occasionally, without interruption to their running discussion, they glanced out the window looking for Annika's car. They were anxious for the women to arrive.

A short time later, the stranger looked up and caught sight of Valerie. She scooted into Annika's car parked at the front entrance of her hotel.

Immediately he stood up, stuffed the book into his coat pocket, and when he turned around and rushed past Greg and Tom, his trenchcoat brushed their table, which caused both men to glance up at the man as he hastened by them.

"Now there's a man in a big hurry on a lazy Sunday morning," Tom commented. "I've never seen anyone move that fast going to church."

Greg checked his watch and said, "And we'll be in an even bigger hurry if Annika and Valerie don't get here soon. I'd hate to miss that 8 A.M. flight to Bergen. I never like to rush."

"Don't worry, Greg. They're due to show up any minute now."

Minutes later, Annika's car passed by their window and stopped short in front of the hotel entrance.

Both men stood up instantly, took quick sips of coffee, and while pulling on their jackets, ran out of the coffee shop.

When they reached the side of the car, Valerie rolled down her window, laughing. "What kept you guys? We're been waiting on you for all of ten seconds now. Annika might have gotten a parking ticket."

"No chance," Greg snapped. "The *politi* would have been so intimidated by your beautiful faces they would have forgotten why they even stopped. They would have excused themselves for the mistake and the intrusion."

"My, my, what nice flattery from such a handsome man on a gloomy Sunday morning." She beamed.

When the men scrambled into the back seat, Annika spun away from the hotel and after a few rapid turns through the downtown city streets, finally sped onto the freeway and headed toward the airport.

Although the early morning traffic was thin, the trailing black car still remained undiscovered in its distant, deliberate, relentless pursuit.

Once Annika exited the freeway and drove onto the airport causeway, the stranger knew exactly where they were destined.

Now he wanted to get to the airport ahead of them, so he pressed the accelerator and raced onto the causeway directly behind them. Then with a burst of speed, the black car overtook the foursome and sped past them.

At the airport parking area, the stranger quickly pulled into an empty parking space, stopped the engine, jumped out, and ran to the inclined walkway leading to the airport entrance.

As he bolted up the walkway, Annika drove past him and stopped directly in front of the entrance. So he stopped short, then proceeded at a very slow gait without taking his eyes off the car.

When Greg and Valerie stepped out from their side of the car, Annika got out from the driver's side and looked across the top of the roof at them.

"Remember, we'll be in the airport waiting for you at 6 P.M.," she said. If you miss the early flight, don't worry about it. Tom and I will stay in the terminal and wait on the later flights. We know you'll be on one of them. You and Greg have fun in Bergen."

"Thanks, Annika, I know we will. You and Tom have a great day, too."

After everyone waved, Annika got back in the car and drove off. They were both anxious to spend the day together.

Upon entering the terminal, Greg and Valerie went directly to the ticket counter to purchase their tickets and afterwards they ambled over to the snack bar, bought their coffee, and sat down at a table to await their flight.

The ever-watchful stranger had taken a seat in the waiting area a good distance from the snack bar. When Greg and Valerie became absorbed in conversation, he hurried to the same ticket counter and spoke to the agent.

"I see by your flight board, your first flight out this morning is to Bergen at 8 A.M., and your next flight doesn't leave for another hour and a half at 9:30 A.M. Is that correct?"

"Yes, sir, the flight schedule is correct."

"Well, I don't want to sit around for another hour, so I'd better take the early flight. Let me have one round-trip fare to Bergen at 8 A.M., in the first rows near first class, if possible."

"Yes, sir, I can accommodate you." She smiled.

After paying for his ticket, he didn't return to the waiting area, but sauntered off down the concourse, keeping his back to the snack bar.

In a short time, a voice on the PA system announced that the flight to Bergen was "now boarding."

Greg and Valerie got up from their table and made their way to the gate where they handed their tickets to the agent and followed the straggling passengers down the tunnel to the exit door.

Once outside the terminal, they hastened to the plane's stairway, climbed the steps, and boarded the waiting aircraft.

The stranger was the last passenger on board and quickly found his seat in the forward part of the plane, but before he sat down, he scanned the faces of the people sitting to the rear and spied Greg and Valerie. They sat midway in the cabin already conversing. Satisfied they hadn't noticed him, he scooted into his seat by the window and fastened his seat belt.

When the aircraft took off and reached cruising speed, the flight attendants served breakfast to all on board.

While eating, Greg glanced out his window and remarked, "Look at all that snow down there. One minute we're in all the greenery of Oslo and minutes later we're flying over a landscape of ice and snow. This country is full of surprises." He turned to Valerie. "That goes for you, too, troll. You're also full of surprises."

"Good or bad surprises?" She grinned with a glint in her eyes.

"Always good surprises from a good troll, I discovered."

Biting into her sweet roll, she sneered, "Maybe I'm an evil vampire troll waiting for the right moment to bite your neck and suck your blood. You don't really know, now do you?"

"Sounds like I'd better be on guard and on my best behavior," he murmured while pecking her on the lips.

Later when the aircraft landed in Bergen, the stranger sat fast in his seat. He waited for all of the passengers to deplane ahead of him so he could follow Greg and Valerie.

As they passed by his seat, his squinty eyes viewed them intently.

The stranger was one of the last passengers to deplane, and as everyone walked up the tunnel, he kept his eyes focused directly on the backs of Greg and Valerie. He had no intention of losing them.

After a short walk through the small terminal, Greg and Valerie ambled out the front entrance to a shuttle bus waiting to transport people into downtown Bergen.

When they stepped through the door at the front stairwell, the stranger jumped onto the rear stairwell and scrambled onto the bus.

As Greg and Valerie took their seats up front, close to the driver, the stranger took a seat in a rear corner of the bus. From that vantage point on the opposite side of the aisle, he could easily keep surveillance of the twosome.

During the half-hour ride into town, Greg and Valerie admired the passing scenes of rugged terrain.

"Beautiful rocky environment," Greg reacted. "The houses appear to be built on rock foundations and even the grass and flowers seem to grow from rocks. No doubt the countryside formed out of the Ice Age, but I'd prefer to imagine it being hewed and sculptured from the axes and spears of the Vikings themselves. Those Vikings, without doubt, were a rough-and-tumble, hard bunch of people."

Valerie added, "To inhabit and survive in this kind of environment, they had to be. The scenery is so exciting and Bergen is so beautiful and homey. I've always felt comfortable and relaxed here. I just love it."

He replied, "Since you're my personal tour guide for the day, you'll have to show me where you live and the school where you teach."

"That's a must." She smiled.

Soon the bus stopped near the city center, only a few short blocks from the fish market, so Greg and Valerie exited the bus from the front doorway while the stranger departed from the rear doorway.

Greg and Valerie began walking toward the fish market, but the stranger, after stepping from the bus, noticed the desolate, deserted streets and not wanting to draw their attention, turned his back to them and walked away in the opposite direction of the fish market.

When he reached the first side street, he turned the corner and stopped behind a building, then peered around the corner of the building to see where they were.

Greg and Valerie had crossed the street from the bus stop and, hand-in-hand, window-shopped the stores as they strolled along.

The stranger emerged slowly from behind the building and since the streets were practically empty of pedestrians, he began to follow them cautiously, on the opposite side of the street. Being aware that he looked conspicuous, he always kept three to four blocks of distance between him and them, but still, whenever he thought Greg or Valerie would turn around, he'd duck into a doorway or dart around the corner of a building.

Greg and Valerie were in no hurry. They walked slowly and at times chased one another, laughing, along the vacant streets. They stopped often to study the merchandise through the windows.

At the fish market, they stopped to view the various fishing boats, yachts, schooners, and sailing boats docked alongside the cement walls that encircled the U-shaped piers.

They continued to meander and window-shopped the small souvenir and gift shops along the piers. Eventually they stopped at Madam Felles cafe on the piers, bought coffee, and relaxed at a patio table with a view of the small harbor.

Greg admired the ever-silent sailing vessels, some stationary, some bobbing, with their shiny white masts stripped of their sails. The pointed stanchions, with their arm-like booms bound securely with tightly rolled canvas, stood with dignity and staunchly pointed straight upward toward the overhanging gray layer of clouds. To Greg, it was postcard scenery.

Behind them, across the street, the stranger sat on a bench reading a newspaper.

"After we drink our coffee, Greg, we can go to Ulriksbanen," Valerie stated. "That's where we ride the cable up the mountain. The view is spectacular."

"Sounds great. I should be able to get some good snapshots up there."

"The bus stop for the drive to the cable car is only a few blocks from here."

"Okay by me. My beautiful troll guide could lead me to all of Norway's mysterious places." Then with a glint in his eye, he added, "And if I get real lucky, maybe you'd take me to a secluded Viking hideaway."

"You are a tease, Greg. When we come back to the fish market, we can shoot up the Funicular also and catch a view of Bergen's harbor from Mount Floyan. That's always fun, too."

Minutes later, they finished their coffee, left the promenade, and crossed the street behind the cafe. As they stepped onto the sidewalk and passed by the stranger sitting on the bench, Valerie casually looked to the side and glimpsed the man's craggy face and beady eyes looking straight up at her. His ugly glare unnerved her.

She and Greg continued strolling the waterfront and window-shopping the gift stores, but several times Valerie turned around curiously to view the man sitting on the bench. Twice, she caught him staring at them and each time he dropped his gaze onto his newspaper.

At one of the shop windows, Greg exclaimed, "Look, Valerie, there's a troll plaque. It describes trolls: 1) They can have nine heads; 2) They have tails; 3) They can have eight fingers and eight toes; 4) They can carry their heads under their arms; and 5) They live in the dark and turn to stone in sunlight. I'd love to buy that plaque, but the shop is closed."

"I'll be sure to buy it and mail it to you, Greg."

"I'd appreciate that. Let's not forget to exchange addresses before I leave for the States tomorrow. You haven't seen the last of me, troll."

When they reached the bus stop, the sun peeked through an opening in the overcast sky but quickly disappeared behind the fast-moving gray clouds.

The bus arrived shortly and upon entering the bus, Valerie led Greg to the back. Before sitting down, however, she glanced out the rear window and saw a man enter a taxicab one block behind them. She thought he looked like the same man who sat on the street bench reading a newspaper and observing them. So after she sat down, she looked out the rear window several times and each time, she saw the same taxicab following their bus. The taxi had made no attempt to pass the bus.

At the same time, Greg's curiosity over Valerie's many glances out the rear window caused him to turn around and stare out the window, too.

"What's outside that's so fascinating?" he queried.

"It's that taxi. It's been following this bus ever since we got on at the bus stop. It won't pass the bus nor will it turn off onto another street."

"So what's strange about a taxicab following a bus? Maybe the driver hasn't had a chance to pass. These streets are very narrow and traffic's flowing now."

"No, Greg, that taxi has had plenty of chances to pass this bus. Back at the fish market, a man sitting on a bench reading a newspaper looked up at me as we walked past him. We made eye contact and while we walked along the store fronts, I turned around a few times and caught him watching us. Then when we got on this bus, I saw that same man climb into that taxicab right behind us. I'm convinced he's following us, Greg."

"Don't be silly. Why would anyone be following us? You aren't hiding a deep dark secret, are you? Like a sordid indiscretion, perhaps?"

"No, Sherlock, I have no hidden secrets or skeletons in my closet." She shrugged, turning to face front. "I'm not paranoid and I don't suffer from any guilt trips, but I DO have a creepy feeling about that taxicab. I know my suspicions will be confirmed at the cable car."

"Don't be too disappointed if they aren't confirmed." He grinned.

At Ulriksbanen, when they stepped off the bus, Valerie immediately looked to the rear of the bus for the taxi. It was gone.

The parked bus also blocked any view of the entrance to the cable car, but when it drove on, Valerie looked across the street to see the taxicab climbing the small hill leading to the cable car.

Instantly she pointed to the taxi climbing the hill, "See! There it is, Greg. That cab is heading straight to the cable car. That man is tailing us, I just know it."

"Just because he's going where we're going doesn't mean he's tailing us. Maybe he's a tourist going for a ride on the cable car, like us. C'mon, Valerie, lighten up."

"Okay, if he's a tourist, like us, why didn't he ride the bus?"

"How would I know why he'd take a taxi? I'm no psychic. He's probably a rich tourist. I think your woman's intuition is getting the best of you right now. Thank goodness we men don't have women's hypersensitivity."

"Too bad for you men. Perhaps if you were more sensitive, you'd understand us women better."

Greg grasped her arm, tightened his lips, and murmured, "Better for us not to be so sensitive."

"What was that?"

"Oh, nothing." He grinned as they crossed the street.

After a ten-minute jaunt up the hill, they arrived at the cable car ticket booth, purchased their tickets, and took their place at the end of the short line of people. Valerie looked up ahead and after spying the stranger standing at the front of the line, elbowed Greg's ribs.

"See, he's up there at the head of the line."

Greg winced while rubbing his ribs and said, "I see him. I see him."

In due time, the cable car descended the mountain and the small group squeezed aboard.

Although everyone was closely jammed against one another, with Valerie's back pressed tightly against one window, she was still able to eye the stranger's profile.

Suddenly the stranger turned his head and made direct eye contact with Valerie.

Immediately she looked away from his steely gaze.

"Omigod, Greg, he stared right at me."

"I'm aware," Greg answered. "He glared at me, too, but it still doesn't mean anything. Look away from him and enjoy the ride."

Valerie gripped his arm, snuggled up close, peered up at him, and purred, "Okay, you win, handsome. I'd rather look into your dark sexy eyes, anyway."

"If we weren't squashed like packed sardines, you'd be in some deep trouble right now, troll. However, for the moment, I DO like these close quarters." He smirked, squirming against her. "Real cozy, eh?"

"Eh, eh, Mr. Ghost, there's people watching."

"Now, don't get sassy, sexy troll."

Valerie pushed tight against him.

"Ooo, now I'm a SEXY troll. I like that."

At the summit, everyone scattered in all directions while Greg and Valerie strolled over to a scenic lookout. With their arms around each other's waists, they stood and admired the magnificent view of the rugged Norwegian landscape. The peaceful fishing town of Bergen laid to their right with the shadowy fjords stretched across the far horizon. For the moment, the stranger was forgotten.

Greg wanted to feel her soft breasts against his chest again, so he impulsively tugged at her waist, pulling her close to him. When she turned to look up at him, he squeezed her waist and pulled her up flat against himself. When he kissed her warmly, she wrapped her arms around his neck and met his lips eagerly. She kissed him back hard on the mouth. Desire welled within them as they clung together in a long embrace, but when she tried to push away from him, Greg wouldn't release her. Finally, she broke away from his vise-like grip.

Panting to catch her breath, she threw her hand to her breasts and gasped, "I must admit, I've never been kissed like THAT before! You literally took my breath away. I can't catch my breath."

Shaking a finger at her, he laughed. "I warned you that you were in deep trouble, sassy one."

"Evidently!" she puffed.

His face sobered as he took her hands in his, looked directly into her eyes, and said sincerely, "Valerie, I really mean it. I've never felt like this for any woman in my life. I truly believe I'm in love with you."

Immediately she reached up and touched his lips with her fingertips and with anxiety in her inquisitive eyes stared hard into his eyes. She searched them desperately in the hope of finding something there to support the truthfulness of his words. Her heart ached to believe him, for in her previous relationships with men, their words had proven to be meaningless and worthless.

"Oh, Greg," she whispered, "think about what you're saying. You've only known me a few short days. How can you possibly know your true feelings for me? How can you say you love me? You don't even know me. Maybe it's all just physical infatuation."

"Shopping for love is like shopping for anything else," he replied. "When we shop for clothes, we know beforehand what we're looking for and when we don't find what we're looking for, we don't buy anything, right? Just like Annika yesterday. However, when we do find what we're looking for, we buy it. I'm a one-woman man, Valerie, and I've found what I've been shopping for–you!"

"I must admit, too, Greg. I've never felt this way about any man, either. But I'm not so sure it's love. I'm not that sure of myself."

They kissed affectionately and when they released their embrace, Greg spotted the stranger over Valerie's shoulder, watching them from another lookout. They eyed each other momentarily before the stranger turned his head away and gazed off into the distance.

Valerie turned around to see that Greg was staring at the stranger.

"When your expression changed, I knew it must be him again. He was watching us, wasn't he?" she quizzed.

"Yes, he watched us kissing, but it still doesn't mean anything."

"Well, that guy gives me the willies." She quivered. "I just know he's following us and I'm not riding back down the cable car with that creep gawking at us. We can use the trails and walk back down the mountain. It only takes twenty minutes to a half-hour. C'mon, let's get some sandwiches and snacks. We can stop and have a picnic on the way down. It'll be fun, Greg."

"Sounds great. Let's do it."

She took his hand and they left for the coffee shop, which lay beyond the stranger's viewpoint. The walkway led directly by him and Greg spoiled for a confrontation, so when they passed behind him within a few feet, Greg turned to say something, but Valerie tugged at his arm to stop him from speaking. She feared the man too much and wanted no contact of any kind with him.

The stranger never turned around or reacted to them. He peered straight ahead into space.

They continued on and entered the coffee shop to buy their food and drinks. After Greg paid the cashier and they stepped outside, he looked to the viewpoint where the stranger had been standing. He was gone. The stranger was nowhere in sight.

Hand-in-hand, Valerie led him to a trail and before long, they had traipsed halfway down the mountainside, laughing and kissing, until they stopped to relax and eat their food. Sitting down with their backs propped against a tree, they munched on sandwiches.

Later, as they rested their heads back against the tree trunk, Greg turned to Valerie's profile and kissed the side of her face. When she turned to face him, they kissed tenderly.

Then he slid his cheek alongside hers and murmured, "Don't you believe in love at first sight, Val?"

"I really don't know if I do or not," she answered, "but I can say, honestly, that no man has ever affected me like you do."

Instantly, he brought his eyes back to meet her eyes directly. Wide-eyed, his eyes flashed from side to side with intense curiosity. In anxious anticipation, he stared deep into those indelible purplish-blue eyes, wanting her to say she loved him.

"How do I affect you, Val? What are you feeling for me right this very moment?"

She stared back, lovingly. "At this very moment, Greg, I'm full of desire for you. I believe it's more than physical attraction, but I don't know if I'd call it love. I'm not quite sure how to define love. It can only be defined with intangibles; that I know."

Greg quickly swallowed her in his arms and laying her back gently down on the grass, he unzipped the front of her jacket and unbuttoned the top buttons of her blouse. As he caressed her soft firm breasts for the first time, desire aroused their passion for one another; kissing fired more excitement.

When he backed away from her, he searched her incredible eyes saying, "Someone once said, 'the eyes are the mir–'" His words cut off when he looked up and spied the stranger. Then he drawled, "–'rorrrs of onnne's soooul'. What the hell's with that guy! He's always gaping at us whenever we kiss. He's got to be some kind of pervert."

High above them, standing on a viewing platform, the stranger observed them through binoculars.

Valerie sat up quickly to button her blouse and zip up her jacket, and when she turned to glare up at the inscrutable stranger, he instantly dropped his field glasses and backed away from the railing, then disappeared from sight.

Jumping to her feet and brushing herself off, she stammered, "Well, that should finally prove it to you, Mr. Ghost. He IS spying on us, so he's the real spook here, not you. C'mon, let's get out of here. He's too creepy for me."

"But why would he be following us, Val?"

"How should I know? Maybe it's you he's after. That would be somewhat of a relief."

"Following me? I haven't got any dark secrets. I'm just plain ol' Greg from Dakota territory, ma'am."

"Well, I don't have any skeletons in my closet, either."

He took her hand and as they hurried down the mountainside, they stopped from time to time to look back up the trails to see if the stranger was following them. He was never seen.

In the meantime, the stranger had already descended by the cable car and awaited them at the bottom of the mountain. He sat with his back against a tree on the sloped hillside in a small park overlooking the bus stop. The tree blocked any view of him from the circular road behind him, the same road that led to the cable car entrance. From his vantage point, he could watch Greg and Valerie when they returned down the road to the bus stop. He opened his newspaper and held it out wide to cover his face.

It wasn't long before Greg and Valerie hastened down the road behind him. She kept checking behind them but didn't see the man sitting with his back to the tree. He made no move to leave his position. He simply observed them from the side of his paper.

At the bus stop, they sat down on the bench with several other people to await the bus and when it approached, the stranger stood up and raced down the hillside toward the sidewalk. At the sidewalk, just as he turned toward the bus stop, the bus passed by him and stopped about one-half block ahead of him.

As the passengers began boarding the bus, the stranger bolted to get aboard but when he reached the front door, it was almost closed and the bus was already moving away from the curb. Running with the bus, he reached up to block the door from closing. Then holding the door back, he jumped up onto the stairwell and barely squeezed inside the door before it closed completely.

The driver checked his side-view mirror and after pulling out into traffic, turned and glared at the stranger, who was looking down and fumbling with his pocket change. Without looking up, the stranger paid the fare and took a seat directly behind the driver.

Greg and Valerie sat in the rear of the bus, and when she saw the stranger get onboard, she exclaimed, "Omigod! Look, Greg, that creep just got on the bus. Do you see him sitting behind the driver?"

"I see him."

"It's all to obvious now. It's by no mere coincidence that he's on this bus. So are you convinced yet that that creep IS following us?"

"You win. Now I'm convinced."

"So what do we do?"

"For now, we'll stay cool, calm, and collected but when the bus stops near the fish market, we'll dash out the rear door. So let me know when we're near the fish market."

Every time the bus stopped to drop off riders, the man's intentions clearly showed when he turned around to eye the people debarking from the rear exit.

"Look at him, Greg. Every time the bus stops, he turns around to see who's leaving by the back door. When we get off, he'll see us for sure."

"Don't worry about it. There are a lot of people on the streets now and I'm sure the fish market is crowded. I don't believe he'll try anything in public because he hasn't approached us so far. I really don't think he wants confrontation anyway, my beautiful troll."

"Not yet, anyway," she replied, "but he may try something later."

"I'm ready at all times now for any moves he might make."

"That creep doesn't seem to be too concerned we're well aware of him, either," she added.

"Nope. He also remains cool, calm, and creepy."

Valerie turned and kissed him on the cheek, saying, "You may think this is all very amusing, Mr. Ghost, but I'm terrified of that man. I don't know what he wants from us."

"Nor do I, but relax, will you? We still aren't absolutely sure he's tailing us. He might only be some kind of weird spying voyeur obsessed with your beautiful body."

"Oh, real nice! That's just what we need. A pervert flasher in a trench-coat following us around Bergen. Makes for a wonderful Sunday outing, Greg."

Greg burst into laughter, then quickly cupped his mouth with his hand to muffle his outburst.

In a short time, the bus stopped a few blocks away from the fish market and the stranger, as usual, turned around to see two riders stepping down into the rear stairwell. Greg gripped Valerie's hand and when the stranger turned back around to face the front, they jumped up and scooted out the rear exit behind the other two people. For a few moments they stood and watched the bus wheel from the curb and drive away.

"Ah-ha, we were too fast for him that time!" Valerie smirked. "By the time that bus reaches its next bus stop, we'll be out of his eyesight. We can forget about him now. C'mon, Greg, let's get to the Funicular. From Mount Floyan, there's a fantastic view of the harbor and fish market."

They hurried along the sidewalk and when they reached the ticket booth and bought their tickets, the tram car sat at the depot waiting for its milling riders to get onboard. Before boarding the car, still skeptical, they scanned the passengers with suspicion.

"Looks like we finally gave him the slip," Valerie chimed.

"For the time being, anyway," he answered.

"What do you mean, 'for the time being'? We better be rid of him for good."

Boarding the tram car, they enjoyed the scenic ride to the summit and stepped off the car to admire the magnificent rocky terrain sprawled beneath them. The rugged landscape provided a perfect backdrop for many snapshots of Bergen's colorful harbor and U-shaped piers along with a few shots of his beautiful troll.

Around midday Greg checked his watch and saw it was growing late, so they decided to return to the bottom of the mountain.

After they descended the tramway and stepped off the car, they walked to the nearest street corner to wait at the curb for traffic to clear. A bus crossed the intersection and passed directly in front of them, stopping at its corner bus stop. The side of the bus remained only inches away from their faces, blocking their view of the street.

After the bus drove away, Greg immediately noticed a man sitting across the street on a bench reading a newspaper. Because the paper was held up in front of his eyes, Greg couldn't see his face, but being suspicious, and before they stepped off the curb to cross the street, Greg hesitated and held Valerie back with his arm.

"What's the matter, Greg?"

"That man across the street, sitting on the bench with a newspaper."

Valerie shot a glance at the man on the bench and cried, "Oh no, it's him again!"

Suddenly the man closed the newspaper, folded it, dropped it on his lap, and turned sideways to watch the motorcyclists congregating in the fish market.

"Whew! It's not him," she sighed. "That's a relief. My heart's pounding fast!"

"He's wearing black pants exactly like him," Greg said. "Because I couldn't see his jacket or face, I thought it was him."

Before stepping off the curb, they scanned the faces of people immediately across the street and beyond to the milling people in the crowded fish market. Without sighting the stranger, they crossed the street and mingled with the throng of people who flowed into the fish market.

Unaware to Greg and Valerie, a lone figure sat by a window in a cafe situated directly across the street from the fish market. When he spotted them, he squinted his beady gray eyes and scrutinized their movements. From time to time, he lifted a stein to his mouth and sipped his beer.

While strolling the marketplace, Greg used the schooners and sailing ships as background for more snapshots of Valerie, and a friendly passerby accepted a request to take a snapshot of both of them.

A short time later they made their way to Valerie's favorite restaurant, the Bryggeloftet. Upon entering the dining room, the hostess led them to a table for two by a window overlooking the U-shaped piers and surrounding marketplace.

She handed them menus, left, and returned shortly to take their order.

Greg ordered two glasses of wine, steak strips for Valerie, and baked salmon for himself.

Then he leaned back in his chair to relax and said, "Well, Valerie, I must say it's certainly been quite a memorable day. A day I'll never forget. You haven't seen the last of me, you know. Will you write to me?"

"Yes, Greg, I will write to you." She smiled.

"I'll like that. We mustn't forget to trade addresses before my flight leaves in the morning."

"I've had a wonderful weekend, too, Greg, but please don't expect too much from me. I'm very attracted to you, but let's look at our situation realistically. We'll be thousands of miles away from each other; you in South Dakota and me here in Norway. Our lives are very different. What could ever come of our two-day relationship?"

"That settles it then. I won't leave tomorrow. I'll stay right here in Bergen forever and ever, so I can gape at those two beautiful blue eyes and auburn hair."

"Don't be silly, Greg!"

"Your eyes wipe me out."

"Do you want them?"

"Heavens, no, they were only created for a beautiful troll like you, not a ghosty like plain ol' Greg."

Valerie turned toward the window and gazed out over the people in the fish market.

"I guess we finally escaped that creep," she remarked. "We haven't seen him since we jumped from the bus."

Greg wasn't convinced they'd seen the last of the mysterious stranger, but he wanted to try and make Valerie feel comfortable with good food and conversation.

"Are you more relaxed now?" he asked.

The waitress had arrived with their wine and as she sipped her drink, she said, "I'm somewhat relaxed sitting here. This wine and a delicious meal will certainly help."

After dinner, while drinking their wine, Greg reached into his pants pocket and grabbed the tiny jewelry box. Pulling it from his pocket, he stretched his arm across the table and presented a clenched fist to Valerie.

"What's that?" she asked.

"Open my hand and see."

Valerie turned his hand over, gently opened his fingers, and picked the box from his palm.

Upon opening the top, she exclaimed, "Oh, Greg! It's lovely. Thank you, so much." Then after slipping the ring onto the third finger of her left hand, she added, "But it's too big for my finger." She held up her hand to admire it. "I assume it's a friendship ring, right?"

"Yep, that it is, and don't worry about it being too big. The clerk in the gift shop told me you can take it back at any time and have it sized free of charge."

"Those index fingers touching fingertips signifies our own personal touching of the two of us," she continued. "I just love it, Greg. Whenever I wear it, I'll look at those two fingers touching and think of this fun weekend we're sharing."

He replied, "To me, it signifies a meaningful and lasting relationship."

"I like that, Greg. That goes for me, too."

"Hey, you put it on your wedding finger. How come?"

"Not in Norway," she retorted. "The third finger of the RIGHT hand is the wedding finger for Norwegians; not the left hand."

As he took a sip from his glass an image suddenly flashed through Greg's mind and he blurted, "That's where I saw that guy!"

"What guy? You mean that creep who's been following us all day?"

"Yes, I thought he looked familiar. I didn't mention it before because I kept trying to remember where I'd seen him. He was in our hotel cafe this morning where Tom and I waited for you and Annika to pick us up. He sat at a table by the window in front of us drinking coffee and when he jumped up and ran by us, his coat brushed our table. Startled, I looked up and glimpsed his face."

"You mean that creep was in your hotel this morning!" she exclaimed. "The hotel where I'm staying is only one-half block up the street from your hotel. How soon after he jumped up and left his table did we arrive?"

"Not more than three or four minutes."

"That's about how long it took for us to get from my hotel to your hotel with all the right turns. He must have been watching my hotel entrance from that cafe window. When he saw me come out and get into Annika's car, that's when he got up and left the table in a hurry. That means he followed us here from Oslo and he's still out there somewhere. Even though we can't see him, Greg, he knows right where we are. I just know it. The question is, why? What could he want with us?"

"It beats me, but I intend to find out. The next time he shows himself, I'm going to confront him. I've had enough of him."

"Now, I'm really scared. I think I'll go and powder my nose. I'll be right back."

As Valerie got up and walked away, Greg turned his attention out the window to the fish market. While sipping his coffee, he surveyed the people intently for any sign of the mysterious stranger.

Around ten minutes later, when Valerie hadn't returned, Greg became concerned about her. He turned around in his chair several times to look for her, but she wasn't coming. After fifteen minutes, he moved around the table to sit in her chair. From that position, he stared anxiously at the hallway Valerie had entered.

Where is she? he thought. *Why is she taking so long? I hope nothing has happened to her.*

At twenty minutes, his imagination was running away with him. He checked his watch frequently.

When twenty-five minutes had expired, he murmured, "That does it! I can't sit here any longer. I've got to find out what's happened to her."

He shoved the chair back and just as he stood up to go and look for her, Valerie emerged from the hallway into the dining room and hastened toward him. Relieved at seeing her, he sat back down in his chair again.

When she arrived at the table, he asked, "What took you so long? I was about to go looking for you."

"I'm sorry, Greg, but I met a friend in the ladies room and we started chatting. You know how women are when we get talking. I lost track of the time."

"It's okay now, but I was very worried. I thought something happened to you."

Valerie gazed out the window at the people in the fish market.

"I wonder if that creep is wandering around somewhere in that crowd," she said.

He replied, "Even if he isn't in the fish market, he could be waiting at the airport watching for us at the departure gates for Oslo. When I spot him, I'll confront him. You can be sure of that, Val."

"I'm not so sure I want you to confront him."

Their conversation soon waned and when they finished drinking their coffee, Greg paid the waitress and they left the dining room.

After they descended the stairs and stepped outside onto the sidewalk, Valerie viewed the fish market.

"I'll bet that creep is watching us right now," she maintained.

"Well, I wouldn't worry too much about him, Val. If he meant real trouble, he would have made a move on us by now."

"That's your opinion," she snapped.

"Why don't we forget about him for now," he said as he checked his watch, "so you can show me where you live and where you teach school. It's just about four o'clock. Do we have time to go there before we head for the airport?"

"Yes, we have plenty of time." She smiled. "My apartment is only a few blocks away. We can walk there from here and the school is not far from my apartment. We can walk there also."

She slipped her arm under his and they strolled again toward the fish market. When they reached the main corner to the marketplace, Greg picked six long-stemmed red roses from a flower cart and handed the flowers and krona to the flower lady.

After wrapping them in paper, she handed them back to him and smiled graciously. "Thank you, sir."

Greg, in turn, handed them directly to Valerie, who reached up instantly and kissed him on the cheek.

"Thank you, Greg, they're beautiful."

Continuing up the street, they came to a tourist information center where they stopped for Valerie to browse through the magazines displayed outside the small building.

"Do they sell street guides here?" Greg queried.

"Yes, they do," she replied. "You can buy one inside. You go ahead. I'll wait for you right here. Maybe I can find this month's issue of my favorite magazine."

As he entered the small shop, Valerie was already thumbing pages, unaware of the stranger approaching fast, within a half-block away. When he saw Greg disappear inside the store, he raced toward her and within seconds, he stood at her back and grabbed her arm.

Instinctively, she shook her arm loose and spun around to stare straight up into the beady gray eyes of the stranger. He glowered at her and smirked.

Petrified at his face, she dropped the magazine and stood frozen for an instant.

Then she jammed the roses straight into his face and screamed, "Get your hands off me, creep!"

He staggered backwards and when he covered his bleeding face with his hands, she shoved him further away from her.

Terrified, she panicked and ran toward a taxicab parked a short block away, yelling, "Taxi! Taxi!"

The stranger quickly regained his senses and raced after her.

Meanwhile, Greg emerged from inside the shop and was stunned to see Valerie gone from the magazine rack with her roses strewn all over the pavement. When he looked down the street, he saw Valerie running for a taxicab, screaming, with the stranger in hot pursuit.

Immediately, he bolted after both of them, hollering, "Valerie! Stop!"

It was to no avail. She didn't stop or even turn around. She kept on running until she reached the taxi safely.

She jerked open the door and scrambled onto the back seat, but when she pulled the door to close it, the stranger's knee shot inside to block it.

"Go! Go, driver!" she yelled.

The taxi screeched from the curb and jolted the stranger back out of the car. Stumbling backwards, he fell flat on his back on the street.

As the cab sped away toward the fish market, the stranger jumped up, brushed himself off, and dashed back to another taxicab parked at the curb.

Pulling open the door quickly, he jumped inside and shouted, "Follow that taxi that just pulled out in front of us."

The driver instantly started the engine and shot away from the curb to speed after Valerie's cab.

When Greg saw the two taxicabs speeding after one another, he stopped dead in his tracks in the middle of the street. He reeled around in search of other taxis, but none were in sight.

Running back, he stopped to stoop down and pick up a rose from the street. As he broke off the long stem, he looked up and noticed a cruising taxicab turn the corner at the next block. Greg jumped to his feet, waving frantically for the driver to come to him, and when the taxi drove up, he stuffed the rose into his jacket pocket, opened the back door, and scooted inside.

"See those taxis moving slowly through the fish market?" he stated.

"Yes, I see them," the cabby said.

"Look, they've turned left on the far side of the market. They're passing by the white schooner now. Follow them, keep them in sight, and don't lose them."

"I'll get right on them, sir. They won't get away from me," the driver announced. "I'll be right on top of them."

Greg rested his chin on the top of the front seat and stared ahead at the racing taxicabs.

At the piers and after Greg's cabby made the same left turn as the other two cabs, he noticed up ahead that Valerie's cab stopped abruptly at the end of the piers.

When she leaped from the car, two tall men ran across the street to her. One of the men wrapped his arm around her waist.

Then the second taxi slid to a stop next to the first taxi and the stranger jumped out.

Immediately Valerie's cab spun around with a U-turn from the curb and sped at Greg's taxi. As it sped past them, Greg turned around to observe the car as it turned right at the fish market and vanished in traffic.

He remarked, "He was in one big damn hurry to get away."

When Greg faced forward and looked ahead again, he saw the stranger talking to the two tall burly men.

Suddenly Valerie pounded the stranger with her fists and kicked at his legs, but the man with his arm around her waist jerked her backwards away from the stranger. He lifted her up sideways, and with her legs still kicking and her arms flailing wildly, carried her across the street. When the other man followed, the stranger stood and watched the three of them disappear from sight.

Greg couldn't believe what he'd just seen.

"Where did they go?" he stammered.

"Down to the water," his driver replied.

"Faster! Faster, driver!" Greg ordered. "She's in bad trouble."

When Greg's taxi screeched to a stop next to the stranger's taxi, the stranger stood at a precipice with his fists to his hips, staring out at the harbor.

As Greg jumped out to confront the stranger, his attention was quickly diverted to a white speedboat skimming across the water in the harbor basin.

Three people sat in the speeding craft. Valerie sat alongside the driver of the boat and the other man sat behind them. As the boat sped for the open bay, Valerie's hair blew wildly in the harbor breeze. When she turned around to catch sight of Greg, she waved frantically to him. All he could do was wave back to her. He stood baffled, unable to save her, and watched helplessly as the speeding boat diminished in the distance.

The chase ended the same way it started–abruptly.

"She's gone! They've kidnapped her, but why?" he murmured aloud. "I don't even know where she lives. I'll never see her again."

Greg quickly emerged from his thoughts to turn and glare at the stranger, but when the stranger saw Greg eyeing him, he instantly hopped into his standing taxi.

"Hey, wait a minute!" Greg shouted at him.

His plea ignored, the stranger's cabby started the engine and spun away from the curb.

Greg turned his attention back out toward the bay. He wanted one last look at Valerie. On the horizon, the speeding craft appeared only as a moving white speck.

Then he jumped into his taxi, demanding, "Go, driver! Don't let that other taxicab get away. I want to talk to the man riding in it."

Wheeling away from the curb, Greg's cab sped off and chased the stranger's cab down the street. With the stranger's taxi clearly visible in front of them, it turned right at the fish market and drove toward the information center.

"Don't lose him," Greg replied.

"I'll try," his driver answered, "but the traffic downtown is very heavy now. There's a big crowd milling around in the marketplace, too."

"Do you know the driver of the taxi we're following?"

"No, I don't know him. He's a new driver."

At the next corner, the stranger's cab made a sharp right turn and sped alongside the piers of the U-shaped harbor.

"Stay with him!" Greg cried.

Greg's driver turned right sharply at the same corner and sped past the restaurant Greg and Valerie had eaten it, while up ahead the stranger's cab slid left around a corner and disappeared from their sight.

Moments later, Greg's taxi turned the same corner, but the stranger's taxi was nowhere to be seen. It was gone.

For the next hour Greg and his cabby cruised the waterfront and hunted up and down the many narrow downtown side streets, but their efforts were fruitless. The streets were deserted and barren. There was no sign of the stranger's cab.

"I guess it's useless to keep driving around these streets," Greg relented.

"It's for certain they're out of the area now," the cabby replied.

"My friend, Valerie, has been kidnapped, so you can take me to the Bergen *politi*. I need to file a kidnap report."

"The station is only a few streets from here."

His driver turned a few corners and arrived at the police station within a few minutes. When Greg stepped out of the car, he asked the cabby to wait for him. Then he entered the station and walked up to the main desk.

"I'd like to report a kidnapping," Greg said. "Who would I have to see?"

"You're American?" the officer queried.

"Yes, I am."

"Is the missing person American, also?"

50

"Yes, she is."

The officer pointed to a bench by the wall and said, "You can wait over there. I'll get someone to help you."

The officer picked up his phone, spoke a few Norsk words, and put the receiver down.

In a short time, another officer arrived and while shaking Greg's hand, introduced himself.

"I'm Officer Stensen," he said, "and I work in the Missing Person's Division. If you'll follow me, we can fill out the necessary papers at my desk."

Greg followed the policeman to his desk and related all pertinent information to him.

"Well, it all does sound very strange, Mr. Ericsen. We'll give it our immediate attention."

"It's more than just strange. There's a kidnapping here," Greg reiterated.

"Do you have any idea who these men are or where they came from?"

"How would I know who they are? I'm an American tourist. I've only been in Norway two days."

"What color was the boat?"

"White."

The officer winced. "Mr. Ericsen, there are hundreds of white speed-boats among all of our surrounding islands; and there are thousands of places to hide within an infinite number of coves and fjords. The task will be almost impossible, but I'll notify the harbor *politi* immediately and see what they can do, if anything. You've given me very little information, so we can't guarantee she'll be located.

"You must understand, even though you've filed a report, there's always the possibility she may not be missing at all. We'll be looking for a needle in a haystack, but I assure you, we'll give it our best efforts. Are you flying back to Oslo this evening?"

"Yes, I'm headed for the airport right now. I'd like to catch the early flight, if possible."

"There's nothing more you can do here. We have your complete statement, so you'd better get going. If you keep talking to me, you may not catch your flight. I'll be here on duty until midnight. Give me a call later this evening. I may have some information for you."

In parting, while shaking hands, Greg replied, "Thank you, sir, I certainly appreciate your help. I'll be sure to phone you before midnight."

"We'll do our very best, Mr. Ericsen."

After leaving the station and upon entering the waiting taxi, the driver asked, "What time is your flight, sir?"

"I believe it's five o'clock."

The cabby checked his watch saying, "It's four-thirty already."

"Do you think you can get me there in time?"

"The airport's thirty minutes away. I've driven it in twenty before, so I'll give it a try anyway, sir."

The driver pulled away from the station and sped off down the street, and as they traveled back toward the airport along the winding road, Greg related his bizarre events of the day to his driver.

"He sure is a strange one," the driver commented. "I wonder what he was up to."

"I never had the chance to find out, but I still intend to if I can catch him at the airport. I'll look for him boarding each flight to Oslo. I'll watch every boarding passenger until I find him. Then I'll confront him to find out where they took my friend, Valerie. I'll even take the last flight out, if necessary."

In a short time their conversation abated, so Greg turned his attention out his side window and admired the passing scenery.

⋯⋯⋯⋯

Somewhere in a distant part of his mind, Greg heard someone faintly calling him.

Then he felt someone shaking him gently; the voice became louder and more coherent. "Sir, sir, please fasten your seatbelt," she said. "The captain just announced we'll be experiencing some turbulence for the next fifteen minutes."

Greg sat straight up in his seat, wiped his eyes, and shook his head groggily.

Then looking up at the gracious flight attendant, he smiled. "Can I make a trip to the restroom first, ma'am? I'm sorry, but nature calls."

In return, she smiled politely. "Of course, sir, but remember to fasten your seatbelt."

Greg slipped out of his seat behind the flight attendant and swayed up the aisle to the men's room.

In a short time, on his way back to his seat, he observed the dark cabin over the steady sound of churning jet engines. Most of the passengers were asleep, but several small night lights glowed from the ceiling.

Back in his seat, he settled into a comfortable position and secured his seatbelt tight against his waist. Then laying his head on the pillow, he closed his eyes and drifted back into deep thoughts.

Once again, he focused on the peculiar circumstances of his early relationship with Valerie.

⋯⋯⋯⋯

At the airport, Greg hopped out of the taxi and paid the expensive fare to the cabby through his open window.

When he offered change, Greg pressed the kronas in the man's hand, saying, "No, no, keep the change for all your trouble."

"No trouble at all." The cabby smiled. "I was only too glad to help. Sorry I couldn't catch that other taxi, though."

"Don't worry about it. You did your best, but I have to run, now. Thank you," Greg replied as he turned and ran toward the airport entrance.

Inside the terminal, he double-checked the departure schedule to confirm the five o'clock flight to Oslo. Then checking his wrist watch, he saw he only had ten minutes to catch the plane. He hurried to the departure gates, but he didn't really care whether or not he boarded the early flight. His main intention was to reach the gate in time to see if the stranger was boarding that flight and, if not, to see if he was in the immediate waiting area.

When he arrived at the gate, the attendant informed Greg there was a mechanical problem with the aircraft, so the five o'clock flight would be delayed.

She also informed him that two smaller planes were now being prepared to handle the unusually large overflow of people for the early flight.

"In a short time, the first aircraft will depart from the terminal," she informed, "and approximately forty-five minutes later, the second aircraft will depart."

When the first plane was ready for boarding, the first wave of people rushed toward the ticket agent standing at the departure gate. Since there were no reserved seats—only first come, first served—everyone wanted to be first through the gate. Consequently, the huge crowd became tightly pressed together very quickly, so everyone shuffled and nudged one another as they inched their way toward the ticket agent.

Meanwhile, Greg simply stood at the rear of the slowly moving crowd and scanned the backs and faces of the throng of people.

He wasn't in any hurry to catch that first plane, especially if the stranger wasn't going to be on it.

Suddenly Greg spotted the stranger. He was up near the front of the moving crowd. There were only a few people between him and the ticket taker.

"He'll get on board, for sure," he muttered. "Now I've got to get on board THIS plane! If I don't, I'll lose him forever."

Instantly Greg merged into the shuffling crowd and as he tried to elbow and maneuver his way though the tightly knit travelers, he waved his ticket high in the air.

"This is an emergency!" he shouted. "Please let me through! I must get aboard this plane."

The packed crowd simply looked ahead as they inched their way forward at a snail's pace. Some passengers, however, turned around to glare and scowl at Greg's impatient pushing and nudging while everyone scuffled along.

Just as Greg squirmed his way into the middle of the crowd, he saw the stranger pass by the ticket agent and go through the gate. He disappeared into the tunnel.

Several more people passed through the gate before the agent stopped taking tickets and announced, "The aircraft is now full of passengers."

With his hopes dashed, Greg thought, *That's it! It's over. I'll never get him. He's gone. Valerie's gone. Now I'll never find her. She's lost for good.*

At the same time, a positive thought also crossed his mind.

His face brightened with renewed hope. *Maybe Valerie gave her address and phone number to Annika,* he thought.

Forty-five minutes later, Greg boarded the second plane to Oslo. During the flight, his mood remained frustrated with preoccupied thoughts still centered on Valerie's mysterious abduction and the men responsible for it.

The aircraft landed shortly and when he walked into the waiting area of Oslo's spacious terminal, Tom and Annika greeted him.

"Where's Valerie?" Annika asked, bewildered.

"She's vanished!" Greg snapped.

Annika's mouth dropped open. Dumbstruck with fear, she instantly cupped her hand over her mouth.

"What do you mean, 'she's vanished'?" Tom quizzed.

Annika cried, "Omigod! Something bad has happened to Valerie! She was with you, Greg. How could she disappear?"

"She's a victim of foul play. The whole thing happened so fast, I'm still in a state of shock," Greg related. "It's one damn mystery, I'll tell ya. She simply panicked and ran away."

"Why would she run away from you?" Annika asked.

"Let's get some coffee and find a table where we can talk. Then I'll explain the whole story. The taxi took the last of my money, Tom, so you'll have to buy my coffee."

"No problem, pardner. It sounds like you had one helluva day in Bergen."

"It was the weirdest day of my life, believe me. I'm so worried and afraid for her, Tom."

They found an empty table in a corner near the snack bar, and when Tom brought the coffee and snacks, Greg recounted the details of his bizarre one-day visit to Bergen.

Afterward, he noted, "And I never did get her address or phone number, either." He turned to Annika. "Do you have Valerie's address and phone number?"

"No, Greg, we never exchanged addresses. I was going to ask her for them when you returned from Bergen tonight. I did give her my phone number when I dropped her off at her hotel last night."

"Well, that tears it! Now I know I'll never see her again. She's vanished into thin air."

"Maybe the police will turn up something," Tom replied.

"I would like to hope so too, Tom, but I really think the situation is hopeless."

After several more cups of coffee, along with more pointless speculation, they finally left the terminal.

It was nightfall when Annika dropped Greg and Tom at their hotel, and as Tom kissed her through her open window, she said, "I'll meet you fellas at the airport in the morning. Your flight leaves at 11 A.M., right?"

"Right," Tom confirmed.

When the two men walked toward the entrance, she called out to them. "I'll be at your departure gate about 10:15 A.M.," and as they entered the building, she honked the horn and drove off.

Once inside their room, Greg went directly to the telephone and immediately phoned the Bergen police station.

When connected to the Missing Persons Division, Officer Stensen answered the phone.

"Hello, sir, this is Greg Ericsen. You asked me to phone you when I arrived at my hotel in Oslo."

"Oh yes, Mr. Ericsen, we notified the harbor police immediately after you left, but they haven't reported anything as yet. I have your South Dakota phone number and address, and I'll personally inform you if we locate her."

"The man who stalked us was in Bergen's airport when I got there," Greg continued. "He caught the five o'clock flight to Oslo, but because the plane was full, I couldn't get aboard, so I lost him again. I only wish I knew what he wanted with Valerie. I fear for her safety."

"I know you do, Mr. Ericsen, and I assure you, we'll do everything we can to find her."

"Thanks for all your help, Mr. Stensen. I'll wait anxiously for any word from you."

"You have a safe flight back to America, Mr. Ericsen. You'll hear from me. Goodbye for now."

Greg bade the officer goodbye and hung up the receiver, saying, "That's that, Tom. It's finished. Nothing more can be done now."

"Don't give up hope, pardner. Let's turn in and get some sleep. It's been a very long day for both of us."

"You're right, Tom. I think I'll take a shower, but I don't think it'll help me get much sleep tonight."

It was a restless night for Greg, with several hours of tossing and turning before he finally fell asleep.

Early in the morning, Greg and Tom arose, packed their bags, checked out of the hotel, and drove to the airport. After returning their rented car to a pre-arranged site, they entered the terminal, checked their bags at the airline counter, and moved along to their departure gate where Annika awaited them.

She greeted Tom with a warm, affectionate kiss. Then she squiggled her nose and asked, "Will you write to me?"

"You bet, crinkle nose," he replied, kissing her again.

"Annika," Greg said, "if you hear from Valerie, will you inform Tom or me so I can get in touch with her?"

"Oh yes, Greg, if I hear anything at all from her, I'll let both of you know, right away."

Greg sat down and wrote his and Tom's phone numbers and addresses on a slip of paper and gave it to her.

In turn, Annika wrote her phone number and address on two separate pieces of paper and gave one to each of them.

Shortly thereafter, a female voice over the SAS PA system announced that Greg and Tom's flight was "now boarding for departure."

As the three stood up, Tom immediately embraced Annika with a prolonged goodbye kiss, and as she ran her hands through his thick blond hair, he whispered, "I WILL write to you, Annika. That's a promise."

Suddenly she pushed away from his chest, declaring, "You just better, you blue-eyed brute. Where did you get that big hard chest, anyway?"

Tom puffed out a cheek and drawled, "From elbow-bending at my favorite waterin' hole, ma'am."

Frowning for the moment, Annika curled a few strands of hair around her finger until Greg smiled. "That means Tom drinking beer at his favorite tavern."

"Sometimes I just don't understand him and all that cowboy stuff." She grinned. "I guess I'll have to call him 'Cowboy Tom' from now on."

When Greg hugged Annika and they kissed each other's cheek, tears streamed down her face.

"I know you care very much for Valerie," she cried, "and I pray she is okay. We will live with the hope that she'll turn up safe and unharmed. I'm so happy to have met both of you."

Greg's eyes filled when he replied, "Annika, please promise me, if and when you talk to Valerie, you'll tell her I love her."

"Oh, I will tell her, Greg. I promise."

Then Greg looked away and he and Tom hurried off to the departure gate.

Before entering the tunnel, they both turned around to see Annika still watching them.

Tom bowed his legs, stuffed his left thumb down inside his belt, puffed out his cheek, and saluted Annika.

With streaking tears, she smiled faintly, blew a kiss, and waved to both of them.

Greg and Tom waved back, turned, and disappeared into the tunnel.

With mixed emotions and feelings, Annika walked sadly to her car and drove away from the airport while up above, their aircraft lifted high into the clouded sky and flew westward.

For most of their flight back to the States, Greg and Tom spoke very little to one another. They slept and read books for most of the trip.

Eight and one-half hours later, early in the afternoon, their plane landed at Newark International Airport.

After the two men retrieved their luggage and checked through customs, they left the terminal and caught a taxi for New York City.

Even though they took in the Yankee and Met baseball games and toured the city's many attractions, they were not enough to distract Greg's mind from Valerie. She was never off his mind.

By the end of the week, they were ready for their plane trip home and boarded their scheduled flight for Rapid City.

While flying home, Greg relied on Tom's confidentiality not to mention Valerie's disappearance to his parents. He would eventually tell them Valerie's story, but for now he didn't want to spoil the happy homecoming.

It was early in the evening when they arrived in Rapid City, and when they walked into the small terminal, they were immediately greeted by Greg's parents. Because Tom was like a second son to Greg's mother, she greeted them both with hugs and kisses.

On the drive to the Ericsen homestead, much laughter followed the candor and unfolding tales of their week's vacation.

At the house, as Greg opened the garage door, Tom gathered his belongings from the trunk of the car and tossed them into the trunk of his own car parked in the Ericsen garage. Because they knew Tom was anxious to get home to Sturgis, Greg's parents bade him good night and went into the house to await Greg.

When Tom slid onto his driver's seat, Greg commented, "It was a great vacation, after all, wasn't it?"

"A terrific vacation, pardner."

"I'll give you a call during the week, Tom."

As Tom backed his car down the driveway, he rolled down the window and stuck his head out.

"Don't give up on Valerie, Greg. She's sure to turn up safe and sound."

"I hope so. I really think I'm in love with her."

After backing onto the street, he honked the horn and drove off toward the interstate.

Greg walked into the house to converse with his parents, and within several hours he grew weary and retired to his bedroom.

Shortly thereafter, as he lay in bed with his hands folded behind his head, his thoughts concentrated only on Valerie. Soon, with his mind exhausted, he fell into a deep sleep.

IV

During the ensuing weeks, Greg's mind constantly stayed on thoughts of Valerie, and one morning while his mother poured him a fresh cup of coffee, he was preoccupied in thought and stared blankly at his coffee cup, fiddling with the teaspoon.

She said, "Ever since you returned from your vacation, son, you seem distant and far away these days. It's not like you to be so quiet and pensive. Are you troubled?"

"Sometimes my head is still back in Norway, Mom."

"Your father and I figured as much. Something's bothering you."

Greg's father stepped into the kitchen and sat down at the table.

"Good morning, everyone," he announced.

"Good morning, Dad," Greg replied, then continued. "There is something bothering me, Mom, and I've been wanting to tell you and Dad, so this is as good a time as any to tell you. It's a woman. A very beautiful woman."

"I thought so," his mother snapped. "Didn't I tell you, Howard? I said 'I'll bet Greg met a nice woman in Norway and he's smitten by her'."

"You and your woman's intuition." His father grinned, shaking his head.

Greg's mother poured her husband a cup of coffee, then poured a cup for herself and sat down promptly at the table.

"Now, tell us all about her." She glowed anxiously. "What's her name?"

"It's Valerie, Mom. She's a school teacher in Bergen and a wonderful woman."

His mother patted Greg's hand, saying, "I know she's beautiful and wonderful because my son picked her."

"Tom and I met her and her friend, Annika, on one of Oslo's tours. For two days, the four of us had a great time. We ate dinners together and went drinking and dancing, but when Valerie and I flew to Bergen to have a day to ourselves, we were followed by a strange man."

His father asked, "What did he want with you?"

"I don't know, Dad. I never found out because Valerie panicked. She fled into a taxicab. Then the stranger jumped into a cab and followed behind her. I followed both of them in a third taxi, but when her taxi stopped at the end of the piers and she emerged from the car, she was quickly carried away and wrestled into a speedboat by two burly men. By the time my taxi reached the end of the piers, the boat was speeding out of Bergen's harbor. That's the last I saw of her."

With her hand to her mouth, his mother gasped, "How terrible!"

"Did you report it to the authorities?" his father quizzed.

"Yes, I did, but they said they couldn't do much with the little information I supplied. They ARE working on it, though, and said they'd keep me informed of any findings."

"No wonder you've been so distant," his mother said. "You must be very worried about her."

"Didn't you get her phone number or address?" his father queried.

"No, Dad, everything happened too fast. I was going to get them before we left Oslo. One minute she was thumbing through magazines at the Information Center, the next minute she was gone."

"So all you know about her is that she's a school teacher in Bergen, nothing else?" his father asked.

"Nothing, except she also told me she grew up in Charleston, South Carolina, and graduated from high school there."

"I'm sure the police will trace all the schools and get her address from the school records," his father added.

"That's one hope right now, and I've also been toying with another idea lately."

"And what would that be?" his mother asked.

"If the authorities in Bergen don't come up with anything soon, I may try searching Charleston for her. I might find someone there who knows her, maybe a friend or relative who could connect me to a relative in Norway. I know it's a shot in the dark, but I have to do something. I just can't sit and do nothing. She's lost her parents. She has no immediate family. She's all alone, so I may be her only hope."

"I feel terrible for you, son," his mother replied, patting his hand.

"It's an awful worry," his father agreed, "but if nothing can be done, you may have to accept it and overcome it in time."

"I suppose you're right, Dad."

Later that evening, Greg joined Tom and their friends at the softball field for their weekly game. Tom's friend Marylou and Greg's friend Kimberly had driven with Tom to meet him at the field for their night game.

Greg and Kimberly had been friends since college, and although they dated often, their friendship remained platonic. That was from Greg's standpoint, anyway, and Kim had never indicated anything different to Greg either. No commitments of any kind had ever been promised or discussed by either of them. However Greg knew of Kim's hope that she had confided to Marylou some years previous.

In the dugout, as Greg and Tom laced up their cleats, Tom said, "Kim's been wondering why you haven't phoned her since we got back from Norway."

"I know, Tom, but I can't get Valerie off my mind."

"I figured that was the reason. I wouldn't dare breathe a word about Valerie to Kim or Marylou."

"How about Annika? Have you told Marylou about her?" Greg grinned.

"No way!" Tom snapped. "Are you crazy? If Marylou found out about Annika, I'd be lassoed, hog-tied, and shipped out on the next cattle truck for slaughter."

"Have you heard from Annika?"

"Yes, I talked to her a few days ago, but she said she hasn't heard anything from Valerie."

"I haven't heard a word from the Bergen police, either."

After tying their shoes, they walked out to the third base foul line where they spread apart to play catch and warm up their arms. While tossing the ball back and forth, Greg looked up in the bleachers at Kim and Marylou sitting together. Greg waved with a smile. Kim waved in return and, as usual, beamed her addictive bright white smile.

When the game started, the other team batted first, so Tom ran out to play shortstop and Greg took up his usual position at third base.

On the first play of the game, the leadoff batter hit a slow-roller to third base. Greg charged in fast, but before he snagged the ball, he took his eye off it and looked up at the runner. He fumbled the ball, so the batter was safe at first base.

Tom ran over to Greg and with his glove, tapped him on his backside, saying, "C'mon, pardner, get with it." Then he quickly ran back to his shortstop position.

As the game wore on into the last half of the ninth inning, Greg had committed three costly errors, which caused their team to be five runs behind.

Greg and Tom sat in the dugout waiting for their turns at bat.

"You hadn't made any errors all season, Greg, now three errors in one game! I can't believe that."

"You and me both, Tom, and they were all easy gimme plays, too. I don't know what's wrong with me."

"You're lovesick, man! That's what's wrong with you. You've got a woman on your mind and it ain't Kim."

"You're nuts! No woman's ever affected my ball playing before."

Tom smirked. "Well, Valerie's affected it, that's for damned sure. You're hooked, pardner."

Suddenly the third batter grounded to second base to make the last out and the game ended quickly, before either of them could bat.

So while changing shoes, they continued to chide each other about their women, and after stowing their gear in athletic bags, they flung them up on their shoulders and sauntered down to the end of the bleachers where their women greeted them.

"Hi, Greg." Kim beamed. "You didn't play very good tonight. I've never seen you play so badly. Usually batters are out when they hit the ball to you."

"I know, Kim. It was a bad night, but I'll get with it next time. It'll be different next game. I'm sorry I haven't called you. C'mon, I'll take you home."

As she and Marylou hopped down from the bleachers, she replied, "That's okay, Greg. Tom said you were busy at the school the past few weeks."

The two pairs walked off toward their cars parked curbside on the street. There was a chill in the air, so Greg draped his jacket over Kim's shoulders. When she slipped her arms through the sleeves, they were much too long for her short arms, so the sleeves drooped over the ends of her fingers covering her hands.

"Baggy hands, eh, short stuff?" he teased.

"Oh yeah, well short stuff can still punch smart guys." She laughed, jabbing him in the ribs.

As they neared the street, they separated from Tom and Marylou, and when they reached their car, Greg opened the trunk and slung his bag inside. Then he and Kim entered the car and drove off to meet Tom and Marylou for sandwiches and coffee at their favorite coffee shop.

During the drive, Kim happened to slide her hands into the slash pockets of Greg's athletic jacket. Feeling something odd, like dried brittle crumbs of some sort that seemed to crumble in her hand, she pulled out the crumbled, crushed rose that Greg had stuffed in his pocked at Valerie's disappearance.

Looking down at the dead flower in her hand, she remarked, "What's this? Oh, it's a crushed red rose."

Because he'd forgotten about the rose, he knew it was now time to be honest with her, so he said, "Ah . . . that's . . . what I wanted to talk to you about, Kim. Let's go to a different restaurant where we can be alone and talk, okay?"

Kim stared at the dried rose, shrugged her shoulders, and replied, "Okay, Greg, if you think you have to explain. We aren't engaged or anything, so you really don't have to answer to me, you know."

"But I want to explain, Kim. We've been together too long. I want to be honest with you."

Instead of meeting Tom and Marylou at their usual rendezvous, Greg drove to another restaurant.

Inside the coffee shop, they took a quiet corner booth and after ordering, Greg explained the rose to her and related his story of Valerie.

"It's okay, Greg. We've both understood our platonic friendship and you've always been honest with me. Lately, I've been seeing someone also, but it's nothing serious, though."

"I'm glad to hear that, Kim. We've known each other too long and I wouldn't want to hurt you. I have too much respect for you."

Kim reached for his hand and squeezed it firmly, saying, "You haven't hurt me, Greg, honestly, and I do hope you find Valerie. You have to find out if she's the woman for you."

"Thanks for understanding, Kim."

When they finished eating, he drove her home and at her apartment door, he kissed her good night, as always, but to Kim, she suspected it to be their last. Teary-eyed, she opened the door and pecked him once more on the lips. Then she turned away and quickly entered her apartment. She leaned backwards to close the door behind her and as she stood frozen with her back against the door, her eyes flooded, then overflowed into streaming tears as she listened to his fading footsteps on the sidewalk.

A few nights later, Greg met Tom at their favorite cocktail lounge for a few drinks. He wanted to inform Tom of his coming departure for Charleston.

While they sat drinking their first beer, Greg said, "I've decided to go to Charleston."

"Charleston? You don't think you'll find Valerie there, do you? That's a long way from Bergen."

"Valerie grew up there, remember? I might make contact with someone who knew her or grew up with her; a relative, perhaps."

"What about the Bergen police? Haven't they come up with anything?"

"I received a call from Officer Stensen the other night. He said they still haven't found her and they're in the process now of checking the schools."

"There can't be many schools in Bergen, so they should easily find the school where she taught, right?" Tom queried.

"I would think so too, Tom, but even if they do find her school, I don't think it would help me. I really need an acquaintance or family connection. She's been kidnapped and I can't wait on the police any longer. God only knows where she is right now. I can't sit still anymore. I have to make a move to find her, NOW."

Tom shook his head slowly and replied, "I wish you luck, pardner, but needless to say, you'll be looking for a needle in a haystack."

Later, as they parted outside the lounge, Greg assured Tom he'd keep him posted on his whereabouts in Charleston.

Then he returned home to plan his search for Valerie.

V

On the morning of his departure, Greg arose early. Being excited and filled with hope and enthusiasm the night before, he hadn't slept much.

After he finished packing his clothes, he shaved and showered, and dressed into a clean pair of Levis and sweatshirt. Then he carried his two suitcases downstairs and placed them by the front door.

When he joined his parents in the kitchen, he saw that his mother had prepared a nice big breakfast for him consisting of sausage and eggs; pancakes; hot, freshly baked muffins with raspberry preserves; coffee; and orange juice.

As he sat down, he said, "Mom and Dad, I hope you understand that this is something I have to do. Maybe I'll find her and maybe I won't find her, but I have to make the effort. Her disappearance has had a profound effect on me as you've seen since my return from Norway. My feelings for Valerie are much stronger than for Kim."

"I do understand, son," his mother replied. "Your father and I agree it's something you must do. You could very well be in love with her; otherwise, I'm sure you wouldn't be going on this wild goose chase."

"I'm all for it too, son," his father affirmed. "If it were your mother, I'd do the very same thing you're doing. I'd have to search for her, too. I can only hope you find her or at least find out what's happened to her. It's the only way you'll have peace of mind."

When breakfast was finished, his parents walked him to his car parked on the driveway and after Greg laid his luggage in the trunk, he turned and gave his mother a hug and kiss on the cheek.

Then as he shook his father's hand and hugged him with one arm, his father whispered in his ear, "I have a feeling you just might find her in Charleston, son. Give it one helluva shot, anyway."

"I will, Dad. You can bet on that."

After bidding their farewells, Greg slid behind the wheel and started the engine, and as he backed down the driveway, he waved through his open window.

While standing on the driveway with their arms around each other's waists, they waved in return and called out, "Good luck!"

"And I'll need a lot of that, for sure." Greg laughed as he honked the horn and drove up the street.

Although his mother and father had encouraged their son's venture, they both remained skeptical about his quest to find her. Having discussed it privately, they agreed with his friend, Tom, that it was nothing but a whimsical adventure with a fruitless ending. However, they didn't want to dash his hopes or dispirit him in any way, so they never tried to dissuade him. It was a forgone conclusion to both of them that it was the only way their son could remove Valerie from his mind and get on with his life; the only way to remove his fixation of her.

Within minutes Greg reached I–90 and sped down the ramp heading east to begin his journey of uncertainty. He depressed the gas pedal until the speedometer read sixty-five. Then he set the cruise control, settled comfortably in his seat, and laid his head back on the headrest. He estimated his time of arrival in Charleston to be sometime on the evening of his third day's travel.

Johnny Mathis was singing "A Certain Smile" on his favorite radio station. Every time he'd hear the song, he'd smile to himself because it always reminded him of Valerie. As he hummed the tune, he imagined her staring at her with those incredible violet eyes along with that magnetic, gracious, and friendly smile.

His first motel stop in Wisconsin ended his first day's travel, and at the end of his second day's travel, he stopped at a motel inside the state of Kentucky.

Early in the evening at the end of the third day, Greg finally drove into the outskirts of North Charleston. He tingled with excitement at the thought of being in Valerie's hometown.

This is her home, he thought. *This is where Valerie actually grew up and graduated from high school. Wouldn't it be great to find her neighborhood and house she lived in. Maybe I'll run into an old classmate of hers, but then again, not too probable since she's been out of high school for seven or eight years.*

He was tired and hungry, so as he passed through the northern part of the city, he decided on Denny's for supper. Since Valerie had done waitress work in Charleston, it would also begin his restaurant searches. So when he spotted a Denny's sign, he pulled into the parking lot, parked the car, and entered the restaurant.

Because studying peoples' faces was one of his pastimes, he quickly looked over the waitresses, and satisfied that none of them looked like

Valerie, he walked to the counter, picked out an empty stool that faced the waitress station, and sat down.

While eating a hot meal, he observed all of the waitresses more closely as they picked up their orders from the cooks. He saw that none of them remotely resembled Valerie.

Later, he bought a city street guide and took a motel in north Charleston. Then after showering he sat at the small table, making notations in his pocket notebook. From the telephone book he noted addresses of restaurants and cocktail lounges and with his street guide, he especially marked off the location of Charleston High School along with the surrounding area. They would be his starting points in the morning.

Afterwards, he relaxed with the TV and fell asleep watching the eleven o'clock news.

He awoke around 8 A.M., shut off the early morning news show, and proceeded to shave. While shaving, he decided he would eat three meals a day, every day, at three different restaurants and would skip no meals, because any skipped meals could easily be the one vital contact to Valerie.

After dressing, he set out for the closest restaurant, and as he sat in a booth eating French toast, he noted the faces of the three working waitresses; none bore any resemblance to Valerie.

Afterwards, within a half-hour's drive he arrived at the high school and since it was the weekend and summer vacation, the grounds were deserted. There was no sign of life. He drove around the school several times hoping to see, perhaps, a groundskeeper or anyone entering the building; nobody came or went.

He hadn't really hoped to gain much if any information with a visit to her old high school anyway. It was mostly to satisfy his personal curiosity.

So he moved on and for the next few hours, he cruised many residential streets in the school's neighborhood. At times, he'd pick out a house and imagine it to be the home where Valerie might have lived during her high school days. Several times, he stopped to ask women on the streets if they knew of the Nielsen family; no one had ever heard of them.

At noontime, he stopped for lunch at a restaurant in the neighborhood and checked out the waitresses—no luck.

After lunch, the humidity lay heavy over the city and Greg found himself moving toward the inner city. A few cold beers on a hot afternoon sounded great, so he decided to frequent some of the downtown bars and cocktail lounges.

While visiting several bars, the beer quenched his thirst, but when Greg showed Valerie's photo to the waitresses, none of them could quench his search. They didn't recognize her nor did any of them resemble her.

After leaving the bars, Greg drove the city center tourist route for possible search areas for another day. Then he headed back toward the northern part of the city, but he quickly found himself imbedded in evening rush-hour traffic and decided to stop for supper.

When he spotted a small diner, he pulled into the parking lot, parked the car, and made his way into the cafe. He took an empty stool at the counter and a pretty waitress took his order of coffee and a chicken-fried steak dinner.

When she returned shortly with his coffee, Greg snatched the picture of Valerie from his shirt pocket and flashed it before her.

"Pardon me, ma'am, would you happen to know this woman? Her name's Valerie."

As she rested the coffee pot on the counter, she took the snapshot from his hand and examined it, saying, "No, can't say I do, handsome. She a friend of yours or somethin'?"

"Yes, she is. I haven't seen her in a few months and I'm trying to find her. She's done waitress work from time to time."

The waitress bent down and leaned her two elbows on the counter. Revealing half of her two bare breasts that bulged from the top of her tight uniform, she stared directly into his dark brown eyes.

Then she propped her chin up with one hand, picked up the creamer with her other hand, and purred, "Cream . . . sugar?"

"Yes, both, please." He smiled.

Without dropping her deliberate eye contact, she poured cream into his cup, grasped the sugar shaker, and poured in some sugar. Still fixed on his eyes and without looking away, she picked up his spoon and stirred his coffee.

"Why are you looking for her? Are you her lover?" she pried.

"Not exactly." He laughed. "I'm just a friend who wants to get to know her better."

"Well, you've found me, sugar, and we're already getting to know each other better—as we speak."

Suddenly, a man hollered from the kitchen, "Betty Jo, pickups! Leave the customers alone and get back to work."

Instantly, she straightened up from the counter and with Valerie's photo in one hand, she primped her hair with her other hand. Then with both hands, she pulled down her tight mini-uniform and wiggled off to pick up her orders.

Greg was left grinning and shaking his head.

When she returned with his meal and placed the plate in front of him, she also handed back his picture.

"The cook has never seen her either, sugar." She winked.

"Thanks, anyway." He smiled.

When he finished eating, Greg left a generous tip under the plate for the sexy Betty Jo and walked to the cash register to pay for his meal.

Needless to say, Betty Jo hurried to the register to take his money with a parting invitation. "If y'all don't find your girlfriend and you're lookin' for a nice friendly girl, I'm available, sugar. Y'all come back and see us now, ya hear?" She winked.

"You betcha." He grinned as he took his change and stuffed it in his pocket.

He returned to his hotel, and later that night when he climbed into bed, his enthusiasm hadn't dampened despite an unsuccessful first day's search.

The next day he traveled Susannah Highway in the northwest section of the city. It proved uneventful and the morning and afternoon passed swiftly.

Having turned up nothing at the end of the day, he decided during supper to have a few beers afterward at the neighboring bars and cocktail lounges with the hope that a bartender or cocktail waitress might provide a lead.

After eating, he stopped at the first lounge he saw on the highway and ordered a beer at the bar. While waiting for his beer, the song "That Elusive Butterfly of Love" played on the juke box. As he listened to the words, he was smiling to himself when the bartender served him his beer. "What are you smiling about, stranger? I've never seen you in here before. Are you from around these parts?"

"No, sir, I'm not from Charleston. I'm a Yankee from South Dakota territory and I was just smiling to that song on the juke box. The woman I'm looking for is another elusive butterfly, I'll tell ya."

Greg pulled out several snapshots of Valerie from his shirt pocket and spread them on the bar for the bartender to look at.

"You wouldn't happen to know her or recognize her, would you?" he asked. "She was raised here in Charleston."

The bartender picked up a couple of the pictures, and while looking them over and scratching his head, he replied, "No, sir, can't say I've seen her in this place at any time nor any place else, for that matter. She sure is a looker. Can't say I blame you for chasing after this little beauty. If I was your age, I'd be hound dogging her, too. No luck so far, huh, son?"

As the bartender laid the snapshots back on the bar, Greg replied, "Not the tiniest clue. I do know she graduated from Charleston High School seven or eight years ago and did waitress work here in the summertime."

"I suppose you're checking all the restaurants, too."

"Yes. For the past two days I've covered most of the restaurants in north Charleston and turned up nothing. I'm beginning to think this is a crazy wild goose chase."

"It may very well be a goose chase, son. If you want my opinion, your chances of finding her after so many years are just plain zero."

With that, the bartender walked away and began wiping glasses at the end of the bar.

So Greg scooped up the photos and stuffed them, along with his note pad, back into his shirt pocket.

After he drank the last of his beer, he backed off the stool and walked toward the entrance.

The bartender was serving a customer when he called, "Thanks for talking with me. It helped."

The bartender looked up and said, "You're welcome, son. If you need any help finding that little butterfly, call on me anytime. I'm always here."

"I may do that."

Greg pushed open the door, walked to his car, and drove off to spend the rest of the evening visiting other neighborhood bars and lounges. It was to no avail, however, since no one at any of the establishments know or recognized Valerie's picture. Every place was a dead end.

He finally gave up and returned to his motel by midnight, and even though he was tired and discouraged and was no closer to finding her then when he left Bergen, he still hoped to get lucky and find a lead to Valerie.

The next morning, he continued with his game plan, so he set out early. His new day's quest would now focus on the inner city.

During a bacon and egg breakfast he speculated if she had no car, the bus would be her means of transportation, so he decided to take a bus ride into the city.

After breakfast, he drove to the outskirts of the city, parked his car, and waited at a bus stop on Meeting Street. When the bus arrived, he climbed aboard, walked to the rear, and took a seat.

At each bus stop all the way into the city center, he observed the faces of the women who got on board. None of them were Valerie.

During the morning, he walked along the downtown streets checking out the bars and restaurants, most of which he merely peeked inside for a quick look-see.

Finally, after a full morning of covering the city, he reached the waterfront gardens to rest on a park bench. Already sweaty, his clothes felt clammy from the heavy humidity. The cool breeze that blew in lightly off the harbor was a welcome relief from the hot morning sun. He was alone with his thoughts as he gazed out over the harbor and observed the slow moving boats and ships.

I'm getting nowhere fast, he thought. *Nobody knows her or has heard of her and she's probably still in Norway. It's looking more like a pipe dream every day. Oh well, I'll give it another day or two and call it quits. Nothing ventured, nothing gained.*

He sat for a long time enjoying the cool breeze, and later took lunch at a city coffee shop.

During the afternoon, he strolled the rest of the downtown area and around 5 P.M., he joined the happy hour city crowd for evening drinks. Frequenting a few lively bars, he focused solely on the faces of the female patrons.

About an hour later, he caught the Meeting Street bus again and rode to the end of the line where he picked up his car and drove to the motel for a welcome shower. Then he dressed for his last night's search of the lounges and clubs.

When he stepped outside into the dank, warm night air—laden with humidity—a fine misty drizzle sprayed against his face.

After fried chicken at a nearby cafe, he drove out the highway scanning for cocktail lounges and clubs, and having spotted the Pirate's Den dance club, he stopped for a drink.

Inside, Greg ordered whiskey at the bar and stopped a passing waitress. He flashed Valerie's picture at her with the same questions, but she simply shook her head and quickly moved on to serve her tray of drinks.

The heavyweight bartender returned shortly to serve Greg his drink and, as usual, he showed the snapshot and asked, "Would you have seen this woman in your club at any time, sir?"

Baldheaded with a round red face, the barrel-chested bartender chewed heavily on his cigar, eyed Greg skeptically, and cupped the picture into a massive hand. He stared intently at her face for a moment, then shook his head and handed the photo back to Greg.

"No, sir, I've never seen that pretty face around here. Are you a cop or somethin'?"

"No, I'm just a friend of hers from South Dakota. I've been all over this city trying to find her."

The redneck bartender bursted into a deep, guttural belly laugh.

"You mean you came all the way down here from Yankee country to snatch one of our southern belles and all you have is a picture? Where did you last see her in town?"

"I've never been in Charleston before now."

"Then where DID you meet her?"

"In Norway."

"Norway!" he exclaimed bursting with laughter. "How long ago did you see her in Norway?"

"About a month ago. She's a school teacher in Norway, but she grew up in Charleston and she's done waitress work during the summertime here. I was hoping she might be working in the city somewhere."

The bartender chomped hard on his cigar, but listened attentively.

"How long you been lookin' for her, now?"

"A week."

The bartender leaned on the bar, flicked his cigar in an ashtray, and slid forward eyeball-to-eyeball to Greg.

"Well, if you haven't found her by now, boy, don't you think you should chuck it and call it quits? I'd say the chances of you finding that filly in this city are absolutely nil. If I were you, cowboy, I'd pack up my horse and head back to Dakota country. It's about time you got your Yankee tail back home to marry that nice little girl next door, don't you think?" He winked, sticking the cigar back in his mouth.

"I have to agree. It's all been a waste of time," Greg agreed as the bartender turned and walked away.

Greg turned to watch the couples on the dance floor, and as he swirled the ice in his glass, he noticed a woman dancing who looked like Valerie.

Quickly sipping the last of his drink, he placed the empty glass on the bar and slipped off the bar stool. He moved directly toward her, but halfway to the dance floor, he saw it wasn't Valerie, so he stopped, turned around, and headed back to the bar.

Since the bartender was eyeing him, Greg hunched his shoulders with outstretched palms and smiled.

Grinning, the bartender hunched his shoulders and drawled, "Y'all come back now, ya hear."

With a wave of his hand, Greg smiled, "See ya."

Outside the club, he ambled slowly to his car through the warm drizzling rain. Dejected and discouraged, he got into the car and after starting the engine, he sat motionless behind the wheel. With the engine idling, he made no attempt to drive away.

He simply stared at the streaming water on the windshield, and thought, *That bartender's right. This search is finished. I've been hoping against hope by chasing a fantasy. The whole idea was crazy and ludicrous. Tomorrow, I'm going home where I belong and, if I never see her again, so be it.*

Feeling like a fool, he shifted hard into reverse and spun gravel backing up. Then shifting into drive, the car lurched forward, spitting more gravel from the back tires before they screeched onto the highway.

He drove straight to the motel and once inside, he fell backwards on the bed. Laying flat on his back, disgusted, he soon feel asleep with his clothes on.

The next morning after a sound sleep, he awoke more relaxed. He felt much better, and in a way felt a certain release from all his worry. He no longer felt like a fool.

After all, he thought, *I sought her out because she's the only woman I've ever been serious about, and those feelings are not dumb or foolish. I still think I love her.*

Being in a better mood, he decided to be a tourist and enjoy the city's attractions and sights, so after he shaved and dressed, he headed for downtown and stopped at Shoney's restaurant on his way into the city.

He would still continue to show Valerie's picture, just in case, but the answer was always the same—no luck.

Later in the morning, he parked his car on a side street in old town Charleston and entered the visitor's center to browse through the brochures. After eyeing all the female clerks, he chose a walking tour and set out to enjoy the historical parts of the old city.

As he strolled along, he observed the old buildings and side streets and imagined old Charleston during the Civil War. The boat ride to Fort Sumter would highlight his afternoon.

Arriving at the city market, he quickly merged into the crowd of shoppers and followed the flow of people down a pathway which led through the middle of the bustling marketplace that stretched for two to three blocks.

Booths and long tables lined both sides of the aisleway displaying a multitude of wares. While strolling with the crowd, he stopped occasionally to examine the many unusual objects and trinkets, along with the faces of all the female clerks.

At the end of the covered marketplace, he emerged into the hot, humid, late morning sunshine, so he decided to walk to the Battery waterfront in the hope of catching a cool breeze off the harbor.

Along the way, he stopped at the Old Exchange building to learn some pirate history, then continued on toward the waterfront.

As he drew near the park and looked ahead for a vacant bench, his attention was drawn to a woman sitting on one of the park benches. With bowed head she read from her book, but Greg focused on her profile and long auburn-colored hair. His heart pounded and his pace quickened as he stepped off the curb and hastened across the street to the park. Nearing her bench, he slowed down and finally stopped within a few feet of her.

"Valerie?" he inquired.

When the woman looked up from her book, he saw instantly she wasn't Valerie.

"No, my name isn't Valerie." She smiled pleasantly.

"Oh, I'm terribly sorry, ma'am. Truthfully, you do bear a striking resemblance to a woman I know and that's not an opening line."

"It's quite all right, sir." She grinned. "But, at the moment, I sort of wish I was her."

He smiled faintly. "Sorry I troubled you, ma'am."

"It's okay," she reassured him again as she bowed her head and returned to her reading.

Greg stood momentarily to admire her beauty and uncanny likeness to Valerie. Then he backed away from her bench slowly, turned around, and walked directly out of the park.

Shaken by the incident, he headed up King Street, depressed, but by the time he arrived at his car, he had chalked it up to simply another dead end road. Since it was noon, he was ready to eat, so he drove off to get something to eat and headed back toward the harbor.

As he drove along the road that skirted the harbor, he looked for that same woman on the bench, but she was gone, so he stopped at one of the umbrella carts to buy a hot dog and drink.

Afterward, he continued along the harbor road and as he neared the boat piers where he'd catch the boat to Fort Sumter, he turned right onto a side street to stop and finish eating. A block in front of him he saw a small park, so he drove ahead, turned left, and parked by the curb close to a vacant bench.

It wasn't until he got out of the car that he noticed the entire oblong park was filled with water. The small pond encompassed one square block with benches surrounding its outer perimeter. The few people who occupied the benches either rested leisurely or read from their books.

Greg imagined it to be a wading pond for children, but no children were present. The water was clear and motionless, like a smooth mirror, sparking flashes of reflected sunlight.

The unique park was quiet and serene, a good place to rest before his afternoon boat tour. So he sauntered up to an empty bench and sat down.

As he munched the last of his hot dog and took a sip of his Coke, he laid his head back on the bench, closed his eyes, and contemplated.

So, I didn't find her. So what, he thought. *I did give it the ol' college try even though it was an idiotic idea and wild goose chase. She's a needle in more ways than one. At least I've got it all out of my system now. Maybe she'll turn up after I get home. How does that saying go? 'Hope springs eternal'. There's always that flicker of hope she'll contact Annika. One phone call to Tom and we'd all know her where-abouts. Tomorrow, I'm homeward bound.*

The sounds of barking dogs broke into his thoughts, and when he opened his eyes and sat up, he observed two dogs—one small, one large—directly across the pond from him. Both dogs faced one another with front legs flat on the ground. Laying steadfast, paw to paw, they snarled and barked loudly, intimidating one another.

An elderly lady pulled hard on her little dog's leash, trying to draw her dog back from a much larger dog. A man holding the leash of the larger dog struggled feverishly to keep his big dog at bay from the feisty little dog.

Greg laughed at the sight of such a little dog taking on the big dog and watched the show.

The elderly lady fought hard, but her efforts were in vain. Her leash fell to the ground and instantly the little dog dashed straight at the big dog. It stopped short in its tracks, however, when they came face to face. They sniffed each other momentarily before the bigger dog suddenly lurched forward, snapped the leash out of the man's hand, and leaped into the pond.

Not to be denied, the feisty little dog darted into the water after the big dog.

Greg, along with other park onlookers, watched with amusement at the unfolding dog show.

Both dogs swam directly at Greg as their two frustrated masters raced around the end of the pond toward Greg in hopes of retrieving their leashes. However, the dogs reached Greg's side of the pond ahead of their masters. The big dog scampered out of the water first and stood fast to shimmy water from its fur. When Greg dashed from the bench to retrieve the leash, the big dog suddenly bolted across the street with his master in hot pursuit.

The little dog leaped from the water barking, and without stopping to shake off water, he shot straight for the bigger dog.

This time Greg dived headlong for the little dog's leash and landed flat on the grass. Everything in his shirt pocket flew out in all directions, but he managed to reach out and grab the end of the leash. Skidding along the grass only for a short distance, his weight finally brought the little dog to a halt. Unable to shake Greg's hold, the stubborn little dog still tugged hard on his leash and barked fiercely.

Hanging tightly to the leash, Greg stood up and brushed himself off, at which point the little dog now decided to shake water from his fur, so the dog showed his "gratitude" by spraying Greg with a nice doggie shower.

Greg stepped back from the spray to notice the man across the street retrieve his dog and continue on down the street.

Seconds later, the elderly lady ran up, picked up her little dog, and cradled it tightly in her arms.

Her exquisitely styled white hair accented a green-eyed round face and thin, tiny figure.

"Thank you so much for catching my dog, young man. I certainly appreciate it."

"You're welcome, ma'am. They put on quite a show, didn't they?"

Kissing the top of her dog's head, she replied, "Yes, they certainly did." Then she shook her finger at the dog. "Shame on you, Simba. How many times have I told you? You can't climb up on that big horse's back and do your stuff."

Greg laughed. "You mean your dog is a male and that huge dog is a female?"

"Yes, and that big dog always seems to be in heat." She tapped the dog's nose lightly, saying, "I suppose you'll never learn. You'll always think you're a big bad stud, won't you, Simba?"

The dog licked her hand and she squeezed him tightly.

When Greg continued to brush off his shirt, he felt his pocket and saw it was empty.

"Oh no!" he declared as he began scouting the grass, "I've lost my pictures and notebook."

"Good heavens, let me help you find them," she replied.

Spotting the notebook and most of the pictures scattered around the grass, he picked them up and stuffed them back into his pocket.

The woman eyed a snapshot floating at the water's edge and stooped to pick it up.

Examining the photo, she tilted her head and smiled, "Oh my, that's a lovely picture of Valerie. She's such a pretty girl, isn't she?"

"Huh—what's that? Did you say Valerie? Do you know her, ma'am?"

"Yes, I do, young man. My daughter brought her to my home just last week. We had afternoon tea and got on very well together. Is she your lady friend?"

Stunned by the coincidence, Greg couldn't believe what he was hearing.

"Uh, well, not exactly, ma'am, but we are acquaintances. In the past week, I've searched all over Charleston for her without any luck. I'd given up hope of finding her here. Did you really talk to her a week ago and can you tell me where I can reach her?"

The woman patted his arm assuredly and said, "Yes, young man, I really talked to her last week. We had a very nice chat. Now you come to my house and I'll phone my daughter immediately. She'll be able to tell you where to contact her. If I remember right, I think she's a waitress."

"Yes, yes, that's her. If your daughter knows where she is, I'd be indebted to both of you for your help."

"You must like her very much, and I can certainly see why. Where are you from and where did you lose contact with her?"

"I'm from Rapid City, South Dakota, and I lost contact with her in Bergen, Norway."

"South Dakota and Norway! What in heavens name brought you to Charleston to look for her here?"

"Well, she graduated from Charleston High School and did waitress work during summers here. She teaches school in Norway and I thought she might return to Charleston during the summer holidays. I had hoped to locate her through a friend or relative or perhaps even find her here."

"Well, you figured right, young man, because today is your lucky day. Now come along with me and we'll reunite you with your beautiful Valerie. I live on the first block beyond the park."

As they began to walk along, she snuggled her nose in the dog's fur, and when the little dog barked and licked her face, she scolded, "And as for you, Mr. Studsville, you won't be chasing any more girls for the rest of the day."

"My name's, Greg. What yours, ma'am?"

"Oh, thank you for asking, Greg. My name is Ella Mae, and I must say, if I were your age again, your Valerie would be in for some tough competition. I've always been attracted to tall dark men, and by no means does that deep cleft hurt either."

"Thank you, Ella Mae." He grinned. "And I do believe with your looks if you were a bit younger, I would have a hard time choosing between you and Valerie."

"Ooo, you're not only a handsome men, but a wonderful flatterer, too," she flirted as she patted his arm again.

When they reached her home and walked into the kitchen, Ella Mae served Greg a cup of tea and cookies. Then she picked up the phone and called her daughter.

"Hello, dear, this is Mother."

"Hi, Mom, how are you today?"

"Oh, I'm just fine, dear, and I'm so excited. You'll never guess what just happened to me at the park."

"Tell me, Mom, what happened?"

"Well, first of all, Simba ran away from me again and chased that same big dog. She's three times bigger than Simba and she always seems to be in heat. Simba will never get anywhere with her, I'll tell ya. When he stands on his hind paws, his front paws barely reach her tail, but you know him, dear. He'll never learn. He really thinks he's super dog, king of the K-9 studs."

After an instant burst of laughter, her daughter queried, "But what's so exciting about that, Mom? That's nothing new. Simba always does that."

"Now here's the exciting part, dear. There was a very nice gentleman in the park who caught Simba after he swam across the pond after that big dog. So when I thanked him for retrieving Simba, I noticed a picture he had lost in the water. Guess who it was?"

"I wouldn't have any idea, Mom. Who was it?"

"Your friend, Valerie. He said he'd been looking for her all week and he's sitting here at the table having tea with me, right now. He would like to know where he can get in touch with her and I said you could help him."

"I don't know about that, Mom. What's his name and where is he from?"

"His name's Greg and he's from Rapid City, South Dakota." She looked at Greg. "What's your last name?"

"Ericsen."

"His last name's Ericsen and he lost contact with Valerie in Bergen, Norway. He's very anxious to find her and renew their relationship."

"Well, I suppose it might be okay. Let me talk to him."

"Yes, it would be better if you talked to him yourself."

She turned to Greg and handed him the phone, saying, "Here, Greg, my daughter's name is Helen."

"Hello, Helen, I'd appreciate your help if you know where I can find Valerie."

"I'm only too glad to help, but I hope Valerie won't be mad at me. That's all. She works at Shoney's restaurant on Savannah highway."

"I can assure you, she won't be mad at you or your mother. I really am her friend. We met in Norway when I vacationed there. Now only this morning I ate breakfast at Shoney's and my waitress didn't know of Valerie. Are you sure she works at that restaurant?"

"Yes, I'm very sure. At least, she worked there last week. When you go back there, ask for Mary. She knows all the waitresses and their shift schedules. When I talked to her last week, she was definitely working there."

"Thanks very much, Helen. It was nice talking to you. Believe me, she's in no trouble whatsoever. I'll go out to the restaurant, right away."

"I'm sure you are her friend and I hope you find her today. Bye-bye and good luck."

"Thanks again, and have a nice day, Helen. Goodbye."

Greg handed the receiver back to Ella Mae, who spoke to her daughter again.

"Thanks for helping Greg, dear, and I'll call you again, tomorrow. Bye for now."

"Bye, Mom, I'll see ya."

As Ella Mae hung up the receiver, Greg drank the last of his tea.

"Thank you for the tea and cookies," he said, "and now I'm very anxious to get to that restaurant."

"I know you must be excited to see her." She smiled warmly. "But to show your gratitude, you must promise that you'll stop by with Valerie sometime for an afternoon tea and chat."

"That's a definite promise, Ella Mae," he stated firmly.

After he left the table and walked to the front door, he stooped down to pet the little dog, who tagged along behind them wagging his tail.

Standing the dog on his hind paws, Greg said, "If it wasn't for you, Studsville, I'd never have found Valerie. I always thought Simba was a lion, so in your case, I'll think of you as a mini-mini lion. Thanks, partner, from now on, you're my best friend."

With his tail wagging nonstop, Simba barked and licked Greg's face.

Ella Mae laughed. "Oh, he may think he's a lion with the females, but they always let him know he can't 'cat' around."

When Greg stood up, he hugged and kissed her on the cheek.

"Thank you again," he said. "And your hairdo is very becoming. Is that a beautician's style or one of your own?"

She primped her hair, tilted her head, and said, "Why thank you. This is my own styling. You really are a lovely man and such a charmer, too. I can see that Valerie is already in trouble. Wouldn't I love to be her age again with the likes of your kind of trouble chasing after me."

They both smiled at one another as Greg stepped out the door.

After descending the steps, he turned around and said, "Goodbye. I'll see you and Simba real soon."

"Goodbye and good luck with Valerie. You'd better come back real soon, ya hear."

Greg waved. Then he turned around and hastened along the sidewalk toward his car.

When he reached the car, he slid inside quickly, started the engine, and drove away from the park.

His heart pounded and his thoughts raced with images of Valerie, especially focusing on his last image of her speeding away in that white speedboat with her hair blowing wildly. At long last, he'd found her, and now he would finally see her again. So with each passing second, as his excitement escalated, the speed of the car also escalated.

It wasn't long before he arrived at the restaurant and parked the car.

He hurried through the front entrance and once inside, he panned around the room anxiously, but he didn't spot Valerie anywhere on the floor, so he walked up to one of the idle waitresses.

"Are you Mary?" he asked.

"Why, yes I am." She beamed. "Would you like a table or booth?"

"No, ma'am, I'm only looking for a waitress by the name of Valerie. Does she work here?"

"We did have a Valerie working here, but she quit a few days ago."

"Do you know if she's working at another restaurant?"

"I don't have any idea where she went, but Jan might know. They worked together on the second shift. Jan's waiting on a customer right now. I'll talk to her after she places their order."

Greg was nervous. He worried he might have lost Valerie before he ever found her.

After Jan placed her customer's order with the cooks, Mary approached her and as they spoke to each other, Jan glanced at Greg several times.

Then they walked up to Greg.

"Does Valerie know you?" Jan inquired.

"Yes, she does. My name is Greg Ericsen and I would like to get in touch with her."

"I'm not sure I should do this," she replied, "but you seem nice enough to me. I don't suppose it'll really hurt. She's working at the House of Pancakes down the road going toward the city. She does work days."

"Thank you for your help," he said. "She's in no trouble or danger, believe me. I really am a friend of hers."

"In that case, you're very welcome." Jan smiled.

As Greg turned and hastened back to the entrance, Jan called, "Come back with Val and have dinner sometime."

"We'll do that," he called back with a wave.

Within minutes, he was back on the road driving toward the city, and when he spotted the House of Pancakes, he turned in and parked the car.

Nervous with excitement, he jumped from the car and hurried through the entrance.

Once inside, he quickly scanned the heads and faces of the waitresses taking orders from the customers.

"Would you like a booth, sir?" a black waitress asked.

Greg glanced sideways, but kept gazing straight ahead at the main dining room, which was half-filled with customers.

"Uh, no thank you," he replied.

"Are you looking for someone?" she asked.

"Yes, I am. Can you tell me if Valerie is working, today?"

"She could be. Who wants to know?"

"My name is Greg Ericsen. I'm a friend of hers."

Offering her hand, they shook hands, as she said, "I'm Valerie's friend Jessica, and you sound like a Yankee. Where are you from?"

"Yes, I'm a Yankee from South Dakota, but can you please tell me if Valerie is working?" he asked anxiously.

"Follow me, and I'll personally take you to my roommate."

As they approached the waitress station, a waitress with long dark auburn hair stood with her back to them. She was busy filling syrup containers.

Greg eyed her hair and knew it was Valerie.

Standing behind her, Jessica asked, "Hey, Val, do you know someone named . . . what did you say your name was?"

Instantly, Valerie spun around and froze. Stunned momentarily with her mouth agape, she stared directly into Greg's eyes. Then threw her arms around his neck and squeezed hard.

"Greg! Where did you come from?" she squealed.

"Finally!" He beamed. "The ghost has caught up with his beautiful troll."

With both arms wrapped around her waist, he squeezed hard, jerked her tight against himself, and kissed her full on the lips.

Wide-eyed with surprise, Jessica did a double-take and exclaimed, "Oh yeah, Valerie, suuuure does know who Greg is. Uh-huh, you betcha."

Their warm and tender kiss calmed both of them, and as they relaxed their embrace, Greg felt relieved and at ease, for he'd found her at last.

Jessica turned aside and ambled back to another smiling waitress who stood nearby watching the affectionate reunion.

With her back to Greg and Valerie, Jessica pointed her thumb over her shoulder, rolled her eyes, and said to the waitress, "That guy ain't messin' around. He's one of them fast-moving Yankees from up north, baby. I know his kind, all right. He's here for some reeeeal serious Valerie business. Oh yeah, uh-huh, honey!"

The other grinning waitresses nodded their agreement with Jessica.

When they broke their embrace, Greg asked, "When do you get off work, Valerie?"

"At five."

Checking his watch, he said, "That's only an hour from now. I'll sit in a booth and wait; that is, if you haven't any plans after work."

"No, Greg, I have no plans this evening. Look, I'm shaking. I'm so shocked and excited at seeing you. You . . . you just dropped out of nowhere. How did you ever find me?"

"To put it mildly, it was not easy, believe me. I've been all over this town the past week. Why I know more street names in Charleston than all the cab drivers and mail carriers put together." He laughed.

"You've been here in Charleston for a whole week looking for me? Oh, Greg, we have so much to talk about."

"You bet we do. Now where's my empty booth, so I can drink coffee and ogle my beautiful troll while she works?"

"Right this way, Mr. Ghost," she replied as she curled her finger and led him to an empty booth in the torpedo room.

She returned shortly with a full pitcher of coffee, and as she filled his cup, she bent over and kissed him softly on the lips.

He grabbed for her waist, but she instantly stepped backward, teasing, "Ooo, not now, tiger. We'll have lots of time for that, later. I'm off work for the next twenty-four hours and you're being abducted."

"Oh, I am? And to where am I being abducted?"

"To Myrtle Beach–in one hour, we're gone, Ghosty."

"How far is Myrtle Beach?"

"About two hours up the coast." She grinned impishly as she turned and wiggled back to her station.

As he sat drinking his coffee, he thought he'd better phone home. He knew Mom and Dad were worried, so he got up and strode to the cashier to get quarters.

While the cashier counted out the change, Valerie walked up to him and whined, "Don't tell me you're afraid of being seduced already, Mr. Ghost?"

"Not on your life, troll, you can't get rid of me that easy. You'll have a much harder time getting rid of me than I had in finding you. I'm just going outside to call home and let the folks know I found you. I'll be right back, so don't go away."

"Oh, I'm not going anywhere. That's a promise."

Greg stepped outside and into the phone booth that sat next to the entrance.

He dialed the number, deposited the money, and listened to their phone ring for long seconds.

Finally his mother picked up the receiver and said, "Hello?"

"Well, it's about time you answered," he chided. "I was about to hang up."

Immediately, she turned her mouth away from the phone and shouted, "Howard! It's Greg. Come quick!"

In the background, Greg heard his father yell, "Where is he?"

"Where are you, son?" she queried.

"I'm in Charleston."

Turning away from the phone again, his mother called out. "He's in Charle–oh dear, that was rude, Howard. You didn't have to snatch the receiver out of my hand."

"Hello, Greg, you've had your mother and me worried sick over you," his father declared. "Why haven't you called sooner?"

"Sorry, Dad, I guess I was too wrapped up in my search for Valerie."

"Well, how are you doing with your search? Have you had any leads?"

"Only one, Dad, and it was the clincher. I just found her not thirty minutes ago."

With a covered mouth piece and muffled words, his dad spoke excitedly. "Martha, he's found her!"

"He found Valerie! How wonderful!" she shouted. "Give me that phone, Howard. I want to hear all about it."

His father spoke into the receiver once again, saying, "You've found the woman who disappeared from you in Norway? She's actually living in Charleston now? It sounds unbelievable. How did you ever find her, son?"

"It was no piece of cake, Dad, I assure you. I had given up yesterday and was going to leave tomorrow to head back home when I literally stumbled into some crazy luck this morning. I'll tell you the whole story when I have more time, Dad. Let me talk to Mom."

His mother replied, "I'm so happy and thrilled with the news, Greg. She must've been shocked to see you. How in the world did you ever find her? You must tell me all about it."

"I can't right now, Mom. I'm in a phone booth outside her restaurant and I'm running out of quarters. I can't talk much longer."

His mother turned away from the mouthpiece, saying, "Howard, Valerie owns a restaurant. Isn't that wonderful?"

"Mom!" Greg shouted. "Valerie doesn't own the restaurant, she works in the restaurant as a waitress. She gets off in about twenty minutes, so I've got to go now. Mom, are you there?"

"Yes, Greg, I'm still here listening to every word. I thought you said she was a teacher. Why would she give up teaching to be a waitress? You must tell me all about her. I'm so happy and excited that you found her and very anxious to meet this woman who has my son all shook up."

"Hey, Mom, that's one of Presley's songs, 'All Shook Up'." He laughed. "Yes, she does have me all shook up, since the moment I laid eyes on her. Now that I've found her, she won't get away a second time."

"Okay, dear, I'll let you go. Call us soon won't you?"

"Yes I will, Mom, and would you please call Tom to let him know I found her? He'll want to phone Annika and tell her the good news."

"Yes I certainly will. Goodbye, son, and tell Valerie we're both looking forward to meeting her. Love you."

"Love you and Dad, too. Bye, Mom."

Greg hung up the receiver and returned to his booth inside the restaurant.

When Valerie ended her shift, she joined him at the booth and said, "It's been busy and steady in this place since 8:30 A.M. I'm sure ready to get out of here. Are you ready to leave, Greg?"

"More than ready," he replied.

"You can follow me to my apartment. I live only ten minutes from here on Wentworth Street."

Greg paid his tab at the cash register and before they walked out, Jessica waved to Valerie and said, "Later, baby. I'll see you two at home."

"Not if I can help it, baby," Valerie quipped.

Jessica shook her finger at them.

"Hey, I know what you two are fixin' to do. You're headin' for some of that messin' around trouble. You just betta mind yo manners now, ya hear."

"And when did you ever mind your messin' around manners, baby?" Valerie laughed.

"Honey, I'm always mindin' my manners, because there ain't no man in Jessica's life. Uh-uh, oh no, baby. I'm a tower of steel."

"Yeah, sure, until a new Mr. Right comes along to melt all that steel. Then you'll be nothing but a puddle of putty," Valerie teased.

"You hush your mouth. You think you know me, but you'll see ol' Jessica standing tough against those sweet-talking mama's boys. They're always lookin' for a new mama and it ain't never gonna be ol' Jessica, oh no. You're lookin' at the tower of power, uh-huh, baby."

"Yeah sure, Jessica, with that beautiful upsweep hairdo and pearly white smile of yours, the guys will never leave you alone. I'll bet you even have a date after your shift, tonight," Valerie kibitzed.

"If I do, honey, you'll never know." Jessica laughed.

"Because you can't admit that to me. You'd never live it down." Valerie grinned as she and Greg pushed open the door.

They waved and left the restaurant.

Before they went to their cars, Valerie directed Greg, saying, "After we drive over the bridge, we'll make a left turn onto Wentworth Street."

"You can lead me anywhere, troll." He grinned.

Shortly thereafter, both cars drove out of the parking lot onto the main street.

VI

Crossing over the bridge, both cars followed the water for a short time. Then Valerie's left turn signal blinked and both cars turned left onto Wentworth Street. A few blocks up the street Valerie parked alongside the curb, so Greg parked behind her.

After exiting their cars, Greg remarked, "I notice the dealer's frame around your license plate reads, 'Tupelo, Mississippi'. Did you buy your car there or here in Charleston?"

"I bought it in Tupelo. My girlfriend lives there. After I returned from Norway, I stayed with her for a while and I needed a car, so I bought it there. At the time, I didn't know whether or not I'd be coming back to Charleston."

"This area looks very familiar," Greg continued while turning around and looking back down the street. "I think I was around here this morning. Isn't there a neighborhood park nearby with a shallow pond surrounded with benches?"

"Yes, there certainly is. It's only a few blocks from here. Why?" she asked.

"That's the park where I met your friend's mother, Ella Mae, and her dog, Simba. She's the woman who led me to you."

"She is? I know her daughter very well. Isn't her mother the sweetest lady you've ever met? She's such a dear."

"She's not only sweet, but one beautiful lady. If it wasn't for her, I wouldn't be standing here right now. Retrieving her dog's leash was a real stroke of luck for me."

"They'll both get a 'thank you' from me, too. You can be sure of that," she declared, "but you can tell me the whole story on the way to Myrtle

Beach. Right now, you have to see my apartment. C'mon, I'll make a quick change and pack a few things in my overnight bag."

"Like what things?"

"You'll find out only in due time, Mr. Ghost."

She pecked him on the lips, took his hand, and led him across the street to her white frame apartment house.

The long, two-story row of wooden frame houses lined the north side of the street both east and west. The consecutive row of white houses stood prim and proper with their distinctive southern architecture, and with an air of southern dignity and charm, they suggested a salutation of southern hospitality to all passersby.

Valerie led Greg across the street and up the few wooden steps into her apartment.

When she disappeared into the bedroom, he stood admiring his surroundings. "I see your apartment has the feminine touch, naturally," he said. "It's very homey and comfortable."

"Thank you," she called out. Then she poked her head around the doorway. "Jessica and I like it very much. Give me a minute to change. You won't go away, will you?"

"No way, you were too hard to find. You're stuck with me now. As Elvis would say, 'I'm going to stick like glue, cause I'm stuck on you'." He laughed.

"What's with you and Elvis?"

"It's just a quirk of mine, I guess. His song titles and words to his songs pop into my head at times."

While waiting Greg roamed the room, casually examining the knickknacks and pictures that hung on the walls.

"Okay, me and the bedroom are decent now," she called out. "You can come in, but only if you mind your manners, ya hear."

"Yeah, I hear." He grinned, walking toward the doorway.

At the doorway, he stopped short and admired her beauty.

"You like?" she asked as she curtsied and fluffed her full skirt. Then she extended both arms upward, curved them in a circle over her head to simulate a ballerina stance, stood on her toes, and pirouetted.

"Wow! You look terrific. You're a knockout in pink, Val." Looking down at his own clothes, he added, "But I'm embarrassed. I can't take you anywhere in these old Levis. I need to get to my motel for some clothes."

"Where's your motel?"

"In north Charleston."

Suggestively, she sauntered up to him, wrapped her arms slowly around his waist, pressed herself against his body, and kissed him teasingly on his lips.

Then lifting one eyebrow, she purred, "Don't bother, tiger. You won't be needing any clothes later this evening, will you?"

Reacting to her sexiness, he playfully pushed her backward, so she grabbed his shirt, and as he pushed her down flat on her back on one of the twin beds, she pulled him down on top of her.

Hugging one another tightly, they rolled from side to side on the bedspread and kissed passionately.

When they relaxed their embrace, she whispered, "Oh, Greg, I'm so happy to be in your arms. I've thought about you so much. I never thought I'd ever see you again."

"I've never stopped thinking about you, Valerie. I thought you'd been kidnapped. I had to find you."

She closed her eyes, rubbed her cheek against his cheek, ran her fingers up the back of his head and through his thick black hair, and smiled contentedly. "I'm so happy to hear you say that, Greg. I feel so safe and secure now that I'm with you, again."

"Why go all the way to Myrtle Beach?" he queried. "Let's just stay here for the night."

As he snuggled his face in her breasts, he closed his eyes, but she quickly pushed his head up.

"Oh no, we can't stay here. Jessica will be here right after her shift. We can't very well kick her out of her bedroom. Besides, you have to see the beautiful sunrise from the beach and we have a lot of talking to do, so get up. We have to get going."

Greg didn't move.

She couldn't budge his heavy muscular body and begged, "C'mon, Mr. Ghost, we have to leave. Get off."

Greg giggled at her inability to move him, so she began tickling him in his ribs. He quickly scooted to his knees, but tickled her furiously in return.

She squealed, squirmed, and wiggled tenaciously to free herself, then finally, slid off the side of the bed landing hard on the floor on her buttocks.

"Ow! That hurt!" she cried. Jumping to her feet, she rubbed her backside, saying, "You play too rough, you big brute."

"Need some help to make it all better?" He grinned while reaching behind her to rub her buttocks. "Ummm, soft buttocks. How nice," he added as he started lifting her dress. "Now let's see what's underneath."

She quickly slapped his hand away, folded her arms, and batted her eyes in mock indignation.

"Bad boy! It seems to me, Yankee, I told you to behave yourself when you came in here. You obviously don't know how to behave yourself in a suth'n belle's bedroom. Now you mind your manners, ya hear."

"Mind my manners? So where were the manners of the prim and proper suth'n belle when she pulled me down on the bed on top of her?"

Valerie straightened her dress, turned her head away, and scoffed. "I did no such thing, suh. You pushed me onto the bed and ravaged a lady's innocence and dignity."

Greg stood up and, with his finger, turned her chin to face him and grinned. "But the lady offered no resistance, now did she?"

He kissed her softly on the lips.

"You took advantage of an innocent belle." She pouted with sly pursed lips. "You don't play fair."

"All's fair in love and war." He grinned.

"It is, is it?" She snickered as she shoved him back hard against the dresser. "Then this is war!" she declared, running from the room.

After slipping on the throw rug, Greg quickly reached back to steady himself against the dresser, and his hand fell into Valerie's open jewelry box.

When he regained his footing, he turned around to view her jewelry, and as he fingered her pretty earrings, necklaces, and delicate gold and silver chains, he spotted the friendship ring he'd given her in Bergen. While picking it up, he admired it with a smile. Then he walked into the living room where she sat on the sofa and handed her the ring.

"I see you still have my friendship ring."

"I sure do." She smiled as she gazed down at the ring and rubbed it affectionately. "Because I never forgot you, I keep it with me always."

"Why don't you wear it?"

Clutching the ring in her hand, she pressed her fist against her breasts and stared up into his eyes lovingly.

"When I realized I loved you, Greg, and because I never thought I'd ever see you again, I kept your ring in my jewelry box. In my own loving memory of you, I had you boxed forever. It also symbolized my boxed love for you. Now that you're back in my life again, it's so fitting for you to unbox my memory and ring. How beautiful that it is you who took my love out of the jewelry case and directed it back on you."

She stood up, brushed her lips softly across his mouth, and asked, "Does the ring still signify a meaningful and lasting relationship, ghosty?"

Welled with emotion, he smothered her in his arms and kissed her passionately.

Upon the release of their embrace, Valerie began to slip the ring onto her finger, but he gripped her wrist and stopped her, saying, "As Presley would say, 'Won't you wear my ring around your neck?'"

"Oh, that sounds even better," she replied as she strode across the room and entered the bedroom once again.

"My, my," she called out, "you do have a thing about Elvis, don't you?"

"Not really, but the words of his songs just seem to apply to us. That's all."

Valerie reappeared in the doorway, and with an impish look in her eyes, she said, "Well, I must admit, he was a verrry sexy man. I like his songs, too."

Leaned back against the doorjamb, she bent one knee and slid her foot up the jamb until she braced her foot against it. With both hands placed on the sides of her dress, she slowly slid her dress up over her knees to teasingly expose her bare thighs. Then she instantly dropped her dress, spread her fingers wide, and pressed both palms to her thighs. Sliding only her hands up both sides of her dress to her face, she rubbed her hands up both sides of her face and up through her hair, at which point she threw her long auburn hair forward over her head to let it drape over her face.

Giggling to herself as Greg rushed up to her, she peered up at him from underneath the thick, messy, fine hairs. When he parted the hair to try and kiss her, she covered his mouth with her hand, lifted a gold chain from her blouse pocket, and dangled the friendship ring in front of his eyes.

She batted her eyes and replied, "Could you be so kind, suh, as to help a damsel in distress by hooking my chain, so I may wear your ring around my neck?"

"I'm much obliged, ma'am," he offered.

Dropping the ring and chain into his hand, she promptly turned around and held her long hair forward to expose her delicate white neck. He drew the chain about her neck, but hesitated before clasping the chain.

"Better yet, ma'am, why don't you put this chain around MY neck and lead me anywhere. Cuz, I'm yo teddy bear," he sang.

"Ah sweah, Mista Ericsen, sometimes you really are impossible. Now will you please behave and hook me up."

Still tantalizing, he kissed both sides of her neck, and after much coaxing and begging, he finally clasped the chain behind her neck.

When she turned to face him, he wrapped his arms around her tiny waist and pulled her to him, so she slapped his cheek gently and pecked his mouth with her lips.

"Don't be too free with your kisses, ma'am, or you'll find yourself in deep trouble again." He smirked.

"And I DO like your kind of trouble," she purred as she slowly rubbed her soft full breasts across his hard chest.

Immediately, he released her waist and kissed her on the forehead, saying, "I think we'd better get out of here right now, beautiful troll, before it gets too warm for both of us."

"Yes, I have to agree, Mr. Ghost," she agreed while straightening her clothes.

She hurried into the bedroom to pick up her overnight bag, and as she rushed out of the room, she snatched a wide-brimmed hat from the closet shelf.

Rejoining Greg in the living room, she plopped the hat on her head and said, "Okay, I'm ready. How do I look?"

"Terrific! I love it, but don't tell me what your hat's made of. Ask me if I know what it's made from."

"Okay, smarty, what's my hat made from?"

"Sweet grass." He smiled. "Because I saw the women in the marketplace weaving them along with various-sized baskets, too."

"Right you are, so now that your Yankee brain's been enlightened with southern ingenuity, let's get moving, or we may not get a room. It's a summer weekend and Myrtle Beach is a tourist resort."

Hand-in-hand they left the apartment, crossed the street to Greg's car, and after entering it, they drove down the street toward the freeway.

Upon turning onto Route 17, they headed toward the two bridges which would lead them over the Ashley and Cooper rivers and take them away from the city.

Crossing the first bridge, Greg observed the harbor and commented, "Charleston is a very pretty city."

"How could it be anything different, suh? After all, it's my home and it's where all the prettiest suth'n belles come from."

"And ever-so-modest belles, too," he added.

"Right you are, Yankee."

As Greg relaxed, putting his arm around her, she turned on the radio and tuned it to her favorite station. Johnny Rivers sang, "Baby, I need your lovin'." While listening to the song, she cuddled into him and neither of them spoke for a long time.

After many miles, Valerie finally broke the silence by saying, "I'm so thankful you found me, Greg. I feel so safe and comfortable next to you."

He squeezed her shoulder and replied, "I've never felt more comfortable and relaxed next to any other woman, either. Don't you think this is a good time to tell me what happened in Bergen. Why did you panic and run away? Did you know that creep? I deserve an explanation, don't I?"

Valerie peered up at him with anxiety and longing in her eyes and said, "Yes, you certainly do, Greg. I was terrified of him."

She sat straight up in the seat, turned off the radio, and began to relate the story of her disappearance from Bergen.

"Do you remember when I went to the ladies room in the restaurant that Sunday?"

"Yes, vividly."

"After I came out of the rest room, I stopped at a pay phone in the hallway to call my boyfriend, Lasse."

"So you were already involved with another man, but why didn't you tell me about him?"

"A few weeks before I met you, I had called off our engagement and we had a big argument over it. I was confused about my emotions so, on impulse, I left Bergen quickly on a weekend. I didn't tell him I was leaving because I didn't want him to follow me or find me. I needed time alone to think and gather my thoughts.

"I didn't know Annika before that weekend. I had just met her on a previous tour a few days before we met you and Tom. I wonder how she's doing? She was so nice. She was very infatuated with Tom. Do they keep contact?"

"Yes, they write letters often and sometimes Tom phones her. They'll be relieved to know I've found you and you're safe. Annika's been very fearful and worried about you. When I phoned home, I asked my mother to inform Tom and I'm sure he called Annika right away."

"I knew you'd all be concerned about me. I'm very sorry about that, but I deliberately didn't contact any of you because at the time I didn't want any involvement of any kind. I was so confused. I found out later how much I missed you, but it was too late. I'm sorry, Greg."

"It's nothing to be sorry about, Val. You were troubled with your problems about Lasse and I was a complete stranger to you. You couldn't really confide in me. I can understand it was a very emotional experience for you, something you didn't foresee and had to work out. I guess we can conclude we were all victims of your circumstances, right?"

"That's right. It's where I was at and we were all victims at the time."

"So what did you tell Lasse on the phone in the restaurant and what about that creep?"

Suddenly, she looked away from him and reached for her purse sitting next to her.

Greg sensed evasiveness, which immediately aroused his suspicions. *She's hesitant to explain. I wonder why?* he thought.

As she took a comb from her purse, she pulled down the sun visor and began to comb and primp her hair in the mirror.

Then she continued to relate, "Lasse was relieved that I called. He'd been very worried, naturally, because he didn't know where I'd gone. I told him I left unexpectedly to be alone to think. Then I told him about the man following me and how petrified I was. I told him where I was phoning from, so he said he'd leave immediately in his boat and wait at the landing at the end of the street. I told him if I encountered that man again, I'd take a taxi to the end of the street and meet him there."

Greg listened intently, but her slow and sometimes hesitant words seemed suspect.

"Well, you saw what happened after the phone call," she added.

"Yes, we both know that part of the story, but what happened with you and Lasse after that Sunday, and did you ever encounter the stranger again?"

"He and his brother took me to his island summer home, and because I was so scared, I asked him if I could stay there for a few days. He said I could stay forever if I wanted to, but I only remained there for a week. Escaping that creep was all I cared about, at that time. I didn't encounter him, again."

Greg replied, "By the way it all happened, it appeared as though Lasse and his brother knew the stranger, so I assumed they abducted you; but I'm real glad I mistook it to be a kidnapping now, because I wouldn't be sitting here otherwise. On second thought, I'm glad you didn't tell me about your engagement problems with Lasse also or again I wouldn't be here right now. I would have chalked off your broken relationship as just a lover's quarrel which would undoubtedly have been patched up later and you two would have lived happily ever after. It must be fate that we're together, eh Val?"

"Yes, and what a wonderful fate it is to have you back in my life again."

"We were meant to be. That's all there is to it." He smiled, squeezing her shoulder again.

Then from the corner of his eye, he noticed her looking down rubbing the handle of her hair brush nervously. He wondered about her nervousness.

Is she telling me the truth about Bergen? he thought. *I'm a little skeptical, but more importantly, we're together again and that's all that matters to us now.*

A short time later they drove into the city limits of Myrtle Beach, and Valerie announced, "Oh, we're already here. That was a fast trip, wasn't it, Greg?"

"Yes, a fast drive with time well spent," he agreed.

"Up ahead, at that next signal light, turn right," she directed. "That road leads to the beach and a string of motels. It's Saturday night in the middle of tourist season and all we can do is hope for a vacancy."

"I hope so, too. I'm not keen on sleeping under any bridge, troll," he mused.

When the road reached the beach, it curved to the left, so they followed it along, viewing the long string of motels to their immediate left, and as they drove slowly past the motels, they also observed all the shining bright signs displaying NO VACANCY.

Suddenly a NO went black on a sign up ahead and Valerie saw it, exclaiming, "Look, Greg! The sign at the Four Seasons shows a vacancy, now. Do you see it?"

"Yes, I see it."

"Hurry up! We don't want anyone to get there ahead of us!"

Greg hit the gas pedal and within seconds, swerved off the road, screeched onto the driveway, and jerked to an abrupt stop in front of the office door.

Jumping from the car, he dashed into the office and rang the desk bell. The desk clerk appeared immediately.

"Can I help you, sir?"

"Yes, I'd like a room if one's available."

"I didn't have anything up to a few minutes ago, when I received a phone cancellation. I've been booked solid since noon today, so you're very lucky. The room has one double bed, if that's okay?"

"We'll take it. It looks like every motel on the beach is also booked solid. They all show 'no vacancy'."

"I'm sure they are. It's the height of our tourist season."

The clerk handed Greg a registration card, and after he filled it out and paid the charges, the clerk also handed Greg the key.

"Thanks for the room." Greg smiled.

"My pleasure," the clerk replied. "Have a nice night."

When Greg returned to the car and climbed inside, he held up the key with a wink to Valerie.

"Whew! That was close." She sighed. "And now we have to get you some beach togs. I know just the place for great mens' beach clothes. Afterward, for a nice supper, we can go to my favorite cozy restaurant with intimate corner booths that are perfect for quiet conversation."

"Sounds good to me. You still need to update me on your great escape from Norway."

"All in due time," she replied as Greg started the engine and they drove back out onto the beach road again. "Keep following the road," she continued. "It will wind to the left and take us back to Route 17, where we turn right. Seventeen will take us to the mall for your beach clothes."

A short time later, at the mall, Greg bought a change of underwear and blue shorts and along with a white t-shirt with blue lettering reading MYRTLE BEACH, SC across the chest, he picked up a baseball hat that also read MYRTLE BEACH.

Upon leaving the store, as he adjusted the hat on his head, Valerie shook her head and said, "Once a jock, always a jock."

"Yep, and now I'm a full-fledged Myrtle Beach jock. Where's the restaurant? This jock is starved."

"It's only about ten minutes from here on seventeen again."

Driving west from the mall parking lot, they arrived at the restaurant quickly and once inside, Valerie led him to a back booth in a far corner of the eatery. It was quiet and private.

After Greg ordered two New York steak dinners with coffee, they returned to their subject of Norway.

"So after one week, you left Lasse and where did you go?"

"During that week at Lasse's I booked a flight to Cannes and also phoned the hotel in Oslo to assure them I'd pick up my luggage in a few days. They were kind enough to hold it for me. Then when I left Lasse's, on the same day I picked up my luggage, I went to the airport and flew to Cannes. I needed to be alone, completely away from Lasse, so at Cannes, I laid around on the beach every day just to think and sort things out.

"Finally, after ten days of heavy thinking and sunbathing, I decided to return to the States and forget about Lasse."

"But what about your teaching job in Bergen?"

Looking down, she fiddled with the handle of her coffee cup and replied, "I had already quit my teaching job. I wasn't too happy at the school, anyway, so my teaching there didn't matter anymore. I was too mixed up over Lasse and very confused at the time."

"I thought you liked teaching the children."

Valerie looked up quickly and snapped, "Don't misunderstand, Greg. It wasn't the children I was unhappy with. I loved the children. Already, I have my resumes out to teach here in Charleston this fall. It was my colleagues. We didn't have too much in common. You know, cultural differences, background, compatibility, interests, things of that sort. I was just tired of teaching in Norway and homesick for the States again. I didn't know if I loved Lasse enough to stay there."

"Well, I can understand all of that," Greg replied.

When the waitress set their plates in front of them, they broke their conversation only to smile and nod to her, then kept talking.

While eating their meal slowly, Valerie continued telling her story with Greg interjecting many questions.

After their meal, Greg suggested dancing and drinks at one of the beach clubs but Valerie, with a gleam in her eyes, declined the suggestion, saying, "Oh, not tonight, Greg. It's been a long, tiring week and I had a very busy day today."

He smiled knowingly at her excuse as they both slid out of the booth, and when they reached the cashier, he paid the tab.

"Look, Greg, it's raining outside. I hadn't noticed," Valerie commented.

Greg winked at the cashier and grinned. "I wonder why? It couldn't be because you never stopped talking all during the meal, could it?"

Instantly, she tickled him in the ribs, chiding, "And what about your wagging tongue, pieface?"

"You two sound like you're married," the cashier noted.

"Not yet." Greg smiled. "But we'll be working on it."

After he pushed open the door for Valerie, they dashed through the pelting rain to the parking lot and jumped into the car.

On their drive back to the motel, Valerie flicked on the radio.

The Cascades were singing "Listen to the Rhythm of the Falling Rain."

"How appropo," she purred, snuggling into his side.

During the short drive to the motel, the rain became heavier and by the time they reached the motel, the rain, pounding hard on the roof, bounced pellets off the hood.

Valerie reached around to grab her hat and beach bag off the back seat and laughed. "Let's make a run for it!"

"I'm game. It's only water." He grinned.

"Ha, ha, but I've got an umbrella." She smirked, holding up her wide-brimmed hat. "It's as good as one anyway."

Suddenly she jerked the door open, jumped from the car, and on the run, plopped the hat on her head. Splashing through the puddles, she bolted toward the back entrance to the motel.

Greg jumped from his own door and splashed after her through the pouring rain and puddles until he reached her at the entrance door.

Just inside the door, they both stood dripping wet, shaking their heads and arms. Then they leaned back against the wall to catch their breath.

After a moment, Greg turned toward her, pinned her back flat against the wall, and kissed her hard on the mouth. She went limp and dropped her arms to her sides. Her hat and beach bag hit the floor.

Holding the kiss with his stomach pushed tightly against hers, he clutched her hands. Pressing them back against the wall, he outstretched her arms and slid them slowly up the wall and over her head.

In her struggle to breathe, she tried to shift her head from side to side, but it was useless. He kept his mouth firmly clamped to her lips. She moaned and groaned, staring at him wide-eyed with pleading eyes, so he finally relaxed his grip. Twisting her mouth away from his, she shoved him backward and slumped against the wall. With a clenched fist to her breasts, she gasped for air.

Laughing and panting, he fell back against the opposite wall, trying to catch his own breath.

With their backs to the walls, they slid slowly down until they both came to rest sitting on the floor. Still huffing, puffing, and giggling, they tried to speak, but couldn't.

Finally, Valerie huffed, "You . . . you literally took my bre . . . breath away, Greg."

"Tha . . . that was the who . . . whole idea," he puffed.

When they quickly regained their breath, they stood up with Greg stating, "Uh-oh, I left my new clothes in the car."

"Too bad, ghosty, I've got mine," she claimed, holding up her hat and bag. "Serves you right after that nasty kiss, but I'll be a sport. Here, take my 'umbrella'," she offered while handing him her hat. "It'll keep those raindrops off that sexy crop of hair."

He snatched the hat from her hand and squashed it onto his head. It was too small. The hat slid down the side of his head, stopping at his ear. There it sat supported by the one ear.

"Why, Mista Greg, you pretty suth'n belle. Ah sweah, you look sooo adorable in your little sweet grass hat. You're just all full of little surprises, aren't you? You little dickens!"

Lifting both sides of her dress, she tilted her head to one side and demurely curtsied to him.

He tossed the hat at her and grinned. "Sassy, are you? I'll tend to you later, troll. There's no bridge around here for you to hide under, either. You're in trouble now, so you'd better keep your dress down. I'll see you in a bit."

He turned around and pushed open the door as she whined, "Don't get TOO wet, pieface."

When he ran out the door into the torrential downpour, she hurried down the hall to find their room, but had to wait at the door since Greg had the key.

He returned, dripping water, and remarked, "My, my, no key, eh? Too bad for you, troll."

She threw her hands to her hips and bent toward him.

"'Too bad,' what's that supposed to mean? You think you're big enough to try something, huh, you cute little suth'n belle," she cooed.

"Still sassy, eh? Well, I'll fix that when we get in the room," he declared as he reached behind her and pinched her buttocks.

"Ow!" she squealed, jumping back and rubbing her backside, giggling.

When he turned the key in the lock and pushed open the door, he suddenly turned and lunged toward her, but she was too quick for him. She sidestepped his lunge, darted past him into the room, threw her hat on the bed, and raced into the bathroom with her beach bag.

Fast on her heels, he chased her up to the door where she scooted inside the bathroom, slammed the door in his face, and quickly turned the lock.

While running her bath water, she unzipped her beach bag and pulled out a pair of white nylon lace panties. Then she listened at the door and when she heard Greg turn on the TV, she opened the door quietly and peeked around the opening.

She saw him sitting up on the bed at the headboard staring at the TV with two pillows propped behind him and his hands folded behind his head.

When he glanced over at her, she poked her head out and dangled her panties at him.

He squinted his eyes, clenched his teeth, and muttered, "Ooo, you really are in deep trouble now, troll."

"Ha, ha, who's afraid of the big bad wolf–pieface!" She laughed.

When she continued jiggling her panties, he dashed off the bed, but she quickly jumped back inside the bathroom and locked the door.

He reached the door too late, so he called through the door, "Who's pieface!"

"That's you, kind suh. You're pieface." She laughed while stepping into her warm bath.

He shook his head, saying, "Your southern expressions are somethin' else. What next?"

From her bath water, she cooed, "Ooo, I'll never tell–pieface."

"I'd watch my mouth, if I were you, ma'am. You do have to come out of there sometime, you know, and you're already in deep trouble."

"Really? And what kind of trouble might that be comin' from a north'n Yankee?"

He drawled, "Real South Dakota lovin' trouble, ma'am."

She lowered her voice and growled, "Well, I've neva been in any South Dakota trouble before, 'cuz I'm from Missouri, pardner, so you'll just have to show me. I'm a 'show me' woman."

Frustrated, he jiggled the doorknob.

"Ha, ha, too bad, so sad. The door is locked, bad boy. After all, a suth'n lady must protect her honor and dignity from the likes of trouble-making Yankees like you, ah dooo declaaah!"

"You are a sassy one!"

"I beg your pardon, suh. I'm not sassy. I'm just a prim and propah suth'n lady, wonderin' what that South Dakota lovin' trouble is all about."

"Well, I wouldn't say you're looking so prim and proper sitting all naked in that bathtub covered with soap suds."

When silence ensued, Greg returned to the bed, and as he waited patiently, strong sexual desire stirred within him. Moments later, he heard the electric sound of her hair dryer.

Eventually the bathroom door opened slowly. One violet-blue eye peeked around the door and peered directly at him.

"What's the matter, gorgeous troll? Afraid to come out for South Dakota trouble?"

"And are you ready for the lingerie show?" she teased.

She stepped out from behind the door and pirouetted in only her bra, half-slip, and panties.

Her long hair flowed to one side of her head and the light shining from the dresser lamp behind her glowed through the fine rose-colored strands of her auburn hair.

"Now, how prim and propah am I? Sexy enough for you?"

As she stood posing at the foot of the bed in all-white nylon and lace, he crawled forward into a kneeling position to admire her alluring figure.

"You are indescribable, Val. I've never seen a more beautiful woman."

"Oh, so how many women have you seen in their underwear, bad boy?"

Lifting her slip to show her lace panties, she sashayed at the foot of the bed. Then dropping her slip, she pirouetted again. After one turn she stopped, lifted one eyebrow, and sensuously slid her slip up her thighs with both hands to show off her lace-trimmed panties again.

"How do you like the show, so far?" she asked.

He growled and scooted to the foot of the bed, but when he made a swipe for her slip, she jumped back quickly and held him at bay with a straight arm to his head.

"Dowwwn tiger, you're too eager!" she squealed.

"Well, what do you expect when you flaunt your sexy wiles in front of me, tea and crumpets?"

The enticing smell of her expensive perfume heightened his passion, and when she fingered and toyed with his hair, he wrapped his arms around her slip and thighs and kissed her soft stomach gently and repeatedly.

She closed her eyes and tilted her head back to enjoy the repetition until he started to slide her slip and panties down her thighs. Immediately she opened her eyes, tugged her underwear out of his hands, and pulled them back up.

"I think it's time for the troublemaker to take his shower and cool down." She smirked.

When she shoved his head back, he scampered onto the floor after her, but she scrambled onto the bed and scooted up to the pillows at the head-board. After fluffing both pillows, she flipped around in a sitting position and leaned back against them with folded arms.

Greg stood with his hands on his hips and grumbled, "First you get me all sexed up, then you dump me to the shower. You're a real sport."

"Now mind your manners, ya hear. You've had your lingerie preview. We have all night for the feature attraction."

"That does it! Now you've had it," he asserted as he hopped onto the bed and crawled up the bedspread after her.

She screeched, pulling her legs up instantly, but he grabbed her ankles and yanked her feet back down. She giggled and squealed and twisted and writhed to free herself, but her feet were caught in two tight vices. She couldn't shake his tenacious iron grip. Slowly, he began his deliberate slide over her legs and stomach, but her efforts to resist were useless against his overpowering strength, so she began beating his back with her fists. He grabbed her wrists and pinned them against her sides.

She squirmed feistily, but to no avail, and when he reached her face to face, he engulfed her in his muscular arms. She couldn't move. She lay motionless beneath his hard, all-encompassing body and comforting grip. Eyeball-to-eyeball, he smirked between pursed lips while she glared with clenched teeth.

"See, you DO have a pieface," she sassed.

With her arms still pinned at her sides, he kissed her softly, and with affection rubbed his body gently over her stomach.

Stubbornly she squirmed and wiggled, but within moments, her arms and body relaxed. She no longer resisted. Filled with ecstasy, she enjoyed his warm lips. Her whole body tingled.

He released her wrists and momentarily withdrew his lips from her mouth. Then he continued kissing her gently. Sliding his hands up her back into her hair, he ran his hands through the soft fine strands.

She kissed him tenderly, caressing his face with her smooth creamy hands.

Suddenly overwhelmed with desire, in a burst of urgency, she threw her arms around his neck, squeezed him tight, and pressed her mouth against his lips.

Greg felt her passion and tried to pull back from her lips. She moaned and tightened her grip on his neck. Seconds later, their lips parted slightly, but she hung tight, groaned, and pulled his mouth back to hers. She nibbled his lips fiercely.

"Oh, Greg, please don't stop kissing me," she begged. "I want so much to love you. I need to be loved."

He knew she wanted him right away, but he wanted more for her to sense his sincerity, to feel safe and secure consumed in his strong arms, so he squeezed her body tight against himself and while kissing her again, held her snugly, keeping her still and motionless for several moments until her passion subsided.

When he released her and they lay together in each other's arms, she stroked his face again with her gentle hands and ran them up through his unruly hair.

"I've missed you terribly, Greg. I need you so much."

With loving eyes, she stared at his mouth and with her fingers, touched his lips gently. Then she lifted his chin and brushed her lips softly across his lips.

For a few moments, they remained calm and contented in the comforting quiet of one another's arms before Greg jumped off the bed and headed for the bathroom.

"Cold shower or hot, ma'am?"

"Hot!" She grinned.

After his shower, he emerged from the bathroom to see Valerie sitting in front of the dresser mirror, brushing her long silky hair.

When she turned to face him, her arm froze momentarily above her head. Then her arm dropped down on the table and with a bracing elbow, she propped the hairbrush squarely under her chin. Immediately, her eyes roamed all over him, examining every inch of his athletic body.

Lifting one eyebrow, she declared, "Well, aren't you a vision in your sexy blue briefs. That's one beautiful bod you have there. Where did you amass all that curly hair on your chest?"

"I eat my Wheaties and drink orange juice faithfully." He smiled.

She stood up and moved toward him.

When they touched foreheads, he placed his hands on her hips and said, "I can't keep my hands off you. All this silky slippery nylon stirs up the hormones."

She batted her eyes and purred, "Isn't that the whole idea?"

Instantly he jerked her tight against his stomach, ran his hands up her back, and kissed her firmly.

Dropping to the floor on his knees, he pulled her stomach into his face. While kissing and running his tongue softly over her stomach, he slipped his arms under her slip and ran his hands slowly up the back of her thighs.

She closed her eyes, tilted her head back, and held his head against her stomach.

When his hands reached her panties, he rubbed his hands over them. The feel of the soft slippery nylon aroused him even more. He caressed and squeezed her buttocks and kissed her stomach harder.

Moments later, he got to his feet, picked her up in his arms, and carried her to the bed. Laying her down on her back, he stood above her, relishing her beauty.

Enjoying his eager eyes, she lifted one eyebrow and brought her arms up over her head. Then she stretched her arms straight out flat on the bedspread and writhed and teased him sensually with seductive body movements.

"Now what, Mr. Troublemaker?"

He gripped her hips and slid her lace slip slowly down her thighs and legs until it dropped to the floor.

Laying there in her bra and panties, she crossed a knee over her other leg to entice his hungry eyes with more thigh and panty display.

When he reached for the elastic of her panties, she grabbed his hand, saying, "Eh, eh, not so fast, pieface. This isn't a one-way street, you know."

She yanked his arm and pulled him forward on top of her, and as they brought their mouths together, they slipped their hands down inside the elastics of each other's briefs and slid them down their legs.

Afterward, Greg slid onto his knees and replied, "Still one more to go, troll. A man's work is never done."

Valerie giggled, sat up, and turned around to let him undo her bra.

While unhooking the clasp, he caressed her breasts with his other hand. When the strap fell away, he dropped her bra to the floor and massaged her soft full breasts with both hands. She closed her eyes, laid her head back on his shoulder, and turned her face up to him. He kissed her warmly. After moments of tender caressing, she twisted around and promptly ran her hand slowly over his chest and through his thick, curly black hair.

He gently laid her back down on the bed, laid on top of her, and kissed her anxiously. He kissed her neck and nibbled her earlobe. Then, crossing over, he kissed her mouth and the other side of her neck and earlobe. His warm breath on her ears excited her. He slid down her body, and when he kissed her breasts and ran the tip of his tongue slowly around her nipples, they breathed heavier.

When he reached her tummy, he moved his tongue lightly all over her stomach and rubbed his hands up and down her legs. As he slid further downward, he ran his tongue ever slightly on the insides of her thighs and kissed them softly. The sweet scent of her body smelled like rose petals and her milk white skin felt just as velvety.

He slid back up to her breasts and fondled them gently in his hands. Then he brushed his lips lightly over each breast and glided his caressing tongue over and around her hardened nipples.

When he reached up to her face, once more, they panted heavily.

Her watery violet-blue eyes beckoned impatiently.

With her petite body smothered in his arms, she murmured, "Oh, Greg, I feel your love. Love me."

She wrapped her arms tightly around his neck, pressed her breasts hard against his chest, and squeezed his neck hard.

With every kiss, passion grew stronger and sexual anxiety intensified in their hunger for each other.

Within minutes, they kissed wantonly, and as sexual desires burned unharnessed, their tightly entwined bodies became as one.

Later, when the rustling of bedclothes and heavy breathing subsided, their warm, stilled bodies lay close to one another in the dark, silent room. The sound of rain pinged against the window.

Shortly afterward, wrapped in each other's arms, they fell sound asleep.

Sometime during the night, Greg awakened in the darkened room and reached out to feel for Valerie. He felt only empty bed clothes and quickly looked to her side of the bed. It was vacant with the bed covers turned back.

Panning the room, he saw her huddled in a chair with a bed sheet wrapped around her. She sat motionless with her feet perched on the edge of the chair and her knees drawn up–her chin rested on her knees–staring out the window at the falling rain. She looked like a big white ball.

Greg turned on the bed lamp and noted the time. It was 4 A.M. He wondered why she wasn't sleeping, so he slid out of bed and went to her.

"It's so early, Val. How come you're awake? Is something wrong?"

Looking up at him, the tears streamed down her cheeks.

"Hey, there IS something wrong. What is it, Val?"

She took his hand and rubbing it with endearing affection she stared at him through blurry watery eyes, saying, "Oh, my dear Greg, you're such a gentle man. There's nothing wrong. I'm crying because everything is so right. At this moment, I'm the happiest woman in the world. I feel so safe and happy with you. For the first time in my life, you've made me feel loved. I feel like a real woman. I'm alive!"

He knelt down by her, wiped her tears gently with the bed sheet, and smiled warmly. "Those dark blue piercing eyes are even more incredible when they're watery. They glisten purplish blue. Now you've got to stop your crying, troll, or you'll have me crying, too, ya hear. We can't both be bawl babies."

He pulled another chair over to the window and sat beside her. For a long time they sat hand-in-hand. They spoke very little, only in whispers, and enjoyed the quiet intimacy they shared with one another. They simply sat staring out the window at the rain beating against the pavement on the deserted street outside.

Soon the heavy rain slowed to fine sprinkling that appeared as a sparkling misty curtain flowing past the glowing street globes.

At daybreak the rain had stopped entirely, so Valerie got out of her chair and dropped the bed sheet.

Still in her underwear, she stretched sensuously in front of him, so Greg instantly put his hands under her slip and ran his hands slowly up the front of her thighs. Then gripping her buttocks, he pulled her toward him and kissed her tummy softly.

She rumpled his hair with her hands, closed her eyes, and whispered, "Ummm, I love it when you do that."

His caressing hands continued to roam underneath her slip, so she slapped his arm, pushed his arm away, and said, "Not now, bad boy! We have to get down to the beach or we'll miss the sunrise. C'mon, let's get dressed."

He stood up, threw his hands in the air, and sighed. "If we must, we must."

"Yes, we must." Valerie laughed while pulling out a bright yellow skirt and white sleeveless blouse from her beach bag.

With a toss of her hair, she held up the skirt with both hands at the waist and shook it for inspection.

"You're wearing a skirt and blouse. Why not shorts?"

"I did bring shorts, but I decided not to wear them today. You make me feel too feminine and womanly around you, pieface, so from now on, I'm wearing only skirts and dresses when I'm with you."

"I'm all for that." He grinned. "You flatter me."

"You deserve it," she flirted.

He stepped into his shorts and pulled his t-shirt over his head, and when she put on her blouse and began to button the buttons, he walked over to her and finished buttoning her up.

"That was a beautiful night we shared, Val."

"Isn't that what all you men like?"

Instantly he stepped back, held up the palms of his hands, and said, "Whoa! Hold on here. You mean much more to me than just sex. I didn't travel halfway across the country and search all over Charleston for you, just to have a roll in the hay and one-night stand. Don't cheapen my feelings, Val. They go much deeper than sex, and don't demean what we shared last night. Didn't you say you felt loved for the first time in your life; that today you feel like a woman?"

Her eyes flashed nervously, listening to his sensitive outburst, so she rushed up to him, covered his lips with her finger, and whispered, "Sssh, my darling, I'm sorry." She pecked his lips. "I didn't mean anything by it. It was a stupid remark. Yes, it meant much more to me than sex, too. Now I know how much you really care about me. I said it without thinking only because it's been so long."

"So long meaning so long since you've slept with a man, or so long since we last saw each other?"

"Does it really matter that I've been with other men, Greg? I'm sure you've had your share of other women."

"Yes, I've had other women, but I've never felt like this for any other woman. It's the feelings and meaning behind the act that means so much. I guess I'm like a young boy right now, wanting to be your very first love."

She cupped his chin, stared hard into his eyes, and smiled sincerely. "You ARE my first REAL love, Greg. You are the very first man from whom I've ever really felt love. You can believe that or not but it's the honest truth."

"So it wasn't just physical. You did feel more than just passion from me?"

"Oh yes, because you were so gentle. From your loving caresses and gentle fondling, I truly felt loved for the first time. I really felt your love, Greg. I've never felt like that for another man. That's the truth. Now, c'mon, let's get down to the beach or we'll miss the sunrise."

While tying his shoes, he replied, "Everything will be wet."

She slipped into her sandals, pulled the bedspread and two blankets off the bed, and said, "We can sit on one of the tables. Here, you take the blankets and I'll take the bedspread and pillows."

They hurried out the door and left by the rear exit so the desk clerk wouldn't see them with all the bedding. Since the office was out of sight from the parking area, they made their way through the parking lot and across the street to the beach.

When they reached a nearby table with a good view, Valerie threw the bedspread over the wet tabletop and plopped the two pillows on top for cushions.

Climbing up onto the table and pillows, they wrapped themselves in the blankets to watch the brilliant yellow ball peeking up on the horizon.

She snuggled into his side and peered up at him. "Now, isn't this nice and cozy, Mr. Ghost?" She smiled.

"Perfect," he replied. "The clouds have broken up and there's the blue sky. It's a great sunrise. It should be nice and sunny today."

"Ummm, nice and warm, just like my man," she replied while rubbing the top of his hairy thigh. Teasingly, she slowly ran her hand down inside his thigh, adding, "Ooo, you're so hairy. Ummm, I love it."

"Better be careful with that hand. You sure like to get yourself in trouble, don't you?"

He bent over, kissing her full on the lips with a long, lingering kiss.

When their lips parted, she lifted an eyebrow and squeezed his thigh, saying, "You wouldn't do anything on a public picnic table, would you, pieface?"

Without looking at her, he gazed straight ahead at the sea and replied, "When I'm with you, beautiful troll, I wouldn't be surprised at anything I might do."

"Ooo, that sounds intriguing. I'll have to keep a close eye on your manners, bad boy." Then she slapped his thigh and sat up straight.

"You're the one starting trouble with that sassy hand. You're the trouble maker right now, but I DO love your kind of South Carolina trouble, ma'am."

"In Norway, you said you thought you loved me, Greg. Do you still think you're in love with me? I've never met a sincere man like you, so I'm very vulnerable right now. Be very careful how you answer, because my heart's on my sleeve."

He lifted her chin and stared directly into her eyes. "I'm crazy about you, Val. That I DO know, but I don't really know if I'm in love with you, yet. We've just discovered each other again, and I'll need more time to know my true feelings. I'll be staying another week in Charleston, so we can spend a lot of time together and get to know each other better. I'm betting we hit it off together, Val."

"You're staying another week!" she squealed. "That's terrific. We'll have so much fun together. I'll be your personal tour guide and show you all around Charleston."

"As if I haven't already seen Charleston," he winced, "but with a beautiful troll as my guide, it'll be a lot more fun the second time around."

She grasped his hand and rubbed it gently along her cheek. Isn't that a beautiful sunrise?" she queried.

"That it is."

During the next half-hour they sat quietly, enjoying their closeness.

While they talked occasionally, Greg continued to ponder his thoughts. He had some reservations. She seemed a bit of a mystery to him.

He thought, *There's something not quite right with us, but what is it? Why am I so suspicious of her story? Because her hands were very nervous when she explained about the stranger in Bergen? She discarded him very quickly. Is she still in trouble and, if so, why? I have to get these doubts and questions answered or there can be no commitment.*

Eventually they gathered up the bedding and strolled back to their room, where they retrieved their belongings and checked out of the motel.

Driving back along the beach road, they took their last look at the ocean and stopped at the same restaurant from the previous evening for a French toast breakfast.

Later, when they neared Charleston, Greg decided to test her.

"I wonder what that creep wanted in Bergen?" he questioned.

Immediately Valerie straightened up in her seat and said, "Just thinking about him gives me the willies. His ugly craggy face is a vivid image in my mind." Then she quickly changed the subject by adding, "Oh, look there's the bridge. We're almost home. What time is it?"

"It's almost eleven forty-five."

"Good, we're in town early. I can call Jessica to find out what shift I work today. The new schedules for the week are always posted on Saturday nights."

"Why call? Why don't we just drive to the restaurant?"

"Because right now I'm taking you to my secret hideout, that's why."

"Whoa! A place of mystery. The plot thickens." He laughed.

Still puzzled with her evasiveness over the stranger, his mind speculated with many thoughts. *Is there more to the story of that creep or did the experience terrify her so much that she's afraid to even talk about it?*

After crossing the second bridge, she interrupted his thinking, saying, "See that Route 26 sign up ahead?"

"Yes."

"Stay to your right and go north," she directed. "That takes us to 526, where you bear right again. From 526 we exit onto Rhett Avenue. Think of Rhett Butler."

"Yes, my dear, I do give a damn." He laughed.

When they exited onto Rhett Avenue, Greg recognized the area immediately as that of his first day's search for her.

Soon they were on a familiar side street, and she directed, "Now bear to your left around that little park and take another left at the first street."

He knew exactly where she was taking him.

"There's my old high school, and on your left is our football field."

"I know."

"How do you know?"

"Because this is where I started my search for you. I had hoped to find someone around the school or neighborhood who might know you or your family."

"Oh, I see. Now drive around the block and get back to Rhett Avenue."

After several turns north of Rhett Avenue, they came to a dirt road, whereupon they drove on it for another mile or so.

"Stop here and park, Greg," she declared. "We can walk from here."

"It's very remote. That's for sure," he remarked.

Snatching her hat from the back seat, Valerie jumped out the door to meet him in front of the car and take his hand.

Walking up the road together, he said, "It's certainly very quiet and peaceful around here. Everything is so still. All you can hear are the birds chirping. So where's your hideaway?"

"You'll see in a few minutes." She grinned impishly, squeezing his hand. "It's my very own secret hiding place. I've never brought anyone here, only you."

When they came to a small pathway lined heavily on both sides with trees and bushes, they followed it along until they came to a clearing with a tree standing in the middle of it.

"Well, how do you like my secret tree?" she quizzed.

"It's looks very skinny and drab to me."

"Oh, but she's a very special tree."

"What kind of tree is it?"

"It's a magnolia tree—the only one—sitting all by itself here in the woods among all these other different trees. It's a mystery to me how it got here. Haven't you ever seen one?"

"No, I've heard of them, but this is the first one I've seen. What's so special about it?"

"It's special because when I was a little girl, I used to come here and dream by it. I even talked to it."

"You did. Why?"

"Well, when I started junior high school, I had a crush on a boy for the first time. His name was Jimmy. One day, I asked him to go bike riding with me. He said he would, but when the day came, he told me he wasn't going riding with me. He was going bike riding with another girl.

"He was mean and rude to me that day and told me not to ever ask him again because he didn't like me or want me for a girlfriend. I was so shocked and hurt. I started crying and jumped on my bike and pedaled away down the street.

"I rode up and down the streets all afternoon until I came up that dirt road and noticed the pathway. I was curious where it led to, so I got off my bike and followed the path to this magnolia tree. I felt so lonely and hurt, and because it stood all by itself in this clearing, it looked lonely, too. It didn't have any magnolia 'friends' and I had no friends, so I made it my friend and sat down under it and cried my eyes out.

"Later, when I stopped crying, I was angry and promised myself I'd never ask any boy to ever go riding with me, again.

"After that day, whenever I was lonely and sad, I'd come to my favorite tree and talk to it. When I was happy, I'd come here too, just to lay under it and dream about traveling to California; about being rich and famous; or about marrying a handsome doctor. You know, little girl dreams. I claimed it as my very own magnolia tree and sometimes I'd kick off my shoes and dance around my secret tree and hum to it, like right now—watch."

She slipped out of her sandals, plopped her hat on her head, and began skipping toward the tree with her arms above her head. Then she tiptoed in pirouetting circles while dancing around the tree.

Greg momentarily imagined her dancing in colonial times as a southern belle in a long, full, yellow dress with yellow shoes and white lace pantaloons, pirouetting with a yellow and white parasol.

When she came around full circle in front of the tree again, she stopped, facing him, on tiptoes with circular arms above her head. She removed her hat, bowed her head, and curtsied gracefully.

Greg clapped his hands, saying, "And a beautiful ballerina she is."

Valerie spun her hat into the bushes and started doing cartwheels around the tree, but when she came full circle again, she was exhausted and fell flat on her stomach at the foot of the tree. Gasping for breath, she flipped over on her back, giggling.

Having retrieved her hat from the bushes, Greg sat down next to her and handed her the hat.

"Do you know the color of the magnolia flower?" she asked.

"No, I've never seen a magnolia flower either. What color is it?"

Valerie lifted her skirt and pointed to her slip. "It blooms as white as my pretty white lace slip." She grinned. Then pointing to her yellow skirt, she continued, "But it can also bloom bright yellow like my skirt, and also pink. I've never seen the yellow or pink flowers. I'd love to see them, sometime."

"Why isn't it blooming now?"

"It only blooms in the spring."

"Then I'll be sure to be here next spring to see your favorite tree in bloom."

"I'd love that, Greg," she replied, "and because today is a very special day, I made sure I wore the same colors of magnolia flowers. Now don't ask me what's pink either, bad boy."

He grinned. "Okay, then I'll ask what's so special about today?"

"On that same day I found my tree, I made a promise to her that I would never bring a boy or man to meet her unless I knew he cared about me. That's been our secret and you're that first man, Greg. You're the only man I've ever brought here. That's the truth."

Greg laughed. "Cross your arms and fingers across your chest. Now close your eyes and swear on a troll's grave that it's the truth."

She crossed her fingers and arms across her breasts, closed her eyes, and stated, "Ah sweah and do deeeclaah with all my heart, on a troll's grave, it is the bare-faced truth, pieface."

With her eyes still closed, he embraced her, laid her back on the grass, and kissed her.

Whereupon her eyes popped open.

Wide-eyed, she batted her eyelids and slapped his cheek, saying, "You are always so eager, young man! You will take advantage of a proper lady when her guard is down, won't you?" She pushed him away, sat up, and fluffed her skirt, adding, "Why must a suth'n lady always have to be so vigilant to protect her honor and dignity against the likes of you Yankees? I must keep my eyes open at all times with you, kind suh."

He leaned toward her and murmured, "We're very much alone here, you know. I dare you to close your eyes again."

"No way!" she cried.

As she stomped to her feet, she brushed off her skirt and said, "You have me at a disadvantage. This place is too quiet and romantic, and my defenses are very weak around you, sexy man." Looking at the tree, she added, "Besides, my magnolia tree is a dignified suth'n lady too, and her leaves might turn pink with embarrassment if we did anything improper. Don't you think she's pretty even though she's wearing her dark green dress today, instead of her green and white one?"

"Yes, although she is skinny and drab, she's still a dignified and pretty suth'n lady."

"Would you like to know one of my little girl's dreams when I came here?"

"What is that?"

"I dreamed of dancing with a handsome prince, and in high school, I imagined myself dancing with a handsome man who loved me."

Greg stepped backward, bowed politely, extended his arm, and offered, "Madam, may I have this next dance?"

She curtsied demurely, fanned her face with her hat, and replied, "I would be most delighted, kind suh. I'm flattered by your invitation."

When he stepped forward and took her in his arms, they began waltzing around the tree, and as they danced cheek to cheek, she hummed and sang a tune in Greg's ear. "When you are in love, it's the loveliest night of the year."

After circling the tree several times, they stopped and sat down on the grass again.

They talked for a little while but finally stood up and sauntered over to the pathway. Before entering, Valerie turned around for a last look at her tree, and with a slight wave, she said, "Bye, sweet magnolia. You're still my favorite, special tree."

They returned to the car, and while driving back down the dirt road, Valerie declared, "I'm hungry. You must be too, Greg."

"I sure am. It's lunch time."

"We can go to my favorite restaurant and I can phone Jessica from there."

Within twenty minutes they arrived at the eatery, parked the car in the lot, and when they stepped out of the car, Greg looked up at the building to a sign that read, CALIFORNIA DREAMING.

"That figures," he commented. "Now I know why it's your favorite restaurant."

"Where else?" She laughed. "When the place first opened, I came here often for dinner to look out the windows and dream about California. Then, when I turned twenty-one, I dreamed over drinks."

"Show me the food. I'm starved," he replied.

She slipped her arm underneath his and led him up the steps of the old restaurant fortress.

Once inside, she quickly scanned the booths and said, "Oh, good, my favorite booth is empty."

When the hostess approached them, Valerie requested the booth, so the hostess led them straight to it and, after seating them, she handed them their menus.

Valerie told Greg to order her a hamburger and coffee and left immediately to phone Jessica. So he placed their order of two hamburgers and coffee and admired the view of the water through the huge bay window.

Valerie returned to the booth shortly to say, "I have the evening shift tonight, so I don't have to be there until 3 P.M. What time is it, Greg?"

"My watch shows one-thirty."

"Oh good, we have over an hour to eat. That gives us plenty of time. How do you like my favorite hangout?"

"Very classy, I must say."

"I knew you'd like it. They have great burgers."

"So did you ever make it to California?" he queried.

"No, I haven't. After college, I headed straight to Norway to visit my grandparents, and when I visited Bergen, I fell in love with it right away. So I immediately applied for a license to teach there, and the rest is history."

After eating, they drove directly to Valerie's apartment where Greg once more parked the car across the street. She informed him it would take only a few minutes to change into her uniform, so he decided to wait for her in the car.

She ran across the street and up the steps to disappear into her apartment, and before long she had returned to the car and they were on their way to the pancake house.

When they arrived, he escorted Valerie into the restaurant. He enjoyed Jessica and wanted to kibitz with her again.

Jessica spotted them first and stood eyeing them with her arms folded.

"Well, well, well, look who's back. The two lovey-dovey love birds have returned from their secret love nest." She shook her finger at Greg. "And I knnnow you didn't mind your manners, boy!"

Greg grinned. "I beg your pardon, madam. I'll have you know I have a most gracious bedside manner around Valerie."

Instantly, Valerie jabbed his ribs with her elbow and snapped, "You hush now, ya hear!"

Jessica smirked while others within earshot nodded their heads and laughed knowingly.

Then Jessica handed Valerie the new shift schedule, and when she and Greg examined it together, Valerie looked up momentarily to speak to Jessica. When she did so, she glanced at a man sitting in a booth by a window reading a newspaper. Instantly she recognized his unmistakable profile.

"Oh no, it's him!" she muttered. "He's found me again!"

Clutching Greg's arm, she jerked him, and as she pulled him, stumbling and bewildered, toward the entrance door, he questioned, "Where? Where is he?"

"Never mind where he is. We have to get out of here, right now!" she blurted.

She squeezed his arm tighter, and after running out the door, they raced for the car.

The stranger, seeing them out the window running through the parking lot, dropped his paper immediately and dashed up the aisle to the cashier.

While the stranger took time to reach into his pocket and throw money and his receipt on the counter, Greg and Valerie hopped into the car, and without waiting for any change, the stranger ran out the door into the parking lot, only to see Greg's car squealing onto the main street.

He pulled a note pad from his pocket and quickly jotted down Greg's South Dakota license plate number. Then he bolted for his car, peeled out of the parking lot, and sped up the street after them.

"Where the hell did he come from?" Greg shouted.

Trembling, she scooted close to his side and squealed, "I have no idea! I'm so terrified of him, Greg, and now he's found me again."

"You've known this all along, but wouldn't tell me. What's going on, Val? You have to tell me what he wants with you. I have to know."

"It's because I was afraid I'd lose you, but please don't ask me to explain right now, Greg. I'll tell you later."

Greg pulled her close to him, stroked her hair, and murmured, "You won't lose me, Val. That's a promise, but we can only build our relationship with honesty. I have to know the truth of what's happening here. Promise me you'll tell me what's going on, okay?"

"Yes, yes, I promise, but right now I'm too frightened."

Greg checked his rearview mirror and saw no car close behind them or racing to catch up to them.

"Okay, you can calm down, now. There's no one on our tail and we're way ahead of him. I'll make a few turns just to be sure. Where are we going, anyway?"

"Please take me to your motel, Greg? It's the only safe place I can go. I'm sure he doesn't know where you're staying, but he might already know where I live, so I can't go home; not yet, anyway."

"That's right, you'll be safe with me."

Turning onto the interstate, Greg headed for north Charleston, and when they arrived at his motel and entered the room, Valerie fell backwards on the bed and sighed with relief.

"We made it! Thank goodness! I'll always be safe with you, Greg."

"Now, will you please be honest with me and tell me what's going on with you and this creep?"

"I will, Greg, but I'm too upset right now. I'll tell you later, okay?"

He threw his hands up and said, "You're getting to be a real mystery to me, Val. You know that, don't you?"

She stretched out her arms, motioning him to come to her, so he climbed onto the bed and lay close to her.

"I'm so nervous. Hold me, Greg. Make me feel safe in your arms. Hold me tight."

Swallowing her in his strong arms, he squeezed her tight and kissed her softly.

"You are going to tell me what's going on with that creep, aren't you?" he whispered. "I need to know, Val. It's the only way we can get our relationship off the ground."

"I will, pieface. I promise, but right now I'm still shaky–see." She held up a quivering hand.

"Okay, okay, I won't pressure you anymore. Tell me whenever you're ready."

She nibbled his lips and smiled. "Thank you, ghosty."

For the rest of the afternoon they lay in each others arms, dozing off several times.

In the evening, Greg went to pick up take-out meals, and when he returned, they spent the rest of the evening with quiet conversation.

While watching television, he asked, "What will you do tomorrow, Val?"

"Let's sleep on it, Greg, and cross that bridge in the morning. We can talk about it over breakfast."

It had been a long day for both of them, and they were asleep by 10 P.M.

Valerie went to sleep with the intention of awakening early, so around 4 A.M., she woke up and slipped out from her side of the bed carefully. Although he slept soundly, she didn't want to awaken him.

Dressing hurriedly, she grasped her beach bag and shoes and hastened out the door.

Once outside, she slipped on her shoes and walked quickly to a public telephone booth at a nearby street corner and made a call.

Within minutes, a taxicab drove up and Valerie climbed into the backseat. The cab pulled away and drove down the deserted street toward the interstate.

Sometime around 8 A.M., Greg stirred from his long sleep, and when he opened his eyes and turned over to face Valerie, he saw she wasn't there.

Assuming she was in the bathroom, he sat up in the bed and called to her, but she didn't answer. So he jumped out of the bed and ran to the bathroom.

"Oh no, not again!" he exclaimed.

He quickly panned the room for her belongings and saw they were nowhere around. He pounded his fist against the wall.

Then leaning against the wall in frustration, he braced his forehead against his arm and muttered, "She's gone, dammit! She's gone again."

CRROCRROCRRO

When Greg bumped his head against the aircraft's window shade, his eyes popped open.

Looking around, he noticed the flight attendant walking up the aisle toward him.

As she approached his seat, he asked, "Excuse me, ma'am, have we passed the point of no return yet?"

"Yes sir, we're closer to Norway than the United States now." She smiled. "We can no longer return to America on this trip. We can only land in Oslo now."

"How long before we land?"

"Perhaps in another three to three and one half hours, depending on our tailwind. Can I get you anything?"

"No, thank you, I'm fine."

When she continued up the aisle, he fluffed his pillow.

With at least three more hours to go, he snuggled his head back into the pillow to get comfortable, and after closing his eyes again, his thoughts drifted back to Valerie's second disappearance.

CROCROCRO

VII

While thinking momentarily, he suddenly jerked back from the wall.

His mind was set on Valerie's apartment.

Getting his clothes, he dressed quickly, packed his belongings, and after flipping the key on the dresser, he dashed out of the room and threw his luggage into the car's trunk. He jumped into the car, started the engine, backed out of his parking space, and screeched out of the motel's driveway onto the street.

As he entered the interstate and merged into heavy morning commuter traffic, he thought, *Why does she run from me? She must be in trouble or she wouldn't run. Why is that creep after her, and why won't she tell me who he is? Why all the mystery? What trouble is she in? Why won't she let me help her?*

When he arrived at her apartment and parked the car at the curb, he saw that her car was gone.

He knocked on the apartment door and Jessica let him inside. She was crying.

"Where is she, Jessica? What's going on here? I want to know," he demanded.

"I don't know," she sobbed. "She wouldn't tell me anything, but I know she's in some kind of trouble. I'm so glad you followed her here. I've only known Valerie for one month and I love that girl like my own sister. I don't want anything bad happening to her, ya hear."

"Did she tell you where she was going?"

"She barged in here about five o'clock and woke me up. I asked her what was going on, but all she said was, 'Don't ask me any questions. I have to get out of Charleston. I have to leave. That's it.' When I asked her, 'What about Greg? You know he'll come here looking for you.' She said, 'I love him dearly, Jessica. He's the only man I've ever felt love from, but I don't want to hurt him. He's a very good man and deserves better than me. He's better off without me.' That's what she said, Greg.

"Then she packed two suitcases, gave me a hug and kiss, and said, 'I love you, Jessica.' I asked her where she was going and she said, 'I don't know. Maybe California; maybe Key West. I haven't decided yet.' When I asked her, 'What's in those places?' She said, 'I have a friend in Key West who might be able to help me, but I don't know for sure.'

"Then, when she ran out the door and down the steps to her car, she was cryin' somethin' awful. I yelled after her to phone me when she got where she was going and she shouted back, 'I will, Jessica, I will.' She drove away, and just like that, she was gone."

"She's definitely in trouble, but that creep isn't going to get her. Somehow I have to get her away from him."

The phone rang abruptly, so Jessica picked up the receiver.

"Hello, this is Jessica." She listened and asked, "When did he leave?"

Then she put down the receiver, saying, "That was Jenny at the restaurant. She said about a half-hour ago, a man flashed a badge at her, asking for Valerie. He wanted to know what shift she worked and where she lived. At first she thought he was a cop and told him Valerie lived somewhere on Wentworth Street, but didn't know her exact address.

"After he left, she and another waitress were suspicious and began to think he wasn't a cop. They decided to phone Valerie and me to warn us."

Greg reacted, "The restaurant is only ten minutes away, so I'm sure he's already out there canvassing the street. My car is parked right in front of this house, so he could be waiting outside to see which house I'll come out of. I've got to go, Jessica. Can I have the phone numbers of the restaurant and this apartment? If I don't find her, I'll want to check in with you to find out where she is. Are you okay with that, Jessica?"

"You betcha, Greg."

She bent over the table and wrote the phone numbers on a pad of paper. Then she tore off the piece of paper and handed it to him.

"Where are you going now?" she asked.

"Since she said she had a friend in Key West, I'll try there first, but if I don't find her, I'll phone you from there. I figure it's about a day and a half drive from here."

After hugging and kissing each other's cheeks, Greg walked to the door, turned around, and winked. "I'll find her, Jessica. I found her before and I'll find her again. Somehow I've got to convince her to stop running away from me. I believe we're meant to be together. Love ya."

"Love ya, too, Yankee. You find her now, ya hear. Good luck," she whimpered with tears streaking down her cheeks.

As she turned her back to him, Greg went out the door and hurried down the wooden steps to the sidewalk. He turned and looked both ways, up and down the street, but didn't observe any suspicious-looking cars, so he walked to the street and entered his car.

After starting the car, he drove slowly down the street toward the boat piers, continually glimpsing his rearview mirror. Before he reached the end of Wentworth street, he saw in the mirror a car turn out from a side-street several blocks behind him. He was immediately suspicious.

So when Greg turned right onto Lockwood Drive and right again onto Calhoun Street and the car followed after him, he knew for certain the creep was following him.

Greg wanted to lose him before heading for Interstate 95 south, so he decided to make a few more fast turns in downtown traffic in order to shake him off his tail.

He proceeded to weave in and out of heavy downtown traffic, and after a few quick turns onto one-way streets, he no longer saw the car in his rearview mirror, so he finally drove south on Route 17.

Eventually he gloated with a smirk on his face as he headed for Interstate 95. He'd shaken the creep, so he thought, but he hadn't shaken him at all. Back in the city, the stranger had also discovered that Greg had spotted him, so he let Greg think he'd lost him by lagging a few cars behind.

While they drove toward the interstate, the squinty-eyed stranger held his position by continuing to keep several cars between them while keeping close surveillance of Greg.

At the interstate, many cars turned onto the south ramp along with Greg, followed by the stranger several cars behind him.

After driving awhile on the interstate, they entered Savannah's city limits and Greg chose to satisfy his suspicions that he wasn't still being followed by the stranger, so he turned off at a few city exits and returned to the interstate several blocks later.

The stranger, however, stayed well back behind him and simply escorted Greg off each exit ramp, then returned to every on-ramp right along with Greg.

After several more maneuvers, Greg was convinced he'd shaken the stranger and continued his drive south on the interstate.

In due time, they crossed the Florida state line, and now the stranger knew Valerie must be in Florida. All he had to do now was to keep Greg in his sights, and he would lead him straight to her.

When Greg stopped for gas, he saw no sign of the stranger, but while eating lunch in the coffee shop, he thought he saw his car parked in a far corner of the food stop. He scanned the busy eatery, but didn't see him anywhere.

After lunch, Greg drove out of the rest stop slowly, observing his rearview mirror. Satisfied no car was following him, he settled back to relax and continued his journey to Miami.

Within minutes, the stranger was back on his tail, keeping well behind him, within a quarter of a mile.

That evening, Greg stopped at a motel in Hollywood. By staying north of Miami, he figured he'd drive through the city early in the morning to avoid the rush-hour traffic.

As Greg checked into the motel, the stranger's car passed by the motel entrance unnoticed by Greg. Several minutes later, it returned and make a left turn across from the motel. Within a half block, it U-turned to park alongside the curb. The stranger's car now directly faced the motel.

The mysterious stranger didn't want to miss Greg when he left in the morning, so he slumped behind the wheel to begin his long stakeout for the night. The only thing on his mind was to get Valerie—and Greg was his only link to her.

Early the next morning, Greg checked out of the motel.

The streets were deserted when he drove out of the motel's parking lot onto the main street. When he turned at the first corner, the stranger's car moved slowly away from the curb, turned onto the main street, and followed Greg to the same corner.

As Greg approached the interstate's south ramp, he easily spotted the car in his rearview mirror. It followed only a few blocks behind him. Immediately he was suspicious so after he drove onto the interstate, he quickly pulled over and stopped the car on the shoulder.

Seconds later, the stranger's car advanced toward him, and as the car sped by, Greg focused on the stalker's face. He merely grinned and continued on his way toward Miami.

"Oh, shit! It's him," Greg mumbled to himself. "He's followed me all the way into Florida and believes I know where Valerie is. He thinks by following me I'll lead him straight to her.

"If this guy is really a cop or private eye and I report him to the police, I could put Valerie in worse trouble. I've got to get to her first. That's all there is to it. What he doesn't know is that I don't know where she is, so for now she's safe. Somehow I've got to find her and hide her out. Maybe then she'll tell me what's going on."

Greg got into the car again, pulled back onto the interstate, and sped after the stranger.

Minutes later, while driving through sparse city traffic, Greg passed the stranger's car but never bothered to look over at him. He stared straight ahead and increased his speed.

By the time he left south Miami, Greg had given up any thoughts of losing his shadowy figure. He decided it was useless, since the creep would know very soon they were on their way to Key West. There's only one highway into and out of Key West and that one highway—Route 1—dead-ends right there. So at the end of the next 156 miles, there will be nowhere to go and no place to hide for the three of them.

Greg now knew he'd have to match wits with the creep in Key West in order to get her off a two-by-four mile island and out of Florida. He had to find her first.

With a three to four hour drive ahead of himself, Greg relaxed behind the wheel and speculated.

She's only a half-day ahead of me, he thought. *Is her friend male or female? Then again, she may not be there yet. Maybe she stopped elsewhere; or worse yet, perhaps she didn't go to Key West. Maybe she went to California.*

He was back to square one again, just like his first search for her in Charleston. He'd never been to Key West either, so he didn't know where he'd begin his search. He didn't know what to expect or what lay ahead of him.

When Greg crossed into the city limits of Key West, followed closely by the stalker, the tiny island teamed with summer tourists. There were people everywhere either strolling the sidewalks or casually riding bicycles. People on motor scooters cruised all over the streets.

Congested traffic with bumper-to-bumper cars clogged the narrow one-way thoroughfares. Greg had no idea where he was heading, but followed the stream of traffic and turned right when all of the cars in front of him turned right. Following the one-way traffic to the end of the street, he finally came to a dead stop at the fishing piers, surrounded by milling people.

The downtown streets bulged and overflowed with clusters of tourists who seemed to wander about aimlessly.

As cars inched their way through the horrendous crowds, Greg eventually made his way to a side street and luckily spotted an empty metered parking space.

He quickly backed into the curb and grumbled, "No wonder they either walk, bike, or scooter in this tourist hot spot. It's the only way to get around."

While putting money in the meter, he looked around for any sign of the stranger, but he was nowhere in sight.

"These crowds worked to my advantage, anyway," he murmured with a grin.

It was extremely hot and the humidity was stifling. Sweat poured off Greg, so he set out to find a bar to quench his thirst. When he saw a soft drink stand, he chose a lemonade instead of a beer.

Afterwards, he walked up Duval Street away from the piers, and since he moved against the steady stream of people walking toward the fishing boats, he assumed he was on the main downtown street. He was firmly convinced when he saw both sides of the street lined with many t-shirt and souvenir shops.

Looking ahead, he noticed a sign displaying La Concha Hotel and hoped he might be able to get a room. So when he reached the hotel entrance, he stepped inside and walked up to the reservation desk.

"I don't suppose you have any rooms available with all these tourists in town, do you?" he surmised.

"As a matter of fact, we do have a vacancy. A customer checked out only an hour ago." The impish blonde-haired girl beamed. "It's for how many nights?"

Hesitating for a moment to think, because he hadn't given any thought to how long he'd be in Key West, he replied, "Er, ah, I don't really know," and when he detected her impatience, he quickly added, "Make it three nights, ma'am. That's good. Three days and three nights should be enough, I hope."

"You hope?" She frowned while handing him a registration card to fill out.

"Oh, yes, I am hoping." He winked as he began to fill out the card.

"Oh, I get it." She smirked. "You're just like all the rest of the bachelor tourists around here. You'll be hitting on all the single women for pickups, right?"

"Yes, I suppose you could say I'm looking for a pickup. It's something like that, anyway."

When he paid for his first night's stay, she informed him there was reserved parking for all hotel customers directly behind the building, and as he walked toward the entrance, she called, "Hey, handsome, if you're still lonely later, I get off at six o'clock."

When he turned around to see her flirty smile with a slight hand wave, he simply returned the hand wave with a smile and walked out the entrance.

Walking back to his car, he stopped at a gift shop to buy a street guide, and when he reached the piers again, he stopped at Sloppy Joe's open patio bar on the corner. While ordering a sandwich and cold beer from the bartender, he inquired about Hemingway's picture hanging on the wall. The bartender informed him Sloppy Joe's was a favorite "watering hole" for Hemingway and that his house was a museum only a few blocks away. Since Greg wasn't a sightseer, the museum was of no interest to him; another time, perhaps. So after the bartender returned and served him, Greg munched on his sandwich and drank a cold beer and proceeded to survey the hundreds of female faces milling on the piers. None of them bore any resemblance to Valerie.

When he finished lunch, he left the bar to drive his car back to the hotel and take his luggage up to his room.

Inside the room, he walked over to the window overlooking Duval Street. Since his room was on the second floor, he could observe the people walking down on the street. He had an excellent view of peoples' faces as they walked along the sidewalks on both sides of the street.

Obviously, Duval Street, with all of its souvenir and gift shops, is the main street for tourists, he thought. *Sooner or later, Valerie will have to walk down Duval Street and her beautiful face would stick out like a sore thumb in any crowd.*

116

He was confident he'd spot her in the afternoon crowds, so as he studied the faces of the flowing people on the street below him, he pulled a chair up to the window and got comfortable. It would probably be a long afternoon.

Late in the afternoon, with no sign of Valerie, the steady stream of people waned, so he opened his street guide and noticed the tiny island had very few streets; most were one-way. Then using the telephone book, he jotted down the addresses of many restaurants, bars, and clubs on his note pad. He check-marked clubs that had dancing and entertainment.

"It shouldn't take very long to cover this tiny island," he muttered.

Afterward, when the heat of the day subsided, Greg left the hotel and walked up one side of Duval Street and down the other noting female faces. He walked for many blocks but had no luck.

Finally he stopped at an open-air cafe to rest and eat supper. He sat at a table close to the sidewalk where he could eye pedestrian faces while eating jumbo fried shrimp.

During his meal, Greg concluded that the fishing piers seemed to be the main tourist attraction, so after eating he sauntered off toward the piers.

At the piers again, he merged into the throngs of bustling people that hadn't thinned out to any degree. The raucous crowd seemed even louder and noisier while enjoying the evening's street entertainment.

While mingling and moving around among the people, he kept checking female faces and eventually emerged from the crowd at the foot of the piers without having spotted her.

While he scanned the various sightseeing and fishing boats docked at their berths, one boat in particular caught his eye as it backed down from the long pier. So he strolled along the wharf watching her back down into open water.

Suddenly his eyes widened. "Omigod! It's Valerie!" he exclaimed.

She stood at the ship's wheel next to a tall, lanky man in a white uniform and captain's hat. He puffed on a pipe sticking out the side of his mouth.

Immediately he raced down the wharf parallel to the retreating boat, waving and shouting, "Valerie! Valerie! It's me, Greg."

When they noticed Greg running on the dock, Valerie stared at him for a moment. Then she turned to the captain, reached up, and put her arms around his neck. The captain removed his pipe, wrapped one arm around her waist, and drew her close to him. Their kiss was deliberate and lingering.

Stunned, Greg stopped dead in his tracks. He couldn't believe what he just saw.

After releasing their embrace, Valerie momentarily pursed her lips, stared straight at Greg, and smiled faintly. Turning back to the captain, she slipped her arm around his waist and gazed up at him. She ignored Greg and never looked back at him. Her eyes focused only upward at the captain as the boat glided swiftly backward through the water.

Within seconds the captain spun the wheel, and as the stern came around, the bow turned away from Greg. The boat kicked into open throttle and churned with a heavy wake toward the open sea.

Shocked and bewildered, Greg sat down on the edge of the wharf and with feet dangling, stared at the water lapping at the pilings below him. He sat there for a long time, wondering why she had done that to him. Her behavior was beyond his comprehension.

Finally he stood up and returned to the foot of the piers where the milling crowds were thinning. Many people had retired to waterfront bars and clubs for their relaxing evening drinks.

Because he didn't accept her actions with the captain and disbelieved what he'd seen, when Greg eyed the ticket booth for that particular boat's tour, he quickened his gait to the booth.

"Who is the captain of the tour boat that just departed?" he asked the booth attendant.

The dark-complexioned young man replied, "Rune Petersen is the captain and owner of the boat."

"He's Norwegian?" Greg asked.

"Yes, he is Norwegian."

"How long has he been running a tour boat in Key West?"

"Oh, maybe eight or ten years."

"Kinda strange for a Norwegian to be running a tour boat among all you Cubans, don't you think?"

The attendant laughed. "I suppose so, but he's been here for so long that he considers himself one of us now. We all love Captain Petersen. He's a kind and generous man and treats all of his employees very well. He's very friendly to everyone on the piers, too. He's our Norwegian Cuban American amigo."

"What time will his boat return from the tour?"

"In about two hours, usually around 9:30 P.M. It's the sunset cruise tour."

"Thank you."

"You're very welcome."

Greg walked away to find a waterfront bar. He needed a drink after the initial shock of seeing Valerie with the captain. Most of the waterfront bars were crowded and noisy, so he ambled farther up the street and found a quieter lounge with an empty stool at the bar. As he sat drinking and awaiting the return of their tour boat, he contemplated a confrontation with Valerie and the captain.

Around 9 P.M., he left the lounge to return to the docks, and when he arrived, he observed the boat already tied up at the wharf. So he continued on to the ticket booth, whereupon he found the booth closed; no attendant was on duty. His confrontation with both of them was now on hold.

Returning to his hotel, Greg entered the lounge to order a drink and ponder his next move. His mind wasn't going to rest until he had his encounter with both of them.

So after only one drink, he'd decided to rent a motor scooter. A Moped was ideal. He would use it to search the bars and clubs on the outskirts of town. It would also prevent the stalker from tailing him in his car should he happen upon him.

Greg left the lounge to find a scooter rental, and by the time he obtained the keys and hopped onto the Moped, black sky blanketed Key West. It was a moonless night. Greg kicked on the muffled engine and scootered slowly across Duval Street. He drove ahead for a few blocks, turned right, and sped away in the darkness.

Greg motored along the dimly lit one-way street heading toward the main highway north of town. On Route 1, he'd seen several cocktail lounges and dance clubs on his initial drive into the city.

Determination burned in his eyes, and with a set jaw and pursed lips, he muttered, "Contrived! That kiss was contrived; a deliberate fake kiss. That's what it was. You're a lousy actress, Valerie. You didn't convince me one bit, and now that I know you're here in Key West, I'm not leaving without an explanation–stalker or no stalker!"

During the next several hours, he stopped at all of the outlying bars and clubs on the highway. In addition, he also checked the few restaurants that were open late, but had no luck.

While entering town again on Route 1, he came upon several of the more exclusive hotels that featured dance floor entertainment, so he turned into the Casa Marina parking area.

As he motored along slowly behind a long row of parked cars to scan the various license plates, he listened to Cuban music emanating from inside the club.

Suddenly he spotted a South Carolina plate. It was Valerie's.

"Bingo!" he murmured. "She's in there."

Being cautious, Greg parked the scooter next to a rear door above which a neon red sign read EXIT in case he needed a fast getaway.

When he entered the hotel through the front entrance, he walked directly toward the entertainment lounge and stepped into a spacious outdoor patio. In an obscure corner of the patio, a Cuban band played a cha-cha. The dance floor was crowded with dancing couples, so as he sauntered toward the island hut bar, he surveyed the entire dance floor looking for Valerie. When he didn't see her dancing, he slid onto a stool at the bar and ordered a drink from the bartender. Then he looked to the opposite side of the patio and continued to pan along the tables. He quickly spied her sitting with the captain at a table partially hidden by the band.

They were deeply engrossed in conversation, so it was obvious to Greg neither of them had noticed his entry into the lounge. They were completely oblivious of him as he glared intently at both of them.

When the band stopped playing momentarily then started playing a mambo, Valerie jumped up impulsively and staggered around the table toward the captain. The captain laughed as she wiggled and wobbled to the rhythm of the music, and with outstretched arms, she gestured for the captain to dance with her. He grasped her hands, got to his feet, and swaggered onto the dance floor with her.

The bartender served Greg his glass, and as he sipped on his rum drink, he thought, *They're both drunk. This is just great. Now I've got a drunken runaway woman on my hands—real fun! This gala happening gets better by the minute. I can imagine Tom, if he were here.* He grinned, sipping his drink. *He'd be out on the floor staggering around with both of them. Then he'd wave his bottle of beer at me, and holler "Hey pardner, it's party time. Gimme another beer."*

With his share of evening rum drinks, Greg wasn't feeling too much pain either, but when he turned on his stool, still grinning to himself, and glanced at the lounge entrance, his grin disintegrated. His eyes froze on the stalker standing in the entrance way, scrutinizing the dancers on the crammed dance floor.

"Dammit! He found Valerie's car, too," he mumbled. "I've got to get her out of here, fast!"

Greg quickly returned his glass to the bar, jumped off the bar stool, and bolted onto the dance floor toward Valerie and the captain.

The stalker instantly spotted Greg pushing couples aside and raced onto the dance floor after him.

When Greg reached Valerie, he wrapped one arm around her waist and shoved the captain hard with his other hand. Greg grabbed her hand and dashed for an open doorway at the end of the patio. The captain stumbled backward and hit the floor in a sitting position against a table leg. Propped against the leg, his head bobbled several times before his chin drooped to his chest and he passed out.

The stalker pushed and shoved dancers out of his way as women screamed and people stumbled and fell over tables and chairs; glasses smashed onto the floor.

With the stalker charging after them, Greg pulled Valerie faster, and when they ran off the dance floor and through the doorway, he looked in all directions for the rear exit door. There were no doors, so they turned and raced desperately down a hallway.

"Where on earth did YOU come from?" she babbled.

"Never mind where I came from. Run faster, will you?"

While stumbling and hurrying alongside him, she managed to keep pace, saying, "Now I've got TWO men stalking me. There's no escape from either of you."

Greg persistently tugged at her arm, goading her to run faster, and blurted, "We've got to find a way out of here. That creep is right behind us."

As the stalker gained ground behind them, they darted down another hallway and zigzagged into other passageways.

Finally bewildered and frustrated, Greg stopped short in the labyrinthine maze to catch their breath.

"That exit door has to be around here somewhere," he puffed.

Suddenly, Greg spotted a door on a side wall in the hallway, and with the stalker right on their heels in another hall, they ran for it. Reaching the door, Greg twisted the knob, which opened easily into a small janitorial closet. Jumping quickly into the cramped closet, they swiped dirty cleaning rags away from their faces and squeezed between mop and broom handles along with various cleaning equipment. After Greg locked the door from the inside, Valerie kicked a pail.

"Sssh!" he whispered.

Everything was pitch black and silent except for their breathing and pounding hearts, while they listened intently for any sound.

It wasn't long when they heard muffled footsteps running in the hallway. The rumbling grew louder until the running feet slowed and the heavy footsteps clumped close to their door. Suddenly the footsteps stopped abruptly outside the door. All went quiet until the doorknob twisted back and forth, clicking repeatedly.

Then the heavy footsteps clumped away from the door and began running down the hallway again. Within seconds the sound of loud rumbling feet quickly became that of muffled running feet and, finally, that of fading footsteps–then silence.

After unlocking the door, Greg slowly pushed it open and peeked through the cracked opening. Staring down the long hallway he saw no one, so he opened the door wider and poked his head out. Peering around the door toward the other end of the hallway, he observed it to be deserted also.

He and Valerie quickly alighted from the closet. He grasped her hand to retrace their path back through the hallways in search, once again, for that secluded rear exit.

Dashing back through the passageways, almost back into the patio, they turned a corner and spied the exit door they were hunting. Greg shoved open the door, hopped on the Moped, and switched on the ignition.

Valerie stared at the scooter, stroked her chin, and giggled. "My, my, a ghost on a scooter. How cute!"

"There's no time for jokes. We've got to get out of here. C'mon, jump on behind me."

"But I've never ridden on a motor scooter. I'll fall off."

"I promise you won't fall off. Just wrap your arms around my waist and hold on tight. Now, c'mon, that sicko may be coming any second."

Reluctantly, she climbed on the scooter behind him. Then she scooted up close to him, wrapped her arms around his waist, and hugged him tight. When she pressed up against his back, cuddled into him, and rested the side of her head on his back, she slurred, "Ummm, this part aaah do like!"

"We're off!" he shouted.

The Moped jolted forward. Greg U-turned immediately, bolted into the parking area, and darted straight for the driveway exit.

As they passed behind the long row of parked cars, suddenly two high-beam headlights instantly flashed directly in front of them.

With Valerie screaming in his ear, Greg hit the brakes, skidded to a stop, and threw his arm up in front of his face to shield his eyes from the glaring, blinding light. He couldn't see the driver's face, but he knew it was the stalker. His car blocked their escape.

Greg squeezed the handle grips, U-turned, and sped back behind the row of parked cars. He scanned the tall thick hedge of tropical plants and bushes in front of the cars anxiously, seeking an avenue of escape.

Suddenly tires screeched behind them, and when the car charged their back end, Valerie screamed, "He's going to ram us!"

Instantly, Greg swerved to the right, scooting between two parked cars. In doing so, he spotted a small tunnel-like opening in the tall hedge and scootered into the tunnel's entrance. He slowed the motor to an idle, flicked off the small headlight, and with both feet on the ground, began to push and maneuver the scooter through the little tunnel.

"Keep your head down low behind my back, Val, and watch out for sharp branches and leaves."

"Be careful, Greg. I hope we don't get stuck in here or he'll have us trapped."

Although he ducked low while inching the Moped slowly through the narrow tunnel, leaves and branches still brushed and scratched his face. Luckily, no large branches blocked their path.

In scant seconds, they reached the main road safely. Greg flipped on the headlight and twisted the handle grip to full throttle. The back tire spattered a rooster tail of dust, dirt, and stones behind them, and when the spinning tire jerked onto the pavement, they shot out onto the road. Greg swerved the scooter hard left to head south toward the water.

Meanwhile, the stalker had jammed his gearshift into reverse, squealed rubber back to the driveway exit, spun the wheel, and screeched onto the main road directly behind them.

With the menacing headlight bearing down on them, Greg accelerated faster.

"This road dead-ends at the water," she called into his ear. "A few blocks up ahead, you can still turn right onto a side street. It's the last street before the water, or we can shoot straight ahead and take a midnight dip in the Gulf of Mexico."

"Gotcha! But I'm in no mood for any midnight swim, especially without a full moon. I'll take that right turn, if the creep doesn't run over us by then. He's almost on top of us."

Nearing the water's edge where Route 1 dead-ends, Valerie pointed over his shoulder.

"Straight ahead, on the left side of the road," she informed, "a stone marker reads 'The southernmost point of the United States'."

"I'm so thrilled to hear that, Val. Like I really care about tourist trivia right now. We're about to be run over by a maniac in the middle of the night and you're playing midnight tour guide."

"Turn right! Quick!" she yelled.

Greg hit the brakes, and with the Moped sliding sideways, he stuck out his leg to avoid a smashup. He held the scooter steady with his skidding foot to keep it upright, and when they straightened up, he wielded the turn and sped off down the darkened side street.

"Hey, that was great!" she laughed. "Where'd you learn a trick like that?"

"Didn't I tell you? I'm a member of a scooter club called 'The Devil's Angels.' I've got a new advocate sitting right behind me."

Valerie ignored his chide, nuzzled her nose against his back, squeezed his waist, and said, "Aaah dooo love this midnight spin with my ghosty on his ghostmobile."

Behind them, the stalker's car skidded and screeched around the same corner, and when the menacing burning headlights came up fast on their back fender, Greg turned sharply to the right onto another side street. The stalker's car shot ahead to make a right turn at the next corner.

Meanwhile Greg doused his headlight, U-turned, and motored back to the cross street from where they'd just turned off. For the moment they had ditched their predator, so instead of turning right to follow the stranger, Greg continued on across the street.

While motoring along in pitch blackness, he asked, "Where can we go, Val? It's too late to get a motel room. We can't go to my hotel. I'm sure he's already seen my car parked there, and he also knows where your car is parked, right?"

"Omigod, Greg, what are we going to do?"

Just then, the menacing headlights swung around a corner a few blocks behind them, so Greg promptly turned right at the next corner and drove down another side street. After one block, he turned right again. As they moved slowly up the street, he noticed a tall shadowy outline of a long row of palm trees lining the side of the street ahead of them. As they drew closer, large masses of high plants and bushes mushroomed beneath the palm trees. A tropical garden park emerged huge in the darkness.

Greg slowed the scooter, turned into the curb, lifted the front wheel and bounced up onto the sidewalk. Then following a pedestrian walkway, they motored into the park. After driving deep into the gardens, he finally silenced the motor. They climbed off the scooter, and Greg hand-pushed the Moped still deeper into the thick shrubbery until they found a small clearing.

Because the tropical alcove was completely hidden from the street, it was a perfect sanctuary in which to hide. When Greg parked the scooter, they both slumped onto the grass with sighs of relief. Now they were completely consumed in blackness. Everything was silent.

The warm night air lay heavy and still, enhanced only by the smell of muggy humidity and dank odors of tropical plants.

"Okay, my beautiful mystic troll, let's have it. I want the truth and whole story this time. Why are you running—and from whom? And who is this Captain Andersen?"

The questions were instantly sobering, so she quickly threw herself at him and snuggled the side of her head against his broad chest.

He felt her trembling against his chest.

Her voice quivered. "I'm so petrified, Greg. He finds me wherever I go. There's no escape from him. I thought I'd escaped from him this time for sure. I mentioned Key West to Jessica because I knew she wouldn't tell anyone except you. I have no idea how he found me here."

"Yes, Jessica told me you might come here because she wanted me to get you away from him."

"But how did he know I was here?"

"He found out you lived on Wentworth Street from a waitress at the restaurant and staked out the street. When I showed up at your apartment, he began following me. Because I couldn't shake him, he trailed me all the way to Key West. He's like the devil himself."

"I can't stay here with that . . . that thing after me," she said. "Now I have to leave Key West. I don't believe I'll ever be safe from him."

Turning to face her, he put both his hands on her shoulders and replied, "Tell me what's happening with you. You know him, right?"

"Yes, I know who he is. I thought when he saw me with you and Lasse he'd leave me alone and get out of my life, but it didn't work. He's obsessed with me, Greg. That's all I can tell you right now."

"So there's more to it?"

"Yes."

"Now, tell me about that fake kiss on the tour boat. I know it was contrived. You're a bad actress, Val. Who is Rune and what does he mean to you?"

Detecting a bit of jealousy, she stroked his chin softly and half-grinned. "He's only a very old and dear friend of the family. He's nothing more than that. We practically grew up together. He's like a big brother to me. I deliberately kissed him when you were looking because I wanted to make you angry. I wanted to drive you away. You're such a loving, considerate man, Greg. I'm no good for you. I don't want to hurt you."

He squeezed her shoulders, and when he shook her hard, she frowned with blinking eyes and a bobbling head. The alcohol hadn't worn off completely.

"Don't talk like that, Val. You're a good woman. I don't care what happened before we met. It doesn't matter to me, but I do need to know the truth. Our relationship is only between us, no one else, and all that counts is where we go from here. Do you understand that?"

Still sobering, she replied, "Yes, I understand it, Greg. I need your love desperately."

"How long has this creep been after you?"

"It seems like forever. About two or three years."

Greg sat up straight. "What! Two or three years!" he exclaimed. "You've become a fugitive of fear. You're his mental and emotional captive. You've got to let me help you, Valerie."

She began to cry. "I'm trapped, Greg. I can't do anything about it."

"Why can't you do anything about it? Couldn't you have gone to the authorities long ago?"

"I can't go to the authorities. He's got me blackmailed. I'm trapped. That's it. That's all I can tell you. Please hold me, Greg."

He embraced her and hugged her tightly.

Overwhelmed with emotion, she trembled and wept uncontrollably. A deluge of unrestrained tears poured from her eyes and streamed down both cheeks.

Greg comforted her in his arms. For a long time he rubbed her back, stroked her long soft hair, and rocked her back and forth like a baby, until the trembling and tears subsided and her body finally calmed down.

"Somehow I'm going to get you out of here. Will you come to Rapid City with me?"

Looking up at him lovingly, she kissed him softly and said, "I'll go anywhere with you, Greg, but won't he follow us there, too?"

"So far, all he knows is that I'm from South Dakota. Now that's a big state. I could live anywhere in it; also, as far as he's concerned, I could take you anywhere. We could even leave South Dakota for points unknown at any time, but the immediate problem is, how do I get you off this dinky little island at the end of nowhere and out of Florida?"

"Do you really think my going to South Dakota would work, Greg? Finally I'd be rid of him. He'd be out of my life forever."

To lighten their discussion, he changed the subject by saying, "Did you really think I was interested in tour guide trivia with a maniac on our tail at one in the morning in pitch-black Key West?"

"I thought it was quite romantic, even without the moon. I had my loving Mr. Ghost all to myself on his ghostmobile. All you needed was a white sheet. A ghost on a scooter, whoa! I imagined myself riding with my personal ghost while he made his ghostly rounds on a dark spooky night."

"Ha, ha, very funny, troll," he said while tickling her. She giggled and squealed as he pushed her back flat on the grass. "For that, you sleep under a bridge tonight." He laughed.

They kissed tenderly.

Being well hidden by thick tropical shrubbery, they felt very safe and assumed the creep had given up on them—at least for the rest of the night.

The alcohol took its toll on Greg and shortly thereafter he passed out in her arms, but Valerie had no such intention. She intended to stay awake.

Since she sobered up considerably, for the next couple of hours she would only catnap.

Around 4 A.M., Valerie's eyes popped open to observe Greg sleeping soundly.

Being careful not to waken him, she gently slipped out of his arms, and on her knees she backed away from him slowly.

At a safe distance, she stood up and quietly left their hiding place.

When she walked out of the park, she quickened her pace on the sidewalk. Time was of the essence. She could never hide from her stalker. She had no other choice but to keep running. She had to get back to her car and get out of Key West.

Since she and Greg had driven only a few blocks from the hotel, she didn't have far to go, so she hastened along the dark, deserted street. The black night sky was now high and clear with rolling clouds; the pinpoint sparkling stars—along with glowing street lamps—lighted her way. At times she ran in her anxiety to get to her car.

In a short time, she arrived at the hotel's parking lot, and as she approached her car, she saw the stalker's car parked only a short distance away from hers.

Bending low, she crept up quietly to the back of his car and peered up through the back window. The stalker's head rested on the back of the driver's seat. He was sleeping with the two front windows rolled down.

She tiptoed slowly backwards, then turned around and walked upright to the front of her car, where she reached under the fender and retrieved a spare key.

Grinning, she held it up, kissed it, and whispered. "Thank goodness for magnets, and I'm so glad I left my purse in the car. It's still on the front seat."

Opening the door, she reached for her purse and pulled out a full set of keys. After closing the door quietly, she went directly to the back of her car, opened the trunk lid, grabbed two old blankets, and crept silently back to the stalker's right rear tire.

Covering the tire stem with both blankets in order to muffle the hissing sound, she unscrewed the cap and began letting air out of the tire slowly. When it was flat, she crept to the right front tire to do the same thing. When it was flat, she crept back to the left rear tire and flattened it also. Since his front window was open and, for fear of waking him, she left the front left tire alone.

Flattening three of them is good enough, she thought, so she crept back to her car and slid inside behind the wheel. She closed the door softly.

Gloating she glanced over at the stalker's car and started her car with a smirk. She kept the headlights off as she backed out of the parking space and moved slowly toward the driveway exit. When she drove out onto the road, she flicked on her lights. She was already on Route 1, so she headed straight up the highway toward the north end of town. Since she'd taken a motel on the outskirts, she would pick up her belongings, check out of the motel, and continue north to Miami.

She relaxed in the seat to breathe in the fresh, exhilarating, early morning breeze and smiled. "At last! I'm free again."

Sometime later, when Greg awoke to find that Valerie had left him once more, he pounded his fist on the ground and stammered, "She's gone again! When will she ever stop running and where did she run to this time? She can't go to her car. The creep has it staked out, for sure, but I'd better check there first to be sure."

He pulled the scooter out of the shrubbery and hopped on. After kicking on the motor, he scooted along the garden walkway and finally drove out of the park onto the deserted street.

When he approached the hotel, he turned off onto a side street, parked the Moped at a curb, and walked the last few blocks to the parking lot. Because he didn't want to be seen, he looked for the small tunnel through the shrubbery that they had used for their escape only hours before.

Finding the tunnel, he passed through it, and at the parking lot, he found two cars parked conveniently in front of him. So he crept between the two parked cars to reach their back ends without being seen. Looking over a car trunk, he saw the stranger standing behind his car with his fists to his hips. At the same time, Greg looked past him but didn't see Valerie's car. Her parking space was vacant.

Focusing back on the stranger, Greg noticed the flat rear tires on his car and grinned. "She flattened his tires and got away. Good for her. That does it. Now I've got to get out of here, too."

Greg backtracked through the tunnel, ran to retrieve the scooter, and motored back to town to check out of the hotel.

Within the hour, he was driving Route 1 north out of town. He wanted to be well out of the city ahead of the stalker.

He won't follow me this time around, he thought, *and why does she keep running away from me? If she's headed for California, this time, where would she go in the state?*

While driving north through the small resort fishing communities, traffic clogged and slowed to a standstill. It was slow going, so Greg checked his rearview mirror frequently. He wanted to be aware of the stranger, should he catch up to him.

When he neared Florida City, he decided to cut away from Miami and head northwest to Naples on Interstate 75. In that way, he would not drive out of the state the way he drove into it. He would travel out of Florida on the Gulf side of the state instead of driving out on the Atlantic side.

The afternoon sun burned scorching hot, along with drenching humidity, so Greg, being from a cooler climate, was very glad to be leaving Florida.

When he reached the top of the state and traveled west toward Tallahassee, the radio music station played the record "That Elusive Butterfly of Love."

Greg smiled. "And Valerie is certainly one of those elusive butterflies of love also. That's for sure."

When he arrived in Tallahassee, he stopped to spend the night, and after a hearty supper, he phoned Jessica to see if Valerie had contacted her.

"Hello, Jessica?"

"Yes, this is Jessica. Who is this?"

"It's Greg. How ya doin'?"

"Oh, it's you, Greg. I'm doin' just fine. I have a new man in my life now. How are you doin'? Not very good, I suppose, without Valerie."

"Did I hear right? A new man in your life? What happened to the tower of steel? Quote, 'No more men for me. They're outta my life for good. I'm the tower of power, baby,' unquote."

"Did I say that? Why, I don't remember saying any such thing, Yankee."

"Oooo, Jessica, your nose is growing long." He laughed. "But I'm very happy for you. What's his name?"

"It's Allen, and he calls me his little queen. Now we both know that's a lie, because I'm no LITTLE mama! He just fusses over me and hounds me somethin' awful."

"I know, like an Elvis hound dog." He laughed.

"Yeah, that's it, Greg, Ah swear, he ain't nothin' but a hound dog in heat. Every time I tell him to quit fussin' over me, he keeps it up all the more. I tried to beat him off with a stick, but he's too irresistible. All I could do was give up and follooow his leeadd, honey."

"'Beat him off with a stick?' Yeah sure, Jessica. You love every bit of that attention. You eat it up. That tower of steel is nothing but a puddle of putty."

"You don't believe me, huh, Yankee? Well, in that case, maybe I won't tell you where Valerie is, since she's the reason for this phone call."

"Now, be nice, Jessica. We're still buddies, aren't we?"

"You betcha, Greg. Now, listen up." Greg pulled his notebook and pen from his shirt pocket and flipped it open to a blank page. "Valerie called me a few hours ago and said, 'Greg has no reason to come after me anymore. I ran off on him again, but if he should call and want to know my whereabouts, tell him I'm on way to meet my friend, Terri, in Tupelo, Mississippi. He can contact me through her. She's a waitress at a steak house on Glouster Street.'

"She told me the name of the restaurant, Greg, but I didn't get the name straight. She hung up before I could get her to repeat the name. It's a complete blank to me, now. She also said Terri works the day shift.

"I know you care a lot for her, Greg, or you wouldn't have found her and tried to help her. I also know she loves you, but right now she isn't showing much love to you. It's because she's so troubled and too afraid of that man who's stalking her. She really needs you, so don't give up on her, Greg. You won't, will you?"

After jotting down his notes, he stuffed the notebook back in his pocket and asked, "Has she ever told you anything about this creep? For some reason, she can't bring herself to tell me about him."

"No, she's never told me anything about him, either. I've asked her several times, but she's never opened up. She's just too scared, I guess."

"Well, so be it, but I won't give up on her, Jessica. You can be sure of that. I care too much for her."

They both promised to keep each other posted, bade their goodbyes, and hung up their receivers.

Then Greg immediately dialed his home phone number, and after a few rings, his mother said, "Hello?"

"Hello, Mom, this is Greg. How are you and Dad doing?"

"We're fine, but still worried about you. Where are you?"

"Right now, I'm in upstate Florida on my way to Mississippi."

"Is Valerie with you?"

"No, Mom, she isn't."

"But I thought you'd already found her and you were on your way home."

"I thought so, too, but she's got some problems and she's run off. I'm trying to catch up to her again."

"Here's your father."

"What's going on with Valerie, son?"

"She keeps running away from me and I have to find out what's troubling her."

"Why don't you go to the authorities?"

"I can't do that, Dad. It might put her in more trouble. I have to work it out with her first. Then maybe we can go to the authorities."

"So where do you go from there?"

"Right now, I'm heading north to Tupelo, Mississippi. If I catch up to her there and she doesn't give me any answers, I'll call it quits. It's all on the way back to Rapid City anyway, so I'll arrive home with Valerie or without her."

"Okay, son, I'll tell your mother what your plans are. Good luck."

"Love you both."

"Love you, too, son."

After hanging up their phones, Greg returned to his motel room for a restless night of sleep.

VIII

The next morning he was on the road early. He wanted to reach Terri before her shift ended for the day. So not having eaten any breakfast or lunch, he arrived in Tupelo by mid-afternoon.

As he entered the outskirts of town on the freeway, he observed Tupelo to be a small town. He grinned at a sign informing him that it was the birthplace of Elvis Presley. Immediately he planned to visit his home, but not right away.

At the next ramp, he exited the freeway and turned left for the city's center. As he passed through the downtown section, he viewed the older buildings; not too many people walked the streets.

Moving westerly, he checked each cross-street sign, looking for Glouster, and when he spotted it, he quickly turned right and drove north. Not seeing any restaurants, only motels, he turned around and drove back south.

Very quickly he came into the newer, more modern section of Tupelo with all of its fast food chain restaurants. Up ahead of him, he spied a STEAK AND BREAKFAST sign, so he pulled into the parking area and parked by the entrance.

Upon entering the restaurant, he met a tall brunette waitress standing behind the register counter and asked, "Would your name happen to be Terri?"

"No, it's Beverly."

"Does Terri work here?"

"No, I'm sorry. There's no Terri working here."

"Are there any other steak restaurants around here?"

"Yes, there's a streak house right next to us."

Greg looked out the window and saw the steak house sitting to the rear of their building. It was set back from the street.

"Oh, now I see it," he replied. "I didn't see it back there when I drove up. Thanks. Sorry to have troubled you."

"No problem." She smiled.

After departing, he drove the short distance next door to the steak house, and upon entering, he was greeted by a gracious black-eyed waitress.

"May I help you, sir?"

While he stared over her head and scanned the room, he said, "Yes, you can. Does a waitress named Terri work here?"

"Yes, I do." She beamed. "I'm Terri, and you must be Greg. You fit Valerie's description perfectly. I must say, they grow 'em tall, dark, and handsome in South Dakota."

He looked down at her short stature with a broad grin.

"And I see they grown 'em dark and mighty pretty and petite here in Mississippi."

"Valerie thinks you've probably given up on her, but she asked me to watch for you anyway in the hope that you might want to see her again."

"I haven't given up on her yet because I need to know why this creep is stalking her."

"Well, I can't help you there," she replied. "Valerie's never told me anything about him either. I'm just trying to be a friend and help her as much as possible, and I'll tell you this for sure. She's not a bad person. We've been friends since grammar school."

"Where can I find her?"

"Have you eaten lunch?"

"No, I've not eaten all day. I've been on the road since early this morning."

"Then pull up a chair, and after I place your order, I'll phone her at home. She'll be so excited and happy to know you've showed up."

"Terrific," he answered pulling up a chair at an empty table.

While pouring his coffee, she smiled broadly and said she'd be right back.

Returning to his table shortly, she related, "Greg, Valerie's been very depressed since she arrived this morning. She's been crying over the mess her life is in, but when I told her you were here in the restaurant, she just screamed and squealed into the phone. She was so happy. She was half-crying and half-laughing at the same time. Wow! She was so nervous and excited, she sounded like a giddy little school girl again.

"She's too embarrassed to see you right now because her face is a mess from crying, but she said she'd meet you at a place called Old County Line at 7:30 P.M., tonight. It's about five miles north of town on the main highway. It's a country and western club where you can drink and dance."

"Why don't you join us, Terri?"

"Oh no, you two need privacy to do your talking. You don't need me there. Now don't worry about me. My shift ends in a couple of hours and I have serious shopping to do. Besides that, my favorite TV shows are on tonight. I can't miss them. You two have fun and enjoy yourselves tonight. Valerie needs you very much, Greg."

"Needs me enough to tell me what's going on, I hope."

He was famished, and after eating a good steak dinner, he left a generous tip for Terri, made his way to the cash register, and paid his bill.

Before leaving, he walked over to Terri, who stood at her station waiting for an order from the cook.

"Nice meeting you, Terri. I'll see you soon. Tell Valerie I'll be at the club 7:30 P.M. sharp."

"Nice meeting you too, Greg. I'll be sure to tell her you'll be there."

He left the restaurant and drove around town to take in the surroundings. Then he drove out the north end of town to find the nightclub where he'd meet Valerie. He wanted to know exactly where he was going that evening.

Later he returned to town and took a room at the Holiday Inn, where he spent the rest of the afternoon watching TV talk shows and newscasts until he showered, shaved, and prepared for his evening with Valerie.

He left the motel around 7:15 P.M., and when he arrived at the nightclub, he saw the parking lot almost full, but found an empty space against the wall toward the rear of the building. He pulled in, shut off the engine, and sat waiting for her arrival.

Several minutes later, Valerie drove into the space next to him and parked the car.

They both jumped out of their cars and ran to greet each other. When they met between cars, they embraced and kissed each other warmly.

Afterward, she hugged him tight, and with her mouth close to his ear, she whispered, "Oh, Greg, I'm so happy you didn't give up on me. When I left you in Key West, I thought it would be over between us. I thought you'd never want to see me again. I don't deserve someone like you, but I need you desperately. My life is such a mess."

Greg broke their embrace and gazed into her watery violet-blue eyes.

"Because your life's a mess, you don't think you deserve me. That thinking is ludicrous and nonsense, Val."

Staring directly at him, her eyes were full. They shifted nervously from side to side as if pleading with an urgent hope to find true happiness with him and to remain together forever.

She began to cry, so she turned away from him and walked to Terri's car to get her purse. When she retrieved it from the front seat, she snatched a handkerchief, and while drying her tears, she said, "I'm so upset, Greg. It's been a very emotional day for me. I can't seem to stop crying, so let's get in the club. I could use a couple of drinks right now. We need to talk."

"Well, I'm ready for that. Bartender, tend your bar, 'cuz here we come." Then he glanced to the side and noticed that she wasn't driving her own car. "Hey, this isn't your car. Where's your car, Val?"

"Terri wanted me to take her car. My car was parked in front of hers in the driveway and she didn't want to get up to move hers, so she told me to use her car tonight."

"Nice car."

Walking toward the club entrance, Valerie was apprehensive. She was worried about his reaction to what she was going to tell him, but she was determined to reveal her situation regardless of how it affected their relationship.

Upon entering the crowded club, they saw most of the tables already filled with noisy customers. However, they were able to find a table for two in an intimate corner of the room.

When they sat down, the waitress was there quickly to take their orders: a strawberry daiquiri for Valerie and scotch and water for Greg.

"You can start talking anytime you're ready, Val. I've got a good ear for listening."

"Okay, I'll start and I'm hoping you'll understand. When I was twenty-two, I was very angry to an unfair–"

"Valerie!" a man blurted as he walked up to their table. "Long time, no see, eh? What a delightful surprise. How many years has it been?" He nudged her with an elbow and winked, "At least ten; maybe twelve, eh? How ya doin' these days?"

"Hello, Ed, nice to see you, too. This is my friend, Greg."

Greg stood up and shook his hand, saying, "Glad to meet you, Ed."

"Nice to meet you, too, Greg."

Ed turned back to Valerie and said, "I see you haven't lost your good taste in men, Val." He nudged her again, grinned, and walked away sipping his drink.

"Who was that?" Greg quizzed.

She shrugged. "Oh, he was just a summer infatuation after high school. In third grade, here in Tupelo, Terri and I became best friends, and after my family moved to Charleston, we still kept in touch with letters and phone calls. During twelfth grade, I planned to stay with her that coming summer so we could work together all summer. It was a fun time for both of us after graduating, and it was during that summer between high school and college when I met Ed here in Tupelo."

"You and Terri must be very close. True friendships are rare after our school days. Tom and I are lucky that way, too."

When she reached for her daiquiri, Valerie's hand trembled, and as she lifted the quivering glass up from the table, some of the drink spilled over onto the table. She managed to steady the glass and get it to her lips to take a sip, but as she returned the shaking glass to the table, she spilled more of the drink on her dress and table again.

While listening to the band playing "I Can't Stop Loving You," it calmed her somewhat, so she asked, "Dance with me, Greg? I need your arms around me right now. I need to be held."

Ed's intrusion obviously broke Valerie's mood to talk. She was nervous and upset.

"I'm always here to help my damsel in distress. Let's go."

When they got to their feet, she grasped his hand and led him onto the dance floor.

Pressed against each other with their heads side to side, they glided around the floor to the slower music.

"Greg, I truly love you," she whispered softly in his ear. "I don't want anything to come between us. I want so much for us to be together."

"I want that too, Val, but I do need to know why all the running and what's going on. We need complete honesty between us or our relationship will never get off the ground."

Rubbing her hand up his back into his thick hair, she kissed his lips softly and stared into his eyes, saying, "I know, Greg. I'm trying hard to tell you, but I'm so afraid I'll lose you. I couldn't bear to lose you. I love you too much."

He kissed her and stared momentarily into her anxious eyes. He yearned for an answer. Then he pulled her tight against himself and continued to dance until someone tapped Greg's shoulder.

"May I cut in?" a voice asked.

Greg turned his head to look at a smiling, ruddy-faced, red-haired man.

Irritated, Greg stopped dancing, dropped his arms, stepped back from Valerie, and replied curtly, "Be my guest, sir."

Recognizing the man as another old acquaintance, Valerie was taken aback, so she hesitated for a moment. Then she obliged the intruder and began dancing with him. While dancing away, her red-headed partner eagerly started a running one-way conversation with her, but she paid no attention to him. She shut off his words easily and gazed over the man's shoulder to focus her eyes on Greg's back as he made his way off the dance floor. She quickly lost sight of him when the dancing crowd closed off her view.

When the music stopped then started to play again, she politely declined another dance, left the man standing in the middle of the floor, and hurried back to their table.

"I suppose that was another one of your long-lost admirers?" Greg declared.

"Yes, he is. He's a very old grammar school classmate."

Greg stared down hard at his drink and turned the glass slowly on the table.

Without looking up at her, he queried, "Any particular reason why these guys are showing up tonight, Val?"

"Why no, Greg. It's just a coincidence, I guess."

"Could it be because you knew it was a popular hangout for all your old acquaintances, you brought me here to make me jealous."

"Certainly not, Greg!" she snapped. "That's school girl foolishness. I'm no school girl anymore. Do you really think I'd jeopardize our relationship with that kind of childish behavior? My love for you goes much deeper than school girl nonsense."

"Okay, I'll accept that, Val, but let's get out of here and find a quieter place to talk. This place is too damn loud."

"Can't we just dance for awhile and talk later? I need your arms around me, Greg, just to hold me, for now."

"No, Valerie! I've waited long enough. I need answers right now. Let's go."

"Please, Greg, I'm so overwrought. Won't you give me a little more time? I need to gather my strength to explain it to you properly. I promise, I'll tell you later tonight."

"More time? I've given you more than enough time." Suddenly he jumped up and shoved his chair back. "I would have thought you'd have wanted to get it off your chest by now." Reaching into his pocket for change, he glared down at her and flipped a quarter onto the table. "Whenever you're ready to tell me what's happening, use the quarter and call me collect in Rapid City. I'll be happy to accept the charges. Until then I'm outta here. I'm going home. You've had plenty of time to square things with me and you keep evading me. I've HAD it with your evasiveness. Goodbye, Val."

He threw some bills on the table to cover the tab, turned, and hastened toward the front entrance.

Stunned for the moment, she sat staring after him. Then she bolted from her chair and caught up to him at the door.

As they left the club, she tugged at his arm, pleading, "Stop, Greg! Please stop! I love you. Please, come and dance with me. I promise. I WILL tell you everything tonight. Please come back."

Shrugging off her arm and without looking at her, he stared straight ahead and continued his deliberate pace toward his car.

"Dancing doesn't get it anymore, Valerie. If and when you find the time, give me a call or drop me a line sometime. Take care of yourself, Val."

She stopped dead in her tracks and watched him walk away.

She stared at his back and called, "I WILL tell you, Greg. That's a promise!" Then she murmured, "I love you too much not to tell you, luv."

Beginning to cry again, she turned around, cupped her hand over her mouth, and rushed back to the club entrance. It had been a hellish day for her, and at that same moment, the mysterious stranger's car was turning into the club's parking lot. She and Greg were completely oblivious to his arrival.

Instantly the stalker noticed Greg hurrying to his car and glimpsed Valerie entering the club. He stopped to watch Greg enter his car, then drove past the rear of Greg's car to park in an empty space a few cars away. The stalker stayed in his car until Greg backed out of his parking space, drove out of the parking area, and disappeared up the highway.

The stalker left his car, smirking. "Well, well, well, it appears as though Valerie's protector lover boy has left her all by her lonesome. Now she's all mine."

When he stepped into the club and surveyed the packed room and dance floor, he didn't see Valerie. So he swaggered over to the bar, slid onto a stool, and ordered a drink from the bartender.

During his early evening's search of nightclubs, the stalker already had had too much to drink. He was inebriated.

When he received his glass and sipped on his drink, he continued to pan the crowded room for any sign of Valerie.

Suddenly at the back of the club, a woman ran up to the front of a small hallway and screamed, "Call 911! A woman just fainted in the ladies room."

As the bartender grabbed a wall phone, people flooded toward the hallway.

Undeterred by the announcement, the stalker paid no attention to the confusion. He merely scanned the flow of peoples' faces.

Minutes later came the sound of a siren; then attendants with medical bags in hand came rushing into the club. The gurney was then wheeled in.

Unaware to the stranger, it was Valerie who lay in the restroom with an empty bottle of sleeping pills at her side.

When the attendants reached her, she was still breathing, so they lifted her onto the gurney and wheeled her out of the restroom and into the hallway.

While pushing the gurney toward the front entrance, people backed away to give them room, and when it rolled past the bar in front of the stalker, he noticed Valerie laying on the stretcher. She laid motionless; her body appeared lifeless, her eyes closed, head turned to one side.

The attendants hurried toward the entrance and quickly disappeared through the door.

Squinting his beady eyes, the stranger mumbled, "So it was her."

He gulped the last of his drink, slipped off the stool, and swaggered behind the small crowd who followed the attendants out of the club.

It was raining now as the ambulance moved through the parking area and when it screeched onto the highway, the familiar red and blue flashing lights and wailing siren signaled its oncoming path.

With his plan thwarted, the stranger stood frustrated and watched the fading red and blue flashing lights disappear into rainy darkness.

The stranger hastened to his car, and after driving onto the highway, he headed south to follow the ambulance to the North Mississippi Medical Center.

At the medical center, the stranger ignored the receptionist. He passed directly by her into the waiting room, sat down, and snatched a magazine. As he thumbed through it quickly, the receptionist eyed him through the doorway.

For the moment, he was stymied. To buy time, he flipped pages nervously while trying to think of a way to get to Valerie. He fidgeted and shifted constantly in the soft-cushioned chair.

Meanwhile, Greg was driving approximately fifty miles north of Tupelo, having second thoughts about his behavior with Valerie.

He talked to himself and thought, *She says she loves me, but keeps running away from me. She says she's going to tell me her problems, but runs away every time. But she runs, because she's running from her stalker—not me! She says she doesn't want to hurt me and thinks she's not good enough for me. She says she doesn't deserve me. She's an emotional basket case. She needs space and more time. I shouldn't have lost my temper and pressured her. I know she'll tell me in time just as she says. I'm a stupid ass. She has nowhere to turn. What's to become of her? I can't go home yet. I feel too guilty leaving her back there. She needs me desperately. I'm going back!*

He slammed on the brakes and skidded onto the shoulder. Sliding sideways, he swung the wheel hard left, bouncing and kicking up a hail of gravel and dust. And when the U-turn was finally complete, he steadied the car on the highway, floored the accelerator, and raced south to Tupelo. He hoped to arrive back at the nightclub before it closed.

Within the hour, he entered the club and when he looked for Valerie at the table, it was occupied by another couple. So he looked for the cocktail waitress, who waited on them.

Spotting her quickly, he walked up to her and said, "Do you remember waiting on me and my lady friend earlier this evening?" He pointed to their table. "We sat at that table over there."

"Yes, I do."

"Can you tell me if she left the club or if she's still here somewhere?"

"Yes, she did leave the club, but not under her own power. She left in an ambulance."

"An ambulance! What happened?"

"From what I heard, they found her on the floor in the ladies room with an empty bottle of sleeping pills next to her."

"Good God! Where did they take her?"

"To the medical center, I suppose. It's Tupelo's main hospital."

"Where is it?"

"When you drive out onto the highway, turn left and drive south. The road becomes Glouster Street at the north end of town. Keep driving straight ahead and you'll come to it. The medical center sits on the left side of the street near the south end of town. You can't miss it."

He reached into his pocket and threw a couple of dollars on her tray, saying, "Thanks a lot."

"No problem." She smiled. "Thanks for the tip."

Turning away, he hurried for the front door, and once outside, ran to his car and climbed inside. After hitting the ignition with the key, he spun tires out of the parking space and sped onto the highway.

Speeding well over the speed limit, he murmured, "Do your job, guys. I hope you got to her in time. Don't let her die. Don't die, Val. Please don't die. I'm so sorry."

When he reached the hospital and parked the car near the rear of the hospital, he raced toward the back of the building to find the ambulance entrance.

Upon entering the hospital through the emergency entrance, he hurried down a long corridor, passing many white-coated people walking in both directions. No one stopped him or questioned his movements.

At an intersecting hallway, he stopped to look left down a short hall. It was deserted but when he looked to his right, he saw Terri leaning on a counter talking to someone.

He was at her side in seconds.

"It's a big relief to see you here, Terri. Where's Valerie?"

Startled, she looked up at him to say, "Greg! Where have you been? I couldn't understand why you weren't with Valerie when they brought her into the hospital."

"Because I'm a damn fool, Terri, but I'll explain it all later. Where's Val? Is she alive?"

"Yes, she's alive and doing just great. The paramedics got to her in time to pump her stomach out. She's resting in her room right now She'll be so happy to see you."

"I wonder about that. I blame myself for what happened."

Terri turned back to the duty nurse sitting at her station and asked, "Can he go in her room with me?"

The nurse nodded. "Yes, the doctor said she's doing very well, so you both can go in her room now."

When they walked into her room, Valerie sat dejected in the bed with her head down, but when she looked up and saw Greg, she squealed, "Greg! You came back. I thought you were gone forever." Dropping her gaze again, she stared down at her folded hands. "I'm so ashamed and so sorry for the trouble I've caused both of you. It was stupid and crazy. I promise I'll never do that again."

Greg rushed to her bedside and grasped her hand.

"I don't deserve your love, Val, because I blame myself. If I hadn't pressured you and walked out on you, this wouldn't have happened. I'm very sorry. I promise you I'll never pressure you again about our relationship. Take all the time you need, because I know you'll tell me the whole story, eventually. Can you forgive me, Val?"

"I'll always forgive you, Greg," she cried. "I love you too much not to forgive you. I'm so undeserving of your love."

He sat down on the side of the bed, smothered her in his arms, hugged her tight, and kissed her full on the mouth.

After their embrace, he replied, "I'm to blame, Val. I provoked your actions because I refused to listen and accept your emotional condition. I rejected you and that will never happen again. That's a promise." He hugged her again. "Terri and I are so happy you're still with us."

Valerie pecked him on his lips, put a finger to his lips, and said, "I give you fair warning, Mr. Ghost. Be prepared for wild emotions when we're alone again, because you're in baaad trouble, pieface."

Backing away with palms up, he laughed. "Now don't be cruel. Treat me nice."

"Oh, you and that Elvis." She winced.

When they kissed again, Terri interjected, "Okay, break it up, you two love birds. We have to get Valerie out of here and home right now."

Terri left the room and returned shortly with the duty nurse, who declared, "The doctor has released you, Valerie. He said you'll be fine, so there's no need to hold you any longer. You're free to leave at anytime. Please stop at the nurse's station and sign the release form when you check out." Then she left the room.

"Terrific!" Valerie cried, jumping from the bed. "Let's get out of here."

Immediately Greg turned around to let Terri help her dress quickly.

Meanwhile, at that same moment, the stranger, being too nervous and fidgety, couldn't wait any longer, so he got up from his chair and walked out to the receptionist in the lobby. Flashing his phony detective's badge, he demanded to know Valerie's room number.

Startled and surprised to see a badge, she stuttered, "I . . . I have it right here in my record book, sir. Yes . . . yes, here it is, Valerie Nielsen. She's in room 106."

The stalker fled from her desk and at the first hallway, he turned left only to see that the room numbers ran higher than 106. He spun around and raced back down the hallway, checking room numbers above the doors, and when he came to room 106, he burst into the room.

He froze, dumfounded! There was no Valerie. The room was empty.

"What the hell! She's not here," he stammered.

Fleeing from the room, he ran back down the corridor to the receptionist's desk again and confronted her.

"Did you give me the right room number for Valerie Nielsen?" he blurted.

"Yes, sir, I did. Here it is right here in my book, see," she explained, pointing to the room number, "but let me double-check with the nurse's station to be sure."

139

She picked up the phone, dialed the number, and when someone answered, she said, "Hello, this is the receptionist in the main lobby. Can you please give me the room number of Valerie Nielsen?"

During the time the stalker was delayed at the receptionist's desk, the threesome left room 108, and after Valerie checked out at the nurse's station, they started to walk toward the front entrance, but Greg stopped them in the hallway.

"Let's leave by the emergency entrance. It's the way I came in. My car is parked in the rear of the building, anyway."

The women agreed, so the threesome turned around and left the hospital through the emergency entrance.

Back at the receptionist's desk on the phone, there was a few seconds pause and a voice said, "That room number is 108."

"Oh, dear, my records show room 106. Someone entered the wrong number in my book. I'll change it, right away. Thank you. Goodbye."

"I'm sorry, sir, 106 is the wrong number. The correct room number is 108. Someone enter—"

"Don't explain, lady. Stupid idiots!" he muttered racing back to the hallway once more.

Meanwhile, outside the hospital, the threesome discussed car arrangements among themselves.

Valerie said to Terri, "I'll ride with Greg and follow you, Terri. That way, if we lose you, I can still show him the way to your house, okay?"

"Fine with me," Terri agreed. "I had to drive your car, Valerie, because you had mine, remember? I'm parked near the front entrance."

Valerie called after her, "Your car is still parked at the club."

At the same time as the threesome entered their cars, the stalker, having found room 108 just as barren as room 106, flashed his phony badge at the nurse's station and was questioning the nurses.

Minutes later, the two cars drove out of the rainy parking lot, turned right on Glouster Street, and traveled north toward the city. Eventually they turned right again and drove east out of the city. It began to rain again, so Greg turned on the windshield wipers.

Valerie directed, "Up ahead, we'll branch to the right onto Briar Ridge Road. If we were to turn left and drive up that street, you'd see Elvis's birth place, Mr. Presley fan."

As she snuggled into his side, he remarked, "His house is up that street, eh? I'd like to visit it before I leave town. I've also come to appreciate another one of his songs that applies to tonight."

"Oh, which one is that?"

"The words go: 'You don't know what you've got until you lose it.' I almost lost you tonight, Val. I don't ever want to lose you. You mean too much to me now."

"Do you love me, Greg?"

"I'm crazy about you, Val, but with this mysterious hang-up of yours and all the unanswered questions, it's like there's a barrier between us. All we have to do is get rid of the barrier and we'll be off and running."

"Do you think when I remove my shroud of mystery and the barrier disappears, you could love me?"

"Remember what I told you in Bergen? I said that I thought I was in love with you. That still goes. Of course, at that time, I didn't know you were a mystery woman, and I still don't care about your past, as I told you in Key West. It's only us and our relationship that counts with me, but we need trust and honesty to build on. I'm sure it's all going to work out for us. I know it will, Val."

Her eyes filled when she looked up at him longingly and said, "Oh, I hope so, Greg. I hope and pray we can work it all out. I love you so very much."

Reaching up, she kissed his cheek.

Outside, it was only drizzling while they continued to follow Terri along the country road to her home. Three or four miles later they arrived at Terri's rented house and she stopped on the right shoulder across from the house to motion Greg to drive ahead first into the driveway and park his car.

So Greg turned left off the road onto the muddy driveway and parked his car. Then Terri drove in behind him and parked Valerie's car.

When everyone got out of their cars, it was raining harder, so they hunched their shoulders and walked up the few steps onto the small wooden porch.

"Nice place, Terri," Greg commented. "It's quiet and peaceful; very country."

"Yes, it is. It's small, but it's very homey and comfortable. C'mon inside and I'll show you my little sugar shack."

Once inside the small wooden frame house, Valerie went to the kitchen to brew some fresh coffee while Terri gave Greg a quick cook's tour of her small one-bedroom home.

In a short time, the threesome sat comfortably in their living room chairs drinking coffee. The conversation focused on Valerie's impulsive and dangerous behavior.

Terri related, "I was shocked when the medical center called me. I couldn't believe what they were telling me when they said you took an overdo–"

Bang! A gunshot cut off her words.

"What was that?" Valerie cried.

"It sounded like a gunshot," Greg exclaimed.

"It did sound like a gunshot, didn't it?" Terri declared.

Terri ran to the window, threw the curtain aside, and peered outside at a lone figure standing motionless in the pouring rain.

"I see a man standing by the back of your car, Valerie," she said, "and he's got a gun in his hand."

The figure staggered toward the rear of Valerie's car and fired another shot into her right rear tire. Instantly, the tire flattened.

When Greg and Valerie dashed to the window, all three of them stood frozen while staring out the window at the gunman.

Then Valerie gasped, "Omigod! It's him. Where did he come from, Greg? How did he get here?"

"Don't ask me, Val, but I can give you one clue. That dealer bracket around your license plate does read TUPELO right? This is the only Tupelo I know of."

"That's right. I forgot about that. He's drunk and he's got a gun. Now, what do we do?"

Terri grabbed the phone, saying, "I'm calling 911 right now."

"No, Terri!" Valerie yelled snatching the receiver away from her. "Don't do that!"

"What's wrong with you, Valerie? He's crazy. He's shooting out your tires. He may try to kill us."

"We have to keep the police out of this. If you call them, I'll be in more trouble," she explained while returning the receiver to its cradle. "Now I'm sure we'll be all right. I know we can handle this ourselves. Trust me on this, Terri, okay?"

Dumbstruck and wide-eyed, Terri shook her head and said, "Okay, Valerie, but I don't get it. What's going on here?"

"That makes two of us, Terri!" Greg affirmed angrily.

Angered by the stalker's presence and belligerence, Greg stepped deliberately and defiantly toward the front door and threw it wide open.

"Well, if it isn't the cowboy!" yelled the stalker. He bowed mockingly from her right front fender. "Finally we meet face-to-face, eh. Hey, Valerie, now you've got a flat tire. Let's try for three. Turnabout's fair play, right? All's fair in love and war."

The drenched stalker stepped back and fired another shot into Valerie's right front tire.

When Greg stepped out of the doorway onto the tiny porch, the stalker waved his gun at him.

"Stay right where you are, cowboy, or you're next," he warned.

Then the stalker slipped and slid around the front of her car to the driver's side and blew out her left front tire.

"That's three, Valerie. How 'bout baby makes four, since the four of us are all nice and cozy on this beautiful rainy night?"

Staggering to the rear of her car, the stalker fired his fifth shot, blowing out her fourth and last left rear tire. Her car lay sunken in the muddy driveway.

The stalker slipped and skidded around the back of her car, and when he gained footing on the grass, leaned his head back. With his face pointing upward, he opened his mouth wide, staggered sideways, and gulped a mouthful of rain.

"Not bad!" he shouted. "All I need is more whiskey to go with it."

The stalker swayed forward toward Greg, and when he was about ten feet away from the porch, he pointed his pistol straight at Greg.

Standing only a short distance from Greg, the creep suddenly flipped his gun over his head and stretched out his arms with open palms. The pistol landed somewhere in the middle of the lawn.

"Well, what are you going to do now, cowboy? I think you're soft Dakota man. You're not man enough to take me. C'mon, take me!" he goaded with beckoning come-hither fingers.

Infuriated, Greg still hesitated.

"What's the matter, cowboy, afraid to take me on? C'mon! Just like the good old days, huh, Valerie, me against your boyfriends. Winner gets Valerie and Valerie knows who always wins–I always win. Don't I always win, Valerie? Tell your nice little cowboy the truth now."

Greg seethed with anger. He wanted to beat him within an inch of his life. So incensed with loathing for the stalker's arrogance and condescension, Greg leaped from the porch with an old linebacker's dive, butted his head straight into the stalker's chest, and he pancaked him flat on his back. Then Greg vented his rage by pounding his face repeatedly with his fists along with fast and furious punches to the creep's ribs.

The stalker writhed and squirmed to free himself from Greg's scathing onslaught, but Greg knelt on top of him and dug his knees hard into both of his outstretched arms. He showed no mercy. With unrelenting fury, his blows snapped the man's face from side to side.

Suddenly the stalker slipped one arm out from under Greg's pressing knee and punched his fist hard into Greg's ribs. Then he continued to push and force him to one side. Greg tried to resist, but the stalker's strength was too much for him. Greg fell to the side. The stalker instantly slid out from underneath him, brought up one leg, and kicked Greg away from him with his foot. The creep got to his knees and waited for Greg's next move.

Greg jumped to his feet and dived at the kneeling man. He drove him onto his back on the wet soggy grass again, but this time the stalker wrapped his arms around his body and locked one hand around his other wrist behind Greg's back. The creep had him squeezed into a tight bear hug. Although Greg was on top of him, his arms were pinned against the sides of his body.

At the house, the two frantic women stood helpless and watched the furious battle from the window. They felt powerless to stop them.

The rain beat incessantly onto the two drenched and muddied men. They rolled over and over and over on the muddy lawn and appeared as one huge log rolling on the grass.

Finally they stopped rolling, but their bodies continued to slide, slither, and writhe on the grass, half-wrestling, half-fist fighting with one another.

At one point the stalker got to his feet and prepared to charge Greg, but Greg quickly rolled onto his back and bent his knees. When the creep dove at him, he shoved his feet up into the stalker's stomach, lifted him up, and heaved him head first over his head. Flying over Greg's head, the creep somersaulted and landed flat on his back beyond Greg's head.

Greg leaped to his feet and when he turned around to pounce on him, he saw the stalker with one of his shoes in hand. He reached up and swung the shoe hard at Greg's face.

As Greg immediately turned his head aside to avoid the swipe, the creep got to one knee and threatened him with the shoe's heel.

"Now I'm going to work over that pretty boy face of yours, cowboy."

The stalker charged Greg, swinging the heel wildly at his face. Greg jumped backward and as he dodged from side to side avoiding the repeated vicious swipes, the creep's arm tired quickly. Within seconds, the stalker's arm swung wildly; the shoe flailed aimlessly in his hand.

In desperation, the stalker lunged at Greg with the shoe, but he grabbed the shoe, twisted it out of his hand, and flipped it over his head into darkness.

With sapped and waning strength, the two men still fought on, each man trying to get the upper hand. Again and again, the two bleeding men locked arms around each other, but were too weak to gain any advantage.

Finally with mouths and faces bleeding badly, both men wavered, slipped, and staggered across the grass, flinging their fists weakly at each other. They were deadlocked. It was a standoff.

Valerie, observing the weakened state of both men, reacted, "I'm going to get the gun, Terri."

"No, you can't, Valerie! He'll kill you if he gets it first," Terri protested.

Terri grabbed Valerie's arms trying to pull her back, but Valerie shook her off and ran out the front door.

"I'm coming, Greg!" she yelled through the pouring rain.

As the groggy tottering men paused to look up at Valerie running toward them, the stalker instantly kneed Greg in his groin. He doubled over in pain and with a swift uppercut to Greg's battered and bleeding face, the blow sent him reeling backwards against Valerie's car.

Valerie was now searching the grass for the gun, but when she spied it lying in the grass only several feet away from them and ran to retrieve it, the stalker turned at the same time and raced after her. Just as she stooped down to pick up the pistol, the creep stomped on it with his foot.

Grabbing her wrist, he twisted her arm behind her back. Then stooping down, he retrieved the gun from the grass while at the same time releasing her wrist, and as he rose slowly, she stared into the gruesome, mud-splattered, smirking face of her stalker. She stood petrified and quivering.

The creep staggered over to Greg, who still slumped against her car. He didn't move. He only held his stomach and glared defiantly at the gunman.

Still smirking, the stalker pointed the gun directly at his face.

"I outta kill you right now, cowboy!"

"No, no, don't kill him!" Valerie pleaded. "I'll do anything you want. I'll go with you, Zach, but please don't kill him."

"You just said his name," Greg exclaimed. "You know this creep, Valerie?"

"Now, Greg, you don't know what's going on, so don't get any wrong ideas or be confused with what's happening here. I loathe and despise him. He's only part of my messed-up life."

Zach interjected, "You mean you haven't told pretty boy all about us, baby? Tsk, tsk, that's not nice. Now tell the cowboy the truth of how much we love each other and plan to get married right, baby?"

"That's a lie! Don't believe him, Greg. I've NEVER loved him or would I even THINK of marrying this animal. He's a despicable liar!"

Having listened to her words, Greg declared, "I believe every word you just said, Val. No woman could possibly love this . . . this thing."

Zach turned around to face Valerie and laughed. "It's just like old times, eh, Val? You and me together, again." Waving the pistol in the air, he shouted, "Yippee! Ya-ha!" Then turning to Greg, he smirked. "I win again, cowboy, just like I told ya. Ol' Zach always wins, especially when I have the boss in my hand, ha-ha."

He kept the gun pointed at Greg while he reached out, grabbed Valerie around her waist, and jerked her toward him.

Seething with anger and indignation, Greg glowered at him but stood fast.

Zach stepped behind Valerie, wrapped one arm around her throat, pointed the pistol to the side of her head, and muttered in her ear, "Okay, baby, just for you I won't kill him. See how nice yer ol' Zach is."

The creep slobbered on her neck and began pulling her backward slowly.

He glared at Greg, sneering, "Stand back, cowboy. It's all over. She's all mine now. Move toward the house and she won't get hurt."

Greg answered gutturally, "She was never yours, creepo, and never will be."

Enraged, Zach screamed through the pelting rain, "I said move, cowboy, NOW!"

As Greg moved sideways toward the house, Zach continued to pull Valerie backward to his car parked behind her car in the muddy driveway.

Upon reaching the driver's side of the car, Zach shoved Valerie into the car first, climbed inside himself, and opened the glove compartment to pull out handcuffs. He quickly clamped one handcuff to her wrist and locked the other handcuff around the door handle. Afterward, he started the motor and backed out of the driveway.

Greg and Terri ran toward the moving car.

When Zach backed the car onto the paved road and paused to shift gears, Valerie pressed the palm of her hand against the side window and gazed at Greg with imploring eyes.

Through the blur of streaming water on the side window, her lips read, "I'm so sorry, Greg. I love you. I love you."

Stunned with disbelief, Greg and Terri stood transfixed by the roadside in the driving rain and watched the car speed away into the darkness. They could do nothing to save her. They stood helpless.

Suddenly Greg yelled, "I've got to follow them."

He raced for his car and jumped inside behind the wheel. After starting the engine, he shifted into reverse and swerved the wheel to back around Valerie's flattened car. Spitting up muddy rooster tails, his spinning back tires dug deep muddy ruts in the driveway. Mud splattered in all directions as he tromped the accelerator. The car swerved and swayed in its backward thrust to meet the pavement.

When the car reached the paved road, Greg shifted gears and with his tires screeching forward, he jerked ahead and shot down the dark, deserted road after Valerie and her kidnapper.

Not knowing the surrounding area or the town's streets, Greg had no idea where the creep would take her, but he had to do something to save her. Because they had disappeared from sight, he followed the main road back into town, but there was no sign of the stalker's car on the deserted streets. He drove past the many motels, but again no sign of his parked car. His car was nowhere around town.

"They've vanished into the darkness," he murmured. "They're ten or twenty miles in any direction by now. They could be anywhere."

Discouraged and depressed, Greg headed back to Terri's house.

By the time he arrived, the rain had subsided. So when he turned into the driveway, parked the car, and got out, it was sprinkling once more. Terri greeted him on the porch.

Greg shrugged his shoulders. "Well, what do we do now, Terri? She's gone, vanished again. The story of our soap opera relationship. Now how do we get her back, if ever?"

Terri patted his bruised and bloody face consolingly, but stepping back, he winced, "Ooo!"

"Oops, sorry," she said, "but the first thing I'm going to do, sir, is clean up those cuts on your face, and after that, I'll throw your clothes in the washer and dryer while you're showering. You look like you've just stepped out of a muddy pigpen after a pig fight."

"Well, haven't I?" He laughed.

Terri led him into the house, and after he'd showered, he sat at the kitchen table wrapped in a towel. He and Terri sipped on their hot coffee.

"Who is this Zachary? Did she ever tell you anything about him?" he questioned.

"No, I don't know who he is, Greg. She's never told me anything about him."

"He's obsessed with her," said Greg. "He'll never leave her alone. Do you think she'll ever get away from him now?"

"Don't worry," Terri replied. "You can rest assured she'll find a way to escape. I'm sure she knows how to handle him. When she gets the opportunity, she'll get away and phone me immediately."

"Do you think she can pull off an escape?"

"Oh, I'm convinced she'll get away eventually."

Feeling relieved at her words, Greg relaxed in his chair, sipped on his coffee, and smiled. "Well, that makes me feel a little better, anyway."

Later, because they were both exhausted from a night of harrowing events, he fell asleep on the sofa. Terri retired to her bedroom.

They both slept late, so sometime around noon, Terri fixed a late breakfast, and afterward she walked Greg out to his car.

"She WILL escape from him, Greg. I just know it."

"I can live with that positive hope," he said as they hugged and kissed cheeks.

"Don't let those piercing black eyes get you in trouble, now," he mused.

"No problem, Greg, unless he's black-haired blue-eyed trouble." She grinned.

When he entered his car, started the engine, and rolled down the side window, Terri poked her head through the open window and kissed his cheek again.

"Goodbye, Greg. Remember, I'll call you as soon as I hear from her. Try not to worry, okay? Drive carefully and get home safe, ya hear."

"I hear." He laughed while backing out onto the road.

After waving to each other, he honked the horn and sped away.

Greg knew it would be a very long and trying journey back to Rapid City. He brimmed with frustration and anxiety. Too many unanswered questions plagued his thoughts.

IX

A few days later, toward mid-morning, Greg crossed the Minnesota/South Dakota state line, and while breathing in the fresh breeze blowing off the great plains of the Dakotas, he thought, *It's great to get back home. Football practice starts up in a couple of weeks. It'll feel good to get back with the kids again. I hope they can at least make it to the playoffs this year.* He smiled to himself. *After that, who knows what can happen.*

He was anxious and eager now to get home and increased his speed.

Early in the afternoon as he neared Rapid City, he counted the exit signs until finally the ol' familiar 59 Exit loomed straight ahead.

Veering off I–90 onto the exit ramp, he stopped for a red light at the end of the ramp.

When the light turned green, he turned left onto La Crosse, still thinking, *It's so good to be home again. These past few weeks seem like a dream now. I wonder if Valerie's gotten away from Zach yet. I can only hope Terri calls me real quick to inform me she's safe with her.*

Since Greg lived only a few blocks off the interstate, he was home within minutes, and when his mother saw him pull into the driveway, she ran out the front door to greet him with an endearing smile.

After hugging one another, she said, "I'm so happy you're home, son. Did you find Valerie again and where is she? Has she stopped running away? You must tell us all about her."

His father joined them on the front lawn and after their usual handshake, declared, "It's always good to have you home again, son, especially after a wild goose chase like that."

"Dad, that wild goose chase has become more like a wild butterfly chase. You can eventually catch a big goose, but how do you follow the erratic flight of a butterfly and snare it without a net? Valerie is more butterfly than goose, Dad, and I haven't found the right net yet."

His father laughed. "By the sound of her elusiveness, you'll need a very large net if you hope to catch up to her."

"She's such a mystery. Sometimes I think I'm the one already trapped in the net. I really care about her, Dad."

Greg's father patted his son's back and as the three of them sauntered toward the house, he wrapped his arm around Greg's neck.

After entering the house, they walked into the kitchen where his mother prepared afternoon snacks and coffee, and for the rest of the afternoon, they sat at the kitchen table discussing Greg's involvement with Valerie.

Greg kept a discreet conversation about Valerie. Because his situation with her would be difficult for his parents to grasp, he revealed only the "surface" content of their relationship. He went no deeper, nor did he divulge anything about her stalker for fear of their lack of understanding. He knew that some things were better left unsaid.

During the discussion, his mother intuitively sensed Valerie's love for her son and because she knew her son had never been attracted to another woman as much as Valerie, she encouraged their involvement. She could see how much he cared for her and approved of his continuing help for her.

His father, however, concluded that Valerie had too many problems and advised Greg to give her up.

"Chalk it up to experience, son," he said. "If you involve yourself any longer, you will only cause yourself heartache and grief. Why get involved with a woman with so many problems when there are plenty of nice young women around Rapid City who, like your mother, don't have problems?"

"I don't have problems, Howard?" his mother snapped. "You've been one BIG one for the past thirty years."

They all laughed heartily.

Then with a twinkle in his eye, his father merely grinned and winked. "But you have to admit, sweets, I've been a big LOVABLE problem, right?"

Nudging him with her elbow, she answered, "Oh, I suppose so. You've probably been lovable most of the time, anyway."

"There, you see, Greg. In thirty years, that's been the only difference between your mother and me. She's always been lovable all the time to me, whereas I've only been lovable *most* of the time to her."

His mother slapped her husband on his back, grinning. "And you're one lovable liar, too, Howard."

Their advice and opinions were appreciated but were no help for Greg. His thoughts and emotions were still with Valerie. He had to find out what he really felt for her and only he could find out that answer for himself. He had to continue to help her.

Two weeks later, Greg started football practice and at first scheduled double-dips—same day sessions, one morning, one afternoon.

Each day, the players showed up anxious and enthusiastic. The hard, tough workouts distracted his thinking from Valerie but only temporarily, during the practices. She preyed on his thoughts constantly. Nighttime was the worst. Every night he went to sleep thinking only of her. He worried about her with the creep, where she could be, and whether or not she was safe.

At one time, he thought about phoning Terri but figured it was pointless. He knew she'd call him immediately with any information.

As he finished up the first week of practice, Greg was home for lunch. The phone rang and his mother picked up the receiver.

A woman's voice asked for Greg, so his mother handed the phone to Greg, saying, "It's Terri."

"Hello, Terri, what a relief to hear your voice!" he said. "But hold on, will you? I'll use the extension in my room, okay?"

"I'll hold on," she answered.

After handing the receiver back to his mother, Greg ran to his room, picked up the phone, and said, "Okay, Mom, you can hang up now. Are you still there, Terri?"

Hearing the line click, Terri replied, "Yes, Greg, I'm still here."

"You must have news about Valerie," he said anxiously.

"Yes, I do. She's safe and unharmed, but she's trapped in a motel in a little town about twenty-five miles west of Tupelo. She says she's doing okay and gave me the name of the motel."

"So she's still held hostage."

"Yes, he's still got her, and he's beginning to believe what she tells him. She's finally convinced him that she'll remain with him. Today is the first day he's trusted her. He didn't handcuff her to the bed. So when he left the motel to go drinking in the bars and buy food, it gave her a great opportunity to call me from a pay phone.

"She told me not to come for her yet because she has a plan. She had to hang up, but said she'd phone again tomorrow or the next day with all the details. Terrific, eh, Greg?"

"You bet! Do you know where that motel is?"

"No, I don't. I only have the name, but I'll find it when Valerie tells me to come for her. It's only a small town, so I'm sure I'll have no problem locating the place."

"Great news, Terri. Keep me posted. Next time, call collect, okay? I'm paying for all your calls."

"Will do. It's your dime." She laughed.

"I'll wait anxiously for your next call, Terri, hopefully within a day or two."

After their goodbyes and both hung up their phones, Greg returned to the kitchen to finish lunch with his mother.

"You didn't listen to our phone call, did you, Mom?" He grinned.

She slapped him with a dish towel and huffed indignantly, "Certainly not! You know better than to accuse your mother of doing such a thing! I don't listen in to my son's personal phone calls."

"I was just checking, Mom. I hear nowadays things are getting so bad in this country that we can't even trust our own mothers anymore."

"With this mother excluded, thank you very much." She smirked.

After eating, he stood up, gulped the last of his coffee, and said, "I have to run, Mom. I'll see you and Dad at supper."

He hurried out the front door to his afternoon practice.

Two days later, after Greg and his parents had eaten supper, the phone rang. It was Terri, so Greg took the collect call in his bedroom.

"Hello, Terri, what's up?"

"Hi, Greg. Valerie phoned me a few minutes ago and told me her plan of escape. It sounds great, if we can only pull it off. She knows my days off from work are Monday and Tuesday, so Monday is our target day.

"Early in the morning, around 5:00 or 5:30 A.M., I'm to meet her behind a cafe directly across the street from their motel. She'll slip out of the room while he's still asleep and be waiting for me in back of the cafe. She says he gets drunk almost every night and always sleeps late, so her plan should work."

"Where do you both go from there?" he asked. "You know you can't go back to your place, because he'll figure you're helping her and go straight to your house."

"Yes, that's exactly what he'll think, but we won't come back here. I'll have her suitcase packed and we'll head straight to the airport."

"Airport? Where is she going?"

"She's going straight to you, Greg. She'll fly to Rapid City first to see you, and from there, she'll fly to Los Angeles."

"Los Angeles? Does she know anyone there?"

"She won't be alone there. She has a girlfriend in L.A. who's told her she can come and stay with her anytime."

"She's always wanted to see California, so now she's got her chance. Hopefully she'll be far enough away this time to rid herself of that creep. Does she have the money?"

"I bought new tires for her car and I'll be selling it this weekend. With the money from the sale, she'll be able to buy her plane tickets and also pay me back for the tires."

"What time will her flight leave Tupelo and when will she arrive in Rapid City?" he asked.

"She'll fly Northwest. It's the only airline out of Tupelo. My friend, Pat, is a ticket agent at the airport and she's given me flight times and a possible itinerary for her. There are only two morning flights: 7:05 and 7:30 A.M. The next flight out is at noon, so I hope to get her on one of the two morning departures. She'll fly directly to Memphis. From Memphis, she flies to

Minneapolis, and from there it's a direct flight to Rapid City. If I get her on the 7:05 flight, she should arrive in Rapid City around mid-afternoon."

"I've given her my phone number, but make sure she has it," he said. "Tell her to call me from the airport. I'll go straight home from football practice and be there after 5:00 P.M."

"Will do," Terri replied.

"I hope your plan works, but I worry that creep will come after you, Terri."

"Don't worry, Greg. Before I return home, I'm staying at my girlfriend's apartment for a few days. That creep is only obsessed with Valerie anyway, so I'm not very worried about him."

"He'll also figure she's coming to me, especially if he checks the airport and finds out she's flying here. I expect him to follow her to Rapid City."

"I'm sure that is exactly what he'll do, Greg, so be careful and get her safely on that plane to Los Angeles."

"You can bet on it, Terri. I'll phone you when she's on her way to L.A."

"Thanks, Greg. I'll be worried about her."

"Me, too, Terri. That maniac won't stop. It's been going on too long now. He's totally obsessed by her. Somehow we have to find a way out for her."

"That's definite. I have to go now, Greg, so I'll say goodbye and talk to you soon."

"Good luck on your plan. I hope everything goes well. See ya."

With their discussion ended, they hung up their phones.

The next day, Greg held his usual practices, and that evening while he and Tom drank beer at their favorite lounge, Greg told Tom about Valerie's plans to come to Rapid City and fly on to Los Angeles.

That following Monday morning, Greg was awake before his alarm sounded. He'd been awake most of the night with worry.

Meanwhile, hundreds of miles away in Tupelo, Terri had already awakened in the dark early morning hours. Sometime around 4:30 A.M., she'd set out on her drive to the little town of New Albany.

When she drove into town, the streets were deserted and she easily found Valerie's motel.

The little cafe across the street was exactly as Valerie had described it, so she drove around to the back of the building and parked close to the back wall. It was before 5:00 A.M. when she shut off the motor and doused the headlights.

While waiting, five minutes led into ten minutes, and very soon one minute seemed like ten minutes.

Being worried, she thought, *What if the cook or owner showed up? What would I do or say?*

She tapped on the wheel nervously with her fingers and by 5:30 A.M., there was still no sign of Valerie.

Suddenly in front of her, a car's headlights flashed against the back fence. Then the lights quickly faded into darkness and a car door closed.

Terri was in luck—the driver parked his car along the side of the building. He never saw her parked behind the building.

Minutes later, lights flicked on inside the cafe, so Terri started her car and backed up to the end of the building, where she turned the wheel left to pull ahead and park alongside the other end of the building. Now she faced the deserted street, still hidden from the motel.

She didn't wait much longer when Valerie ran toward her from across the street. She ran barefooted carrying her shoes in her hands.

"YES! She did it!" Terri murmured excitedly.

Instantly she turned the ignition key, started the engine, and without turning on the headlights, drove forward slowly to meet her.

Valerie jerked open the door, jumped into the passenger seat, and after they slapped palms, ordered, "Go! Go! Let's get out of here, fast!"

Terri spun onto the street, flicked on her headlights, and headed east for Tupelo.

"Rapid City, here I come, baby! Oh yeah!" Valerie yelled.

"Have suitcase, will travel!" Terri shouted. "Big bird, here you come."

Upon entering Tupelo's city limits, Valerie said, "It's too early for my flight. Where can we hide out until the plane leaves?"

"That creep doesn't know my car," Terri replied, "so let's get some coffee and donuts. We can park out by the airport on a side street until it's time for your flight."

Later, while parked near the airport and with the coffee and donuts consumed, Terri noted, "It's about 6:35 A.M. Pat said to arrive around 6:50 and she'll board you immediately. I've described Zach to her, so she's already on the lookout for him."

"He's probably awake and furious by now," Valerie speculated. "He'll go straight to your house, I'm sure. After that, he'll check the airport and bus station for sure. I'm so nervous and afraid he'll already be waiting for us at the airport, Terri. He said he'd kill me if I ever tried to escape from him again."

Terri patted Valerie's hand reassuringly and said, "You'll make it, Valerie. You'll make it. You'll see."

Being only a short distance from the airport, Terri started the car, pulled away from the curb, and drove down the street. After making a few short turns, they turned onto the circular drive that leads to the airport's passenger entrance.

Valerie looked behind them several times to check for Zach and nervously viewed the entire public parking area. She didn't spot his car anywhere.

Terri complied with Pat's instructions to park in a reserved parking space by the terminal's entrance, and when they jumped out of the car, Terri snatched Valerie's suitcase from the back seat. The two women dashed for the entrance doors.

Once inside the small terminal lobby, Pat eyed them instantly and waved them to her.

They raced to the ticket counter, where Valerie turned to Terri and huffed, "Thanks for all your help, Terri. I owe you for all of this. I promise, I will phone you when I get to Greg."

"I'll be waiting anxiously for the call," Terri smiled.

Valerie ran to the gate, handed her ticket to the agent, and disappeared through the open doorway.

Terri quickly turned to the ticket counter and handed Pat Valerie's suitcase, saying, "Whew! She made it, Pat."

While tagging the suitcase for Rapid City, Pat replied, "Yep, she's safely on board now. They'll be backing away from the gate at anytime. That was no problem at all. I'm ready for that creep, too. If he shows his ugly face around here, he'll get nowhere with me."

"Thanks loads, Pat. I've got to run too. I'll see ya," Terri replied as she turned around and ran for the entrance.

"See ya," Pat called as she began waiting on a new passenger.

Meanwhile, the stalker's car fast approached the airport, and as Terri left the terminal entrance and raced to her car, Zach turned onto the circular driveway and headed for the front entrance.

After Terri entered her car and started the engine, she looked behind her before backing up but didn't see the stalker's car fast approaching her back end.

He stopped instantly when he saw her backing out. He wanted her parking space, so he waited to pull in. As she backed out, he glimpsed her face but she didn't notice him and turned her head quickly to look ahead while turning the wheel. Because he didn't know her car, he didn't recognize her as she drove ahead on the terminal drive.

When she glanced into her rearview mirror, she saw him cut sharply into her parking space and thought it to be him, so she slowed down to see who would get out of the car.

"Omigod! It's him," she muttered.

At the same moment, she heard the roar of jet engines.

Looking to her right, she observed Valerie's flight taking off from the runway and laughed. "She's out of here now, creep, and so am I."

Terri accelerated and headed for town.

The stalker, upon entering the airport lobby, was noticed immediately by Pat and as he walked toward her counter, she quickly posted a CANCELLED sign next to the 7:30 A.M. flight.

At the counter, he demanded, "The plane that just took off. Where is it going?"

"It's going to Memphis," Pat said.

"And where does it go from there?"

"From Memphis, connections are made to anywhere in the country." She smiled.

"That was a Northwest Airlines flight and their headquarters is in Minneapolis, right?"

"That's right, sir."

"And from Minneapolis, Northwest flies into the Dakotas, right?"

"Yes, sir, Northwest does service the Dakotas."

"Did a woman by the name of Valerie get on that plane? She had dark reddish-brown hair and blue eyes. You couldn't miss her eyes."

"I didn't notice. I don't watch my customers that closely."

He flashed his badge immediately and demanded to know if Valerie's name was on the list of passengers.

Pat, flustered and frightened by the sight of the badge, nervously checked her computer.

"Yes, a Valerie Nielsen is listed as being on board," she said, perplexed.

"I want the next flight out of here," he declared.

"It's . . . it's been cancelled," she stuttered nervously. "See, it's posted there on the outgoing departure board."

While groping in his pocket for money, Zach glared at the departure board and said, "Then give me a ticket on that noon flight."

Still jittery, Pat processed his ticket and handed it to him.

He hastened away from the counter and out of the terminal.

Befuddled by the whole incident, Pat stood behind the counter, bewildered and confused. She simply shook her head when she turned aside and removed the CANCELLED sign from the departure board.

Meanwhile, in Rapid City, Greg held his usual morning football practice, but his instruction was halfhearted. His mind was on Valerie and whether or not she'd gotten away safely from Zach and onto the plane.

During the afternoon practice session, while demonstrating offensive plays to the team in the middle of the field, Greg noticed a taxicab drive up and park alongside the curb at the south end of the school's parking lot.

The cab driver got out, and when Valerie stepped out, she fumbled in her purse to pay him.

With a sigh of relief, he whispered, "She made it."

Instantly he blew his whistle and announced, "That's it for today, guys. Take a lap around the field and hit the showers. See ya, tomorrow, same time, same place."

As Greg walked toward Valerie and the kids started running, several players sprinted by him.

One player called, "Hey, thanks, Coach!"

Another kid yelled, "See ya tomorrow, Coach!"

One big lineman jogged next to him and said, "Great practice today, eh, Coach?"

Greg didn't say anything. He merely held up his hand to acknowledge their remarks, gazed straight ahead, and quickened his stride to greet Valerie.

Behind him, he could hear his players' fading comments.

"Hey guys, look! Coach has a girlfriend."

"So that's why practice was cut short."

"He's been holding out on us."

"Wow! What a fox!"

"Coach has great taste, eh, guys?"

Catcalls and whistles followed his footsteps all the way to the goal post where he met Valerie and embraced her. When they kissed affectionately, the shrill whistling escalated, while their lips parted into smiles. She was overwhelmed with relief. She felt secure once again and safe in his protective arms. She savored his warm tender kiss.

After their embrace, Greg laughed at the players who had finished their laps and stood whistling and gawking at them. He pointed deliberately to the school to indicate shower time while Valerie waved to them with a friendly smile.

Then turning to Valerie with concern, he asked, "Are you okay, Val? Did he harm you in any way?"

"I'm okay and no, he didn't harm me."

"Does he know I live in Rapid City?"

"Yes, he threatened to beat it out of me if I didn't tell him who you were and where you lived in South Dakota. So I told him you were a coach in Rapid City and that's all I knew. He accepted it but warned me if I ever tried to escape from him, he'd kill both of us. He said if he couldn't have me, nobody else would have me, either."

"Did he follow you?"

"I don't know, but he wasn't at the airport when I boarded the plane."

"He knows you'd head straight for me, that's for sure. So he's on his way here. I've got to get you to a safe hiding place. We're going to Keystone. It's near Mount Rushmore. Since he won't know the area and won't know where you're at, you'll be safe there for the night."

"But what about you, Greg? He'll be searching for you, too."

"Of course, he'll come for me first. He figures when he finds me he'll also find you, but I'm already expecting him." He grinned sheepishly.

Sticking his hand into the pocket of his shorts, Greg pulled out his car keys and handed them to Valerie, saying, "Take the keys and wait for me in the car. It's parked in the employee's parking lot near the end of the building where the taxi dropped you off. I'll take a quick shower and meet you at the car in about twenty minutes."

She stroked the side of his face lovingly, kissed him softly on the lips, and said, "I'm so happy to be with you again, Greg. I feel so very safe now."

"You are safe, Val, and I intend to keep you that way. See you in a bit."

As he ran off to the locker room, Valerie turned around and walked toward the parking lot.

In a short time Greg returned to the car, slid in behind the wheel, and started the engine.

"Here we go. We're off to Keystone," he announced. "I called Mom and Dad to tell them I wouldn't be home for supper and I'd be late getting in."

"Did you tell them I was here in Rapid City?"

"No, it might worry them and I wouldn't want them worrying about us. You're mystery enough for me. There's no need to create more mystery for my parents. What they don't know won't worry them." He smiled, pecking her on her lips.

As Greg turned onto the main street, her eyes filled when she replied, "I'm nothing but trouble for you, Greg, but I'm so afraid I'll lose you. I keep hoping you'll understand my screwed-up life when I explain it to you."

He reached over behind her head, tugged at her shoulder reassuringly, and whispered, "Sssh! You're in safe keeping. I'm just happy you're here with me. Now let's enjoy the ride."

Since they were already on the main highway–Route 16 west to Mount Rushmore–they drove straight ahead, passing the many signs advertising tourist attractions in the area.

Soon they arrived in Keystone, where Greg stopped to register Valerie at the Miner's Motel, and afterwards they entered the adjacent restaurant and took a booth in a secluded corner of the room for quiet conversation.

When the waitress left with Greg's order of two steak dinners and red wine, he reached across the table, grasped her hand, and squeezed it tightly.

"So why Los Angeles?" he queried.

"My girlfriend there said she could help me."

"I hope so," he replied. "Somehow, we have to find a way to get that creep off your back or you'll never have any peace in your life."

"He's so obsessed with me, Greg. I don't know if I'll ever get rid of him. Sometimes I believe there's no escape from him. He finds me wherever I go."

"There HAS to be a way and we WILL find it. I believe that, Val."

"Oh, Greg, I hope so, but now I have to tell you another reason why I'm going to California."

"What's that?" he asked as the waitress set their plates down in front of them and left.

"I'm pregnant."

"Pregnant!"

Shocked and disappointed, Greg slumped back in the booth.

Instantly Valerie threw up her palms and anxiously assured him, "It's not yours, Greg. Don't worry, it's not yours."

"Well, if it isn't my baby, then it must be Zach's. We've got to get this son-of-a-bitch off your back, Val. This is an on-going, never-ending mess for you."

Valerie's gaze dropped.

She stroked her wine glass and replied, "No, it isn't Zach's baby, either. I can't tell you whose baby it is right now, but I'm not what you think I am, Greg." She lifted her glass to take a sip of wine. "I'm not a whore sleeping with all kinds of men. When I get to Los Angeles, my friend knows of an abortion clinic. I'm going to abort the baby."

"An abortion? It's none of my business. That's your choice as a woman, but why an abortion? Couldn't you adopt the baby out to a childless couple?"

"It's because I feel dirty and ashamed," she sobbed. "You have no idea what I've been through, and I want so much to tell you, but I'm still not able to. Eventually I will explain all of it. I've promised you, and I am getting there. Please be patient with me, Greg. I just need a little more time."

Their heavy discussion was interrupted by the juke box playing "Feelings."

Valerie looked down and fiddled with her wine glass again. She hummed along with the tune and sang the words softly.

Then she looked up at Greg, tossed her hair to one side, lifted one eyebrow, and half-grinned, "How come your Elvis isn't singing?"

"With this newest revelation of yours, I'm already all shook up," he mused. "Who needs Elvis. What I REALLY need is another drink."

After "Feelings" the next record was Johnny Mathis singing "The Twelfth of Never," and after another drink and more conversation, they finally left the restaurant.

The dance club was only walking distance away, but Greg chose to drive and parked by the building.

Upon entering the club, already half-filled with people, they took a table by the dance floor, and Greg ordered their drinks.

Not long afterward, the country band began to play and the singer sang, "For the Good Times."

Valerie wanted to dance, so they were the first couple on the floor. Other people joined them, and soon the floor was filled with dancing couples.

The next song, "Oh, how happy you have made me. . . ." was followed by the up-tempo, "Don't stop thinking about tomorrow. . . ."

Greg and Valerie were a handsome couple as they clung to one another and glided swiftly over the dance floor.

Soon the singer sang, "Wise men say, only fools rush in. . . ."

Greg remarked, "Finally, she sings the king. There's hope for the band yet."

"Oh, you and Elvis, but I did like him, too. I think every woman loved Elvis. His death was so tragic."

Throughout the evening, they completely immersed themselves in each other and laughed and drank the evening away.

At the end of the evening, he escorted Valerie to her room and kissed her goodnight.

After entering his car, he rolled down the window and said, "Tomorrow, we can lunch at Mount Rushmore. It's only a few minutes up the hill. See you in late morning tomorrow. Good night, Val."

"I'll be waiting, Greg. Good night."

On the drive home, Greg pondered his many questions about Valerie, and to some degree understood her dilemma.

It appears as though she truly is a victim of circumstances, he thought.

Upon arriving home, Greg went straight to his bedroom to make a phone call.

His father, being awake in the next bedroom, heard only indiscernible muffled dialogue coming from his son's bedroom, but ten to fifteen minutes later, when he passed his son's bedroom coming back from the bathroom, he overheard his son say, "Goodnight, Tom. See ya tomorrow."

His father heard the receiver placed back on the cradle and saw the light beneath his door snuff out.

Both men retired for the night.

CROCROCRO

Greg was being shaken gently, and when he opened his eyes, the flight attendant stated "I'm sorry, sir, but the captain has just turned on the sign requesting everyone to fasten their seat belts. We'll be experiencing some turbulence."

"How long before we land?" Greg asked.

"We should arrive in Oslo in approximately an hour and a half, possibly a little sooner depending on our tail wind. Would you like a hot towel?" she offered.

"Yes, thank you."

Greg took the towel from her hand and placed it across his eyes. It was warm and soothing, so he leaned back into his seat to enjoy its comforting effect.

After a few brief minutes of relaxation under the soothing towel, the attendant returned to retrieve the towels from the passengers.

At which point Greg propped his pillow, laid his head back on the pillow and closed his eyes. Once more, he returned his thoughts to Valerie.

CROCROCRO

The next morning, Greg was on the practice field with his team and was unaware when a particular car drove into the employees' parking area and parked in a space clearly visible to the playing field. The stalker sat behind the wheel, keenly observing Greg's football session.

Even though Greg expected Zach to seek him out at the school, he didn't know what kind of car he'd be driving, assuming it would be a rental, anyway.

He was too involved with the boys' play calling to notice anything, but near the end of the morning's practice, he did scan the parking area and observed the one car facing the field.

Instantly the car was suspect. He sensed he was being watched by Zach.

Fifteen minutes later, Greg blew his whistle, ending the practice, and called the players around him.

"That's it for this morning, guys," he announced. "I've got some personal business I have to attend to, so I won't be here this afternoon. Coach Richardsen will take over the afternoon session. I'll be here tomorrow morning So take your usual two laps around the field and hit it hard this afternoon. Have a good practice with Coach Richardsen."

When the team started running, Greg headed for the locker room to take his shower, and twenty minutes later he emerged from the back exit of the building.

As he walked toward the employees' parking area at the end of the building, he saw that the suspicious-looking car wasn't parked in that same parking space anymore. So when he reached the end of the building, he stopped to peek cautiously around the edge of the building.

That same car now blocked the driveway exit from the parking lot, and Zach, with folded arms, leaned against the passenger side of the car, waiting.

Greg muttered, "So he's got the exit blocked, eh?"

He ducked down low and scooted alongside the building in front of the row of parked cars.

When he reached his motorcycle, parked between two cars, he unstrapped his helmet and jammed it on his head. After fastening the strap under his chin, he hopped on his Harley and turned the ignition key. Instantly the motor kicked on. Greg twisted the handle grip for power and jerked out of the parking space. Turning sharply to his left, Greg bolted for the walkway curb directly behind the stalker's car. Just before hitting the curb, he lifted his front wheel up onto the walkway. His rear tire bounced over the curb behind him. A sharp right turn took him to the exit driveway and out onto Route 16 where he made another immediate right turn. With a convenient green light, he shot ahead through the intersection, and within seconds, he was gone.

Dumbstruck, watching Greg fly past the rear of his car on a bike, Zach stood frozen momentarily with a gaping mouth, but he quickly recovered and ran to the driver's side of his car and jumped in behind the wheel. After switching on the motor, he squealed out of the parking lot in hot pursuit of Greg.

Screeching rubber as he turned right onto Route 16, Zach raced ahead through a yellow light at the intersection and tore after Greg, who was two to three blocks ahead of him. He kept Greg in his sights.

Greg knew exactly where he was going. He'd planned his complicated route days before Zach's arrival.

Greg made a right turn onto a side street, which took him into the residential west side area of the city. Afterward he made more left and right hand turns in order to lose the stalker in a maze of residential side streets.

When Zach reached that same side street, he peeled right, but had lost him.

After Greg zigzagged many side streets, he finally backtracked to Quincy Street and headed west up the hill to Skyline Drive. Zach was nowhere behind him. Greg had lost him in short order.

By the time Greg reached the top of the hill, he was satisfied he'd shaken the stalker, so he cruised Skyline Drive admiring the beautiful view above the city. He always loved that view of his hometown. The city lights were gorgeous at night, and during the summer, it was a lovers' paradise. Greg wanted to show off his city's night scene to Valerie. To him, Rapid City was his Scandinavian Brigadoon.

Eventually Skyline Drive merged into Route 16 west, so he continued on his way to meet Valerie in Keystone.

He was at the Miner's Motel within the half-hour, parked his bike near her door, and shut off the motor.

As he climbed off his Harley and removed his helmet, Valerie appeared in the motel doorway.

With folded arms, she leaned against the doorjamb and, as usual, with one eyebrow lifted, she commented, "Now it's a ghost on a motorcycle. You don't really expect me to get on that thing, do you?"

"I sure do, Val. It's fun. You'll like it better than the scooter." He laughed.

"Oh, I think not!"

"Get your suitcase. I'll fit in on the back of the bike, so we can go straight to the airport from Mount Rushmore. What time did you say your flight leaves?"

"Two-forty P.M. to Minneapolis. From there I connect to L.A."

Valerie retrieved her suitcase and joined him at the bike for a quick morning kiss.

While he strapped her bag on the back of the motorcycle, she asked, "Did the creep show up today?"

"He sure did. He showed up at practice this morning and blocked the exit driveway with his car. He got a nice surprise when I flew by him on my Harley, though. He wasn't expecting that. I gave him the slip back in town. He has to get lucky to find us now, or he may just camp out at the airport, hoping."

"Omigod! What if he's at the airport when my flight leaves? What will we do?"

"We'll cross that bridge when we come to it, but right now, strap on this helmet and hop on behind me. Since it's your first time on a bike, I'll take it slow up the hill for you."

After handing her the helmet, he put his leg over the bike, clumped down on the seat, and strapped on his own helmet.

Since she was all thumbs, he helped her snap the chin strap and made sure she was seated comfortably behind him.

"Now wrap your arms around my waist and hold on tight," he instructed.

When she slid her arms around his waist, scooted up close to him, rested her head on his shoulder, and closed her eyes, she purred, "Ummm, this is the part I like. I could go right to sleep."

Greg walked the bike backwards a few feet, started the motor, and twisted the handle grip hard for fast thrust. The bike jolted from a standing start along with Valerie's curdling scream. Wide-eyed with mouth agape, she hung on tightly as they bolted into the street where Greg swerved sharply to the left. With an ashen face and two bulbous eyes, she squeezed tight against his back until he slowed down to let her catch her breath.

"You maniac!" she yelled. "I'm terrified! Can't you go slower?"

He dropped his speed slower and laughed. "Okay, okay, is this slow enough?"

Regaining her composure, she relaxed, sat up straight, and replied, "Yes, much better. You did that deliberately. Ha-ha, aren't you the funny ghost on his motorcycle."

"Beautiful trolls aren't supposed to get scared."

"Well, right now I feel more ugly than beautiful, so I'm entitled to be afraid riding with a maniac. It is fun, though. It rides very smoothly."

"See, I told you you'd like it."

Meanwhile, back in the city, Zach still searched the streets for Greg. The frustrated stalker scoured the same streets over and over, finding no sign of Greg. Eventually when he found himself on Quincy Street, he noticed that the street climbed upward at the west end, so he decided to see where it would lead him.

Reaching the top of the hill, he continued along Skyline Drive until he drove next to parallel traffic and read a Route 16 sign.

"This has to be how he vanished from those side streets so fast," he mumbled. "This was his escape route, which also goes to Mount Rushmore. He may be taking her there to sightsee. I might as well check it out. I've got all day. I'll find that cowboy at the school tomorrow, anyway. He must hold football practices every day now."

The road eventually merged onto Route 16 west, so Zach continued on to Mount Rushmore.

When Greg and Valerie arrived at the remote parking area near the historical site, they found no parking, so they continued up the hill to the bigger parking lot closer to the tourist center.

After parking the Harley, they strolled the surrounding grounds and admired the four president's faces sculptured into the mountainside.

Soon they wandered aimlessly into the gift shop where Greg wanted to buy something for Valerie. He also wanted her to choose her own gift, so she selected a tiny, inexpensive charm bracelet with the four president's faces attached.

Afterward, they sauntered back outside with Valerie saying, "It's very hot. Are you thirsty, Greg?"

"You just read my mind, Val. I'm not only thirsty, but hungry, too. We need lunch and it looks like the cafeteria is straight ahead."

Inside the cafeteria, the line was short as they each took a tray and pushed them along the metal track, and after choosing the same meals–sandwiches, chips, and soft drinks–Greg paid the cashier and they made their way to an empty table.

When they sat down, Greg noted the time on his watch and said, "It's getting close to your flight time, Val. We'll have to head for the airport after we eat."

She reached across the table and grasped his hand. "So soon? I always hate to leave you, Greg. I hope someday I'll never have to leave you."

"I want that, too, Val. Once you're free of that creep, I know everything is going to work out for us."

During their meal and conversation, they gazed out the window, periodically, to admire the carved faces on the mountainside.

Meanwhile, the stalker drove into the parking lot and smirked at the sight of Greg's Harley.

While parking and shutting off the car's motor, he muttered, "So they did come here. I'm sure they're not expecting me either. This time the element of surprise is mine."

He checked the pistol for bullets, slipped the gun under his shirt, and tucked it down inside his belt. Then he was out of the car, hastening for the tourist center.

Valerie opened the small gift box and dangled the tiny bracelet in front of her face. She fiddled with the tiny bracelet and admired its craftsmanship.

As she examined the four miniature faces closely, she fingered each one, saying, "Let's see: First, there's George Washington; second, Thomas Jefferson; then, Theodore Roosevelt; and finally, good ol' Abe Lincoln. They're all in the same order as they are on the mountain." She stared out the huge window and added, "It really is a spectacular sight, isn't it, Greg?"

"That it is; an amazing piece of creativity. It boggles my mind as to how it was accomplished."

While eating the last of his chips, Greg casually glimpsed over Valerie's shoulder toward the cafeteria entrance. Wide-eyed, he exclaimed, "Uh-oh, he got lucky!"

"Omigod! He's here?" she cried.

"Yes, he just went by the cafeteria entrance into the men's room. Let's go. I have to get to a phone, fast!"

Jumping up from the table, they ran out an exit door where Greg found a public telephone just outside the building. He quickly phoned his friend Tom.

When he answered, Greg simply said, "It's a go!"

"Gotcha!" he replied.

Greg slammed the receiver back on its hook, grabbed Valerie's hand, and raced down the walkway by the side of the building toward the parking lot.

Almost immediately Zach emerged from the men's room and walked briskly toward the end of the building, scanning the many faces of the mingling crowd. When he reached the end of the building, he glanced to his right and saw Greg and Valerie running fast along the building's walkway.

"Dammit! They must have seen me," he sputtered as he turned and ran after them.

When Greg and Valerie disappeared among the strolling people, the stalker, knowing they were headed straight for the Harley, ran faster.

Reaching the bike, Greg and Valerie hopped on, fastened their helmets, and within seconds streaked out of the parking lot onto the highway.

The stalker got to his car in short order and spotted them as they shot out onto the road. He jumped into his car, started the motor, and peeled out of the parking lot onto the highway. Being only seconds behind them, he sped down the same road back into Keystone.

While passing through Keystone, Greg had to slow down to 25 M.P.H., which enabled Zach to get them in his sights. However, there were many cars between them.

Driving east out of Keystone, Greg accelerated, then spoke into his CB radio.

"Breaker, breaker, are you there, Tomcat?"

"What's going on?" Valerie yelled.

Greg ignored her question and heard only crackling static. There was no reply.

Turning around, she looked for the stalker's car, which was right on their tail and gaining fast. The speeding car closed the gap between them.

"He's gaining on us!" she screamed.

Over his shoulder, Greg hollered, "It's okay, Val. Don't worry. Help is on the way."

"Help! What help?"

"Breaker, breaker, do you read me, Tomcat?" he blurted into his radio.

Through heavy static, Greg heard an inaudible reply, but he knew it was Tom. He was on his way.

Valerie squealed, "He's almost on top of us!"

"I know, Val. I see him in my side mirrors."

Greg twisted the hand grip hard to power the bike ahead and spread the gap between them and their maniacal stalker.

At 80 M.P.H., he was well over the speed limit, but he didn't care. He held the needle steady in an effort to evade the menacing car that jeopardized their lives.

Unyielding to Greg's accelerating speed, the stalker increased his own speed. Glaring with determination, he tromped the gas pedal with only one deliberate and ultimate purpose: to diminish the gap between them and run them off the road.

Again Greg called into his radio, "Breaker, breaker, do you read me? Come in, Tomcat."

Tom answered, "I read you loud and clear, Hound Dog, and shooting straight at ya. It's party time, pardner!"

Greg replied, "We just passed a crossover on the center divider. There's another one up ahead of us."

"Gotcha sighted, Hound Dog, and I see that puppy's tail wagging behind you. It's show time!"

On the opposite side of the highway, a hoard of motorcycles loomed up ahead. Thunder grew louder as the swarm of cyclists roared straight at them and the marauding car.

Valerie yelled, "Look at them! There must be forty or fifty bikers. Where did they come from?"

Greg laughed, "Out of the Pied Piper's woodwork. See the mice run!"

"What are they up to?" she shouted.

"You'll see the mice play in a few seconds."

As the swarm of bikes streaking in the opposite direction thundered by them, Greg saw Tom leading the pack. They acknowledged one another with a wave of hands.

Valerie eyed the hoard of cyclists as they slowed down to cut across the median behind the stalker's speeding car.

When they advanced rapidly to the back bumper of the stalker's car, Tom announced into his radio, "It's all over now, Hound Dog. You're free and clear. Have a nice ride. Our party's just begun."

"Thanks, Tomcat, we're on our way."

While Greg relaxed and slowed the Harley to within the speed limit, Valerie kept her eyes glued on the bikes behind them. With intense curiosity, she watched the bikers split into small groups. One group remained close behind the stalker's car while another group drove up alongside the driver's side of the car to escort the stalker, but the escort group quickly split into a third group and shot ahead of the stalker's car. Now the car was boxed in and completely surrounded on all sides by the cyclists who slowed down their bikes and forced the stalker's car onto the shoulder of the highway. All of them came to a dead stop, but Valerie still viewed the bikers as they got off their motorcycles and completely encircled Zach's car.

Amid growing static on his radio, Greg heard Tom say, "Okay, Hound Dog, the wagging tail has stopped and droops behind its back wheels."

Greg mused, "As Tweety Bird would say, 'I tought I thaw pooty cats go by, or were dey hogs?'"

"Hogs to you, pardner. You know that. You ain't nothin' but a hound dog. You and that Elvis are spooky."

"You're right, Tom," Valerie shouted into the radio. "He tells me all the time he's a ghost."

"What was that?" Tom queried.

"Nothing, Tomcat. Just an inside joke," Greg answered, and over his shoulder, he said to Valerie, "You'd better mind your manners back there, troll, or you could slide off that seat anytime, you know."

Squeezing his waist tighter, she relaxed, snuggled her head against his back, and cooed, "Oh no, not if I can help it."

Greg smiled and spoke once more into his CB.

"If you can hear me, Tomcat, give us a ten- to fifteen-minute delay and we'll be home free."

Through loud crackling static, Greg heard a faint, "Roger."

Valerie quizzed, "Won't someone report your friends to the highway patrol for running the creep off the road?"

"Yes, they will, but Tom knows that, too. In a few minutes, before the cops arrive, they'll split up and speed off in all different directions, giving us enough time to get you to the airport and safely on that plane."

"All those motorcycles looked scary roaring toward us." She shivered. "I'm sure glad they were on our side."

Greg laughed. "Yeah, like some kind of a mega-beast swarming toward us."

"That's putting it mildly." She winced.

They cruised along Route 16 east until they were within the city limits. Then they turned onto St. Patrick street and continued east toward Route 44.

Turning right onto Route 44, Greg checked his watch and said, "It's 2:15 P.M. now, but we've got plenty of time. We're only a few minutes away from the airport."

In the distance, they heard the shrill of whining police sirens, and minutes later arrived at the airport, where Greg parked the Harley. After unstrapping her suitcase, he and Valerie walked into the airport lobby.

Upon checking her bag at the counter, a voice on the terminal's PA system announced, "Northwest Airlines is now boarding Flight 247 to Minneapolis at gate one."

While running for the gate, Valerie pulled her ticket from her purse, and when they reached the gate, they stopped and kissed one another goodbye.

"I'll miss you, beautiful troll. You'd better phone me."

Her eyes filled when she stroked the side of his face and said, "I'll phone you as soon as I get there, Mr. Ghost. I'll miss you, too. I love you dearly, Greg. Do you think we'll make it someday?"

"Let's keep working on it, okay?" He smiled warmly. "Have a safe flight and I'll call Jessica and Terri to let them know you're on your way to Los Angeles."

"Please do that, Greg. They'll want to know I'm safe."

After she handed her ticket to the agent, she turned around at the gate, waved, and blew him a kiss.

He returned the blown kiss and called, "I'll be waiting anxiously for your phone call."

Once she disappeared from sight and because he anticipated Zach's arrival at the airport, Greg hastened toward the terminal entrance.

Within minutes, he reached his bike in the parking lot, hopped aboard, and quickly donned his helmet. While fastening the strap, he observed the stalker's car moving along the roadway that led to the parking area.

Greg started the motor and slowly moved the bike between the parked cars until he found a spot far from the front entrance where the cars hid him from view. Then he cut the motor and watched the stalker's moving car over the tops of parked cars.

After parking near the entrance, Zach emerged from the car and briefly scanned the parking lot, and when he walked to the terminal entrance, he turned around again to pan the parking area before entering the terminal.

"Too late, creep," Greg murmured while starting up the Harley. "She's already on the runway waiting for takeoff."

Greg drove to the exit gate, paid the attendant, and casually motored on the service road back to Route 44. He relaxed and headed for home.

Driving north, he heard the roar of jet engines and smiled when he saw the plane's takeoff. She was safely airborne.

That evening, Greg met Tom and all the bikers at their favorite lounge for celebration drinks where they rejoiced over Valerie's victorious escape. While drinking away the evening, they all laughed and bragged with intoxication while Greg stayed sober. Despite all the joking and laughter, his mood remained pensive.

Greg knew Valerie's dilemma with Zach was not over with. She was still in grave danger from her tormentor; he worried for her safety; and her freedom constantly nagged his thoughts.

The next morning it was practice as usual at the school. Greg was in the middle of the field with his team when Zach's car drove into the employees' parking lot again.

When the stalker exited the car, Greg knew it was trouble, so he left their instruction to his assistant coach and walked toward the end of the field to confront him.

Before reaching the goal post, Zach demanded, "Where is she, cowboy? I wanna know."

"Forget it, creep," Greg shouted back. "She's long gone where you'll never find her again."

At the goal post where they confronted each other, the stalker shook his finger in Greg's face, yelling, "When I get my hands on her, she's dead and so are you, dead man!"

Greg blurted, "Why not now, creep? Where's the gun?"

Hearing the exchange of shouts, his coach and all of the players raced up and encircled both men.

"Anything wrong, Greg?" Coach Richardsen asked.

"Yeah, Coach," one burly player interjected, "is there a problem here?"

Another tall, lanky player queried, "What's going on, Coach?"

Greg's glowering, fixed glare never deterred from the stalker's menacing squinty eyes when he replied, "No, no problem, guys. This man's about to leave now, aren't you, Zach?"

When the circle of players closed in to crowd closer to the two men, the stalker's face became ashen as he nervously glanced from side to side at all the tall and husky, burly players.

Zach stuttered, "Ye . . . yeah, I was just leaving. I'm going now."

Immediately the players opened ranks, creating a short pathway through which the stalker could pass.

He raced between them all the way to his parked car, jumped inside, and squealed out of the parking area. He vanished quickly in downtown traffic.

Greg thanked his coach and all the kids for their concern, then dismissed everyone until the afternoon session.

When Greg headed home for lunch, he figured Zach wouldn't be back to harass him anymore. He knew Zach was too obsessed with Valerie. She was still his prime target, not him. He worried for her.

X

A couple of weeks passed, and because he hadn't heard anything from Valerie, he was beside himself with worry. He had no idea where she was.

On Friday night after the team won their second game of the season, he returned home late. He'd just gotten to his room when the phone rang.

He picked up the receiver to hear Valerie say, "Hello, Greg?"

"Yes, it's me. What a relief to hear your voice! Are you okay? Where are you?"

She was crying. When she spoke, her voice trembled. "I'm okay and I'm in Reno, but Zach knows I'm here. I'm very afraid, Greg. He swore he'd kill me the next time he got hold of me."

"Reno? Why Reno? What are you doing there?"

"It's a long story as always, Greg, and I really need you, desperately. It's only a matter of time before he'll find me here."

"How did he know you were in Reno?"

"I don't know. Ah sweah, he's the devil himself. He always finds me."

"Did you have the abortion?"

"No, I had second thoughts about it. I wanted to have the baby. I never went through with the abortion."

"That's great!" he exclaimed.

"You didn't let me finish. I miscarried the baby and that's the God's honest truth, Greg, ah sweah. There was no abortion. Could you come and help me, Greg?"

"I don't know if I can get away, Val. School has started. I'm tied up with classes and the football games have started now."

"If you can come to Reno and help me, I promise I'll tell you my whole sordid story this time. That's a promise, Greg. I know I can now. I need you terribly."

"Since the team doesn't have a game next week, I might be able to leave for a few days. It's our bye week and my defensive coach could handle the practices."

"Does that mean 'yes' you'll come?" she asked.

"Yes, that means I'll come and right away, Val. I'll leave early in the morning. If I drive hard, I should be there in a couple of days."

"Oh, thank you, Greg," she cried. "I love you so much. You're so good to me."

"Where will I meet you?" he quizzed.

"Right now, I'm staying downtown at the Holiday Inn, but that can change at any minute because I'm always on the run from him. If I've checked out when you get here, remember to see Danny. He's a bartender on the evening shift in the main lounge. I'll inform him you're coming and he'll tell you exactly where I am."

"Should we use a code word or something to identify me?"

"Good idea," she agreed. "What could we use?"

"How about a Presley song title? 'Kentucky Rain' maybe?"

"Yes, I'll tell Da. . . . Omigod! He's here! Goodbye, Greg."

Instantly he heard a click and shouted into the receiver. "Valerie? Val, are you still there?"

There was no answer. The line was dead.

Immediately he dialed Tom's number. After several rings, Tom answered, "Hello?"

"Tom, this is Greg. Valerie is in danger from that creep again. Somehow he followed her to Reno, so I have to leave early in the morning. Would you phone Coach Richardsen and ask him to take over the team for a few days? Also, could you call the school and ask them to provide a substitute teacher for my classes? I'll be back later in the week."

"You betcha, Greg, and be careful, okay? I don't want my best friend getting himself killed. I don't like funerals. Give Valerie my best."

"I'll do that, Tom. See ya in a few days."

"Bye, Greg. Drive safe."

After hanging up the phone, Greg went straight to bed but couldn't sleep. He tossed and turned until approximately 3:30 A.M. when he finally got up and dressed. After throwing some clothes in an athletic bag, he went down to the kitchen and wrote a note to his parents informing them of his sudden trip to Reno to help Valerie. He left the note on the kitchen table where they would easily see it, then left the house quietly through the back door.

Outside it was still dark with a bright half-moon and a night sky flooded with stars. When Greg lifted the garage door, he figured if he needed another getaway, the motorcycle would give him the best advantage. So he wheeled the bike onto the driveway and closed the garage door. After strapping on his helmet, he hopped on the Harley, started the motor, and drove onto the street, heading south from the city.

Once again he was traveling to help Valerie. He was too emotionally involved and couldn't deny her. He had a long trip ahead of him.

After his first day's journey, he stopped at a motel for needed sleep, and on the evening of the second day, he drove into Reno on Interstate 80. Since he'd never been to Reno, he'd have to search for the Holiday Inn. He'd also decided to rent a car because he knew the stalker would always be looking for his car or motorcycle. A rented car would not be recognized.

Driving closer to town, he noticed planes taking off and landing on his left, so turned south at the interchange to seek out the airport entrance. When he saw the airport exit ramp, he turned off, made his way into the airport parking area, and parked the bike. Afterward he walked into the terminal, secured a rental car, and was back on the interstate again, headed for downtown.

As he merged onto Interstate 80 driving west, he spotted the Holiday Inn and assumed it to be the downtown motel. So he exited the next off-ramp to follow the downtown streets back to the inn's parking lot where he parked the car and entered the building through the rear entrance.

Greg went directly to the lounge bar to find Danny, the bartender. When he stepped to the end of the bar, an attractive female bartender approached him.

"Does Danny work this bar in the evening?" he asked.

"Yes, he does. His shift starts at six." She smiled.

Greg noted his watch and saw he was early.

"I'll come back, thanks."

Greg left the bar to saunter around the casino and put a few quarters in the slot machines. Having no luck, he sat at the snack bar to have a sandwich and coffee while waiting for Danny, who arrived shortly.

At 6:05 P.M., when he finished his coffee, he approached the lounge bar again to find a male bartender serving customers.

When he came over to Greg, he asked, "Are you Danny?"

"Yes, I'm Danny."

Greg leaned close to him and said, "My name is Greg Ericsen. I'm looking for a woman who disappeared in a 'Kentucky Rain'. Her name is Valerie and I understand she's here in Reno. She told me to look you up and you'd tell me where I can find her."

Danny replied, "Yes, she did, but she was in a hurry to catch a cab and ran out of the lounge. She barely had time to give me the message. She said for you to meet her at the Clown Bar in the Circus Circus Casino. She said she'd go there at 7 P.M. every night to look for you."

"Where's the Circus Circus?"

Danny pointed to the wall behind Greg and continued, "If you take Sixth Street north of the building and drive west to Virginia Street, you'll run right into Circus Circus. You can't miss it. There's a huge clown sign on the building."

Greg slapped a couple of dollars in Danny's hand and said, "Thanks a lot."

Then he hurried out the rear entrance to his car, and within minutes he drove west on Sixth Street toward downtown.

However, he was unaware that on the same day that Valerie ran from Danny's lounge, the stalker flashed his badge to Danny, tipping him with a large bill. In return, Danny revealed Valerie's same information to the stalker that he just conveyed to Greg.

At Virginia Street, the Circus Circus Casino stood directly in front of him.

After driving one block through the intersection, he saw casino parking, so he turned left at the signal light and drove into the parking garage. He drove up several ramps on the numbered parking levels but found no parking spaces available. He assumed the casino to be busy and when he arrived at the top of the garage, he spotted an empty space, pulled into it, and parked the car.

From the rooftop he promptly took the elevator down to the street level and crossed the one-way street to a rear entrance of the casino.

Upon entering the casino, he struck a bit of luck. There was no need to search the casino. The Clown Bar lay to his immediate right and stretched against the back wall between two rear casino entrances.

He looked for Valerie at the bar, but she wasn't sitting there, so he checked his watch and noted the time. It was 6:50 P.M. Since he had ten minutes to wait, he walked to the end of the bar, slid onto a stool, and ordered a drink from the bartender.

During the next ten minutes, he scanned the crowded casino floor several times, looking for her. She was nowhere around. He ordered a second drink and nervously checked his watch every few minutes.

Finally around 7:05 P.M., he felt tapping on his shoulder and turned around to gaze straight into her incredible blue eyes and beautiful smiling face.

"Buy me a drink?" She grinned.

"Anytime, for a beautiful troll." He smiled.

After ordering her drink, they began to talk, but when Greg reached for his glass on the bar, he glanced up and eyed the ugly face of their stalker. He'd just stepped through the rear casino entrance doors at the opposite end of the bar. When he turned to one side and immediately spotted Greg and Valerie sitting at the end of the bar, Greg threw bills on the bar to cover the drinks, grabbed Valerie's hand, and jumped off the stool.

"C'mon, he's coming straight at us. We've got to get out of here."

They fled for the second pair of entrance doors behind them. When the stalker saw them fleeing through the other doors, he turned around, ran back out his same entrance doors, and gave chase up the sidewalk after them.

While Greg and Valerie raced across the street to the parking garage, Zach angled across the street behind them.

They reached the elevator ahead of Zach, but the doors were closed. They froze momentarily, staring up at the dim white light above the door which read "2."

"Is it going up or down?" Greg shouted.

The light changed and lit up a white "3."

"Damn! It's going up! Quick! Up the stairs, Val."

Turning on their heels, they dashed for the stairs, and when Greg threw open the door, he jerked Val's arm and bolted up the stairs.

At the fourth floor, Greg shoved open the exit door to see the elevator doors closing. He raced to the elevator and stuck his foot between the doors to stop them from closing. Someone pushed a button, opening the doors wide.

As he and Valerie squeezed onto the already packed elevator, Greg puffed, "Many thanks. How ya doin', troll?"

"Hangin' with ya, pieface."

Suddenly the stalker burst open the fourth floor door and darted for the closing elevator doors. He grabbed for the opening, but he was too late. The doors shut in his face.

The elevator moved upward to floor five but paused momentarily to allow a few people to exit. The agonizing seconds frustrated the impatient pair, but the elevator quickly lifted upward again.

Luckily, no other people exited until the elevator finally arrived at the rooftop. When the doors opened, Greg and Valerie were the first to emerge and dashed hand-in-hand to Greg's waiting car.

Meanwhile the stalker, observing the elevator's climb, saw no one exiting until it stopped at the rooftop, so he raced to the top and slammed open the exit door to see Greg and Valerie running for their car.

Instantly spinning around, he ran back down the stairwell to the next lower level. There he shoved open the exit door and raced for his own car.

After the pair jumped into their car, Greg started the motor, backed out, and sped down the incline ramp. Following the one-way arrows, he swerved around a corner onto another downward ramp. At the next lower level, he suddenly saw the stalker's car backing out onto the ramp directly in front of him.

Instinctively Greg hit the brake pedal, screeching rubber, but with a split-second reflex, he instantly tromped down hard on the accelerator. They shot ahead.

Zach saw Greg coming fast, so he floored his gas pedal to slam him broadside. With back tires screeching and spinning black smoke, his car jolted backward at Greg.

Valerie saw the back end of Zach's car barreling toward her side door, threw her hands up to her face, and screamed, "He's going to ram us!"

"Hang on!" Greg hollered.

As they bolted past the stalker's rear end, spinning tires and a back bumper shot straight at them but missed their back end by scant inches.

The stalker slammed on his brakes, jammed the gears forward and slammed his foot hard on the gas pedal, racing down the ramp after them.

With the near miss, Valerie trembled uncontrollably as Greg continued cornering the curves. While he skidded and slid around the sharp corners in their downward circular path, the tires screeched and smelled of burning rubber.

When they finally reached street level, Greg peeled to the right on 5th Street. At the first corner, he made another right turn, and at the next block, one more right onto 6th Street.

Greg anxiously eyed the cars in front of him. "I know the interstate on-ramp has to be somewhere around Virginia Street because I used that exit ramp," he mumbled.

"Yes, the interstate is to your left," she instructed. "Go ahead to Virginia Street at the second signal light. Turn left there. We should see Interstate 80 signs."

When they stopped for the red light at Virginia Street, Greg checked his rearview mirror and saw Zach swerve around the corner and stop at the red light behind them.

When the light changed green and they turned left onto Virginia Street, Valerie pointed. "There's the I–80 sign, Greg. Stay to your left."

In all the traffic congestion, several cars now separated their car from the stalker's car as everyone lined up left in their approach to the interstate. All cars waited for the red light to change. When the green light flashed on, all cars turned and headed for the on-ramp.

After Greg and Valerie drove down the ramp and merged onto the interstate, Greg tromped the gas pedal, turned on his turning indicator, and sped out into the far left lane.

At the same time, he glanced into his rearview mirror and saw Zach speed out into the left lane behind them.

The stalker was gaining on them, so Greg pressed harder on the accelerator. When his speedometer hit 75 M.P.H., the gap between the two cars held steady.

Speeding west on I–80, Greg quickly noticed the Sierra mountain range looming straight ahead of them.

"This is no good, Val," he declared. "We're already out of town and heading into the mountains. We've got to get back into the city. We can only shake him on city streets. I'm exiting the next ramp and maybe we'll find a road back into the city."

Greg exited at the next off-ramp, turned left, and raced through the first green signal light.

The stalker's car peeled left at the end of the exit ramp, only forty to fifty yards behind, and shot ahead to catch up to them.

At the next red signal light, Greg saw no cars coming toward him, so he floored the gas pedal and swerved, skidding sideways onto the dirt shoulder. Upon meeting pavement, his spinning tires jolted them forward. They barreled east, back toward the downtown streets.

In the rearview mirror, Greg watched a cloud of dust billow from behind Zach's car as he skidded off the road while making his left turn at the signal light. He quickly regained friction and bolted after them.

Seconds later, Valerie noticed an Amtrak train running next to them on their immediate right side. It traveled parallel to them moving easterly.

"Greg, there's a train running next to us. You'd better look for a crossing up ahead."

"I see it. I'm looking for the flashing lights."

Cars were stopped at the upcoming red signal light, but there was a fork in the road. He wasn't about to wait for Zach, so without stopping to yield, Greg bore off onto the right fork. It was an older two-lane blacktop that appeared to lead back into the city.

As they sped under a trestle, the train passed overhead. Now the train was on their left side.

The stalker remained directly behind, bearing down on them.

Up ahead, another traffic light. The green arrow pointed left, so Greg stepped on the gas. At the intersection, when Greg turned left, the arrow turned yellow, then red.

Zach's car shot into the intersection on the red arrow, skidding sideways into his left turn. A driver slammed his brakes to avoid hitting him broadside. All cars screeched to a halt with loud honking horns.

When Greg raced over the railroad tracks ahead of the crossing lights, they looked to their left to see the train's large brilliant headlight bearing down on them, then heard the overpowering blare of the train's whistle.

Instantly the red lights began flashing, but the stalker flew across the tracks and closed in on their back bumper, whereupon Greg swerved right at the next corner and shot ahead.

"I've got an idea, Val. I'll make a sharp right at the next block and see if we can make it across the tracks ahead of the train. If we make it, we'll have the train between us and the maniac. We'll be home free."

At the corner, he turned sharply to the right; the red crossing lights were flashing, but the gates had not dropped.

Another blare of the train's whistle ignited his move. Greg floored the gas pedal and they shot ahead.

Just then, the stalker slid around the corner behind them within yards from their back bumper.

While darting across the tracks, the converging engine charged their car with a steady deafening whistle. Less than sixty feet from the side of their car, blazing blinding light burned before Valerie's eyes. The first gate dropped behind them.

Frozen with terror, she threw her hands up to the side of her face and shrieked, "It's going to smash us!"

The second gate was dropping, but in a split second they were over the tracks. The second gate dropped only scant inches from their back end.

"Whew! We made it," Greg gasped while stopping the car.

Suddenly, behind them came a loud crash followed by screeching metal.

Greg and Valerie winced, then blocked their ears from the piercing, ear-splitting squeal of metal against metal.

After many seconds, when the screeching subsided, they unblocked their ears and turned around to see the train slowing to a stop.

When they stared at each other in disbelief, Valerie said, "It sounds like that crazy fool tried to drive around the gates. They barely missed us."

"You're right, Val. I saw him get around the first gate, but he never made the second gate. He got crunched head on. Finally you're rid of him. I hope he's a goner."

"Do you think so?" She grinned. "He was nothing but an obsessed maniac. I hope it's finally over for me, Greg. It's the only way I could ever be free of him."

"If he's dead, it IS over, Val. You're free. Now let's get out of here before the place is crawling with cops. I'm sure we were seen by passengers."

They drove away, merging quickly into city traffic, and minutes later they cruised the residential streets in the southern sector of the city.

Had they been seen by passengers, Greg wanted to return the rented car as soon as possible, so in a while, they traveled east toward the airport.

Before long they were at the airport, returned the car, and proceeded to the parking lot for his motorcycle. After they hopped aboard and motored from the airport, they began cruising the streets once again. Now they felt safe and wanted to calm down after their harrowing chase. They relaxed with one another to explore some of the city.

With the warm breeze blowing through her hair, Valerie squeezed his waist, saying, "Oh, Greg, I'm so happy, I could scream."

"Go ahead, scream it from the housetops." He laughed.

"I'm free! I'm free!" she yelled. "I've never felt so free."

"Let's hope you really are free," he cautioned. "We don't know yet if he survived."

Later, south of the city, Greg followed the road up a hill to a viewpoint where he turned off the road and parked the bike. They hopped off the Harley and sauntered over to a nearby bench to admire the view of the sprawling valley and downtown city skyline.

A warm summer breeze graced their faces as they sat down in quiet, serene solitude.

"It's a beautiful view, isn't it, Greg?"

"Yes, very beautiful and interesting, and an ideal spot for you to reveal your deep, dark secrets. You owe me that. You promised, remember?"

"Yes, I owe you and I promised you, Greg, and now that it's all over, I can tell you everything. I'm so happy again.

"To begin with, I'm an escapee from a mental clinic in Columbia, South Carolina."

"What! I don't believe it."

"It's true. I was remanded there by a judge, but I'm not crazy, Greg."

"Of course you're not crazy. I know that. How the hell did that happen?"

"When I was a young girl, I confused sex with love, and because I always wanted to be married and have babies, I thought by letting a guy get me pregnant, he'd marry me. It never worked.

"I learned that fact the hard way. They were attracted to my beauty, but wanted no part of marriage. My beauty became my handicap. Sometimes I hate my looks. They've always caused me trouble between my emotions and desires.

"My doctor suggested professional help, which ultimately led into the court system through the social services.

"At first, I was declared an unfit mother because I couldn't support the babies. Then one thing led to another, and with all the social workers, psychoanalysis, and red tape, the court recommended me for a few months of analysis in the mental clinic.

"I thought it unfair and was adamant and resistant, but it didn't matter what I thought.

"Those few months turned into twelve months. I believed I was trapped in the system and they weren't going to let me out. I knew I wasn't crazy and I wasn't going to let them drive me crazy, so I planned an escape."

"What happened to the babies?"

"Two were adopted by foster parents. I miscarried the third," she replied, then continued, "Last spring I stowed away on a delivery truck and made my escape. I've been on the run ever since."

"How about the creep and why Norway?"

"He was the main reason for my escape." She sneered. "He was one of the clinic attendants. He raped me several times. To him, it was fun and games. He felt power because his position was a great cover-up for his sexual perversion. I loathed and hated him."

"Didn't you report him to the clinic authorities?"

"Certainly, from the first time it happened, but they only sloughed it off with disbelief. I was supposed to be mental, remember? Who would believe me? It was supposed to be why I was there in the first place. He laughed at all of it.

"After I escaped, because he was so obsessed with me, he quit his job at the clinic and set out to find me. He acquired a false police badge and started playing detective for his cover-up."

"So why Norway?"

"My relatives are all Norwegian, remember? Through friends here in the States, I obtained a passport and flight ticket for Norway. I thought by leaving the country and visiting my relatives, I'd be rid of him."

"Then you never were a schoolteacher. Everything you told me in Norway was made up."

She drooped her head, nodded slightly, and said, "Yes, I'm ashamed about all that, Greg. I used whatever it took in Norway to complete my escape from the clinic and that pervert, but somehow he followed me and found me there. He must have dug into the clinic's records for addresses of family members and relatives."

"So who drove the speedboat in Bergen?"

"He's my cousin, Lasse, and he does have a summer home on a small island outside Bergen's harbor. When he was sure I was safe, he helped me get back to the States, again."

"And you no sooner arrived back in the States then you got yourself pregnant. What am I supposed to think, Val?"

"I'm not a whore, Greg! What I've learned from all this mess is that I have a misperception of love and sex, but oh, how I've learned. Indeed, I've learned the hard way what a fool I've been. All I've ever wanted was to be loved and married."

Yearning for his belief and trust, she searched his eyes and spoke sincerely, "It's only from you, Greg, that I've ever felt real love for the very first time in my life. That's the honest truth. No man has ever cared about me as you have or treated me so tenderly with so much respect. You didn't even know me and yet you helped and protected me without my answering up to you. No man has ever done anything like that for me. You really are a good man. I fell in love with you and will always love you for that."

She reached up, kissed him warmly on the lips, and whispered, "I'll always love you. Greg, even if you don't want me anymore. Because I lied to you, I don't deserve a man like you. I don't deserve your love. I'm sorry for all those lies, but I couldn't bear to lose you; and if I've lost you because of them, I deserve that, too. I've always done everything wrong, anyway, starting with men, because lies will never work. I'm guilty of loving and wanting you too much, I guess. Thank you so very much, Greg, for saving my life and giving it back to me."

Greg grabbed both of her shoulders and shook her gently, saying, "Stop it, Val! There you go again. You're a good woman, but you've victimized yourself with wrong decisions. We both know you're not crazy. You got yourself messed up in psychological mumbo-jumbo and paperwork caused by the authorities for which you should NEVER have been institutionalized. Then because of it you're victimized, raped, harassed, and stalked by a pervert from the institution. You are a victim of circumstances, a fugitive of fear, but hopefully it's all over with and you've got your life back. You need time to get your life in order, Val."

He embraced and kissed her, leaned back on the bench, and squeezed her shoulder.

It was turning dark when she snuggled into his side and said, "Look, Greg, the city lights are coming on. Reno is beautiful at night."

"And with a beautiful troll at my side, it makes those lights burn that much brighter." He grinned.

He looked her in the eye and winked and pulled her closer to his side, saying, "What you just told me is very difficult for a woman to admit. Now I see why it was so hard for you to tell me, but that's honesty and I do believe you. Thanks for finally telling me, Val."

They stopped talking for a long while and simply relaxed and admired the lights of the city.

Finally Greg broke the silence. "Let's do the city, Val. Let's celebrate with drinks and gambling. What do you say?"

"I'm for that!" she exclaimed. "I'm ready to get drunk."

He smiled. "You're already drunk—with happiness."

"You bet I am. Let's go."

Before long, they rode under the famous arch stating THE BIGGEST LITTLE CITY IN THE WORLD on Reno's brightly lit Virginia Street.

After reserving a room in a downtown motel, they spent the next few hours playing slot machines with no luck. Greg tried the blackjack and dice tables, again with no luck. They didn't care. They shared a closer relationship now. She was free and they were having real fun together for the first time. They laughed, drank, and gambled the evening away.

When they retired to their room around eleven o'clock, Valerie flicked on the TV immediately.

The newscaster's top story was the train wreck.

"Our top story tonight is a train wreck in downtown Reno," said the newscaster. "A man was killed when a train hit his car in west Reno. His identity is still unknown at this time. Eye witnesses observed the car trying to drive around the gates at a train crossing, but because the train was unable to stop, it smashed headlong into the car, killing the driver. Apparently the car was chasing another car in a race to beat the train across the tracks. The first car barely escaped being hit also. The second car wasn't as lucky. The driver died on impact. At this hour, police are still trying to identify the driver."

Valerie stood, shaking her head at the TV, and said, "That crazy fool. He was so obsessed. He did die. At last, I'm free of him. Now I can get on with my life."

"Yes, you can, Val. He'll NEVER harass you anymore. He's out of your life forever."

She headed straight to the bathroom for a shower while Greg flopped backward on the bed, flicked off the lamp, and clasped his hands behind his head to watch the rest of the news.

A short time later, Valerie appeared in the bathroom doorway, her figure silhouetted by the glowing light behind.

In bra and panties, she leaned against the doorjamb and stated, "The bathroom is all yours, Mr. Ghost."

Later, after his shower, he joined her in bed and murmured, "Come back to Rapid City with me, Val."

"I can't do that right now, Greg. In order to escape from Zach, I had to escape from the clinic and now that my escape from him is over, I have to get back to the clinic. Don't you see? I have to get my life straightened out."

"Now you're talking crazy. You intend to walk right back into that psychological mumbo-jumbo and authoritative quagmire. You already know your escape goes against you. It'll be more entrapment for you, Val. Not to mention that the same thing could happen all over again with another Zach. You'll always be accused of inviting rape with your illicit pregnancies being their airtight cover-up for raping you. You may never get out of that place."

"It's the chance I have to take, Greg. The purpose of my escape was to escape from Zach and that's over with. It's pointless to run now. I can't keep running for the rest of my life, whether it's from Zach or the authorities. I can't live that way, looking over my shoulder all the time. I have to go back and fight for my freedom, Greg. I have to straighten it all out. It's the only way I'll ever have complete freedom. Can you understand that?"

"Yes, I can understand your thinking. I guess it's the only way you'll ever have peace of mind and freedom, but because I realize you're a victim of circumstance, I'm afraid to let you go."

Valerie touched his mouth gently with her fingers. "I've never known more peace nor felt more love from any man, Greg," she whispered softly.

She wrapped her arms around his neck, pressed her warm full breasts against his hard hairy chest, and hugged him tightly.

"Oh, Greg, I love you so much. Do you think someday we can be together and live forever and ever with each other."

With reassurance, he squeezed her tiny waist firmly with his muscular arms and replied, "I know we can, Val. Now I want you and need you more than ever before."

He tightened his grip, pulled her in against his warm body, and kissed her long and hard. With heavy breathing, their bodies squirmed and writhed with delight; they moaned in ecstasy.

He broke their embrace, saying, "And what is all this leading up to, beautiful troll?"

She batted her eyes, lifted one eyebrow, and cooed impishly, "Up to whatever you'd like, ghosty."

Then she closed her eyes and tilted her head back submissively.

Instantly he smothered her neck with kisses, nibbling her earlobes gently. When their eager, open mouths met, their fluttering tongues flicked around one another. Impassioned and impatient, he unsnapped her bra, and while fondling her breasts, wildly kissed her neck again. His warm kisses slowly moved down her neck and chest until he caressed and kissed each soft breast gently. Enraptured with the fondling and kissing, she pressed his head tight to her bosom and ran her hands up the back of his head into his thick crop of black hair. She tingled and writhed with excitement.

While stroking his hair with closed eyes, she murmured, "Oh, Greg, I feel your love."

Greg continued to go lower, caressing her stomach with the tip of his tongue until he reached her panties. As he rubbed her buttocks, the slippery feel of the nylon aroused him more. With increasing frustration, he slid her panties down her legs with the tip of his tongue following along down the inside of her thighs. Her body shivered and quivered as her underwear dropped to the floor. He kissed her thighs and calves and ran the tip of his tongue up to her stomach again, where he pressed his body tight against her.

When their anxious, open mouths met once more, their bodies squirmed; their legs sliding up and down against one another.

She caressed his back, slowly running her hands down into his jockey briefs.

"Turnabout is always fair play," she purred sexily, and as she slid his underwear down his legs, she added, "ummm, I didn't know ghosts had such warm hairy legs."

"And I didn't know trolls had such alluring sexy bodies."

He kicked off his underwear, swallowed her in his arms, and squeezed her tighter. They kissed with abandon; their tongues fluttered with anticipation. Their frustrated bodies yearned and ached to be sexually gratified, and with sexual desire and arousal at its peak, they writhed in loving, euphoric intimacy.

Later, entwined in each other's arms, they lay silent and drifted off to sleep.

Around 6 A.M., Valerie awoke and carefully slipped out of his arms and off the bed. She didn't want to waken him.

She dressed quickly, and when she was ready to leave, she sat down at the small table to write Greg a short note on the motel's stationery.

It read:

Dear Pieface,

Yes, I have to leave you again while you're sleeping, but this time it's for positive reasons. I promise you, I'm not running FROM my life; I'm running TO my life. With all the love in my heart remember, luv, now I'll always be running TO you, not FROM you.

I left before you wakened because I couldn't bear to look into those irresistible, kind, and caring brown eyes staring at me while you pleaded with me to go home with you. I would only cry, weaken, and break down and end up going with you. I wouldn't have the strength to resist you.

Don't worry. I'm returning to the institution, and from time to time, I'll phone you to keep you abreast of my situation.

I'm hoping when I reach the end of the long dark tunnel, you'll be standing there, bathed in sunlight, waiting to greet me with open arms, a hug, and huge kiss.

My heart will live and ache for that wonderful happy day in the hope that it's very, very soon, if not sooner.

Till then, I'll hold your precious love captive within my heart.

You remain my ghostly lover forever.

Your loving troll,
Valerie

When she ended her note, she kissed him softly on his cheek and left the paper on the night stand.

Picking up her suitcase, she walked to the door, but stopped to turn around for one last look at his handsome face sleeping soundly on the pillow.

With a slight wave, she blew a kiss and whispered, "Bye-bye, luv. See you soon."

She opened the door, left abruptly, and hurried to the phone booth standing next to the motel office.

In a short time, her taxi arrived, but as she was getting into the cab, Greg awoke to see she'd left him again.

While trying to pull on his pants, he hobbled to the door, and upon flinging it open, he immediately saw Valerie's head through the rear window of the car.

She sat on the back seat and as the taxicab drove away, Greg ran after it, shouting, "Valerie! Valerie, don't go!"

She heard his shouts, turned around, and when she peered out the rear window, tears streamed down both cheeks. She cried irrepressibly, blew a kiss, and waved. Her silent moving lips read, "I love you."

His eyes filled when he stopped running. He could only stand and wave and wipe tears from the corners of his eyes.

He knew she was on her way to the airport, but he didn't chase after her. He knew he had to let her go.

Returning to his room, he picked up her note from the night stand, and as he stood reading her loving words, he couldn't hold back the tears. He desired her more than ever now.

Later, after checking out of the motel, Greg drove out onto Interstate 80 and traveled east, away from the city. Once again, he headed home without Valerie. Dejected and empty and with Reno to his back, he cruised slowly along the interstate. He knew it would be a long and depressing ride home. He left the city in the hills behind him.

Zach's dead and out of her life now, he thought. *She's free. She didn't have to go back to the institution. She could have come home with me. The authorities wouldn't have found her up north in South Dakota. Damn those people! She's so vulnerable. I believe I love her now, I know I love her and I can't live without her anymore. I know we can make it together.*

All the way home, mixed emotions and nagging thoughts constantly ate at him, but inevitably the two-day journey ended. He arrived back in Rapid City to return to work.

In the days that followed, his teaching and coaching deferred his persistent thoughts of Valerie, but only during the daytime; at nighttime, he thought only of her. He wondered and worried as to how she was doing and whether or not she was safe.

XI

The football team had already won the first three games of the new fall season, so during the ensuing weeks, Greg worked hard with his players in practice. He wanted them sharp and psyched up for all their Friday night games.

It was the middle of the week, sometime around 6 P.M. Greg and his parents had just sat down to enjoy supper when the telephone rang.

Greg conversed with his dad about the day's practice while his mother got up and answered the phone.

"Hello?" she replied. "Yes, this is the Ericsen residence. Who is this? Yes, he's sitting right here."

Greg stopped talking and looked up at his mother.

"Yes, I'll give him to you. Hold on for just a moment, please."

A look of concern crossed her face as she held the phone out to Greg and said, "She asked for you, dear. It's a woman, but I couldn't make out her name. She's crying and very hysterical."

Greg jumped up from his chair, took the receiver from his mother's hand, and said, "Hello, this is Greg. Who is this?"

"Greg, this is Jessica!" she screeched. "Valerie's dead!"

Greg's jaw dropped.

With twisted expression, in shocked disbelief he yelled, "What are you talking about, Jessica? She can't be dead, I was with her only a few weeks ago in Reno."

Jessica screamed hysterically, "But Greg, they found her body only hours ago in an alleyway behind a bar."

"Where? What bar? What alleyway?" he shouted.

"Her body was found behind a bar in Columbia. I don't know the name of the bar, but it's near the clinic."

"I can't believe that. Why would she be in that bar? She went back purposely to turn herself in to those mental health people. It can't be her. It's got to be mistaken identity. They've got her mixed up with someone else."

"No, Greg, it's true. It is Valerie's body. She came here to Charleston first to tell me she was returning to the clinic. I drove her to Columbia myself."

"When did you drive her there?"

"Just a few days after she arrived in Charleston. She was such a good and generous person," she sobbed. "I can't stand it, Greg. She was my friend. Why did this happen to her? Why would anyone kill her? I don't understand."

Greg bellowed, "No, it can't be her! It's not Valerie! She can't be dead. I don't believe it."

Shocked with anger he dropped the phone, ran to the front door, and threw it wide open. With the receiver dangling from its cord, he stormed out of the house and dashed to the garage where he shoved open the door and hopped on his Harley. Fury burned in his eyes when he strapped on his helmet, started up the bike, and squealed out of the garage down into the street.

Jamming gears, he wheelied the front wheel before reaching the first corner. Skidding sideways in his turn, he straightened up and jolted ahead to the interstate.

He didn't know where he was going. He just wanted to keep on driving until he dropped. So for the next few hours, Greg covered Rapid City's whole surrounding area. He drove the interstate and around and around the city's streets. He wouldn't accept any thoughts of Valerie being dead. He only wanted to be alone with his happy living memories of her.

When the hours grew late, he eventually rode up on Skyline Drive to stop and park the bike at a turnout. He was very much alone, so he climbed up on a large boulder to sit and stare at the city lights below him. Within seconds, he doubled over with his head between his knees and the tears flowed without constraint. He wept uncontrollably. He loved and wanted her.

Late into the night, Greg sat as a lonely, slumped figure slouched over on the huge rock.

It was after midnight when he came down off the boulder and climbed back onto his Harley. He continued driving west toward Keystone until he turned off the highway onto a side dirt road. When he spotted a flat, open patch of grass, he stopped and parked the bike along the shoulder.

With tears streaming down his cheeks, he wandered into the clearing of grass to lay down on his back and stare up into the dark; blackness covered the night sky.

For several hours, he lay there weeping incessantly until exhausted, drained, and emptied from the shock of her death, Greg fell asleep.

He awoke to an early bright sun, and as he rose slowly from the ground, he snatched a blade of grass to chew on while sauntering back to his bike. He didn't want to return home right away. He had to make plans. He knew he'd have to face up to her death somehow and wanted to drive immediately to

Charleston to see Jessica. He had to know what happened to Valerie and why she died.

While he straddled the bike, strapped on his helmet, and started the motor, he convinced himself that he had to definitely go to Charleston to personally confirm her death. He had to see for himself that she was out of his life forever.

Later in the morning, he returned to the house, wiped his face and eyes, and entered the front door.

"Where have you been, son?" his mother asked. "Your father and I worried about you all night. We haven't slept a wink. I spoke more with Jessica, trying to console her before she hung up. A sudden death is always a shock and so difficult to accept. I know you loved her very much, Greg. It must be terrible for you."

"I cried all night, Mom, and now I have to go to Charleston to see for myself that she's really dead. I can't go on until I do. I can't teach. I can't coach. I can't do anything until I get some answers. It's the only way I'll be able to accept and face up to the reality."

His father replied, "I fully understand what you're saying and going through, son. You have to go there and see for yourself to overcome it."

That night, Greg called Tom to reveal Valerie's numbing death. Tom, also being shocked, still managed to console his friend in an overwhelming time of grief and despair.

That weekend, after another winning Friday for the team's fourth straight win, Greg bought his round-trip ticket to Charleston.

When he phoned Jessica to inform her he'd arrive that Monday evening, she said she'd meet him at the airport and invited him to stay at her apartment. He graciously accepted her offer.

Afterward he again made arrangements with Coach Richardsen to handle all practices in the forthcoming week.

Monday morning didn't come too soon for Greg. His father drove him to the airport, where he caught the early flight to Charleston.

When the plane landed that evening at the Charleston airport, Jessica was there to greet him with flowing tears. She wept openly as they embraced one another with comforting hugs along with fond kisses on the cheeks.

"It's not fair, Greg," she cried. "Just when you two were coming together and her life was straightening out, she has to die. It's not right. It's all so wrong and unfair, Greg."

"I need to know what happened, Jessica. I have to find out all the facts and details."

"So far, the only fact is that they found her body in the alleyway behind that bar in Columbia. If there are any more facts or details, the police aren't releasing them."

"So no information or reports were given to the newspapers? Was it on TV?"

"I only saw it mentioned on one Charleston newscast. It was mostly covered on Columbia television with a write-up in Columbia's newspapers. I cut out the clipping for you, Greg."

"Thanks. I'll want to read it, but I also want to drive up to Columbia and talk to the bartender who was on duty that night. He might know more than what he told the police. Would you mind loaning me your car, Jessica, so I can drive up there for a day?"

"Of course not, Greg. I can't get away from the job, but I can always catch a ride to work. You can have the car anytime you want it; stay overnight if you like. I want you up there nosing around. Maybe you'll get some real answers."

"Has there been a funeral yet?"

"Yes, after the autopsy, the police released the body and there was a small service at the funeral home. She's buried in the family plot with her mother and father. I'll take you there now, Greg, if you like."

"Yes, I'd like that, Jessica. I'll also want to know the results of the autopsy."

She wept as her lips quivered. "All they told us was that she was shot twice in the back of the head. Why, Greg? Why would anyone want to do that to Valerie?"

His eyes filled as he said, "Hopefully, we'll find out, because I damn sure want some answers."

Putting an arm around her waist, he squeezed her tight while they walked toward baggage claim. After retrieving his suitcase, they continued on to Jessica's car in the parking area.

On their way to the cemetery, Greg asked Jessica to stop at a florist shop to buy a bouquet of roses.

At the cemetery, she led him to Valerie's grave site where they stood for a few moments staring at her gravestone. She quickly turned her back to the stone and threw herself into his arms, weeping, but he couldn't console her. She ran off to the car to wait for him.

Greg knelt on one knee, laid the roses on her grave, and said several silent prayers.

"As Jessica says, it wasn't fair for you to die, Valerie. Why? Why now, Val? Just when you were beginning to get your life straightened out, this happens. I intend to find out what happened to you."

Tears poured from his eyes when he continued with hesitant, trembling lips.

"When I found you in Charleston, I never told you I love you, only because I wasn't sure myself. Now I know I did love you, Val. I want you to know that and believe it. It's true. I know we could have made it together. We would have made it happen for us, luv. I'll never forget you, Valerie. You really were a terrible victim of circumstance in your short life. I know, wherever you are, you're happier than you were here on earth. You've finally found peace and happiness, I'm sure. Goodbye for now, luv, and maybe someday we'll be reunited in the hereafter. I really did love you, Valerie, but I think you already knew that in your heart. So long, my beautiful troll. Your loving memory will remain forever in my mind and heart."

Praying silently for a few more minutes, he then stood up and with bowed head, wiped his face with his hands and strolled slowly back to the car dwelling on her memory.

Still feeling the numbing effects of her shocking death, those solemn moments weighed heavily on Greg and Jessica.

They drove from the cemetery to a nearby restaurant to eat supper and talk about their good times spent with Valerie. Afterward they went to Jessica's apartment and spent the rest of the evening in conversation concerning Valerie's mysterious death and watching television. Jessica provided Greg with his sofa bedding, and since she had the morning shift, they both retired early.

Early the next morning, Greg drove Jessica to work, and with her as his waitress, he ate breakfast at her restaurant.

After breakfast, he set out on the short trip to Columbia, and when he arrived, he found the mental health clinic to be a large building within the confines of the inner city.

Upon entering the building, his first purpose was to approach the division of records to see if Valerie had checked back into the clinic. He learned that she had reported back and was indeed listed as a patient.

That afternoon he visited the bar where her body was discovered to have a few beers and examine the alleyway.

In casual conversation with the bartender and his usual daytime customers, the issue of her murder was still the topic of discussion, but Greg learned nothing from them.

He phoned the police station and spoke with the detective assigned to the case, who related to Greg that all information pertaining to the case had already been released to the media, it was an ongoing investigation and so far no new evidence was forthcoming.

Greg did not give his name. He didn't want his name linked directly to Valerie, nor did he need his life disrupted with the police investigation since he wasn't connected in any way to her mysterious murder.

Later that evening, he returned to the bar to talk to the second shift bartender along with the evening customers to see if they could offer any information.

All he learned was that on the night of her murder, Valerie was in the bar drinking with a dark-eyed, blond-haired man in one of the booths. Neither the bartender nor the customers knew her or the man with whom she was drinking. They were both strangers to the bar. They didn't stay long and left the premises after two drinks. That was all everyone in the bar could tell him, which only created more questions in his mind concerning her presence in the bar that night.

He thought, *Who was the man she drank with in the bar, and why was she outside the clinic drinking in a bar anyway?*

When Greg left the bar, an elderly female patron followed him outside to his car and asked, "Are you a relative?"

"No, I'm not," Greg replied, bewildered. "Why do you ask?"

"Oh, that's too bad," she said while walking away.

He thought quickly and blurted, "But I was her fiancé, ma'am. I loved her very much."

"Well, in that case," she replied, returning to his side. "I have something for you."

"You do?"

Opening her purse, she handed him a small sealed envelope, explaining, "They got into an argument in the booth, and when I looked over at them, this bracelet happened to fly off her wrist and slide under a table. She was unaware she lost it."

"A bracelet?" he quizzed.

"Yes, it's a charm bracelet. The charms are faces of some kind," she answered.

"They must be presidents' faces. Those same faces are carved into the mountain at Mount Rushmore, ma'am. I bought that bracelet for her when we were there."

"Whatever," she replied. "I've never liked politicians anyway, so I wouldn't know. Then I've given it to the right person after all. You're the rightful owner. It's yours, my boy."

"But why didn't you return it to her?"

"Because it's so dark in the damn place, I didn't see exactly where it slid to. I found it by accident after they'd left. At first I was going to keep it myself, but decided to give it to any family members who might come snooping around. Since you bought it for her, you're the one who should have it back."

"Thank you, ma'am, very much. What can I do to repay you?"

"Well." She smiled, "You could buy me a drink."

"Great." He grinned, pulling out a twenty dollar bill. "Here's a twenty. They're all on me."

She snatched the twenty dollar bill from his hand and said, "And much obliged to you too, sir. Thank you. I'm sorry you lost your loved one so terribly. I lost my sweetie, too, to the sauce many years ago. We all get over it in time. Bye-bye now."

As she turned and headed back to the bar, Greg called, "Thanks again, ma'am, but I didn't get your name?"

With her back to him, she kept walking and lifted one hand, waving him off, and called back, "No names, my boy. I want no involvements. Let it be."

When she entered the bar, Greg ripped open the envelope, held up the bracelet by its broken chain, and whispered, "It's the same bracelet, all right."

He saw no need to give it to the police, so he dropped it back into the envelope and stuffed it into his pocket.

On the drive back to Charleston, many questions crossed his mind, especially that big persistent one. *Why was she outside the clinic?*

Although he arrived back at her apartment very late, Jessica was awake and waiting for him. She was anxious to learn of any new information, but was saddened and disappointed when Greg could offer no new information.

So for the next hour, they sat at the kitchen table, drank coffee, and analyzed her suspicious behavior on the last night of Valerie's life. Of course there were no answers, so the analysis remained moot. They retired for the night.

The next morning, Greg again dropped Jessica off at the restaurant and said he'd return at lunch time.

When he left her, he drove directly to the dirt road that led to Valerie's secret magnolia tree.

At the tree, he lay on his back on the grass, closed his eyes, and smiled broadly as he visualized her dancing around the tree, then saw her image of happiness when they danced around the tree together.

Teasing, laughter, and sexual euphoria flashed through his mind when he thought of their shared private intimacy in the motel at Myrtle Beach.

He savored the seclusion and memorable thoughts of their fleeting happiness, but eventually he had to leave. So when he got to his feet and before he departed through the little path, he turned around for one last look at her favorite magnolia tree. It seemed lonely and sad and so forlorn standing there thin and drab without a pretty white dress under an overcast sky, as if it knew that neither her friend, Valerie, nor Valerie's friend, Greg, would ever return to visit her.

He left her quiet sanctuary of childhood dreams behind as he returned to the car and drove to his next stop, "California Dreaming."

While sitting at the bar, he lifted his glass slightly with a toast and thought, *Here's to us, Val, for the short loving relationship we did share; a loving memory that remains with us forever.*

Once again, he dwelled on images of her happiness: her shocked happy expression when he found her at the restaurant; their happy embrace and first ecstatic kiss; the camaraderie at her apartment; giggling and rolling kisses on the bed; the pirouetting of her Myrtle Beach outfit; Elvis song titles; the clasping of the friendship ring necklace around her neck; modeling her sweet grass hat; the laughter in the store when buying his beach clothes.

He smiled outwardly as he reminisced and thought of their many happy moments together. At times he gazed at the table where they sat eating lunch together; he imagined her beautiful face smiling at him. Those incredible blue eyes would remain etched in his mind forever.

He remained drinking at the bar for the rest of the morning, but when lunch time arrived, he left the restaurant to have lunch with Jessica.

At her restaurant, Jessica greeted him with the newspaper article about Valerie's murder. As he leaned on the counter reading the clipping, he overheard one of the waitresses remark, "I swear, that little boy sure loves banana splits."

Jessica replied, "It's his favorite dessert."

Greg paid little attention and remained absorbed in the article.

When he finished reading, Jessica pointed to the back of restaurant and said, "Do you see that little boy in that back booth? The one eating a banana split with those two elderly people?"

"Yes, I see him."

"Now you tell me who he looks like, Yankee."

Greg shrugged his shoulders, saying, "No one I know."

"Why you men can't see anything even when it's staring you right in the face, I'll never know. If the devil himself jumped up and slapped you in the face, you'd pay him no mind."

A burst of laughter followed from all the waitresses while Jessica playfully scolded, "Ah sweah, Yankee, can't you see that little boy is the spittin' image of his mama? Why that boy is Valerie's son. Now you get your pretty little fanny over there and take a closer look at him, ya hear."

"That's Valerie's son!" Greg exclaimed. "Val never told me about him. Where's he been living? How come he's here?"

Jessica continued, "He's been a ward of the court in a foster home. On her visitation days, she'd always bring him here for a banana split. He was her pride and joy. She was always so proud to show him off to all of us. She loved him so much and doted over him all the time. The court had hoped to return him to her custody someday, but now they've placed him in the guardianship of his Norwegian great-grandparents. He's in their care now.

"They're taking him to Norway this evening, and because they had time before departure, they brought him here for his ice cream. He wanted to come for one last banana split in loving memory of his mother and to say goodbye to us.

"The grandparents can't speak English, but I'm sure the boy would love to talk to you about his mother."

While Jessica was talking, Greg never took his eyes off the boy and said, "And I definitely want to talk to him, too. What's his name?"

"Kristian. C'mon, I'll introduce you."

When they walked up to their booth, Greg and Jessica smiled at the elderly couple with a nodding gesture. The couple smiled and nodded in return.

"Kristian, I want you to meet your mother's most dearest friend. This is Greg. Greg, meet Kristian."

As Greg extended his hand and looked down at the boy's face, he saw an immediate resemblance to Valerie. His dark blue eyes, chin, and mouth were the exact image of his mother.

"I'm very happy to meet you, Kristian."

The boy laid down his spoon, and as he shook Greg's hand, smiled broadly. "I'm glad to meet you too, Greg. Did you love my mother?"

"Yes indeed, I certainly did; very much so." Greg smiled warmly. "She was the most beautiful woman in this whole world."

"Nobody was more beautiful than my mom. Were you and Mom going to get married?"

"We were working on it very hard, Kristian. I know we would have made it happen."

"I miss her so much. Why did she have to die, Greg?"

"Well, we all have to die sometime, don't we? We just never know when or how. That's what we don't like, but we have to keep living; and we can live with all those wonderful happy memories of those we loved when they lived with us on earth."

Kristian puckered his lower lip, drooped his head, and said, "I hate Mom being dead. She was my best friend. Would you be my friend, Greg?"

"You bet, Kristian. I'm already your new friend, if you'll have me."

"Hey, that's great! We're friends right now, Greg," he exclaimed while anxiously shaking Greg's hand.

"Yes, we are, and now you have to promise me something, starting today."

"Anything," Kristian replied.

"I want your promise that you'll write to me from Norway now and then to tell me how you're doing in school and any new friends you make. Do you like sports?"

"I love soccer, and I promise I'll write to you, Greg. Will you write to me, too?"

Greg smiled. "That's an absolute guarantee. Put 'er there, partner."

While shaking hands again, Greg ruffled the boy's thick shock of hair hugged his shoulder reassuringly, and said, "Don't go away yet, Kristian. I'll be right back."

Greg left Kristian to join Jessica in a nearby booth where she handed him her pencil and a sheet torn from her order pad. Greg jotted down his mailing address, returned to Kristian, and handed him the slip of paper.

"That's my home address, so don't lose it," he said.

"No way!" cried Kristian as he folded the paper in squares and stuffed it down in his jeans pocket, adding, "You're my pen pal from now on, Greg."

Greg smiled, patted him on his shoulder, and returned to Jessica to say, "You're right, Jessica. He looks exactly like his mother; a handsome boy. Do you know why Valerie never told me about him?"

"She had reservations about it, Greg. She didn't know if you'd accept him. You know, being another man's son and all. At times she thought she'd surprise you, and other times, she thought she'd better not. She was betwixt and between."

"I suppose so, but she knew I'm a coach. I love kids. She shouldn't have worried about it. He's part of her, so I want to develop a close relationship with him. Wherever she is, I know she's happy I'm taking up with him. He's a fine boy."

Jessica's eyes filled when she replied, "She must be so happy, Greg. I know she would've loved for you to be his father. She was hoping for just that."

Shortly thereafter, Kristian and his great-grandparents got up to leave, and as they passed by Greg and Jessica, the boy smiled, then offered Jessica a big hug and goodbye kiss.

"Now, remember to write as soon as you get to Norway," instructed Greg. "I'll need your new address to write back to you, right?"

"Right, Greg, I'll write as soon as I get there. That's a promise."

"I'll be waiting, Kristian. Have a safe and fun plane trip. I promise you'll hear from me, too."

After Kristian said his goodbyes with hugs and kisses for all the waitresses, he and his new elderly guardians left the restaurant.

Needless to say, while Greg and Jessica ate lunch, their buzzing conversation centered around the delightful reality of Kristian.

After lunch, while waiting for Jessica to finish her shift, Greg spent the afternoon strolling Charleston's battery park and waterfront. He reminisced about his chance encounter with Ella Mae and her dog and how she directed him to Valerie. When he drove by Ella Mae's home, he had an urge to visit her but drove on by. He wasn't in the mood to discuss Valerie's death.

Later he stopped at one of the cocktail lounges where he had searched for her and sat for a long time drinking and listening to the juke box.

At one point, a record played Barbara Streisand's "The Way We Were." It was comforting for him to dwell on their relationship and the way they were.

He picked up Jessica at the end of her shift, ate supper at her apartment, talked for a while, and retired before midnight.

Early the next morning, Jessica drove him to the airport in plenty of time to catch his flight.

At departure time, they hugged and kissed one another fondly, but after their embrace, Jessica bowed her head and sobbed, "I suppose I'll never see you again. I'll miss you, Yankee, ya hear."

Greg lifted her chin with his finger and grinned. "Hey, hey, don't say that, tower of mush. We'll still keep contact. How about sending cards at Christmas and Easter; Valentine's, too? Let's promise to do that."

"I'd like that, Greg, but let's keep the Valentines silly and foolish, okay? I don't want my man getting jealous and going funny style. You know what I mean."

"You bet, Jessica, and the sillier the card the better." He laughed. "It's a great idea. It would be our way of keeping her memory alive between us; our three-way friendship. Friends forever, Jessica?"

"Friends forever, Yankee." She laughed as they slapped high fives.

A bear hug sealed their bonded friendship, with Jessica saying, "You're a good man, Greg, just like my man, Allen. I love both of you."

"Thanks, Jessica, but it's us men looking for you good women, too." He winked. "We're looking to find you and when we do, we snap you up like a crawdaddy snapping his claws at a mini fish."

She shoved him away, turned her head, and smiled sheepishly. "Go way with you, you flatterer, and it's not a crawdaddy. It's a crawdad. How do you come by all that suth'n talk, anyway, boy? You're a damn Yankee."

"Suth'n damn Yankee to you, ma'am." He laughed. "I'm working on it all the time. I'm being brainwashed by all you suth'n folk with all your wonderful southern hospitality."

Together they walked to the end of the line of people passing through the boarding gate. After handing his ticket to the agent, he stopped at the tunnel entrance and turned around to say, "Remember, we men will always find you good women."

With flowing tears when he showed snapping scissors claws with his fingers, she managed a smile, waved, and blew a kiss.

Greg blew a kiss in return and disappeared down the tunnel to the waiting aircraft.

That evening, Greg's father greeted him at the airport, and within the hour, they arrived home.

The next few weeks were solemn at the Ericsen household. Greg's parents shared their son's grief, but they knew that time cures, so it would only be a matter of time before their son's emotional scars would heal.

During that time, Greg had phoned Terri in Tupelo to inform her of Valerie's shocking, tragic death, and the football season ended successfully for Greg and his players. They had suffered only one loss all season. Greg saw to it that all team members received their letters at the football banquet. He and Kristian wrote each other regularly, and Christmas seemed to come quickly that year.

For a Christmas present, Greg shipped Kristian an electronic soccer game. Kristian sent Greg a warm Norwegian stocking hat.

Throughout the following year, their pen pal relationship grew stronger; their letter writing more frequent.

At Thanksgiving, Kristian's envelope bore a new return address, and inside his letter read:

Dear Greg,

I have been assigned to a new foster home in Oslo. Grandpa has become ill. He's in the hospital for an operation. It's for a bad kidney

194

or something like that. So Grandpa and Grandma had to give up their guardianship of me. They're very old.

Right now there are four of us here at my new home. So far it's okay. Since I'll be attending a new school, I'll have to make new friends. Everything is all new and kind of lonely without Grandma and Grandpa. I miss them both.

I'm wondering if I could ask a big favor of you, but you don't have to do it if you don't want to. I won't be mad or anything.

Could you, perhaps, come and spend Christmas with me this year? It would be so great if you could come.

My foster parents are having a big Christmas dinner with gifts and everything. Family and friends are also invited. The other kids have friends and relatives to invite, but all my friends and relatives are up north now. I haven't anyone to invite except you, Greg.

I would be so happy and grateful if you could come and visit me for Christmas. We would have a great time together. I would be so proud to show off my best friend from America to my new foster family.

Of course, I'll be disappointed if you can't make it, but I will understand, because I know you're very busy being a school teacher and coach and all.

Please answer soon so I can let my new foster family know.

Even if you can't come, I promise I won't be mad. You're still my best friend.

As always, with friendship and love,

your best friend and pen pal,
Kristian

While reading the letter, love and heavy emotion welled within Greg for Valerie's son. His eyes filled for there was no doubt or hesitation in Greg's mind. He'd make the necessary arrangements immediately to spend Christmas with Kristian.

When he informed his parents he'd be spending Christmas in Norway with Kristian, they were thrilled to hear the news. They knew it would mean so much to the boy. They would have a wonderful Christmas together.

Greg promptly phoned the airlines to reserve a seat for Oslo on the evening flight of December twenty-third.

That same day, he wrote Kristian to accept his invitation and that he'd be honored to be a guest at his foster family's home on Christmas. He informed him he'd arrive in Oslo on December 24, Christmas Eve.

So in addition to Thanksgiving and all of the holiday shopping and excitement, Greg now prepared for his spontaneous trip to Oslo. Needless to say, December 23 arrived swiftly.

Early that morning, Greg's parents saw him off at Rapid City's airport, where he caught his flight to Newark International Airport.

In Newark, Greg easily made his connection to SAS airlines and was now flying to Oslo, Norway, to spend Christmas with Kristian.

XII

Greg felt his arm being shaken gently. Stirring listlessly, he opened his eyes to stare directly into two almond-shaped, chocolate-brown, friendly eyes staring back at him.

His flight attendant smiled graciously. "Sir, we are now in our final descent. Please fasten your seat belt. We will land in Oslo shortly."

"What time is it?" he asked.

"It's 7:40 A.M. We'll be on the ground in approximately twenty minutes."

"Thank you."

Greg fastened his seat belt, leaned back, and rested his head on the headrest. Turning his head to one side, he slid up the window shade to gaze out at the passing clouds and early morning sunlight.

Soon I'll be seeing Kristian again, he thought. *It'll be nice to see him and how he's doing in his new home.* A slight smile crossed his mouth while thinking, *It'll be a fun Christmas for both of us. We can get to know one another better and strengthen our friendship. It'll be interesting to observe any of his mother's traits and how much he favors her.*

When the aircraft touched down, an attendant spoke into the intercom, "Good morning and welcome to Oslo. It's 8 A.M. We'll be arriving at the gate shortly. Please keep your seat belts fastened until the aircraft has completely stopped. We hope you enjoy your Christmas here in Norway. Thank you for choosing SAS and have a very merry Christmas."

After deplaning, Greg retrieved his luggage, hailed a taxi, and directed the driver to the Bonderheimen Hotel in downtown Oslo. It was the same hotel—comfortable and moderate and short blocks to the city center—where he and Tom stayed only a short eighteen months before.

Riding into the city, he once again enjoyed Norway's unique beauty. On a bright sunny morning, its rugged snowy terrain provided a continuous flow of picturesque images and postcard snapshots.

In due time they arrived at the hotel with Greg paying the driver his fare. After giving a generous tip and "Merry Christmas," he picked up his luggage from the curb and entered the hotel.

The desk clerk confirmed his reservation, issued him a room key, and upon entering the room, Greg stowed his luggage and lay on the bed for a short rest.

As he lay there thinking back to the initial meeting of the Oslo foursome, it all seemed like one big dream. Their relationships were too short-lived.

After his brief rest, Greg got up to open his suitcase and take out Kristian's neatly wrapped Christmas gift. He would carry it with him since he'd be catching a taxi to the foster home later.

He left the hotel shortly and walked the few blocks into the busy downtown shopping district. Merging with the heavy, scurrying, last-minute Christmas shoppers, he made his way toward the boat landings. He wanted to trace and revisit and savor the happy memories of those same places he and Tom and Valerie and Annika enjoyed together.

Most main streets were wet from a recent snowfall, some side streets still slushy from meltage.

When he reached the piers, he stared out into the harbor at the distant vigilant fjords and visualized all the laughter on their initial harbor boat cruise.

Afterwards he strolled amid the shoppers at the marina shopping mall, and when he came upon the gift shop where he'd bought Valerie's friendship ring, he paused to admire the fine display of jewelry. Periodically he stopped to examine and study the unique Scandinavian Christmas offerings displayed everywhere.

At noontime, he ate lunch at the same restaurant where the foursome had eaten supper and laughingly revealed their deep, dark, "sordid" pasts.

After lunch, he walked again on Karl Johans Gate to enjoy the bustling crowds of eager Christmas shoppers. He studied Norwegian faces as they hastened toward him and hurried past him. Their healthy complexions never ceased to fascinate him. It was fun feeling "unhealthy" among so many healthy, ruddy Norwegian faces; especially the bright children's faces. He enjoyed being envious.

While enjoying the excitement of Christmas Eve shoppers, Greg stopped to have a drink in the heart of the downtown district.

Upon entering the lounge, he stepped to the end of the bar, which was near the front entrance, and chose a stool next to the wall. As he laid Kristian's gift down on the bar, he ordered a shot of cognac from the bartender.

While observing the continuous flow of last-minute shoppers through the large front window, his mood was pensive, and when the bartender served him his drink, he turned on his stool to focus on the outdoor restaurant on the corner across the boulevard. The same outdoor restaurant where the four of them drank beer and wine and ate pizza.

Glistening drops of water dripped from the snow-covered roof of the barren building to join the melting snow covering the entire deserted patio.

Greg envisioned images of the laughing foursome toasting their glasses to a bonding friendship amid the happy faces of summer patrons.

The wintry scene of scurrying passersby paid little attention to the gloomy outside patio of emptiness that projected an air of sadness. The destitute patio restaurant would have to remain closed until the end of winter when all of its happy summer clientele would return once again.

Only the soothing sounds of Christmas carols emanated from the juke-box while Greg sat drinking at the bar with three other customers.

After a while, Greg approached the juke box, looked over the selections before dropping his coin, made his choice, and returned to his stool.

His eyes grew misty as he listened to Elvis sing his song of "Memories." His only thoughts were on Valerie. The emotional pain of her sudden, shocking death still beleaguered him; he missed her terribly.

The bartender abruptly interrupted his thoughts, saying, "That Christmas present looks like it may be for someone very special."

Greg didn't realize the bartender was talking to him until he looked up to notice that he and the bartender were the only two people left in the tavern.

He quickly responded, "Why, yes it is a special gift. It's a camera for a very special boy."

"Could that special boy be your son?"

"No, it's not for my son. I've never been married. It's for the son of a very close friend of mine. I'm on my way to spend the Christmas holidays with him now."

"That's nice," the bartender commented. "When we were children, Christmas was always our favorite time of year, wasn't it?"

"Yes," Greg agreed, "it was certainly my favorite time of year."

The bartender added, "Christmas is really for the children, isn't it?"

Greg paused, slowly nodded his head in thought, and said, "Yes, I suppose it is when you really thing about it."

"Well, I hate to rush you out the door, but it's time for me to close up. Tonight is a very special evening and meal for all Norwegians and we bartenders like to be home with our families on Christmas Eve, too."

"Oh, I'm sorry for detaining you," Greg apologized.

"No, you haven't detained me, because I still have to clean up. I'll be home in plenty of time."

As Greg swallowed the last of his drink and walked toward the door, the bartender called, "You must have loved her very much."

Greg smiled at his insight and said, "Yes, I did. She was a very loving woman, to be sure."

"A merry Christmas to you and the boy."

"And a merry Christmas to you and your family," Greg returned.

When he opened the door and stepped outside, Greg joined the last-minute stragglers hurrying to get to their homes.

Many of the stores had closed earlier and now the last of the shopkeepers closed their doors. Store lights began to flick off spontaneously, accenting an overcast, gray, wintry sky.

Within minutes, the streets darkened with only the bright glow of the street lamps to light the way for the last scurrying shoppers.

A slight cool breeze blew softly against Greg's face.

Just as a clerk closed his doors, Greg dashed inside the store to buy a bottle of table wine for the evening meal at Kristian's foster home.

When he returned to the street, the air had turned colder. It was beginning to snow, so he pulled the stocking hat from the pocket of his jacket; the Christmas present Kristian had sent him the previous year. He jostled the hat onto his head, pulled up his collar, and drew the open ends together snugly around his neck.

As he walked to the corner to catch a taxicab, snow flurries swirled about him gently in their erratic zigzag descent to the ground.

When Greg entered the taxi, he instructed the driver to Kristian's address and soon found his foster home to be in the older, more central residential section of Oslo.

Upon arrival at the home, Greg paid the cabby from inside the car, so when he stepped out onto the snow-covered sidewalk, the taxicab quickly drove away.

The breeze had faded; the air calm; large snowflakes floated heavily to the ground.

In this quiet, peaceful, and serene Christmas atmosphere, Greg stood momentarily to observe his surroundings.

He looked up and down the street to view the large, stately homes decorated with Christmas lighting. The tiny multicolored lights blinked their Christmas greetings to all passersby.

Thin-layered snow now covered the sidewalks and long walkways leading up to the big homes. The lawns, also thinly snow-covered, appeared as newly spread sheets of snowy white linen, soon to become that of a brand-new thick white comforter.

He turned his attention to the Swensen home, standing large in front of him with its long walkway leading up to the front door steps.

On the front lawn, lights twinkled from four naturally growing Christmas trees along with the blinking lights on several trees lining both sides of the walkway. All of the lower front windows of the home were also framed with bright but non-blinking multicolored lighting.

As he sauntered up the walkway, he murmured, "With three floors, their home is certainly large enough to accommodate four to five foster children."

Nearing the front door, he noticed their large Christmas wreath hanging on the door. Above the wreath, a shiny gold banner with red lettering read MERRY CHRISTMAS, while on the porch lay a WELCOME mat.

Greg rang the bell.

Moments later, a tall, slightly gray-haired, middle-aged woman opened the door; another healthy, ruddy, Norwegian face smiled broadly. "You must be Mr. Ericsen from America. I'm so glad to meet you."

Offering his hand, Greg shook her hand firmly and said, "I'm pleased to meet you, too, Mrs. Swensen. Your home is beautifully decorated; very colorful."

"Thank you," she replied graciously while momentarily admiring the heavily falling snow and twinkling lights with Greg. "My husband and I always enjoy decorating at Christmas time. The children love to help, too, but come inside, and welcome to our home here in Oslo. Kristian has been so excited and anxious all day waiting for your arrival."

As he stepped through the doorway, she walked ahead, saying, "Come this way. I'll show you to our parlor. We use it as a waiting room for the relatives and guests of the children. They also use it for personal conversation and private time with the children."

"That's good. I prefer to be alone with Kristian at first so we can reacquaint ourselves with each other."

"That's our first rule with all the children." She smiled stopping at the parlor door. "May I take your jacket?"

"Yes, thank you," he replied while handing her his jacket along with the bottle. "And here's some wine for the table."

"Thank you, Mr. Ericsen, I'll make sure we enjoy it with our Christmas meal. Now please sit down and make yourself comfortable. I'll be back with Kristian promptly."

When she turned and retreated down the hallway, Greg stepped into the parlor but didn't take a seat.

He walked to the window overlooking the front yard and admired the snowfall through the large picture window. While waiting patiently, he tapped Kristian's present against his leg.

Suddenly, from behind him, Kristian exclaimed, "Greg, you really came to see me. You're here for Christmas."

Greg turned around to see Kristian standing in the open doorway.

"You betcha." Greg laughed. "Didn't I promise you I'd come? I always keep my promises."

Suddenly, Kristian tossed his troll onto an empty chair and ran to him with open arms. Greg opened his arms wide to catch him as Kristian dashed headlong straight into Greg's outstretched arms.

Hugging each other tightly, Kristian cried, "Oh man, what a great Christmas this is going to be, Greg. I'm so happy you came. I have a present for you, too, Greg."

"Now, we can become closer buddies, eh, Kristian?"

"Oh boy, will we ever."

When they broke apart, Greg handed him his gift with a smile. "This is for my best buddy."

"For me? Gee, thanks, Greg. Can I open it right now?"

"Yes, I'm sure you'll want to use it tonight, so you'd better open it, right now."

Kristian ripped off the paper and blurted, "It's a camera! It's even got film and batteries. Now I can take pictures of everyone. Oh man, thanks a lot, Greg."

"You're welcome, Kristian. Merry Christmas."

As Greg stooped down to help the boy load the camera, Kristian hugged him around the neck and said, "Merry Christmas to you, too, Greg."

While helping him with the camera, Greg glanced up, casually eyeing the troll on the chair, and said, "I see you have the troll I gave to your mother, Kristian."

Suddenly, a woman stepped into the open doorway and with hands on her hips, snapped, "I beg your pardon, sir, but that troll was given to me, not to his mother. Don't be telling lies to the boy."

When Greg looked upward, he was instantly stunned and astonished at whom he was staring. He face turned ashen.

Wide-eyed, he dropped the box of film and gasped, "Omigod! Valerie? But it can't be you. You're dead! I saw your gravestone in the cemetery. You're a ghost."

Natalie was dumbfounded. She queried, "Valerie? What are you talking about? I'm not Valerie. I'm Natalie. How do you know Valerie?"

Suddenly, she thought she recognized him. Immediately, she cupped her mouth with one hand and with her other hand, quickly covered her breasts. "Greg? Good heavens, is that you, Greg?" she muttered between her fingers. She crouched down and stepped forward to look closer, but Greg threw up a hand and scooted backward several feet.

He fell on his backside and with both palms up cried, "Stop! Stop right there! Don't come any closer."

"Greg! My God, it really IS you!" She giggled slightly. "Where did you come from? How did you get here? I can't believe you're here in Oslo."

She stepped forward again, but Greg dug his heels into the carpet and scooted backward several more feet, huffing, "I said, don't come near me. You're not real. I'm hallucinating or dreaming. This can't be happening. You must be a ghost."

Natalie beamed with a warm smile. "No, Greg, you're the ghost. I'm the troll, remember?"

Transfixed, he couldn't believe he sat staring at her beautiful smile and incredible blue eyes again.

Bewildered he asked, "What's going on here? It's uncanny. You look exactly like Valerie. Who are you?"

"I'm Natalie." She grinned happily. "I'm Valerie's identical twin sister, but how do you know Valerie?"

"Natalie? Who's Natalie? I don't know any Natalie and how do you know me?"

She replied, "Don't you remember, Greg? We all met on the tour boat two summers ago, you, me, Tom, and Annika. You also gave me this troll and friendship ring, remember? And how do you know Kristian?"

As Natalie extended her hand to show him the friendship ring, Greg threw up his palms again, snapping, "Whoa! Just wait one large minute here. I'll ask the questions. Someone has some tall explaining to do and the answers better be damn good."

As Greg got to his feet, Kristian looked at Natalie, and asked, "You already know Greg, Aunt Natalie? I didn't know that."

"Oh yes, Kristian, we already know each other." She smiled. "We met right here in Oslo over a year ago."

"Wow!" he exclaimed. "This is great! I thought I was bringing both of you together for the very first time at Christmas, and you already know each other. What a terrific Christmas this is turning out to be."

"Hold on," Greg interjected, "you're both going too fast for me. I need some answers here, and I haven't got any yet. What do you mean, Kristian, when you say you brought us together?"

"Well, my plan was to bring you two together to meet each other," he related. "I invited you and Aunt Natalie here so both of you could meet each other at Christmas. I thought because both of you loved Mom so much, and you being my best friend and Aunt Natalie looking exactly like Mom, it would be terrific if you two hit it off together. I wrote the same letter to both of you."

Greg grinned. "Who do you think you are, Cupid's right hand man?"

"And what a great surprise it all turned out to be; everyone knows everyone." He laughed. "It turned out better than I had planned."

Kristian picked up his camera, grabbed the troll by the nose, and ran out of the room shouting, "I can't wait to tell everybody about this."

Befuddled, Greg plopped down into a comfortable easy chair and stared at Natalie.

"I'm stunned and dumbfounded by all of this," he said. "I can't believe this is happening–that you're alive and that your name is Natalie or who-ever you are in this mystery game of tag. It appears I'm IT, so I wish you'd tell me what this is all about."

Natalie started to approach him, but he stopped her by pointing to a chair, saying, "No, no, you sit right there in that chair. I need answers and an explanation to all this."

Natalie's eyes sparkled as she stared warmly at him and replied, "Greg, you don't know how happy I am, right now. I never knew I could ever miss anyone like I have you. I've never stopped thinking about you since that awful day in Bergen. I never thought I'd ever see you again. I thought you were gone forever."

"Okay, Bergen is exactly where to start when you supposedly sped away in a speedboat. That is, if you are who you say you are. You say you're Natalie, not Valerie, but I really don't know who's who anymore. This is more like a game of 'Pin the Tail on the Donkey' with Greg being the jack-ass. Only moments ago, I heard your new name, Natalie. So where did Valerie come from and why?"

She related, "First, let me explain what identical twins like to do grow-ing up. They like to play games with parents and friends by making them guess which twin is which. It doesn't last long with parents, though, because they get to know our little traits and mannerisms, especially with mothers. They know us too well.

"Then when we reach puberty and boys come into the picture, that's when the real fun starts. We loved to fool the boys. We were so identical that the boys could never guess which of us was Natalie or Valerie. On double dates, we'd switch places with each other and our boyfriends could never guess who was who. Half the time, they didn't even care. It also became a useful tool when we got older and relationships with men were more serious.

"When I met you on that tour, Greg, I didn't want you to know my real name, so I told you I was my twin sister, Valerie."

"What about Annika? Did you ever tell her you were Natalie, or did you continue letting her believe you were Valerie?"

"No, I never told her my real name. I also let her believe I was Valerie."

"Why? Why all the mystery?"

"At the time I met you, I had just broken up with my fiancé. I had also recently quit my teaching job. I needed a vacation away from all the stress I was under. I needed to be by myself. I was very mixed up and full of indeci-sion. I didn't know what I was going to do with my life. I needed time to think.

"Those were the reasons I couldn't get involved with you; especially when you said you thought you were in love with me. We met at a very bad time, Greg. I thought it wouldn't work and made it a point not to give you my real name. I gave you my sister's name, so you wouldn't know who I really was. I purposely didn't give you any address or phone number because I didn't want any contacts with you after that weekend. Little did I know how much I'd think about you and miss you after I sorted things out. I could've kicked myself a hundred times over for not giving you a relative's address in order to make contact with you."

"I'm assuming it was your ex-fiancé who rescued you in that speedboat, right?"

"Yes, it was. When I made the phone call in the restaurant and told you I was chatting with a woman friend, that's when I phoned him to meet me with his boat. I had to get away from that man who followed us all day. He terrified me.

"So, because Lasse rescued me that Sunday, he naturally wanted to renew our engagement, but I couldn't do it. My feelings toward him had changed.

"After staying with him for only a week at his summer home on a near-by island, I left him to pick up my belongings at the hotel in Oslo. From there, I flew to southern France to rest and think and decide what I wanted to do. Finally I decided to return to Oslo to continue teaching and settled back down to a permanent address, again."

"That story of Lasse is the exact same story I got from Valerie," replied Greg. "How did she get the same story?"

"With Mother and Dad gone, we've only had each other to depend on, so I've always kept contact with her by phone. We've always known each other's whereabouts at all times. A week before I met the three of you, I phoned her from the hotel in Oslo and told her I'd probably be flying to France in a few weeks. I gave her the hotel name in Cannes where I'd be staying.

"It was either that same night or the next night she escaped from the clinic. Somehow she obtained a passport and plane ticket and flew to Cannes to meet me.

"During our two weeks together, I told her how you and I met; what a sweet man you were; and how I lost you when her stalker tried to find out from me where she was. That's why her stalker was following us in Bergen that Sunday. Somehow he found out about me in Norway and wanted to talk to me about Valerie. I guess he figured he'd find Valerie through me.

"Val wanted to know all about you, so I told her everything I knew about you. At the time I didn't think much about it. It was all sister talk, like always. Like school girls again, we giggled when I told her I hadn't given you my right name. I told her I gave you her name, Valerie, instead of my name because I thought I'd never see you again. You were past history, or so I thought at the time.

"When she left Cannes, I never heard from her again. Apparently, she was always on the run from her stalker. I had no more contact with her until the mental clinic informed me of her death. Needless to say, I was terribly shocked when I heard she was murdered. The last information I received was that the case still remains a mystery and is unsolved to this day."

As Natalie related her story, Greg gazed into space, preoccupied with his own thoughts.

He wasn't listening; her words incoherent as he thought, *So Valerie and I might never have made it after all. Love can't grow on deceit. It can only grow with honesty and truth. I now believe my love for Valerie was a misconception. My protection for her was based on pity—not love. Perhaps in time we might have fall-en in love with one another, but did she really love me or did she only love what I did for her? I'll never know that answer.*

Suddenly, when he heard her say, "Greg?" he abruptly turned back into her words. "Are you listening to me? You seem to be miles away."

"Er, oh yes, I did drift off there, didn't I. Where were we? So that's how Valerie found out about me; through you, naturally. She used all of your information about me to her advantage, but how did she know what I looked like?"

"She didn't know what you looked like. She only knew my description of you and that your name was Greg Ericsen. She also knew you were from Rapid City, South Dakota, and of course imagined you to be a handsome man since we always seemed to have the same taste in men."

"How did she get the friendship ring I gave you and how did you get it back? Maybe it's a different ring."

"No, it's not a different ring. She stole it from my jewelry box in Cannes just in case she would run across you for any reason. She might have even gone to Rapid City to look you up, if I knew her.

"Ever since high school, she was always so jealous of me and my boyfriends. She liked to steal them from me. I don't know why. She was so insecure. The ring would be her convincing proof to you that she was me, but I have it back now. She was wearing it on a chain around her neck when the police found her body, and they eventually returned it to me, along with all of her other personal effects from the clinic."

"So, you never knew who that creep was who followed us from Oslo to Bergen that Sunday, eh?"

"No, Greg, truly I didn't know who he was at that time. In France, Valerie informed me he was an attendant at the clinic who quit his job after she escaped. She assumed he found out my Bergen address through clinic records. He obviously flew here and somehow discovered the four of us here in Oslo. He must have figured I'd be his link to her. If he found me in Bergen or Oslo, he probably thought I'd tell him of Valerie's whereabouts in the States. That's all I can conclude. I didn't know who he was until Valerie told me he was a medical attendant who raped her at the clinic and quit his job to stalk her. She said he was a real nut case, insanely obsessed with her. Do you think that insidious maniac killed her, Greg?"

With a wave of his hand, he sloughed off her question.

"I know for a fact he didn't kill her," he replied. "I'll tell you why he didn't someday."

"Greg, I can't believe I'm sitting here talking to you again. It's all so unbelievable to me. What a wonderful shock. I know we're both here because of Kristian, but how did all of this come about? It's so exciting to me. How did you meet my sister?"

"It's a very long story, Natalie, and I'll get to it all in good time. You have no idea what I went through with Valerie and in all that time I thought she was you!

"After your disappearance, I found her in Charleston the next month, and we were involved for that whole summer, right into September until her death. Not to mention we covered half the country."

"You were involved with her that long before she died?" Natalie exclaimed. "You must have loved her. Did you love her, Greg?"

Pondering momentarily, he replied, "I'd say based upon our involvement in a misdirected relationship, I did love her, but I don't think I was IN love with her. I was really chasing you and your love—not Valerie's. There's no question in my mind about that. All the time I thought I was chasing you, it turned out to be a stolen, confused, and misconceived involvement with your twin sister."

Suddenly, Natalie realized in Greg's pursuit of Valerie, he truly believed he was chasing her, not Valerie, and all of his anguish and heartache with Valerie had been caused by herself. She was responsible for all of it.

Impulsively, she wanted to rush to him and apologize for all the grief and heart-wrenching sorrow she'd caused him in his involvement with Valerie, but she was reluctant to approach him. She feared a negative response. She had no way of knowing what his reaction might be in her compassion and affection for him, so she sat fixed in her chair. Loving anxiety welled within her.

When they stopped talking and sat silent in their chairs, Greg simply stared into space, contemplating his varied thoughts.

Soon Mrs. Swensen entered the room and asked, "Would the two of you like a drink of some kind?"

"Oh yes, thank you, Mrs. Swensen," Natalie snapped. "I'd love a drink. Do you have any brandy?"

"Yes, we have blackberry brandy, if you'd like."

"That would be splendid."

"I would not only enjoy a drink, but I NEED a drink," Greg mused. "Would you happen to have a straight shot of cognac with a water back?"

"Yes, we have cognac, too. I'll be right back with your drinks."

Mrs. Swensen left the room and returned shortly with a small tray of drinks. When she served the drinks, Greg and Natalie lifted their glasses and toasted her with a "Thank you and merry Christmas."

After she smiled graciously and left the room, Greg and Natalie also toasted one another.

"Merry Christmas, Greg." Natalie smiled broadly while lifting her glass. "With the hope of many many more happy ones to come."

"Merry Christmas to you, too, Natalie." He smiled warmly. "And to our surprise rediscovery of each other on Christmas Eve."

They both sipped from their glasses but Natalie overwhelmed by emotion, immediately placed her glass on the table and rushed to the side of his chair.

Looking up into his eyes, she reached up to hold his face in her hands. The tears flowed freely as she hoped for forgiveness.

"Greg, I'm so so sorry for everything that happened between you and Valerie. I feel so guilty for all the pain and heartache I've caused you. Can you ever forgive me?"

When she bowed her head, Greg tipped her chin up with his fingers, nudging her mouth toward his. They closed their eyes and kissed tenderly.

Suddenly, a bright flash of light popped!

"Hey, man, great shot!" Kristian's friend cried.

Kristian lowered the camera from his eyes, declaring, "You bet, partner. Slap me five. We gotta see that one."

All Greg and Natalie could do was look at each other and laugh. They'd been caught red-handed.

"Hey, you guys," Greg teased, "if you do that again, we'll get the trolls after you."

The boys laughed impishly, with their planned mission accomplished–a victorious prize snapshot of Greg and Natalie kissing on Christmas Eve. They ran from the room.

"I'll bet they were right outside the door listening, just waiting for their big chance." Greg grinned.

"You know they were, the little stinkers." Natalie smirked.

Moments before, Greg liked what he felt when he kissed her. It felt exactly the same as it did that Sunday in Bergen. He wanted to kiss her again, so he stood up and as he pulled her to her feet and kissed her once more, his emotions burned strong.

Responding to his kiss, she squirmed in his embrace, pressing her breasts hard against his chest. They kissed each other longingly for they both yearned to renew their loving relationship.

After a long embrace, they released one another with Natalie asking, "Was my kiss as good as Valerie's?"

"Much better than Valerie's," he replied, "but keep in mind, whenever I kissed Valerie, my thoughts and emotions were always centered on you. To me, I was always kissing you–not her. Now, I'm really kissing you again.

"Because you're still alive, I'm already emotionally involved with you, thanks to your sister. It's always been you with whom I've really been involved. It's a case of mind over matter, right? All I have to do is get used to you still being alive. Ummm and I can see that won't take too much longer."

He grabbed her waist with both hands and pulled her tight against his stomach.

"That is true, isn't it, Greg?"

"What's that?"

"When you kissed my sister, you were really kissing me?"

"Absolutely. We could actually say we've been mentally involved with each other, right from the beginning; now we're physically involved again. All we have to do is build on it. As the song says, 'Give Me a Kiss to Build a Dream on'. Ummm," he smiled, "so let's start building, partner."

As Greg tried to pull her in close for another kiss, she resisted by pushing on his chest and saying, "Since we're renewing our courtship, I get to ask the first question. Ladies, first, right?"

"Right you are, troll," he agreed while releasing her. "Shoot; what's your first question?"

"Did you make love to my sister?"

Stunned momentarily, instant silence ensued. His mind went blank. He couldn't think quick enough for an evasive answer. He simply stared at her expressionlessly, but his silence was her answer.

"I knew it! I knew it!" she blurted. "You DID make love to her. Your silence speaks for you. If you hadn't made love to her, you would have denied it instantly, and tried to worm your way out of it. You're a worm, anyway," she teased.

"I'm not a worm. I'm a ghost. No, you're the ghost. No, that's not right, either." He laughed shaking his head. "Now, I'm all confused. I'm Mr. Ghost, alias confused. Now I've got it straight."

"Don't try to worm out that way. Admit it, worm! You made love to her, didn't you? You did. You did. You did!"

"I take the fifth." He laughed, putting up his right hand. "I refuse to speak on the grounds that I might incriminate myself."

Just then Mrs. Swensen appeared in the doorway, laughing. "Who's incriminating who? We certainly don't want anyone incriminating themselves on Christmas Eve. Come now, you two, and join us for the church bells. On Christmas Eve in Oslo, all the churches ring their bells at five o'clock. It's our tradition, you know. Hurry! They've already started."

Greg mused, "Ah-ha, I'm literally saved by the bells."

Natalie clenched her teeth and as they quickly followed Mrs. Swensen down the hallway, she pinched his ribs and muttered, "You're not getting out of it that easy. I will find out sooner or later, you know. We women always find out."

While rubbing his side, he winced. "How well we men know."

Once they reached the front door, they stepped outside onto the porch where the house guests, the foster children, and her husband had gathered together.

As everyone listened to the thunderous ringing of bells, the children couldn't resist packing snowballs with the new snow. They scampered onto the blanketed white lawn where a free-for-all broke out but was squelched quickly by the foster parents.

Since it was Greg's first experience, the awesome simultaneous soundings were especially enjoyable. At times unified, the various unique ringing bells mesmerized the entire small group.

Mrs. Swensen stood tall and proud, saying, "It's Oslo's way of heralding the Christ child's birth."

Mr. Swensen added, "It's like the whole city is one big church and we're all inside one huge dome."

"Yes, it certainly gives one that impression, doesn't it?" Greg agreed.

Natalie grasped Greg's hand and commented, "There's a certain feeling of reverence and holiness to it, also."

Listening intently, everyone stared skyward as if searching the night heavens for the appearance, perhaps, of an ethereal or spiritual being.

When the bells grew silent, the small group of children and adults reentered the house, led by the Swensens, who directed everyone into the dining room for the specially prepared Christmas Eve dinner.

After the meal, the dishes were cleared and the gift-giving began with each person taking a turn in opening their own present.

When it was Kristian's turn, he opened Aunt Natalie's large gift first. Inside the box were new books to read, a soccer ball, and a big ugly stuffed troll. After everyone laughed and Natalie assured Kristian he was a good troll, Kristian promptly returned Natalie's troll to her, since it was only on loan. It was really her troll, originally given to her by Greg.

Then it was Natalie's turn, so she opened her present from Kristian first. Inside her oblong box she discovered a new addition to her porcelain doll collection. Dressed in older, more traditional Scandinavian costuming, the pretty female doll displayed a colorful Norwegian dress.

Eventually, it was Greg's turn to open his gift from Kristian, and inside his wrapping he also found a stuffed troll. Grabbing it by its long ugly nose, he yanked it out and held it high for everyone's laughter, after which Kristian also assured Greg that his new troll was also a good and happy troll who would bring his best friend good luck and good fortune.

The three trolls, in the possession of Natalie, Kristian, and Greg, would now symbolize their new bonding and happy friendships.

After the gift-giving, all the guests prepared to leave, so the children and the Swensens escorted everyone to the front door where everybody bade one another a "Merry Christmas."

Natalie patted Kristian's head and stroked his hair, saying, "Thank you for inviting me to your Christmas Eve party, Kristian. It's all because of you that Greg is back in my life again. You're a real Christmas angel who brought me so very much happiness tonight."

She stooped down, hugged and squeezed him tight, and whispered softly in his ear, "I love you, Kristian. Thank you, so much."

He kissed her on the cheek and smiled affectionately. "I love you, too, Aunt Natalie, and I'm so happy that you and Greg already knew each other. We're going to have a great Christmas together, aren't we?"

"You bet we are, my little Christmas angel," she asserted while shaking and jostling his waist.

Greg replied, "And I absolutely agree with Natalie, Kristian, you really are our Christmas angel. You're the messenger who brought us back together again. If it wasn't for you, we wouldn't be standing here." Then he bent low and tapped Kristian on the nose, adding, "Of course, God's real angels are his special messengers and maybe, just maybe, your mom might have put in a special request for all of us to be together tonight. What do you think?"

"Really, Greg? I want to believe that, too. Maybe Mom helped me write that letter to both of you. It could be Mom's Christmas present to all of us. She was so great."

Natalie squeezed his hand and smiled. "Well, I like to believe that, too, Kristian."

"And I do, too." Kristian smiled back.

Greg and Natalie bade the foster family a "Merry Christmas" and shuffled down the slippery front walkway to the car, climbed inside, and drove away.

On the drive to Natalie's apartment, they shared the warmth and togetherness of their surprise Christmas reunion.

"Seeing you alive tonight, Natalie, was a wonderful shock. I feel like I'm dreaming right now, and I don't want to wake up on Christmas morning for fear you'll be gone out of my life again."

She grinned. "I thought I was going to faint when I saw you in the parlor with Kristian. I couldn't believe my eyes that it was really you down on the floor. It was an inexplicable feeling. It does feel like a dream, doesn't it? What an ecstatic experience. Why would you think I'd be gone from you tomorrow when we've just rediscovered each other?"

"I suppose it's because of my experience with Valerie. She was always running from me during the night. It's a bit of insecurity I'll have to get over."

"Oh, Valerie was always running, huh? That makes sense because of her stalker. Now that reminds me. We do have an unfinished question that you have to address in the morning, don't you, worm?"

Immediately Greg slumped down in the seat, pretending to pass out.

"Go ahead, Mr. Ghost, act like you're sleeping, but remember, there's no escape from the Christmas troll. You will be in the witness chair with your morning coffee." She smirked.

The streets were mostly deserted, so Natalie enjoyed the quiet drive observing all the colorful twinkling lights on the houses and newly fallen snow covering the trees and streets.

When they arrived at her apartment, Natalie prepared the sofa for Greg since he'd decided to stay the night and not return to the hotel. Still feigning a sleepy stupor, he crawled under the blankets, and Natalie tucked the covers up under his chin.

She kissed him on the forehead and whispered, "Thank you for coming back into my life, luv."

As she turned away and walked to her bedroom, Greg shifted to one side, grinning.

"Thank you, too, troll, for still being alive," he called, "but you won't get it out of me."

"Oh, yes I will, you faker. Good night, worm."

On Christmas morning, in between preparing the ham and eggs, cereal, juice, and coffee, many stolen kisses were shared.

While eating breakfast, they reminisced about their initial meeting on that first happy weekend they shared with Tom and Annika; and after breakfast, while enjoying their coffee, Natalie would not be denied her explanation.

"As you can see, Mr. Ericsen, I didn't abandon you during the night. We're both here and very much alive on this beautiful Christmas morning. And now that I've found you again, I assure you, you won't be able to get rid of me, so fess up," she cried. "Did you make love to my sister?"

"Whoa, now I'm Mr. Ericsen. Such formality on Christmas morning."

She took a sip of coffee, peered at him over her cup, and said, "Yes, and it will continue to be a formal morning, Mr. Ericsen, until I get an answer to my unavoidable question—a satisfactory answer, that is, one that I'll accept."

"Okay, okay, so I did have sex with your sister, but I didn't make love to her."

Natalie shook her head and squinted. "What's that supposed to mean? You're worming around again."

He continued, "I never told Valerie I loved her—no, that's not true, either. I did tell her I loved her, but what I'm trying to say is that I never told her I loved her when we were having sex."

She took another sip of coffee and still peered at him, gloating over her cup. She enjoyed watching him squirm.

"Talk on, riddler," she taunted smugly.

He continued his explanation, "Because she kept running away from me, I had my doubts about her and was never real sure about my feelings. She wouldn't tell me about her problems with her stalker, so her background was suspect to me. Until I found out more about her, I couldn't bring myself to say I loved her. When she finally told me the truth about her life, I felt I did love her, but I still never told her.

"At her grave site, I told her I loved her, but when you told me about her deceitfulness last night, I'm not so sure it was love. I now believe I was emotionally involved by pity, not love.

"Keep in mind, Natalie, that I always thought you were her. I did have sex with Valerie, but I never made love to her. There is a difference. Remember, too, that when we did have sex, I really believed I was having sex with you; the same as when we kissed.

"However, love and sex don't always go together. By natural law, everyone has sex. Sex is tangible; love is intangible. Even the animals have sex, but they are incapable of love. Love also grows—sex does not. I only hope our intangible love we share will continue to grow stronger in the weeks and months ahead.

"To love is to give, and what better gift can a man and woman give at Christmas time, than their precious gifts of love to one another? Your gifts of life and love to me today, Natalie, are by far the best Christmas presents I've ever received."

Even though he'd been talking about his involvement with her sister, Natalie had known all along he was really explaining his love for her. Tears welled in her dahlia blue eyes when he left his chair and moved to her side.

"Thank you, Greg, for that loving explanation."

"You mean I'm qualified again? I've been reinstated?" he quizzed.

"You were never disqualified, Mr. Ghost; and always with the highest of ratings, but why do I still have this feeling that somehow you wormed your way out of it?" She laughed.

"Great! Now that I'm out of the witness chair, I rest my case. Merry Christmas, beautiful troll," he replied, kissing her softly.

She nodded her head in approval, saying, "And I dearly loved your testimony, luv. You wormed your way out of it perfectly."

"How can I still be a worm on Christmas morning? Don't I qualify for something better?"

"Okay, you'll be my Christmas present and ghost for a day. Tomorrow, I'll decide what your new status will be, based upon how we get along today."

When he bent over and kissed her again, she purred, "Ummm, how I do love your ghostly kind of work."

"Now before this passionate, forbidden relationship gets off the ground, I would like to ask you a few points of information concerning your lurid past, ma'am," he inquired. "Namely, any stalkers? Institutions? Illicit pregnancies? Hidden lovers? Deep dark secrets?"

"Nothing to confess or report, sir. My slate is clean." She saluted with a grin.

Shortly thereafter, Greg phoned home to tell his parents the wonderful shocking news of Natalie.

Later, he phoned Annika since Tom had given him Annika's phone number and address before he'd left home with the hope they could meet and spend a day or two together.

Greg broke the good news to Annika about Natalie and at the same time, invited her to dinner at Kristian's foster home the day after Christmas. The Swensens had graciously made the invitation for Annika to join them at the Christmas Eve meal.

"Yes, yes, of course I'll come," Annika squealed. "I can't believe you and Val . . . I mean, Natalie are back together again. I'll have to get used to her name. I'm so happy for both of you. It's all so exciting, and on Christmas, too. Give me the address and I'll be there, with Christmas bells on, too. Oh, I'm so excited, Greg."

"I'm still in shock myself, Annika." He laughed.

After giving her the Swensen's address, they wished each other a "Merry Christmas" and hung up their phones.

In the afternoon, Greg and Natalie spent a memorable and fun Christmas day with Kristian and all the families at the Swensen foster home.

In the evening, before leaving the Swensen home, Natalie posed a suggestion.

"Greg, why don't you, Kristian, and I fly to Bergen the day after tomorrow and do some after-Christmas shopping there?" she offered. "Wouldn't it be fun to shop in Bergen?"

"That's a great idea," Greg agreed.

"I've never been to Bergen," Kristian replied. "Can I go, Mrs. Swensen?"

"Yes, you certainly may go." She smiled warmly. "Bergen is so beautiful in the wintertime and especially at Christmas with all the snow."

"Then it's settled," Natalie snapped with a nod.

The next day, when Greg and Natalie met Annika at the Swensen home, Annika and Natalie screamed and squealed as they ran to greet each other on the walkway with open arms. Embracing one another, they hugged tightly with tears pouring down their cheeks.

They wouldn't let go of each other until Greg, with filled eyes, broke them apart to hug and kiss Annika on her cheek.

Emotions ran deep with all three of them while wishing Tom could be with them to experience their happy moment.

To Kristian and the Swensens, it was also a touching moment, while they stood on the porch watching the emotional reunion of the threesome, but afterward, fun and laughter ruled the day for everyone.

Late the next morning, Greg, Natalie, and Kristian flew to Bergen to spend the afternoon with all of the after-Christmas shoppers returning their purchases. Other shoppers, of course, took advantage of the usual after-Christmas bargains and sales.

At a fine jewelry store, Greg bought Natalie a Christmas gift which consisted of four small tennis bracelets in one bracelet. Within their tiny inlays, the rhinestones circumvented the bracelet and sparkled brilliantly in their deep vivid colors of ruby red, emerald green, royal blue, and crystal.

After strolling around the U-shaped harbor, they window-shopped the waterfront gift shops until they stopped at the same shop window where Greg had spied the troll plaque listing the description of trolls. The store-keeper still had one plaque left, so Natalie bought it for Greg as his Christmas present.

For lunch they ate at that same restaurant where they had eaten on that fateful Sunday afternoon when she disappeared from his life. To them, it seemed like only yesterday.

Later, before catching their flight back to Oslo, they stopped at the Tourist Information Center to stand on the same spot from where Natalie had run from the stalker only eighteen months before.

Greg stated, "So, you're the real ghost of my Christmas past and Christmas present, eh?"

Her incredible loving eyes glistened bluish purple when she looked up at him, smiled confidently, and said, "You better believe it, Greg Ericsen, and, hopefully, for all of your Christmases yet to come."

Embracing one another, they kissed tenderly with Kristian snapping their picture to freeze their loving image forever on another prize photo.

The loving relationship between Greg and Natalie had now begun anew, but this time from a mutually honest and truthful beginning.

A new light snowfall drifted down from the overcast sky, and with the floating, fluttering flakes swirling all about them, as if shedding their silent, serene blessing on the bonding threesome, Greg grasped Natalie's hand while at the same time, Kristian peered up at her and with a warm exchange of smiles, took her other hand in his.

It was Kristian's hopeful wish that perhaps someday soon all three of them would always be together.

Hand-in-hand, within the light drifting snow, the three of them strolled toward the bus stop for their return to Oslo and their new beginning.

The End